D0443917

THE PEACOCK SHEDS HIS TAIL

The PEACOCK
Sheds His Tail

ALICE TISDALE HOBART

THE BOBBS-MERRILL COMPANY

INDIANAPOLIS   *Publishers*   NEW YORK

Copyright, mcmxlv, by Alice Tisdale Hobart

PRINTED IN THE UNITED STATES

To

MY HUSBAND
EARLE TISDALE HOBART
and
MY FAMILY
MARY,
RAY,
TYLER,
and
EDWIN NOURSE

FOREWORD

It is perhaps unnecessary to state that except for the historical figures in this book all the characters are fictional. Should the name of any fictional character be that of a living person it is by coincidence.

For the purposes of fiction I have found it necessary in a few cases to shorten or lengthen the time between historical events. For instance, the celebration over the confiscated wells came sometime after the taking over, whereas I have placed it on the next day. Also I have not always adhered to the exact dates in the historical events of the Church.

I have also not differentiated the customs of the Indian villages as an anthropologist would. Rather I have tried to catch the significance of the Indian life, accrediting to one village the customs that best illustrate the Indian outlook. The hacienda village is thus a composite one.

The material for the celebration of the dead on All Souls' Day in Chapter 6 is taken from René d'Harnoncourt's article "The Fiesta as a Work of Art," from the book *Renascent Mexico*. The material is used by permission of Mr. d'Harnoncourt and the Crown Publishers.

The poem "Sister Water" is taken from the book *Some Spanish-American Poets*. It is a translation by Alice Stone Blackwell of a Spanish-American poem. It is used by permission of the University of Pennsylvania Press.

THE PEACOCK SHEDS HIS TAIL

I

THE GREAT land mass of North America, which in the United States offers vast stretches of fertile prairie and productive valleys, tapers out in Mexico. As the continent narrows down, the Sierras take over shaping the land. Huge blocks of rock and earth, tilted at precipitous angles, thrust the valleys up—five, six, seven thousand feet above the sea. From the central plateau, the mountains drop away like steppingstones, valley by valley, to the lowlands lying along the coasts.

Mexico is strangely different from the States except where the two countries join. There the earth is a flat, sandy desert, with no outstanding feature to mark the difference between the two nations sprung from such unlike roots.

Each of these nations has gone through a series of struggles for liberty—the last phase of Mexico's struggle so recent that in 1925 the country still reeled from the fierce internal strife. In 1910 the centennial of Mexico's freedom from Spain was observed. There was elaborate celebration in Mexico City. But in the villages over the country the *rurales,* in dove-colored uniforms with silver buttons and silver-mounted revolvers at their belts, held the Mexican people in subjection. Opportunity, under Díaz, president in name, dictator in fact, was for the native Spaniard and the foreign businessman. The Mexican, in bitter mirth, called himself the stepchild of his own country.

In that centennial year revolution broke out. There was a decade of fighting and bloodshed; then the generals made peace among themselves. It was an uneasy peace, for the cry of the revolutionists, "Land, work, and liberty," was still but half answered.

It was September—season of harvest and of festival in Mexico. All over the country, on the big estates and the small plots of the peasants, the corn stood high and golden under the sun.

The clouds which only a few weeks before had arrayed themselves each morning behind the piled-up jumble of mountains that encircle the city of Mexico, waiting to advance in the afternoon and drench the earth, had retreated to the four points of the compass. The rainy season was over. The sun day after day spread its uninterrupted brilliance over the lofty city set in its valley seven thousand feet above the sea. In the thin air, the rose and gray volcanic rock of the colonial dwellings, palaces, and churches took on a luminous, opalescent tone. The cleansing sunlight fell, too, over the rim of the city—a recently shrinking circle of poverty where men lived in caves hollowed out of slag heaps or huts roofed over with tin and straw.

Don Julián Navarro's colonial house, one of the oldest in the city, was a thing of austere beauty. Usually it looked proudly aloof, held to itself behind the iron grilles of its windows placed one above the other, story upon story, its great iron gate, leading to the street, closed except to admit family and guests. But today from morning until night it stood open. While the patio was still heavily shadowed by the high walls of the house, the gatekeeper Francisco rose from his sleeping mat and picked up his keys, grumbling. "The roosters have not begun their crowing on the housetops of the city, and yet I must open the gate."

Alejandra the cook stood, baskets in hand, waiting for him to find the keyhole. "Old fool," she muttered, angry with his clumsiness. He should have the Indian's skilled hands, like hers when she deftly patted out *tortillas*. "Since a very long time have you been fitting the key in," she scolded. "You're drunk, fumbling like that for the hole. I'm the one to grumble, with my tired legs going to the market before they stopped moving yesterday in preparations for today's fiesta, but I do not grumble—because it is for our Conchita." She pulled her blue *rebozo* tighter over her shoulders and across her broad, stout back and went out.

All morning servants and messengers passed back and forth, bent on important affairs. Don Julián's granddaughter Concepción—Concha as she was lovingly called by her family—was fifteen today. At noon there was to be a special Mass at the Church of San Francisco, and afterward, here at the house, the fiesta—Concha's coming-out party— would be held. There would be a banquet and dancing.

The service at the church was in fulfillment of a vow Concha's mother had made when her daughter was eight. The child had been very ill. The last Sacraments had been given her. Then Concha's mother had besought the Virgin to intercede for her recovery, taking a vow that if the child were spared, her womanhood should be dedicated to the Virgin.

Concha's grandmother, Doña María Navarro, had arranged that the vow should be carried out in a public ceremony similar to a wedding. Such a dedication of the young girl's maturity would signify her readiness for marriage. The Church had willingly granted Doña María's request.

Don Julián made his own interpretation of this service. He knew his wife was anxious to bring to fruition a long-cherished plan to unite the two great Spanish-American families—her own and that of her friend, Doña Leonora Fuentes de Lara. Ramón, Doña Leonora's son, was a few years older than Concha. By this emphasis on Concha's maturity, her grandmother hoped to bring Concha's betrothal to Ramón to the point of immediate negotiation.

Now, as the day drew on toward noon, Doña María led her family down the long flight of stairs to the patio where automobiles stood ready to take them to the church. First came Don Julián and Doña María, then Concha's father and mother, then Concha herself in bridal white, followed by her brother Ignacio and her sister Louisa.

"Concha, you will ride with your grandfather and me. I wish to see that your dress is not crushed before you enter the church. And you, too, Louisa. I want your dress to be fresh." Doña María motioned the others into the second car. Francisco threw wide the two halves of the gate and the cars rolled out.

At the church Concha, leaning on her father's arm and followed by her friends, Louisa among them, in fragile dresses of blue, pink, and green, and wearing large picture hats, walked up the aisle to the front of the church.

The priest, preceded by acolytes, came to the altar alight with candles and placed the Chalice before the tabernacle. Reverently he began the Mass, the choir reverently accompanying him. The Kyrie, Gloria, and Credo came to an end. *"Sanctus, Sanctus, Sanctus,"* chanted the priest as the bell rang thrice. Concha and all the rich and poor filling the great church knelt, as silently they joined the priest in his spoken prayers of commemoration. Placing his hands over the bread and the wine the reverend Father whispered, "This is My Body. . . . This is the Chalice of My Blood. . . ." In adoration all lifted their eyes to the Host and then to the Chalice as each was elevated. The sacred moment passed. There was a slight stir. The choir began the beautiful Agnus Dei.

The time for Concha's dedication to the Blessed Mother had come. Slowly she walked beyond the communion rail, knelt at the top of the altar steps. Two, then three, then four, then six of her maids knelt on the steps below. They were like a court train feathered with color spread out behind the small, white, kneeling figure above.

The tabernacle had its gem-encrusted door closed now, protecting the consecrated bread and wine. Three gold candlesticks with tall wax tapers flanked the tabernacle and to the left and right of the altar, slender tapers set in seven-branched candlesticks mounted on gold pedestals threw their shimmering flames upward. On each side of the step where Concha knelt one great candelabrum completed the path of light from the altar to her.

The priest stood facing her. His white alb and gold chasuble shone as if compounded of light itself. The bright red cassocks and lace surplices of the acolytes blended their color into the radiant scene.

Now the priest instructed the kneeling girl in the duties of womanhood and accepted her promise to be guided by the Virgin Mother. Then he recited the communal prayer:

"Hail, Holy Queen, Mother of mercy, our life, our sweetness, and our hope; to thee do we cry, poor banished children of Eve;

. . . .

Turn then, most gracious Advocate, thine eyes of mercy towards us, and after this our exile, show unto us the blessed Fruit of thy womb, Jesus. O clement, O loving, O sweet Virgin Mary."

The prayer ended, the priest raised his right hand, brown against the white sleeve of his alb, in blessing: *"In nomine Patris, et filii, et spiritus sancti. Amen."*

Seated below among the family, Concha's mother prayed. "O all understanding Virgin Mother, who conceived without sin and who has borne sorrow in the death of thy divine Son, intercede for this small sweet child of mine, that she be given purity of mind and grace and simplicity, and if it is the will of thy Son, may she know love."

Mamá Grande's shrewd eyes took in every detail. Concha was just as she had intended she should be—not merely a beautiful girl as others were beautiful, but a figure distinctive and touched with mystery.

Don Julián stood by the railing of the gallery on the second floor of his house, where he could see the spacious patio below. The two stairways curving to the landing and the single flight which led to the second floor were filled with guests. Young girls, their mothers, fathers, and aunts were ascending. When Ramón's family came up the stairs,

Don Julián met them and escorted them into the drawing room, where Concha stood between her mother and grandmother. Doña María welcomed Doña Leonora and her son, her face set in traditional well-bred serenity.

"María," Ramón's mother exclaimed, "how touching the presentation in the church! You have set the families of the city an example of piety."

Doña María Navarro did not reply. She was exasperated with her friend. What pig's eyes Ramón's mother has, little black balls with no white! she thought maliciously. She knows I want her to say how desirable Concha was in her bridal white, kneeling at the altar.

Don Julián's gaze rested on his granddaughter. She still wore the white dress, but not the white lace veil, she had worn in the church. Her great black eyes were bright now, not somber as they had been just after her dedication to the Virgin. But whatever their expression, he felt they gave her the innocence of his favorite Madonna, the beautiful little Virgin of white alabaster which stood in a niche in his library at the top of the house.

Not so Louisa, her sister. Although Louisa was two years younger than Concha, her knowing agate-colored eyes made her seem older— older even than Ignacio, their brother, who was seventeen. Louisa's dress of jade green set off her delicate olive skin strikingly in contrast with her pale yellow hair. She was aware, Don Julián could see, of the effectiveness of her costume, as she talked with a group of young men. From their delighted faces, he gathered that her witty, sometimes sharp, tongue was not well under control. Her mother evidently was aware of it, too, for she went over to the group. She would see that Louisa held strictly to the conventions. A young girl's acquaintance with the other sex must be held within the bounds of propriety, a courtly bow, graceful conversation. To many of these young men, already familiar with Paris and the Riviera, knowledge of women had already reached the point of satiation. The attraction of marriage lay in the inaccessibility of these wellborn girls, their exquisite innocence.

All of his grandchildren were handsome, as Don Julián appraised them this afternoon—his grandson, who was the center of a group of admiring young women, perhaps the most handsome. He had the long narrow face of his Spanish ancestors and their aristocratic features. If only Ramón were as distinguished-looking as Ignacio! Ramón was the short, compact type of Spaniard. He looks durable, was Don Julián's conclusion, but not romantic.

At last everyone was seated around the table that ran the length of the banquet hall. Gratefully Don Julián broke his twelve-hour fast, kept in preparation for Concha's consecration. He tasted the dry Spanish ham of the entree. It was perfect; aged for years, deep red, sliced to paper thinness. He sipped his wine. His wife, Doña María, knew how to provide.

Ramón's mother, sitting next him, said, "I hear there has been some surveying of your sugar land. You are intending to sell?" Her eyes were bright with cunning.

"You know as well as I do the surveyors are government-sent. This Calles they made President last year has a passion for the reforms started during the Revolution. He'd give all our land to the Indian villages if we'd let him. I'm ready for his representatives next time. My overseer has orders to shoot anyone who trespasses."

"Gently, gently," Doña Leonora cautioned. Then, leaning near, she said in a low tone, "There are better ways, Julián. Have you ever known a Mexican who could not be bought—little officials, big officials? Why not try it? And visit your haciendas. It is not good to be absent." She shrugged her shoulders, turned to the man on her right.

Don Julián fiddled with the food on his plate, his mind caught again in a web of nostalgia for the days of Porfirio Díaz, eight times made President. Opportunity then had been for the native Spaniard like himself and the foreign businessman. All had seemed so gay in that year of 1910, with Mexico City given over to celebration. The marble opera house built to commemorate the anniversary gleamed white in the sun. Floats and pageants passed in review. The "strong man" and Señora Díaz presided over a wealthy and brilliant society.

A few weeks, and cries of "Down with Díaz!" rang through the capital. The "great man" lay ill in his house guarded by cannon. It was the beginning of the Revolution and the taking of authority away from the *hacendados* and the Church. With a sigh Don Julián roused himself. Today was a day of festivity. He must not cloud it with vain regrets for the past or fear for the future.

It was six when the banquet was over and the dancing began. As Don Julián stood at the end of the drawing room, he felt Concha's narrow hand slipped into his. "Grandfather," she cried, "it's such a beautiful party! I am so happy."

He drew her to him. A fierce hatred filled him for all things connected with the Revolution. He would leave no stone unturned to keep security for his family, especially for Concha. He and his family had spent the worst years of the Revolution on the Riviera, but lately it had seemed safe for them here in Mexico City. "My dear," he said, releasing her, "Ramón is waiting for you."

Concha wondered, as she danced with Ramón, why her grandmother had chosen him of all the sons of their friends. She wished he were tall like her brother and had Ignacio's smoldering eyes. Ramón had beady ones like his mother. His hand, as he took hers, was so different from Ignacio's. It was solid, compact, and it grasped hers too firmly.

Ramón, for his part, was coolly appraising Concha. He respected his mother's judgment. Yes, she was right. When he took over the management of the estate, such a wife would be an asset. She would add distinction to the family. Her gentleness would serve him. With her as wife, he would be free to live his own life. Thus both he and his mother would be satisfied.

With his arm at her waist he had a sudden sense of her extreme femininity. For a moment he looked down at the folds of her dress, slightly curved by the shape of her young breasts. Desire awoke in him.

Silently they danced together. Concha could think of nothing to say. It had never been like this before; they had known each other all their lives. She was glad when the *pieza* was over and her brother asked her to dance with him.

Ignacio frowned. "I don't like the idea of your getting married. I suppose that's what Mamá Grande has in mind."

"It won't make any difference," Concha assured him. "Besides, you'll be married too, and then you won't need me."

"Do you know if Mamá Grande is thinking of anyone for me?" asked Ignacio. "Because," he went on, "I intend to choose my own wife. Mamá Grande chose once, and that's enough. I'm really a widower," he added with mock seriousness. "I've heard the aunts say so."

"You're not! You can't forever be bound to a girl who is dead!" Concha exclaimed. "That's an outworn custom. The aunts are a hundred years behind the times."

"So is Mamá Grande, selecting the ones we shall marry. Many people in this city are choosing for themselves."

"Not our friends." Concha glanced about the room, knowing it included all the rich Spaniards of the city.

"We're just a tight knot in the midst of—well——" Ignacio did not know how to finish his sentence. He had not told even Concha of the

young men and women, filled with new ideas, he had met at the preparatory school he was attending. "Anyway, remember you're not to
marry before I do," he added.

"How can I help it? How do you know Mamá Grande won't have
it happen very soon?"

"You can make Grandfather not let her." Ignacio's interest shifted.
"Look at Louisa! She is a shameful flirt. She's flirting with Ramón, the
little demon! See how demurely she lowers her eyes when Mamá
Grande or Mamá is looking at her."

"Is Mamá Grande watching her?" asked Concha, anxious to shield
her sister.

"Oh, Louisa can take care of herself," replied Ignacio. "Only when
she and her partner are in the middle of the floor, where she knows
neither Mamá nor Mamá Grande can see her, does she even lift her
eyes."

Ramón, dancing with Louisa, murmured, "I shall be outside the
Church of San Francisco tomorrow morning at the time of early
Mass."

"I shall insist that I go to early Mass." Louisa let the fringe of her
eyelashes rest on her cheeks, hiding her eyes, but not before she had
seen a small flame kindle in Ramón's. Was he in earnest, or was she
simply a child in his eyes?

"Concha will be with you," he added. He was thinking, I'd like to
have Concha for my wife, but always have Louisa to flirt with, too.

Don Julián and the priest, Father Cristóbal, paced up and down the
balcony outside the drawing room. They were two old men whose
friendship had deepened through the years, both Spaniards, both
against the changes the Revolution had brought. Father Cristóbal
welcomed the opportunity to enlist Don Julián's help in a new problem
facing the Church. "I am fearful that this President Calles may enforce
the anticlerical clauses of the 1917 Constitution," he said.

Don Julián did not answer immediately. He stopped, one hand resting on the railing of the balcony. His fingers beat out the rhythm of
the music coming from the great *sala.* "If he does?" he asked finally.

"We must not wait for that. We must move first. We are thinking of
calling the people's attention through the press to the laws which are
against the Church."

"But they are not being enforced now. Would it not be better to
avoid such open opposition? This Calles is hotheaded and given to

sudden violent acts," Don Julián cautioned. "And it is possible," he added, "that if we do not set him against us his wife may, in time, influence him to accept the guidance of the Church. I have heard she is a devout woman."

"Sometime we must take our stand," the priest answered. "Ever since that Indian, Juárez, made laws divorcing Church and State, the Church has suffered. Magnificent, our holdings until then. A third of the land of Mexico belonged to us at that time, as you know."

"Yes," said Don Julián sadly, "the rich and the Church walked together behind the Cross in those days." Melancholy settled over him. Now Mother Church was poor, and he too might become poor. His mind went back to the things Doña Leonora had said to him at the table. Had government surveyors marked his land for distribution? He had an uneasy sense of the lawsuits he and his father before him had engaged in, to get Indian holdings.

"Most of my land came straight from the Spanish Crown. In the family for centuries," he said aloud.

Father Cristóbal's face wore a quizzical expression. So my friend has been thinking about his wealth all the time he has been talking of spiritual things, he reflected. Well, we both love riches, but I only for the Church.

There was a burst of music and laughter from the room beyond, and a flood of bright color seemed to inundate the two as the dancers poured through the French doors out onto the gallery.

~~~~~~~~~~~~~~~~~~~~ *2* ~~~~~

THE fiesta was over. Don Julián closed the door of his library, seated himself at his desk, and picked up the book he had put down the evening before. It was a history of the Spanish people. He made a point of reading it each autumn.

The house was very still when he finished the story of the thousand years Spain held back Mohammedan hordes. Out of the centuries of bloodshed, Spain and the Catholic faith had emerged triumphant. Shutting the book, he felt his mind going on with the magnificent story. Spain had spread her power into the New World. Again there had been the spilling of precious Spanish blood, but fifty thousand Indians had been baptized in one day. This was the miracle of half a continent brought under the Catholic faith—the mother country and the mother Church again triumphant. Both had become fabulously rich, possessing the riches of the New World, gold and silver and land.

He remembered his youth, the four matched horses which had pulled his father's carriage when he went to visit his haciendas, the silver mountings on bridle and harness, the engraved crest, the hundreds of peons who dropped to their knees when the carriage entered the hacienda gates. Both the country estates and town house had come to him at his father's death, with their many servants bound to him by their families' debts, still serving him faithfully with Indian submissiveness.

He looked about the great library with its chandelier and its candelabras on tables and mantel, now fitted with electric globes. In memory he saw their hundreds of crystals lighted by the flaming candle points. The gentle face of the maid who, in his young manhood, attended them seemed illumined in the soft yellow of his bedroom candle. For years she had serviced the candles, her mornings devoted to replacing the burnt-out ones, her afternoons to setting them alight, her nights to seeing the last one extinguished in his own chamber. She had grown old in his service, bowing to his will.

He rose and stood before the portrait of a young man above the stone mantel. He wore ruff and wrist ruffles; his long, aristocratic hands rested on a sword. He was the Spanish ancestor who had gone on pilgrimage to the Holy Sepulcher.

Then Don Julián walked to the end of the book-lined room and stood before a picture, studying it for a long time. The somber browns and dull opaque reds of the background merged with the sorrowing face of the Virgin. All the light seemed concentrated on the figure of the crucified Christ lying across her knees. Staring up at the heavy patches of blood on feet, hands, and side, the drawn suffering of the face, he felt death in all its dread reality.

Turning, he gazed at the lovely alabaster figure of the young Virgin in the niche on the opposite wall, eternally young' in her radiant purity. He walked the length of the room and knelt before her in veneration.

Then rising, he flung back the curtains closely drawn across the window. In the glow of a street lamp directly opposite he saw two figures crouching, wrapped in their serapes. At every festival time the streets were full of Indians, come to worship at the shrine of the Brown Virgin, asking for her intercession. Like a great dark wave they inundated the city. Why should they thus crowd the city simply because the Virgin of Guadalupe had appeared to an Indian boy and asked for a shrine? The Church of Guadalupe had been built with the money of men like himself.

Then he noticed a Mexican man and woman standing half in the shadow. They were looking up at the house. Why were they there?

3

BETWEEN the dwellings of the rich and the very poor lay narrow streets flanked by rows of adobe houses, lime-washed in amber, rose, and green. There was a stir, these autumn days, in these homes where life had once been sustained just above want. The Revolution for which the people had fought was bearing fruit. Until the Revolution no Mexican could hold a position in the foreign banks higher than that of clerk. In express, railroad, mine, and oil offices, too, a Mexican was allowed to hold only the most lowly position. There had been no freedom of speech, no freedom of the press.

But now Mexicans could work and speak. The native banks and all government offices were staffed by Mexicans. Women were teaching in the new schools, attending colleges of medicine and law. Upon the walls of public buildings artists were painting the symbols of freedom, thrice-sized figures of peasant, miner, and artisan, in past servitude and present productivity. In the modern scenes, a new character loomed large—the teacher. On the walls of a hacienda taken for a school of agriculture, Rivera painted Great Mother Mexico, fertile again, released from the chains of the money-changer.

Artists, looking like laborers with their shoes white with lime dust, their bodies sweaty with toil, thronged up the scaffoldings erected in public buildings, contented, happy. What did it matter that they worked for plasterers' wages? They were participating in such a renaissance of art as the world had not seen for a very long time.

Guadalupe Villar, a government surveyor, had been married today and had brought his bride home to one of the tiny pink-walled houses. This very morning he had paid the first rent in advance. The house had three rooms grouped around a minute patio. Behind was a dark kitchen, where a barefoot Indian girl was even now arranging her griddle and grinding stone. There was almost no furniture in the house, but there would be. For several months young Villar had had a position with the government, and Soledad, his stout little wife, hoped to teach in one of the public schools of the city.

As she surveyed the patio, with its one scrawny cypress tree, Soledad puckered up her brows. "When you do your surveying, you'll bring back ferns and orchids, won't you, my husband?"

"If the government gives me time," he replied.

"Against the wall here, we could put pots of orchids. If you go south, you could bring me some, couldn't you?"

Guadalupe watched her. When the deep black pools of her eyes held light, as they did now, he hoped she had forgotten the hard years of the Revolution. She had been intimately a part of it, from the day the federal troops had entered the town where she lived and shot her father as he sat in his place on the bandstand, waiting to play the drum for the Sunday-evening promenade. Afterward she had searched for him, walking among the dead, thrusting her candle into the face of one after another of those who had come to his defense. At last she had found him, his music rack fallen across his chest.

After this she had insisted that her brother, one of General Pancho Villa's men, take her with him. He had not wanted to. "Only the women of the common soldiers follow their men," he had explained. "So far as our meager resources have allowed, you have been brought up as a gentlewoman. I will put you under the care of the good Sisters at the convent."

"No, no," she had cried, "I will not go to them! I don't like the Church. It is on the side of the rich and privileged." She would be proud to be a *soldadera* following the ragged troops of the Revolution, cooking for her brother.

Thinking of these things, Guadalupe shuddered. He came of a Protestant father. During the years of the Revolution he had been in the States at school sent there by a rich North American woman who belonged to his father's faith. Though he believed in the Revolution, he found its violence shocking.

He had met Soledad a few months before, when the government had sent him to survey Don Julián Navarro's great sugar plantation. As he passed through the village, near the gate that led to the hacienda dwelling he had seen her standing in the door of a hut. As she was dressed in the garb of the city, with shoes and stockings, he knew at once she did not belong to the village.

"Why are you here?" he had asked her.

"To teach," she had said simply, and then her eyes had taken fire. "I fought," she told him, "to bring freedom to my country. What would be the sense of fighting if no good came of it, if the Indian villages were not ministered to?"

Soledad was a widow when he met her, with a little girl to care for. At least she stoutly called herself a widow. But during the fighting there had never been a chance for the marriage ceremony. They had planned to have a civil service after the fighting was over. But long before that the man had been killed.

A few days after Guadalupe had first seen Soledad, her child had died. "I could not care for her properly in the village—malaria here is very bad—and I did not have enough money to buy medicine," she had told him. It was the rainy season, and over the floor of the hut where Soledad lived there was water. Guadalupe felt it, wet against his ankles, as he stood looking down at the dead child, doll-like in her immobility.

Now, so bent was he on exorcising his mind of these scenes, he all but shouted, "I'll get you every kind of orchid growing between here and South America. You'll be the envy of all the women of Mexico City."

"Really, my husband!" Soledad exclaimed, clasping her hands.

"Wait!" he cried, and dashed out of the house and down the street to the market. That morning, on his way to his office, he had seen a row of orchids in wire baskets hanging from a support of the market roof.

Only after he had bought one did he reflect that he had broken the peso which had been solemnly set aside as the first little saving toward the buying of a desk. When could he save another? But he forgot his disappointment when he saw Soledad's eyes and her hands as she fondled the tuberous branch which had thrust forth a delicate yellow-green bud.

Together they hung the orchid against the wall of the *corredor*—the gallery which encircled the patio—and then, as the sun had sunk behind the house wall and the air was getting chilly, they went into their *sala*. They laughed at its emptiness. The orchid would bloom tomorrow, or the next day surely. They were safe here in their house; and the past could be forgotten, even those very last days of Soledad's in the village, when, instigated by the hacienda overseer, the village had driven her out.

Later in the evening, they went forth to wander about the city.

"It's wonderful, isn't it, my husband?" Soledad kept saying. "I am a part of this city. Here is the center of the Revolution, and I am a part of the Revolution." After the years spent in the hot lands she was stimulated and renewed by the cool, crisp air of the mountain valley. The malaria, which for so long had held her in alternate fever and chills, was miraculously gone. Nothing was impossible for her here. "Let me pass the house of Don Julián Navarro, husband of Doña María Salcedo de Navarro." With light mockery she pronounced the mouth-filling names.

"Why do you torment yourself?" asked Guadalupe. "Let us forget!"

"Forget!" Soledad's laugh was tinged with bitterness.

Her husband made no further protest, realizing it would take time to erase from her mind how Don Julián's overseer had seen to it that she was stoned and driven from the village.

As they stood silently before the Navarro house, tall and dark, an upper window was illumined and, for a moment, the figure of Don Julián was silhouetted against the lighted room.

"So he does not sleep peacefully," said Soledad, turning away. "Rightly so. Six months, is it, since you surveyed his land, my husband? Surely soon Calles will make him divide it with the villages."

THE morning after Concha's party Francisco again rose from his sleeping mat and picked up his keys, grumbling. "The *gachupines* never leave us in peace." The word *gachupín,* although it was only the Indian word for Spaniard, sounded like an oath as spoken by Francisco. "Yesterday it was a fiesta, the new wagons of the rich crowding each other in and out. Hardly had an old man a chance to lock the gate when it must be unlocked and at an hour like this!"

Again Alejandra the cook stood, baskets in hand. With an angry jerk she pulled her *rebozo* tighter over her shoulders and back. "There is food at the hacienda, is it not so?—but the *gachupín* insists on city foods." Once more the word *gachupín* sounded like an oath.

A bell rang sharply. Francisco moved quickly to answer it, but before he could ascend the stairs Doña María called out, "We must be off in an hour."

"*Sí, sí, Señora,*" Francisco assented with false humility.

The women of the household were going to the family's little hacienda today. It lay beyond the city close against the great mountains which circled the valley of Mexico. It was the only one of Don Julián's haciendas he considered it wise to visit at present. He would have preferred that all his family remain safe within the city, but he could not prevail upon the women to give up their customary harvest-time visit. Doña María had declared her intention several days ago, insisting that the overseer was not performing his duties properly. The dairy at the hacienda was not yielding as much profit as she believed it should. (Long ago Don Julián had surrendered to her the accounts of the overseers.) Concha had begged to be allowed to go too, and Concha's mother wanted release from the city.

Despite the early preparations it was afternoon before the grandmother took her seat beside the chauffeur. Louisa, sitting between her mother and Concha on the back seat, cried, "I don't see why you take us away from the city, Mamá Grande. You give a party for Concha one day, and the very next you hide her away." For Louisa everything was spoiled by the trip to the country. Ramón had tossed her a flower as she entered the church this morning. Tomorrow . . . but tomorrow she would not be there.

"Hush," said Doña María. "It's not for my granddaughter to tell me what to do."

As they left the city behind, Mamá gave a sigh of delight. To the encircling mountains stretched the fields. The rows of sage-green cactus, looking like giant artichokes, set the maize off into yellow squares. Some sensitive chord in Mamá vibrated to the ancient and beautiful scene of fertility. So, she thought, had the Aztecs looked out upon their harvest, celebrating in festival the green corn mother and the young corn god.

As they neared the edge of the valley the snow-wrapped mountains Popocatepetl and Iztaccihuatl, the god mates of Aztec legend, towered over them in majestic grandeur, dwarfing the crenelated wall of their hacienda. The car passed through the first gate, down an avenue of trees, and through the second gate. It came to a halt before the low flight of steps leading to the high-pillared veranda of the house. By the front door, dutifully outlined in flowers as a sign of welcome, the servants were grouped. They moved forward now, welcoming the family with soft words. *"Buenos días, Señora; buenos días, Señoritas.* God go with the Señora," they murmured as the "Old One" passed through the doorway. Louisa skipped along after her grandmother, hoping for activity of some kind after the long tedious ride.

At the end of the veranda the door to the family chapel stood open. The fragrance of flowers, herbs, and incense reached Concha as she followed her mother into the dim room and knelt beside her. Through a window behind the altar a shaft of sunlight fell. Concha, lifting her head, saw it rest on the still, rapt face of her mother. At last the older woman rose, and took her daughter's hand. Together they passed through the first and second patios. Mamá fingered the flowers and the leaves as she went. When they reached the wall at the back of the hacienda she took from her handbag a key and opened a gate half hidden in honeysuckle, and they went out.

For a long time they stood without speaking, watching evening come down over the fields. The two high mountains, the sleeping woman and watching man, cast longer and longer shadows until the great plain was a monotone. "It is time, my daughter," the older woman said at last, "that you should be aware of your heritage. In the days of the Conquest, as you know, in many families Aztec blood was joined with the Spanish. It was so in my family. Some claim that in the long succession of Spanish marriages since then the Indian strain has been bred out. I do not share that belief, nor do I wish my children to. Our destiny and the Indian's are one. I have studied for many years the history of the Aztec people. It is a noble race. I see in you, my daughter, many of its traits. You have the Indian's capacity for profound abnegation. I hope you have its proud independence. I hope you will love the earth with Indian passion." She stooped, scooping up a handful of the soil, letting it filter down through her fingers back to the ground. "Remember, my daughter," she said, "all life the Aztecs knew is contained in the land. In marriage a woman joins it in productivity."

Concha did not fully comprehend the meaning of her mother's words. But something in her mother's face held her from asking. As she looked at her mother she seemed changed. All the urbane, city

look had gone from her. In its place was the immobility Concha associated with Indians. She seemed taller, too, standing so straight and
still.

After breakfast the next morning Concha pulled a table to the open
window. With determination she set to work to write the essay she
had promised her grandfather would be finished when she returned
to the city.

Don Julián had not wanted Concha to interrupt her studies, so
when he gave his consent that she visit the hacienda he had inflicted
upon her this task. Since she left the convent a year ago he had insisted that she study with him. "You are as intelligent as your
brother," he had said, "and I don't see why just because you are a girl
you should be ignorant in the higher matters of learning." Each
morning since she had gone to his library and taken the old man's
instruction.

The only sounds that reached Concha were the cheep of insects
from the earth not far below her window sill and the rhythmic *pat-pat*
of women's hands shaping *tortillas* into paper-thin cakes. The window
was open, making a mirror for the thick walls of the house, reflecting
the branches of trees and the calla lilies growing along the garden wall.
A sudden consciousness of the beauty and power of her body broke
through Concha's will to work. She stretched her hands over her head.
A stirring sensation of growth spread through her and a longing for a
completion that lay not within herself.

Then the moment was gone. She reached for its magnificence. But
the events of the last two days crowded her mind—her dedication to
the Virgin, Ramón's presence, everyone's emphasis on her marriage to
him, and her mother's words to her last evening. She had a confused
sense of pain and trouble.

"Concha, Concha," Louisa called through the window. "Why do
you stay here going over a lot of musty papers as if you were still a
schoolgirl when you aren't any more?"

Concha did not answer.

"Sometimes I think you were born just to make robes for the saints,"
Louisa cried, impatient with her sister when she did not answer.

"But I'm not. Mamá Grande already has my marriage arranged."
She was thinking of the aunt who attended Louisa and herself, took
them to Mass and to parties and shopping, always in black. Always,
always just an aunt! Many such black-clad figures moved about in

the houses of the family. The women belonging to the Navarro and the Salcedo families were legion, so it seemed to Concha. Everyone had an unmarried aunt or two. And added to those were the aunts on her mother's side. No, she would not be like them. Certainly she would marry.

Louisa laughed at the expression on her sister's face. "Well, then, hurry and marry."

"I shall, but only when Mamá Grande decides the time," Concha answered. "But I won't marry Ramón, if that is what you want to find out." Concha didn't know why she had said that. It had never occurred to her until now to marry anyone except the man selected for her by her grandmother.

There was the rustle of skirts behind them. They looked up to see their grandmother, a mixture of amusement and annoyance on her face.

"You'll do what I say, Concha, and you will too, Louisa. Now let there be an end to this idle talk." The amusement faded out of her face. In its place came the hard look of the tribal woman.

"Yes, Mamá Grande," the two girls chorused demurely.

"And now go out in the garden," commanded Doña María.

Concha sat on the edge of the fountain staring down at the blue and yellow tiles that paved it. Louisa, in a kind of irritated excitement, darted about, moving with quickness and grace but with a restless energy that seemed never to be satisfied. At last she sat down on the coping across from her sister. She was a little uneasy over Concha's withdrawal.

"I didn't mean to tease you," she said, "about always dressing the Virgin. But when you were a little girl you liked so much to carry flowers to her in May that I thought maybe you'd like to do it all your life. Maybe become a nun." Louisa's face brightened. The idea interested her, and it would leave Ramón free.

"Louisa, why should you even think I want never to marry? Please go away," begged Concha.

Louisa ran swiftly through the garden, stopping once to fling a tiny stone back at her sister. Concha did not notice. She reached down and stirred the water, watching the troubled reflection of the calla lilies which encircled the base of the fountain. The tall yellow pistils within the great waxen flowers swayed and blended. Why, she wondered, did I say I would not marry Ramón?

5

THE DAY after her return from the hacienda, as she walked along the gallery of the third floor to her grandfather's library, Concha stopped and leaned over the rail to see the bright blue sky roofing the patio and to feel the sun on her head. Very distinctly from the gallery below she heard the words of her father's customary farewell to her mother, "Now I am going." Leaning farther over, she caught a glimpse of him walking down the stairs. His soft fedora hat was jauntily tipped to the side of his head. Only one of his bold black eyes was visible. The sunlight touched his hand as he raised it in brief, final salutation to her mother. The long, tapering fingers were delicate but strong; the wrist and the palm were in perfect proportion. She saw her mother looking after him, resignation in every line of her face. In that instant Concha understood where her father was going. Things spoken quietly among the servants of the household took on meaning—whispered words of his "little home" and another woman. She had a sudden understanding of what that salutation meant to her mother.

Concha turned away, hurrying to keep her appointment with her grandfather, wishing to forget her mother's face. She listened intently this morning to his discussion of Sor Juana Inés de la Cruz, Mexico's great poet and nun. Under Concha's evident appreciation Don Julián's enthusiasm grew. His faded blue eyes filled with light. "My child, you make me very happy with your interest in your studies."

"Grandfather," she answered, "please may I study with you for many years? I am not fitted yet for marriage."

"Would you, then, wish to take vows?" he asked gently.

Concha shook her head. "It is not that I do not care to marry."

"Is Ramón, then, not acceptable to you?" he asked.

The question threw Concha into confusion. "I don't know, Grandfather. I—I——"

"We will leave the matter undecided for the present," he said. "You may go now."

As she moved toward the French door, Concha saw Ignacio just outside in the gallery, summoning her with an imperious gesture. She understood that he wanted her to join him on the flat roof of the house, their usual meeting place. Then he disappeared.

She found Ignacio standing behind a long line of clothes the laundress had hung on the roof to dry, his back toward her. "Is anything wrong, Nacho?" she asked with concern.

"You must help me!" Ignacio turned and faced her. "I have a plan. I've worked hard at the preparatory school, and now I want to go to the States for my university training. Will you intercede for me with Grandfather?"

"But Nacho," Concha exclaimed, overcome by the enormity of the request, "I've heard Grandfather say that we are not fitted for the way of life of the States. Their efficiency and drive, he says, aren't healthy for us. Suppose you should come back to us made so—what shall I say —so driving?"

"Strong, do you mean? It's they who aren't strong. They talk about compromise all the time," he answered, scorn in his voice. "It's cowardly."

"Then why do you want to go there?" asked Concha.

"Because you are your own master there."

"But that's bad, Grandfather says, especially for women."

"Well, I'm not a woman," Nacho retorted. "Of course a woman shouldn't be her own master."

"But Nacho, Spain is our mother country. I could ask Grandfather to send you to Spain, if you prefer not to go to the university here."

"You don't understand—it is freedom I need!" Ignacio had never spoken to Concha of the young people at the preparatory school who had shaken off the confining customs he was still subjected to. There was a girl named Berta Mendoza who was going to New York to study medicine. He had even walked home with her several afternoons. She lived in a small house with her father, who, she told him, had been an exile in the States during the last years of the Díaz regime. He was a scholar and almost the whole of their small house was filled with his books. The picture he drew of life in the States had fascinated Ignacio, and so did the girl Berta. She was pretty in an odd way. She had large dark eyes that had none of the calm he had been trained to admire. They sparkled with life and mischief and then would sober. They were more the eyes of a boy trained to think, and yet they were tender the way his own mother's were. She was a tiny person, afire always with some cause or project. When he was with her he sometimes disliked her, for she was always saying things that annoyed him, but when he was away from her he longed to see her. If he went to the States, he meant to take rooms near the Mendozas and see her all he wanted to. Thinking of her now, he forgot about Concha.

Then he heard his sister say, "Grandfather will never consent."

"But try, Concha," he pleaded. "He'll do anything for you. You wouldn't stand against me, would you? You wouldn't let me be unhappy, would you?"

Concha's love for Ignacio rushed up in her the way it had ever since she could remember, offering him fullness of service. Ignacio had been an unhappy youth, misunderstood, he thought, by his grandparents and father. It was Concha who had assured him over and over that both his grandmother and grandfather were proud of him. If his father did not entirely approve of him, it was only because he thought him too serious. "And it is good to be serious," Concha comforted him. And was he not the most Spanish-looking of them all?

Of his mother's love Concha never had to assure him. But his mother was a person too beautiful, almost too sacred in Ignacio's eyes to be burdened with his difficulties. She was one to be protected and shielded. Concha was his confidante, his companion, and his go-between in matters that involved his elders.

"I'll try," she told him at last, "but Grandfather won't listen, I feel certain."

"If you try, you'll succeed," he answered. "If you don't get him to let me go, I'll know it's because I don't come first with you any more, or because you are afraid."

Ignacio walked away. He didn't want to see her eyes. He knew how stricken they could look when she was hurt, and he knew he had hurt her, doubting her devotion and her bravery. But she must do what he to'd her. Not once looking back, he tramped angrily away over the sheets the laundress had soaped and laid on the floor to bleach in the strong sunlight.

Concha was troubled. She felt inadequate to deal with a contest between the proud wills of her grandfather and her brother. Somehow she must persuade Nacho to give up his plan. She started to follow him, in her hurry running straight into a line full of clothes. As the wet surfaces struck her face and her hands, she drew back. After all, it would do no good to follow Ignacio unless she could give him what he wanted.

She went over to the parapet and, resting her elbows upon it, her chin in her hands, stared out into the brilliant intensity of the autumn.

sunlight streaming down upon the city. Surrounded by the blue-black mountains, the city and the valley seemed a luminous caldron, the downflaming sun meeting the upspringing brilliance thrown off from the myriad flat roofs. She felt herself caught up into the lively splendor of light, into happiness that outdistanced the perplexities of the morning.

"Concha!" She swung around to see Ignacio with the scarlet *muleta* of the bullfighter in one hand, a short sword in the other. "I want you to help me practice."

So it was not always necessary to surrender entirely to Ignacio's wishes! With a sudden rush of renewed devotion to her brother, she exclaimed, "We don't need the horns! I can be quicker without them, as a good bull should." This was something she had shrunk from before in their practice.

With grace and art, they executed the final movements of a bullfight. As Ignacio slowly moved the *muleta* Concha lowered her head, followed unerringly the hypnotic movement of the scarlet cloth. Closer, closer he led the bull to his body. With a quick movement he raised his right hand. For a split second, he let the sword's point touch Concha between the shoulders, then threw down *muleta* and sword and stood back. The tactical advantage was his—the danger of death had passed from him to her.

Concha stood up, faced him. Her hair had escaped its pins and tumbled down in a glistening black mass around her face. She tossed it back. With her two hands she grasped her brother's shoulders. "I *am* brave, Nacho! This you can see. If I fail with Grandfather, it will not be because I do not dare to plead for you. Say it, Nacho, it will not be because I am not brave."

He laughed. "Death doesn't mean anything to a Spaniard. Besides, we were only practicing."

"Death means less to a Mexican. I am a Mexican," said Concha proudly.

6

It was November. Tomorrow would be All Souls' Day. Mexico would visit her dead. Many would feast at the graves; many would watch at the graves until the candles burned lower and lower and finally went out. Each would keep the day according to his traditions. But in every household a macabre note would be added—candy coffins and skeletons given as presents.

The Navarros' old servant Francisco was leaving that evening for his village just outside the walls of the Navarros' great sugar hacienda, situated beyond the barrier of the mountains where the land begins to drop down toward the sea. It was essential that he should be there for tomorrow's tribute to the dead, for he was one of the village elders. By hard walking he could reach the village by tomorrow afternoon. He was strong and well, albeit he had told Doña María of a serious complaint which had seized him at this festival time and also that his wife was very sick. He could not tell her the real reason. She might deny the necessity of his going.

In the late afternoon Concha went to the gate and gave him a package. "Take these sugar dainties to your wife, Francisco. Tell her it grieves me that she is ill. But couldn't you bring her back with you? I have not seen my *nana* for a very long time." Francisco's wife had been Concha's nurse, and she loved the wrinkled old woman.

"I fear the distance is too great. Her sickness is the cause of my journey."

"I understand," Concha answered. "But remember to give the package to my *nana*."

"*Sí, niña.* When I reach the village it will be my first consideration." His eyes were soft and warm as he watched her cross the patio. She understood his necessity to go to his village.

It was late when the Navarro maids, housemen, and chauffeurs had finished the day's work. They always hoped that the meal served to the family at ten would be the last call upon them for the day, although Doña María, Louisa, or Ignacio, even Don Julián himself, too impatient to wait for the ringing of bells, might any moment come to the balcony rail and call up to them, demanding some last personal service. In many of the great houses the servants lived in the dark basements, but ever since there had been an epidemic of typhus in the city Doña María had lodged her servants on the roof, contending that no Indian could live without sunshine. He might not have it in his village hut but for centuries he had spent his days in the sun.

The evening was warm. The window and door of the servants' kitchen were open. The women loosened their hair. All had taken the cramping shoes off their feet. They were feasting before Francisco left.

A small charcoal brazier in the corner of the kitchen sent forth its glow. A young girl knelt before it, deftly turning *tortillas* on the griddle. Cleofas, Concha's maid, put candles before the shrine of the Virgin of Guadalupe; Alejandra, the cook who ruled them all with her sharp tongue, set a bowl filled with hot *mole* on the table. The men drew up chairs, resting their bare, strong feet on the cool floor.

When the feast was over, Francisco set out. He should have left earlier, but he had lingered over his drink. He was the oldest man of the village, and he must lead the procession on its calls upon the dead. He waited on the edge of the city until daylight for the bus which would take him over the mountain barrier. In the rocking, swaying vehicle he alternately dozed and prayed to the Brown Virgin, special protector of Indians, catching glimpses of her picture framed just above the head of the driver. In the early morning he started his long walk, covering the ground rapidly with the quick running step of the Indian.

The road dipped down from valley to valley. The earth, replete with water after the long summer of rain, was brilliant with shining green foliage. Shrubs and trees were festooned with red and purple flowers and berries. The harvest, later there than in the valley of Mexico, had just begun. He saw golden heaps of corn. People thronged the roads going to their villages carrying bunches of marigolds, the flower of the dead. In the towns, the rich rode past him, their cars piled with floral pieces.

A little reluctantly he turned from the companionable main thoroughfare into the private road that led to the Navarro hacienda. High on either side of him stood the sugar cane, walling him into the sea of green. Mile after mile he walked, the only sound the rustling of myriad narrow leaves, one upon the other. Late in the afternoon he toiled up a low hill and looked down on his village. Its huts hugged together as if against a common foe. Beyond stood the walled-in hacienda buildings. Towering over all was the domed church. Tiny figures, white specks in the distance, were moving upon the churchyard. Quickly he made his descent. Pausing only for a moment at his own hut to change clothes, he went on to the churchyard. Everything, he saw, was in order. Bunches of marigolds hung on the surrounding walls. Crosses made of the yellow blossoms lay on the graves. Quietly the elders of the village, clad in clean pants and shirts, gathered around him, giving him dignified salutations. The unworthy humility he showed to Don Julián and Doña María was gone from his mind. He straightened his shoulders.

The bell in the church tower began to ring. And after a little it was answered by another far away across the valley. Another and another, until the air was filled with the sound of the bells.

Minute after minute, fifteen, twenty, the clanging echoed and re-echoed over the valley. Then suddenly it ceased. Into the silence fell the *beat-beat* of an Indian drum. Another and another. The hollow, echoing *pound-pound* spoke to Francisco. The drum was the voice of his people; its inherited rhythm throbbed in his veins. Then it, too, ceased, and in the unbroken stillness Francisco, followed by the other men, moved forward, walking the path of the dead marked by the bright marigold petals, a yellow thread leading out of the churchyard, down the village street, to the first hut where death had entered during the year.

A woman stood in the doorway to greet them. "We have come to visit the Little Dead One," said Francisco.

One by one the men stooped and entered the low doorway. Marigolds adorned the walls, and the Brown Virgin looked down upon them from her shrine. On the table stood an earthenware jar filled with turkey *mole*. Francisco longed to taste it, for he had not eaten since last evening. But first he must speak to Cruz, the Little Dead One. He was glad his departed friend had his food, too, on a small table beside the big one. And there too were the things that Cruz, the dead man, loved. A nice sombrero! He would like it. He'd put it on jauntily over one ear. Francisco was pleased with the presents for Cruz, the food, and the yellow candles set in the black candlesticks flanking the earthen jar of *mole*.

He approached the low table, the other men at his side, their hats held close to their breasts. "How are you, Little Dead One?" he asked. "I haven't seen you since that day we drank *pulque* together in the shop not far from the great house in Mexico City. You told me then that the crops were good, that the corn stood high this year."

This was Francisco's last talk with Cruz. Turning now, he addressed the men gathered around him, telling them to eat of the food for the living. When they had finished, they followed the bright petals over the village until all who had died during the last twelve months had been visited and feasted with. Darkness was long fallen over the valley, for there were many dead this year.

Now Francisco was ready to go back to the service of Doña María. He was content. He had had his moment of dignity; he had had time for the fellowship of sorrow. The dead had been courteously entertained by the living. He would meet the men of the village again when they came to the city to make application for a portion of the land to be returned to them from Don Julián's many acres.

All through the winter, month after month, the men of Francisco's village and delegations from other villages came to Mexico City to present their needs, to ask that their communal lands, left to them by the Spanish Crown but in the centuries since filched from them, be given back. They filled the official waiting rooms. They wanted fields; they wanted water; they wanted teachers. Dressed in their white trousers and colored shirts, serapes neatly folded on their left shoulders, their high-crowned hats in their hands, they entered the buildings of their government.

"God go with you!" they murmured in their soft musical voices as the men of the government, their representatives for whom they had fought in the Revolution, passed by. Then they sat on chairs or, when the chairs were filled, squatted on the floor, waiting. Some bowed themselves low when they saw President Calles, who was their present hope. In the days of Porfirio Díaz' regime such as they had been reduced to serfs, impressed into the army, sold to work in the tropics. After the fighting which freed them from such slavery had ended, there had been a series of generals in power. General Obregón's administration had been bright with promise. In his budget for government he had allowed as much for schools as for the upkeep of the army, and he had appointed state commissions to deal with the problems of villages. President Calles, too, had distributed much land. But Francisco's village as yet had received nothing.

Pedro, an old man from the village who had served with Zapata, the violent peasant leader of the Revolution, and had been with him when he was treacherously killed, was getting impatient. Often, he said, he met his general at night in the deep ravine beyond the village, where he went with only his gun for companion. Zapata never allowed his old friend to see him, but the voice that spoke to Pedro was the voice of Zapata, and the words were Zapata's: "The land belongs to him who works it." Had Zapata returned to tell him he should fight again in order that his village might be given back its rightful possessions? Or did Zapata wish him to await the *Ingeniero*?

At the market place on Sunday men talked of the *Ingeniero*. Not one man but many was the *Ingeniero*. He carried great rolls of blue paper, on which were marked out in white lines acres that were to be taken from the haciendas and returned to those villagers whose portion, guaranteed to them at the time of the Conquest, had been lost to them. Precious sources of water, also, marked out in white lines, were to be restored. The *Ingeniero* had made such a picture of Navarro holdings. At least Pedro had seen a man with a roll of blue paper going over the hacienda, and he had stopped in the village. "But why then," Pedro asked Francisco, "is the land not yet ours?"

"We must be patient, give the government time," Francisco told him over and over as the two sat in Don Julián's gatehouse after a day spent by Pedro at the government offices.

7

Autumn passed into winter. The bougainvillea vine which had twined itself around the colonnades of the balconies of the Navarro house and climbed three stories, spreading itself along the parapet surrounding the roof, hung its wine-red clusters of flowers against the gray stone. White honeysuckle, weaving itself into the wrought-iron railings, scented the air with its delicate perfume. Pots suspended from walls and railings were filled with bright flowers.

From week to week Concha put off asking the boon for Ignacio. All the family stood in awe of its austere head. Don Julián's son and his grandchildren, with the exception of Concha, used the polite "you" in addressing him, never the more familiar "thou," the accepted salutation between members of a family. Although Don Julián had given

Concha permission "to break the you" when speaking to him in private, only occasionally did she do so.

To incur his displeasure was something avoided even by Doña María, his wife. How then, thought Concha, can I, the most submissive to his will, ask a thing so clearly in opposition to his wishes? But as the winter term at the preparatory school drew to a close, Nacho left her no peace, each day demanding that this be the day she speak. He had followed her this morning into the music room, where she always prepared the essays her grandfather gave her to write. The room, a few steps above the level of the library, was itself on two levels, with a door leading out of the upper level onto a bit of roof several feet lower than the main roof of the house.

Just as she settled herself on one of the steps leading to the higher level and spread out her papers, the door to the roof was jerked open and Ignacio strode in. Leaning on the rail that divided the two halves of the room, he looked down upon his sister. His fine, thin mouth was petulant, his nostrils expanded slightly. "So you are afraid after all?" he said in a tone of disdain.

Concha looked up. "Do be quiet. Grandfather will hear you, and then you won't have a chance. You know we are not supposed to talk here. It disturbs Grandfather."

"I don't care whether it does or not. I want to know what you are going to do."

"I'm going to do what I said I would."

"Today?"

"Yes, today!" Concha saw she could no longer delay. If she did, Nacho might do something reckless. Getting up, she moved toward the library door. Simultaneously Nacho withdrew to the roof.

Concha was a particularly apt pupil this morning, both eager and responsive. Don Julián was pleased. At the end of the hour, as she stood by his desk waiting for tomorrow's assignment—waiting, too, to quiet her heart so that she might speak of Nacho's desire—he said, "I wish all my grandchildren loved learning as you do."

"Nacho does more than I, Grandfather. He loves it for itself. I love it because I love to be with you." She had a feeling that in depreciating her own abilities she could build up Nacho's. "He has told me how he longs to study and perfect himself."

"I am gratified to hear it." There was a slightly ironic note in her grandfather's voice.

"He has talked often with me, Grandfather. He is really bound up in his studies. He says he wants to take his place in the Mexico of today. And to do it he longs to study in the States."

"That is enough, Concha." Don Julián's white brows drew together. A stern look came into his eyes. "You whom I have trusted with my ideals, you who, I thought, would always remain loyal to them, have allowed a willful youth to turn you to his purposes, purposes that would destroy those ideals. I have told you what the country to the north is like. How can you choose for Ignacio a godless country?"

"Grandfather, I——"

"There is nothing more for you to say, Concepción. Ignacio must be trained to take his place as the eventual head of the family. Only Spain can give him the discipline he needs. As for you, my child, go to Father Cristóbal and tell him of your lack of understanding of my wishes. You have indeed erred in this matter and in spoiling Ignacio. You may go now."

Her grandfather no longer trusted her. He believed she had harmed Nacho! Concha stumbled from the room, her eyes filled with tears.

"Well?" said her brother, blocking her way as she ran along the gallery toward her own room.

"Oh, Nacho, it is just as I said," she cried.

Ignacio's lips curled. "It seems I can't trust you any longer. I'll talk to him myself. I should have done it in the beginning. It's probably too late now."

"I did try. But it wouldn't matter what anyone said. Grandfather would never consent. Nothing would make him let you go there. Please don't think it was my fault." She reached out her hand, trying to take his, but he brushed it away and ran down the stairs. It eased Ignacio's burning disappointment to make Concha suffer too.

As soon as the door closed on Concha, Don Julián summoned his wife.

"It is of Nacho I wish to speak," he said, once he had led her to a chair opposite his own. "I have never approved of this preparatory school with its new ideas. Now we are reaping the result. It seems Nacho has plotted and planned to go to the States with some unfortunate friends he has made at the school."

"Why do you blame me?" Doña María lowered her eyes, speaking in a voice that indicated how injured she felt. "It was your son Vicente who decided the matter with you. It is you—and against my advice— who decided that Concha should continue her studies after she had finished at the convent. It is the men of this household who plan the education of my grandchildren."

"Not entirely," Don Julián answered in a dry voice. "But let that pass. I want Ignacio to go to Spain as quickly as it can be arranged."

It was the wish of Doña María that Ignacio should go to France for his studies. She was half French, all French in her loyalties. She had seen to it that her son Vicente, Ignacio's father, was educated there, and she had intended all along that Ignacio should be. Furthermore, she and Ramón's mother had decided that the two boys should go abroad together. It was a part of their plan for Ramón and Concha. Upon the boys' return the marriage would take place. But she mentioned nothing of this to Don Julián today. "You wish me to make the arrangements?" she asked. "In every way I shall try to please you, my husband."

But a few nights later she said to him, "I have made careful inquiry, and the influences you deplore here seem to be at work in the universities of Spain, forces moving to end the monarchy. Why not send Nacho to France? I have relatives there who can see he is carefully guarded."

Don Julián was distraught. Where could he send Ignacio to escape all the dangers he feared the youth might encounter? Although he regarded France highly as a Catholic country with a culture he admired, he feared its influence on Ignacio. "Exposed to the rationalism in French universities, might not Nacho throw off the authority of the Church?" he asked. "Many of our young men have."

"We have to risk something," Mamá Grande answered, a note of resignation in her voice.

"We risked too much with our son Vicente," Don Julián answered.

"You forget there have been other influences there—perhaps a too devout wife——"

Don Julián frowned, and Mamá Grande left her sentence unfinished. "Then on the whole you think it best to send him to France?" she asked.

"It might be wiser after all to send him to the university here." Don Julián was not ready yet to surrender to his wife's will.

"I have learned through Ramón he has cast off our authority to such an extent that he visits at the house of a man who was one of those Porfirio Díaz exiled. Would you leave him here to associate with such men?"

"Let it be France then," cried Don Julián, filled again with fear.

8

CONCHA's world seemed to have fallen in bits about her. She waited each morning, hoping her grandfather would send for her to begin the lessons again. "This is just one of the periods," she told herself, "when he is too tired, or too busy. Grandfather never does anything day after day. Nobody does." But after a while she knew he had aban doned the lessons. She thought it was because of his anger toward her. In reality there was a pressing, absorbing emergency that claimed all his time and attention. Conflict had again arisen between the State and the Church. The appeal to the people through the press, of which Father Cristóbal had spoken the autumn before at Concha's party, had been made. Such open expression of hostility to the anticlerical clauses of the Constitution had angered President Calles, even as Don Julián had feared it would. He was threatening to have the laws enforced.

Concha saw little of Ignacio, and never alone. Now that he was really to go abroad, he was excited and busy with last arrangements. But when he walked home with his friend Berta, and she talked of how she was going to New York in a few weeks, then his disappointment threatened to engulf him, and he hardened his heart against Concha.

"But surely he'll set things right between us before he goes," Concha told herself. "He always has."

Ignacio was to sail from Veracruz. Concha longed to be one of the party to go down on the train in their private car. Even Ramón's presence would not matter, if only she could be one of the family to wave Nacho farewell. She gained her wish finally by suggesting to Mamá Grande that Ramón might like to have her see him off.

But a few days before they were to leave, word came that the steamer was sailing two days ahead of schedule. It was decided to send the boys down immediately in the regular coach. In the hurry Ignacio found no opportunity for a separate farewell to Concha. He had meant to find one, if he could bring it about without seeming to seek her out.

Ignacio's and Ramón's relatives and friends gathered early under the train shed next to the track where the Veracruz train would pull in. The strong sunlight filtered down onto the empty steel rails, making them glisten. Concha, on the edge of the group, felt a fascination in their glittering length. Those rails leading out of the station, on, on, held tremendous meaning for her. Along them both Ignacio and Ramón would go to a world separate from hers, a world she might be going to, if it had not been for the Revolution which had taken so much of their wealth that years on the Riviera were no longer possible for the whole family. Then there wouldn't be this break in the family, this separation. She looked up to see Ramón regarding her. She flushed, and moved into the group gathered around Ignacio.

Mamá Grande's eyes followed her with satisfaction. She was pleased with the effect she had obtained in Concha's costume. It was Mamá who had proposed that the close-fitting hat, the coat with its sleeves cleverly simulating a cape, and the chiffon dress be in the moss green they usually chose for Louisa. But it was the Parisian shop which had perfected the idea with that bit of mole fur on the collar dyed to match the cloth of the coat. The result was enchanting. The soft green surface against the clear brown of Concha's skin gave her an odd beauty. Mamá Grande had not failed to notice Ramón's interest in Concha today, something lacking in his attention heretofore.

Ramón circled the group until he stood at her side. He had of late been uncertain whether it was she or Louisa he wished to marry. He had brought with him today a beautiful sapphire ring, meaning to slip the small package containing it into the hand of one of them. If he gave it to Concha, it would signify his acceptance of the arrangement between the two families. If he gave it to Louisa, it would be one of a number of amusing small happenings between them which neither he nor Louisa would take too seriously and of which her family would not know. He would be left free.

Looking at Concha now, he had the feeling he had never seen the real Concha before. Or was it that she had changed in the last months? Physically she was taller and more slender. He moved back into the shadow of the train shed. Her dark eyes grew soft as she listened to Nacho.

"I tell you," Ignacio was saying, "I mean to take a trip on foot over Spain."

"Better spend your time in Paris," his father advised.

As he spoke, Concha's eyes became somber. But even in sadness her mouth with its full underlip was sweet and sensuous. Watching her, Ramón believed it held promise of a passionate nature. He knew definitely now he wanted to be the one to awaken her. Moving over to her side, he slipped his gift into her hand. "Just a farewell token," he said. "Open it when you are alone."

The train swept in, darkening the platform. There was a rush of farewells. Don Julián embraced Ignacio. His tall, stooped figure seemed taller as he bent over his grandson. Then the strong form of Vicente moved in vigorously, embracing his son, giving him a farewell whack on the back. "Learn to enjoy yourself, my son! We'll try to have Mexico in such shape that you can do it elegantly and gracefully on your return."

"Gracias," Nacho answered, adding, "I'll obey."

It was time now to say good-by to his mother. He saw she was in tears. "Mamacita," he whispered, embracing her. His voice was choked with emotion. How could he leave his mother? How could he let himself cause her suffering? He called her "Sweetheart, my most beloved, the first in my heart now and always."

Louisa threw her arms around him. But where was Concha?

He stood on the steps of the train, watching both his and Ramón's friends surging forward for a last farewell. Then, at the back of the crowd he saw his more beloved sister standing between Mamá and Ramón's younger brother Augusto, the delicate oval of her face set off by her close-fitting green hat. It was too late to reach her. "Concha," he called, "Concha, good-by!" Light leaped up in her eyes.

Looking down at his friends and family, with their proudly set heads, long, narrow faces, aquiline noses, deep-set, almost fierce eyes— about them all a quality uniquely Spanish—Ignacio wondered that he had ever wanted to go to the States. Europe was his natural home. A throb passed through the train and through him. The faces on the platform receded, were gone.

To the family, as they filed across the patio on their return from the station, the great house seemed terribly empty without Ignacio, the center of all their lives. Mamá went immediately to her own rooms and was not seen for the rest of the day; Don Julián went to his library. Vicente departed. Concha hid herself in the music room next to the library. There was no one to seek her out here, now that Nacho was gone, no one to lean over the railing. She seated herself on the middle of the three wide steps, leaned her head back against the iron railing, stretched her feet straight out in front of her, let the small package Ramón had given her fall into her lap. She would open it after a little.

All her thoughts were occupied with Nacho. He had called out to her. It was once more all right between them.

How bitterly she would miss him! But gradually a sense, almost of relief, stole over her. She no longer seemed involved with her brother's tempestuous personality, but given over instead to a young girl's dreams, dreams tied into this shining valley of Mexico. This land was a part of her, this city with its old streets, its saints set in niches at the corners of colonial dwellings, its purple shadows in recessed doorways, its clear mornings when roosters in their coops on the tops of houses crowed out the dawn, its clanging church bells heralding early-morning Mass. Yes, and its wide new avenues, its park on Sunday morning with her grandfather riding with other *charros,* the band playing. No, she would not wish ever to leave this city. Happiness, her own home, a son to love her as Nacho loved Mamá . . .

Her hand touched the package in her lap. She lifted it, opened it, took out Ramón's ring. As she looked at it her dreams narrowed until they could be drawn through a marriage ring—the marriage of convenience. Ramón was the man she was to marry! Then again her spirits lifted. Time for her as yet had no edges over which one stepped into catastrophe. Ramón had sailed away, not to return for two years.

The library door opened, and her grandfather stood regarding her. She stared back at his faultless figure dressed in gray-striped trousers and cutaway coat. The flesh framing his eyes was fretted with shrewd lines, his eyes were stern.

"Why do you sit here dreaming?" he asked. "These are grave times. Again the Church must fight for its life."

"Yes, I know, Grandfather." Like stitches dropped and hooked back her mind picked up the old man's forebodings.

"Come," he said. Taking her hand, he led her into the library and to his desk, saying, "Sit here while I am gone and read this infamous Constitution. By it even the lowest Indian is made free to worship as he pleases, bring back his idols if he wishes. I have told you how we opposed it before, how the Archbishop refused the Sacraments to anyone who swore allegiance to it. I must go now to a meeting of the clergy."

Concha listened to his footfalls receding down the stairs, then to the sound of the motor as the car passed out of the gate. Dutifully she picked up the paper he had laid before her. *Article 3,* she read: *Primary schools shall be secular. . . . Article 130: Before dedicating new temples of worship, permission must be obtained from the De-*

partment of Interior. Publications of a religious character shall not comment on political matters. Political assemblies in churches are forbidden. State legislatures have a right to determine the number of ministers of each creed according to the needs of the locality.

She sighed, then went on with her reading. Soon, sooner than she had expected, she heard her grandfather's steps on the stairs. The door behind her opened, and he strode into the room. He seemed to be talking more to himself than to her. "President Calles has acted. He says we have too many priests trying to dictate how the country shall be run. He is deporting all foreign priests. To enforce this, he has commanded that all priests must register. This is infamous! We cannot have the State so dictate to us. The episcopate has ordered the priests not to comply and to withdraw from the churches on the day the order comes into effect. No church bells will sound in the city of Mexico then." Don Julián's voice came to a sobbing halt.

Unable to speak, Concha stared up at him. Suddenly a wind swept in through the open window, out the door Don Julián had left open, scattering papers, fluttering the leaves of books. Through the window Concha could see black, rain-filled clouds racing across the summer sky. "Shut out the storm, Grandfather," she cried.

9

Across the city the pink walls of the Villar house lay under the shadow of the advancing storm. Soledad stepped out into the patio to rescue a new orchid hanging from one of the posts of the *corredor*. She had two now. "Flower of the Soul" this was called, because it blossomed in the autumn at the time of the festival of the dead. She placed it on a hook against the house wall, gathered up some small, newly potted plants from under the cypress tree and ran with them to the shelter of the gallery, out of range of the wind.

The gate bell tinkled. She heard the quick step of the maid on the tiles of the *corredor* and then Guadalupe's voice calling, "Where are you?" She went forward to greet him. Then the storm broke, sending the rain in driving sheets, wetting them as they fled through the door into their sitting room.

"And tomorrow we start, Lupe," she cried, laughing up at him.

"Yes, but not a vacation, a business trip." He shook the rain from the sleeve of his coat and put his arm around her.

"So we cannot go to my home!" The disappointment in her voice hurt him but he did not give in to it.

"I am needed in some of the Indian villages. There is trouble over the land. The hacienda people say the villagers have falsified their records; some of the land they claimed never belonged to them, and they lied, too, about the number of heads of families in the villages."

"I'm tired, Lupe," she protested, "and what are you accomplishing?" She shook off her husband's arm. "This slow change you accept, but I cannot. I am a product of the Revolution." Her voice broke. "The Revolution is not just a plan on paper. Fighting, bloodshed if necessary, but glorious action! And we'll fight again if we have to, fight until everyone has land and the power of the Church is destroyed," she cried fiercely. "We should have killed all the *hacendados* when we had a chance, given the land back to the villages right then. Now we wait and wait."

Suddenly she stopped, seeing the look in her husband's eyes. She was all warmth now. She had been angry with him about the vacation, but she could not even remember the anger. "It will be very good, Lupe, just to go with you," she cried.

Guadalupe again put his arms around her. He felt the strong, compact, small-boned body beneath his hand. He knew the ardor and warmth and willingness to sacrifice—yes, and the flaming violence that made up her nature.

Would she never be able to forget her childhood, the life in the colonial city far to the south where the people crossed themselves in fear of evil every time they passed her father—her father, a liberal, ostracized by priest and parish and at last betrayed? Even more he wished she could forget those years in the army of Villa—cruel, brutal Pancho Villa. Guadalupe could never believe in what Soledad told him of Villa's kindness.

"Listen, Cholita," he said, using the diminutive of her name to lessen the sternness of his tone, "you are to recite this after me. 'One thousand schools have been started in the villages.'"

"'One thousand schools!'" she repeated.

"'Fifteen hundred villages have received land. In four years eight million acres distributed.'"

" 'Eight million acres distributed!' " she mocked. "Listen, my husband, sing this song we sang in the Revolution." Strumming on an imaginary guitar, she began:

> "The little tree has fallen down
> Where the peacock used to sit.
> Now like any humble beast
> It must sleep upon the ground."

She broke off, crying, "It's not true, though! We didn't cut the tree down. We just made more fine peacocks to sit on it. Calles is getting rich. And Morones *is* rich, and he's the labor leader!"

"But Calles is pulling the country together. You know that. There's money in the treasury at last. He's building roads, doing big things in irrigation. And Morones is bringing wages up among the laborers."

"It's not fast enough," sniffed Soledad.

"You're tired and discouraged, my wife. It's stopped raining. Let's go out to eat." Again he relinquished the idea of a desk. He had saved two pesos for it. Not much, but so many things had had to come first. Chairs to sit on, and a bed; they had slept on mats at first, as the Indian maid did.

"Could we?" Soledad whirled twice round, executing with grace the steps of a dance.

They called to their servant. "We're going out, Lupe." She, like her young master, bore the name of the Brown Virgin.

Out on the street they walked hand in hand on the pavements still wet from the rain, feeling rich going out for dinner, rich in contrast to those among whom they walked. Soledad had a coat; she had shoes and stockings.

A woman, a child slung in her *rebozo,* another clinging to her skirts, accosted Guadalupe. "We have nothing to eat. Neither corn nor salt."

Soledad pulled back the tightly drawn *rebozo.* "Oh, look, the baby is just bones, and it has malaria! Give them something."

Twice they gave. Poverty, sunning itself in the daytime, forgetting its ills, pressed in upon the well-to-do at night.

"We haven't enough left for gaiety," said Guadalupe. They turned toward home.

"We're back, Lupe," they cried when the little servant opened the door.

"Your evening meal is ready," she said. It had happened like this before.

And then, just as they finished, a friend came to see them. "We almost went out to dinner, Pablo," cried Soledad. "How glad we are we didn't! We would have missed you if we had."

In the *sala* the three sat on gaily decorated chairs Soledad had bought in the market. Guadalupe was slender with large gentle eyes and quiet ways. Soledad and Pablo were more alike, the strain of Spaniard and Indian less blended in them. In both was the magnetism that leaders have. In Pablo it was especially marked, and there was a little boasting note in his voice as he said, "Morones has given me a job."

"You are to help in the labor movement?" said Guadalupe. "Work for Article 123?" Guadalupe was proud of Article 123 in the Constitution. No other nation in the world had put into its Constitution such protection for labor. He got up and went round to Pablo, who had risen too. They embraced.

Soledad's eyes widened. "You mean you are no longer to work with the independent unions?"

"We can't do anything," said Pablo, "separate from the others."

"And so you joined Morones?" Soledad asked scornfully.

"Pablo has his own conscience," said Guadalupe, turning to Soledad. Pablo was studying his hands. What chance was there for a man like him unless he joined the strong? The powerful labor leader Morones had entered the cabinet as Secretary of Labor. He was trying to recruit every independent union into the government-controlled National Federation of Labor Unions. Pablo wanted to be an official, to erase the insignificance of his position in his father's family. He belonged to Vicente Navarro's little household. Today the son of the big house had left for his studies abroad. Pablo had stood far back in the shadows of the train shed and watched his half brother's departure. Pablo was the elder, born three years before Ignacio. Pablo's mother had often told him how important he had been to his father until the birth of the legitimate son. "He thought he was to have no child but you. Two children had been born dead to his wife."

Guadalupe brought from the corner an old and battered harp. "This is music I made last night," he said. "It's for Soledad." All things were for Soledad. He began playing wandering little phrases; then they seemed to join into a martial air and then into tenderness like a lullaby.

Pablo had moved closer to Soledad. He put his hand on her shoulder, touched the lobe of her ear. Her husband smiled. All his friends made a little love to her when they were frightened, when they were tired, when they needed to feel strong. Guadalupe did not mind. He had dark thoughts only of the dead man she had called husband; he sometimes seemed to stand between them.

But even that bitterness was lost in music and in dreams about villages like those in the United States. Because of the kindness of a North American woman, for four years he had lived in the midst of Iowa's plenty, with its snug farmhouses, its prosperous towns. In Mexico someday there would be a great middle class, well shod, well clothed. All would have homes like this one. So he dreamed, making his music fit his dreams.

"In this new fight with the Church we'll enforce all the anticlerical laws," said Pablo, breaking into Guadalupe's dreams.

"Splendid!" cried Soledad.

Guadalupe put down his harp. His face lost its look of happiness. "It is not good that we should go so far. Intolerance is never good."

"Why not?" cried Soledad. "In a right cause?"

"You forget, Cholita, the school to which I went is also a religious one. If these laws are enforced, it will be abolished too. All that I am, I owe to that school. Separate Church and State, yes—but let people worship, let people think as they wish."

"Anyway Calles is doing things for us. He's trying to get back the oil wells. Díaz broke the law when he sold them." Pablo had changed the subject, not liking to be put in the wrong by Guadalupe.

~~~~~~~~~~~~~~~ *10* ~~~~~

The two years of Ignacio's and Ramón's absence had lengthened out to nearly three, but now at last they were coming home. On the dock at Veracruz, Concha with her mother and father, Mamá Grande, Louisa, and Ramón's mother, waited for the steamer to dock. The boat was swinging round to its moorings. Near the prow stood two young men, waving.

"There they are!" Louisa exclaimed.

Concha felt her heart beat in her throat, and then almost immediately it seemed to her that Ignacio and Ramón were in their midst. Mamá had her arms around her son. Nacho was laughing and crying all at once, embracing her again and again. "My Mamacita, my darling Mother, not for a day have I ceased to miss you."

"Nacho, Nacho," Louisa cried. "I think you are very much a man, and I have grown to womanhood since you went away, do you not see?"

"As if a little hoyden like you would ever grow up," her brother told her, pinching her cheek.

She made a face at him. "You don't deserve the present Grand-father has sent you."

"And what is that?" he asked.

"A car all your own."

"Oh, Louisa," cried Concha, "it was to have been a surprise!"

Ignacio turned to Concha, and they put their arms around each other. "I have come back," was all he could say. She was mute with joy.

Ramón watched them. His mother's persistence did not now seem misplaced. He had not expected to see so finished a young woman as Concha here in Mexico. She might just have arrived from Paris. She was dressed in black, and there was no ornament other than her own beauty. That beauty he could not quite analyze in the little time he saw her before they started on the trip to Mexico City. Louisa was the one he talked to most.

Ignacio's new car led the way. What a glorious home-coming it was! It had been good to feel his father's strong arms embracing him. The final pat on his back had been vigorous and friendly, giving him a sense of comradeship which he had never before felt with his father. The present of the car told of his grandfather's affection. Mamá Grande had had tears in her eyes. He had feared her greeting, because in the last year he had taken matters in his own hands and attended the University of Madrid.

Vicente and Ramón, sitting on the back seat of the car, were talking to each other. It left Ignacio free to study the country from his vantage point on the front seat beside the chauffeur. Letters during his absence had told him nothing of Mexico, except the exclusive life of the closely guarded Spanish families and the struggle of the Church. The liberal student movement in Spain with which he had recently identified himself and the conservatism of his people had lain side by side in his mind without either disturbing the other. Now, signs of poverty everywhere manifest came like an assault upon him. He could not ignore them in the light of his study of economics and sociology at Madrid.

His country's beauty, which he had remembered, seemed to recede. In his longing he had idealized Mexico, and now his first feeling was an overwhelming shame for its shabbiness. But then, as the image gave way to the reality, he grew excited again. His country had a wild beauty he had forgotten. In the steaming jungles through which they were passing, coconut palms reared their voluptuous, rounded tops, giant ferns crowded the ground, rare orchids hung from the branches of trees, there was the sudden flame of tropical flowers. "But there is so much poverty!" he exclaimed, looking at the huts, their walls nothing more than brush or openwork bamboo, their roofs of leaves.

As so often in the two years together, Ramón silenced Ignacio with his one argument. "If you were more completely patriotic in your outlook, Nacho, you would see clearly that there is just one thing we need to think of in coming back. Our class represents the brains of Mexico. We are the country's aristocrats. That we are only five percent of the people bears out our aristocracy. Aristocracy is never numerous. Spanish culture and religion—they are ours to preserve. What does this *canaille* we see here mean to us, except that we still have a race that can serve us? There is money to be made in this country, just as there always has been, if we go about it correctly."

Ignacio did not answer.

They had ascended a little now from the coastal plain. Ravines cut the land apart. At the base of the deep clefts where the sun did not penetrate, the tropical growth hung in dark, festooned, tangled masses. High on the steep side of one, among the delicacy of sunlit leaves, he saw a moving white speck—a solitary Indian. These canyons, slashing across all Mexico, were the cause of much of its backwardness, he thought. Nature seemed to repudiate the social law of communication, setting little village away from little village. He stared out at the masses of coffee shrubs intermingled with the broad leaves of bananas, the pale green acres of sugar cane they were now passing.

"There," said his father, breaking the silence and pointing to the fertile fields, "there is our wealth! If we could only stop this land distribution and put the Indians' miserable little *milpas* into sugar and coffee and cotton, we could make ourselves as rich as we ever were."

"That's what I've tried to tell Ignacio," exclaimed Ramón.

Ignacio, conscious as never before in his life of the poverty of villages standing amid plenty, overshadowed by the great domed churches, again did not answer.

"Labor," Vicente said, "has had almost everything in its hands—still has, to some extent, although it's not so strong under Portes Gil. The great Morones you'll see riding through the streets in his fancy car. As for his gaudy attire——" Vicente gave a low laugh. Then he sobered, saying, "These have been hard years for us, these years you've been away. Your grandfather, Ignacio, you will find greatly changed. The closing of the churches has aged him."

"It's the fault of the Church, isn't it? There was no reason why the episcopate should refuse to register the priests, was there? And we did have too many priests. As in Spain they have kept the people poor with their demands for money." Ignacio spoke with confidence, remembering how little interest his father took in religious matters. But to his surprise Vicente's face darkened.

"That's not the attitude you should take," he answered curtly.

"The law of God always should come before the law of the State," said Ramón.

"Going back to the labor business—" Vicente went on— "it renders business pretty difficult. There have been a good many strikes, and although there is an arbitration board, we Spaniards always lose out unless——" He hesitated.

"Unless you know the right people," Ramón finished the sentence for him.

"Yes. The Ministry of Industry is beginning to find it more advisable to co-operate with employers than with employees." Vicente eyed his future son-in-law with considerable satisfaction. Until now he had been the only member of his family who believed they should make friends among the new politicos. He saw Ramón would work to keep their footing in a changing society. He would make an excellent member of the family.

Because of a bad stretch of road it was late when they reached the small city where they were to spend the night. The next morning as the two young men, Paris-fashion, sat over their rolls and coffee at a small table on the balcony outside their room, they saw coming slowly across the plaza Mamá Grande and Doña Leonora, walking together, Concha and Louisa following behind. It's as if they'd just been to Mass, thought Ignacio, but the churches are closed.

As they came under the balcony, Ramón threw a flower down, hoping to attract Concha's attention. To both young men Concha was proving strangely disturbing! To Ramón, because she was beautiful and he could have her if he wished for his wife; to Ignacio, because she was deeply reserved, so quiet and submissive. Was it the work of

Mamá Grande thus to overlay the warm loveliness of Concha, as he remembered her, with this secret, careful expression?

This beautiful but withdrawn young woman was not the impulsive Concha who had challenged him after their improvised bullfight. He hated the change in her with all his soul. In these years away from Mexico his sister had always been his imaginary confidante. He had looked forward to the long talks he would have with her on his return. She would admire and agree as she had in the past. And now he couldn't reach her! He did not realize that, so far, there had been little opportunity for conversation with her.

Louisa's roving eyes caught sight of the two young men on the balcony. Keeping well behind the older women, she waved to them.

Concha gave no sign of interest, lost completely as she was in her own perplexities. She had not slept that night, fighting to get her feelings under control. With Ramón far away, she had found it easy to be submissive to Mamá Grande's wishes. She had only to follow the example of her own mother, to whom submission had become an art.

But now that she had seen Ramón again, she knew beyond a doubt she did not wish to marry him. He answered no single conception she had of what a husband should be, except material security. She instinctively knew he would always provide luxury for her. He was the shrewd, money-making Spaniard, the type that in Mexico had concentrated big and little business in their own hands. Despite his aristocratic forebears, he was the counterpart of the Spanish shopkeepers. His face was not a narrow oval, as she deemed an aristocrat's should be, nor had he the smoldering black eyes. His face was round; his eyes were small, filled with a shrewd wisdom.

According to the traditions of family and Church, the union, once made, could never be broken. For a lifetime she would be submerged in this shopkeeper's personality. Once she was married to Ramón, the things her grandfather had taught her to love in those hours they worked together, the things which by instinct she and her mother loved, even the stormy matters that had always filled Ignacio's life and her own would never be articulate again. Ramón would dictate her tastes, her occupations. Her life would of necessity take on the color of his. If only she could talk to Ignacio! But Ramón was Ignacio's friend.

Later, in their room, as she and Louisa gave little touches to their toilets before starting on the day's ride, Louisa coaxed, "Let's not wait for the others to go down. We haven't seen Ignacio yet to talk to—you know, the way we used to."

In the *corredor* outside the hotel they found Ignacio and Ramón. They were laughing and talking together. But when Ignacio saw them a mask of reserve closed down over his face. "Mamá Grande," he said, ignoring his sisters to address his grandmother, who followed close behind the girls, "do my sisters never go unattended?"

"You forget yourself, Ignacio," she replied.

That day the scene that passed before Ignacio's eyes changed to one of restraint. As the car ascended from one plateau to another, the young green corn was a foot high, mammoth gray-green cacti spotted the roadsides, edged the fields, covered whole hillsides. It was Mexico! Had he seen only the spiny maguey and the blue sky over it, he would have known he had come home. This was his country. He had been born out of its very earth.

Seven thousand, eight thousand, ten thousand feet over the passes, the cars labored along high ridges with stunted pine. Shelving up against the sky at precipitous angles, the mountains stretched away to the horizon in jumbled magnificence.

Night had fallen when they came to the mountain-rimmed valley of Mexico. In the thin air of the high plateau the lights of the distant city took on a luminous glow, blending the flames of street lamps and the bright windows. The city was like light itself. Ignacio felt his heart choking him.

They drove into the patio of their home. He felt the familiar cobblestones under his feet. Francisco had marshaled the servants in a row at the foot of the first flight of stairs to welcome him. The young master of the house had returned. There were the familiar marble steps, the shadowed galleries, the scent of honeysuckle as he ascended to the door of the library where his grandfather awaited him. Deep emotion trembled in his grandfather's voice welcoming him. Ignacio felt how thin the body was which he embraced.

"Sit down, Ignacio," said the old man, releasing him and leading the way into the great room. He tipped the shade on the lamp, throwing his grandson's face into relief. "And have you come back," he asked, "prepared to serve your Church and your country?"

Ignacio hesitated. He had returned prepared to fulfill his part in the family, make the proper marriage, care for the estate when his time came. In that he would comply, but the Church—— "I will carry out the family design, sir, as it is laid down for me. As to my own personal beliefs—in that I have not yet fully decided."

His eyes are the eyes of the crusader who looks down on us from the wall, thought Don Julián, but he is a crusader without belief. The old man was bitterly disappointed.

"The car," he went on, ignoring Ignacio's final remark, "has been given you so that you may take your place here in the city and at the haciendas. All of them can be visited now."

~~~~~~~~~~~~~~~~~~~~ *II* ~~~~~

IGNACIO was awakened the morning after his return by a strange silence—no bell in all the city of Mexico rang out its call. The silence seemed to beat against his eardrums. There was no Mass this morning. He turned over for another nap.

A peremptory knock upon his door, and his grandfather's voice reached him through its heavy oak panels. "I wish you to be in the chapel in half an hour."

Mamá met him as he came from his room, saying, "The entrance to the chapel had to be changed." She led him into a little-used room. Swinging back a panel in the wall, she preceded him down a curving stairway into the chapel, a chapel unfamiliar to him in its beauty, richness, and secrecy. The place as Ignacio remembered it had been simple almost to bareness. Now the vessels on the altar were of gold, and so was the altar rail. The Stations of the Cross were paintings of incomparable beauty.

Father Cristóbal, assisted by Don Julián himself, had already begun the Mass. So my grandfather, thought Ignacio, is evading the edict of the State, hiding a priest in his house in order that Mass may be observed. Don Julián had written him that many of the devout rich were doing it, but he had never guessed his grandfather was one of them.

After the service Ignacio followed Don Julián about, as he explained the changes which had had to be made—the windows on the street bricked in, a wall erected to cut the chapel off completely from the patio. "Seemingly there is no chapel," he said. "Everything I have made beautiful and gorgeous except Father Cristóbal's room. He asked that it be of monklike simplicity."

Ignacio soon discerned that a change had come over the entire household. Where once the Church had been one part of their lives, it now seemed to be the whole. Don Julián insisted that all the family each morning attend the early Mass. Whatever duty any servant was performing stopped, except the duties of the man at the gate and the servant who took up his watch on the gallery of the second floor. In case the authorities should come to search the house, he must reach the chapel in time to warn the worshipers to silence.

As the weeks passed, Ignacio's discontent grew. He had come home with the idea that he could take his part in the new Mexico, as the young men he had met in Spain were taking theirs. Although in 1929 Spain was still a monarchy, the republican movement was gaining headway. He had been in Madrid when the government had closed the university and had partaken of the high sense of purpose of the students and professors when they quietly took up their work in private buildings.

But here, in his home, there was no interest in anything that had to do with reform. There seemed no possible way for him to take part in the liberal movement ushered in by the Mexican Revolution. There was a deeper, more personal disappointment, too. He had always thought his entree into that group would be through his old friend Berta Mendoza. He thought, of course, she would be back from the States by now. But when he went around to their home, he found other people living there, and they knew nothing of the Mendozas.

He had lost Concha too. He felt she had become entirely the tool of Mamá Grande. How could she let herself be so changed? In his disappointment he did not try to pass beyond the mask of her acquiescence. It was more fun now to be with Louisa than with Concha. Yet at the same time he had a feeling he was deserting Concha. But she was always in service to her grandfather, or to the hidden Church. Ignacio was not long in discovering that it was Mamá Grande who was the instigator of such continual service. Through Concha's love for her grandfather, Mamá Grande was training her in docility and pious devotion to please Ramón's mother and to please Ramón. Unsullied, lovely womanhood to stir his jaded desires, was Ignacio's savage comment to himself.

Ignacio's reaction against the Church was now bitter and profound.

One night he came on Concha just within the outer gate, leaning against it, breathless.

"I've done it," she whispered. "I've done what I promised Father Cristóbal I would do."

"You mean you've been out in the streets alone, distributing pamphlets for the Church, as you told me you meant to do?"

"I was almost caught. Two men followed me. They stood in a doorway, and they saw me leave some, and they followed me. I had a bundle in my arms. I dropped it and ran."

"Why did you do it? Why did you do it?" demanded Ignacio, but without waiting for her answer he turned and went in search of Mamá Grande. "Grandfather and Father Cristóbal are carrying this rebellion against the State too far," he told her. "Suppose Concha had been caught? Do you think that would further your plans for her marriage?"

Mamá Grande was a little frightened, but she did not intend that Ignacio should know it. "I will arrange matters in this house as I always have," she told him.

Ignacio acquired the habit of occupying the small music room that adjoined his grandfather's library, playing the piano, painting a little, reading, idling. One day the door into the library was left ajar. Another priest, he saw, had joined Father Cristóbal and Don Julián. He was small, dark-skinned, shabbily dressed in a frayed suit of black which had evidently been intended for a larger man.

"If you must come," Don Julián said to him, "why don't you come at night?"

"I will not hide," said the man. "I serve God and my people. No law shall keep me from that. But I say we should not have left our churches."

"You have no right to be a priest of the Church if you deny its mandates," said Father Cristóbal coldly.

The shabby little man's hands lay palm down on his knees, but as Father Cristóbal spoke he lifted his fingers as if to throw off some sticky substance. "I have never believed in temporal power," he said quietly. "When we are rid of it, we will make better martyrs than we do now."

A few days later Ignacio was sitting with his grandfather when the shabby little priest came again.

"It will be only a short time now," he told Don Julián, "before the episcopate will agree to registration."

"We shall win if we hold out," cried Don Julián. "Underground, the Church has grown strong. Our young people are more devout. In the darkness we have grown in strength and fervor."

"You speak of the rich like yourself who can afford the ministrations of a priest. It is not so in the Indian villages over the country. They have learned to do without the Church. There are no weddings or christening services."

"I have understood they are very devout," answered Don Julián.

"Ah, yes," the shabby little man answered. "It is only the priests they have forgotten."

"Is this so?" asked Don Julián, turning to Father Cristóbal who stood by the mantel playing with a gold trinket.

For a moment Father Cristóbal seemed too engrossed to speak, then he laid the trinket down. "I think, if the Church is not gradually to be stamped out, we must surrender on this point to the State."

Ignacio, looking at his grandfather, thought he aged in that moment. It was as if the flesh all at once shrank, leaving too large a skin to cover the bones of his face. Ignacio felt a twinge of remorse. He had been no comfort to his grandfather since his return. But he was glad the Church was going to capitulate. It would free his home for a little gaiety.

In reality the re-establishment of the Church did change things in the house, but the change was not to Ignacio's liking. Mamá Grande immediately turned her attention to his marriage. He insisted on liberty to choose whom he should marry and when. He insisted, too, that there should be more freedom for him and his sisters. The arguments between his grandmother and himself were frequent and bitter.

"I cannot understand where in Paris you have learned to be so lax in the proprieties," she scolded. "The Paris that I know guards its young women as closely as I do."

"There are several Parises," Ignacio answered, "just as there are several Mexicos. I belonged to the young Paris. It's silly to keep Concha and Louisa hidden away. They are both too beautiful for that."

"I recognize only one Paris, one Mexico. Your sisters are not hidden. How many parties have you and Ramón taken your sisters to since your return?" she demanded.

"Private hings, yes, but we want to take them out to dine and to the cinema."

"To the cinema!" exclaimed Mamá Grande, holding up her jeweled hands. "Those terrible pictures that the States send down here to pollute our womanhood? Nacho, I am ashamed for you."

"At least let us go to the opera on its opening evening," he countered. "That would be safe."

"I have explained to you, Ignacio, that the President will be there, and your grandfather has not paid any President since Díaz the courtesy of his presence. Certainly your grandfather would not bestow the courtesy of his presence on any man who curtails the powers of the Church."

"Then if Grandfather doesn't wish to attend, we four could go. It is becoming very fashionable in Mexico City for young people to go out by themselves," urged Ignacio.

"Not in the society which I represent." Mamá Grande rose and was sweeping majestically toward the door when Ignacio's words brought her to an abrupt stop.

"It is Ramón's wishes that I am presenting. Of course if you do not care to consider them——"

"You and Ramón take with you Concha and Louisa? You'll go only if I am there as chaperon. And I will not go without your grandfather. As he has said he will not go, all is settled. I wish we had back the days when courtings were carried on from a safe distance outside our grilled windows," she added.

Ignacio laughed and, leaning over his grandmother, smoothed back her gray crest of hair. "You are still a very strict chaperon, Mamá Grande. With you we'll be safe anywhere."

12

Ignacio left Doña María, feeling a sense of triumph, almost certain despite her protest that she would arrange the party. Hurrying down the stairs to the second gallery, his attention was caught by the sound of Louisa's voice. In the shadow of one of the great pillars of the veranda he saw her and Ramón. His sister looked flushed and happy. Seeing him, Louisa disappeared into the house, and Ramón came nonchalantly toward him. Ignacio waited until Ramón was close beside him; then he flicked his cheek with his glove.

Ramón's face turned a dark purple. "This is an unwarranted insult," he said in a low voice, not letting his anger go, fearful that Mamá Grande might be near.

"Not unwarranted. This clandestine affair you are carrying on with Louisa has got to stop."

"I am leaving this house, and I shall never return until I have an apology from you," said Ramón, walking stiffly along the gallery toward the stairs.

"You won't get it," cried Ignacio, giving vent to his anger and the distaste he had begun to feel for Ramón. "And I tell you right now I intend you shall not flirt any more with Louisa."

When two days had passed and Ramón had not visited them, Mamá Grande grew suspicious, and she called Ignacio to her. "What has happened to Ramón?" she demanded.

"We have quarreled."

"And over what, I should like to know?"

"Suppose I should say it was over the opera because I sided with you?"

"You are keeping something from me, Nacho. I know where you stand on the opera."

Ignacio did not reply.

"Do you defy me?" demanded Doña María.

"In this case, yes." Ignacio meant to protect Louisa at all costs.

Mamá Grande appealed to her son Vicente. Ignacio was jeopardizing all their plans for Concha.

"I can do nothing," Vicente answered. "When young men quarrel, they must settle it between themselves."

It was useless to depend on anyone but herself, Mamá Grande decided. She must see Ramón's mother. They often spent the afternoon together, drinking coffee and talking over their plans, so there was nothing unusual in asking Leonora Fuentes to come to see her.

When they were comfortably seated in her private sitting room, Doña María asked solicitously for Ramón. "We have not seen him for many days, and we miss him."

At these words Doña Leonora's placidity was gone. "María," she said, "I shall speak plainly. Neither I nor my son will submit longer to the indignities heaped upon him by your household."

"My household!" exclaimed Mamá Grande, throwing up her hands in a gesture of protest. And then remembering the importance of reconciliation, she said humbly, "It is only Ignacio. He is a fiery and impetuous youth, but surely your Ramón, older and wiser, will not let a quarrel with a foolish boy jeopardize the happiness of my Concha. Ramón is too wise, too kind, to let that happen."

"Humph," said her friend. "It cannot so easily be explained away—this quarrel, María."

For many years the two friends had planned together the lives of their children and grandchildren, and each was familiar with the steps that must be taken before agreement could be reached on any point. But today they were on uncharted ground. Does *she* know why they quarreled? wondered Doña María, studying her friend. It's quite likely to have been Ramón's fault, but she wouldn't admit anything was wrong with him, even if I could prove it.

It was late in the afternoon when Mamá Grande decided she must play her trump card. "I have been thinking for some time, my dear Leonora, that I should like to add to Concha's dowry. These have been good years for us." She named a considerable sum above the original agreement.

Doña Leonora had just lifted her coffee cup to her lips, and Mamá Grande caught only a glimpse of her little round eyes, but it was enough. There was an unmistakable gleam in them.

"And now," she said in a gay tone, "let us forget there has ever been even a wee quarrel between our children to darken our friendship. I have a little surprise for Ramón. The family is going to attend the first night of the opera, and I especially desire him to escort Concha. Will you be my emissary and arrange the matter with him?"

"I cannot refuse such a gracious gesture on your part. I shall try to make him forget that there has been any unpleasantness. I know he would like to escort the lovely Concha," answered Doña Leonora, as she rose to go.

13

SECRETLY Vicente determined to take a hand with Ignacio. He was tired of his son's silly little rebellions. Certainly there was plenty of opportunity for him to enjoy himself without infringing on the traditional pattern of family life. He could set up a separate household like Vicente's and nothing would be said. He could carouse with other rich young men, and nothing would be said.

Vicente decided to fulfill an already half-formed resolve to put Ignacio in touch with the mistress of his little home. Elena would know how to manage the boy. She had managed their son Pablo. Pablo had his own interests. He never troubled Vicente or his mother with his affairs. Three years older than Ignacio, he behaved like a man. No silly outbursts of rebellion on Pablo's part! Yes, the lowborn, comfortable Elena was the woman to make Ignacio into a man. The boy need not know of the relationship between his father and Elena. At least Vicente would say nothing of it. If Ignacio guessed, that was another matter. It might give him an idea how to make himself more comfortable.

Ignacio guessed the significance of the household to which he was now introduced. He, much earlier than Concha, had learned something of Vicente's life. He felt not a little pleased that his father was taking him into his confidence, but he experienced distaste for the whole affair when he entered Vicente's little house. The stout woman to whom he was introduced was obviously of the people. So was the house, with its overdecorated sitting room, a cheap image of the Virgin standing on the lace-draped piano, crude holy pictures on the walls.

But, strangely enough, he realized that his father seemed more of a person here than he did at home, where he fawned on Mamá Grande when he needed money, and gave lip homage to Ignacio's mother. Vicente gained by the sincerity here which was lacking in his other relationship.

The door opened, and a young man entered. Vicente was taken by surprise. He had not expected Pablo home at this hour. As Elena said, "My son, Pablo," Ignacio knew that without doubt he was being introduced to his half brother.

He is spoiled, Pablo said to himself, noticing his brother's discontented mouth, but his eyes belied his mouth. They burned with a strange, restless fervor which made Pablo covet him for the labor movement.

Ignacio felt superior to Pablo with his stout, strong, low-hung body, his round face with the high cheekbones of the Indian. The close-growing, soft, fine, black hair was Indian, too, but there was an innate quality of power in the man which claimed respect and made Ignacio unable to patronize him.

After a little Pablo said, "I'm meeting some friends for coffee. Would you like to come along?" Ignacio found himself accepting the invitation. Outside, Pablo asked him what he was doing with his time.

"What would I be doing with it?" Ignacio answered. "What do you do with yours?"

"Oh, I have to earn my living. I have a job in the Department of Industry that keeps me busy all day," Pablo answered, ignoring the truculent note in his brother's voice. "The reason I asked is that I thought with your knowledge of conditions in Europe you would be a real asset to the labor movement, if you'd throw yourself in with us."

"You belong?" exclaimed Ignacio. "Then there is something to it except a lot of graft, as I've been told?"

Pablo's voice was steady and cool. "Anything to it besides graft! It's done a lot for the people of Mexico."

They were entering the café now, a large dim room crowded full of round tables and men seated, drinking coffee. Slender pillars broke up its space, some of them twined with artificial flowers; at the base of others rather dreary-looking palms had been placed. Ignacio noticed, as they walked through the crowded room, that the white tablecloths were cheap and coarse and stained from repeated use. Many of the men were in working clothes. So this was the kind of place his half brother frequented! thought Ignacio.

Pablo walked over to a table by the window. Most of the chairs around it were already occupied. There was an argument going on, and without introducing him Pablo motioned Ignacio to be seated.

Ignacio's eyes wandered around the group of young men. Most of them were engaged in spirited debate over a moot labor point. His attention was caught by a North American sitting beside a slight young Mexican whom Pablo called Guadalupe. The man from the States is the only well-bred one at the table, Ignacio thought.

The man's face and head were narrow, his nose thin, his blue eyes well placed, and his delicate mouth finely modeled. His face was one of distinction. About him was an air of reserve that seemed to emanate not so much from his personality as from an inherited assumption of position. This Ignacio could understand. And yet there was something simple and approachable about him, too. This was not understandable to Ignacio. He wondered idly who the man was. Then he was nettled that the North American was there at all.

Feels superior to this group, I imagine. Intends to tell his countrymen we are a nation of half-breeds when he goes back home, thought

Ignacio, suddenly feeling himself the ardent ally of his countrymen on whom so recently he had looked down.

Listening to the men's talk, Ignacio learned that they were all government employees. One was a minor member of the Labor Department. The man they called Guadalupe surveyed haciendas for the purpose of land distribution. There was a painter who was working on murals depicting the events of the Revolution, one of the younger artists helping Diego Rivera; he was proud that the master painter had belonged to the *Sindicato de Pintores,* a branch of the labor union. What Pablo's position was, Ignacio did not learn. Obviously all of them were the products of the Revolution. Many of them had recently left small towns and come to the city seeking better opportunities. Guadalupe Villar spoke of an agricultural school he had attended in the States.

The discussion grew more heated. It was over the meager opportunities open to men like themselves. The new regime was proving disappointing. The men who ran the government were developing into a wealthy class of their own. There was little for men like them.

He noticed that the young North American had leaned forward, deeply interested in the discussion. In exceedingly good Spanish he asked, "Why do you all work for the government if you feel that way? This glue, you might call it, that is pulling the two extremes of your country together, the rich and the poor, would it not be more effective glue if some of you went into the mining business, or railroading?"

"Why don't you ask your own people that question, Señor Buchanan?" asked the young labor man in suave tones. "Who owns our mines, our railroads, our oil wells? Who are the executives, the engineers in these great businesses? All the bloodshed of the Revolution has not given us back our subsoil rights. Your present ambassador has seen to that."

Ignacio inwardly applauded the clever trouncing the man was giving the North American. He too resented the power the United States held in Mexico, although he knew his grandfather owned stock in several companies in the States. He was pleased when Buchanan, as they called him, rose, pleading another engagement.

14

GUADALUPE VILLAR followed the young North American out. "I regret that you were misunderstood. I asked you to come so that we might understand each other better. Be patient," he pleaded. "I know your people are good. These others have never seen your country." He smiled a disarming smile.

"I quite understand," said Buchanan, as he bade Villar good-by at the corner.

It was the hour when all Mexico City seemed to be on the streets. Men and women going home from work, families enjoying the cool upland evening, all crowding into the bread shops, buying a prodigious assortment of rolls to eat with their ten-o'clock coffee. Too early yet for the rich restaurant crowd, but handsome automobiles filled the streets. At every stop, boys and men thrust books of lottery tickets through the windows, begging the occupants to buy.

As people passed under a street lamp, or their faces were caught in the glare of motorcar lights, Jim Buchanan studied them, noting the separate racial strains. Not often did he recognize the lean lineaments characteristic of the pure Spaniard, like those of the handsome young man at the café.

An Indian passed, treading lightly, moving forward in a swift trot, bearing on his back a great load of corn. The light from the street lamp shone down upon his feet. As he lifted them the callused soles were gray with dust. James Buchanan was aware now of other like figures slipping silently along, weaving in and out among the city people. Women, too, with uncovered heads and bare feet, their *rebozos* drawn tightly around their shoulders and around the small forms of babies carried within. The opaque black eyes of these men and women seemed not to look out but in. Through the streets they moved like some old, half-buried, powerful river, its source hidden deep in the earth.

Seeing them, the present was telescoped for James Buchanan into a residue of subtly beautiful experiences left over from his childhood, of the natives who cared for his mother's land, the Indian woman who nursed him, her soft voice. Indian words, bits of song came back to him. The Indian heart was not closed to him then. He remembered how they had danced and sung. It delighted a little boy to be with people who were always dancing and singing. Mexico was not closed to a little boy.

Immediately after his mother's death Jim had been sent to the States. Always he had dreamed of coming back to Mexico. He had worked hard to train himself for the diplomatic field. But now that he had been assigned to the Embassy in Mexico he was not finding it the country of rich Spaniards and docile Indians he remembered.

The rank and file who passed him were neither Spanish nor Indian, but a blend of the two and handsomer than either—black-haired, warmly brown-skinned, intelligent-looking people like Guadalupe Villar, the Mexican who had taken him to the café.

Interesting, Jim thought, to see how quickly they have acquired the city polish. Some of the older members of the American community had told him that only a year or two ago such men dressed like desperadoes, revolvers slung from their belts, rounds of ammunition in bandoleers over their shoulders. Now, although the clothes of many of them were cheap, they wore city dress and wore it well. They carried no firearms. But they were still revolutionists. That he had learned this afternoon. Also that he and his people were not altogether acceptable to them. Nor were they to him, he decided.

He thought of himself as a victim of revolutions. The Civil War in his own country had left his father's family in the South poor and embittered. His father had come to Mexico solely for the purpose of recouping the family's fortunes. Wealth he had finally gained, but at the cost of his own life, for he had died of a tropical fever when Jim was six. In Jim's tenth year, the first year of the Revolution, his mother had fallen from her horse at the gate of their ranch, shot by one of the marauding bands of Zapata's men.

Quickly the servants had drawn her within the hacienda grounds and shut the gate. He remembered the old Indian manservant, tears running down his cheeks as he carried her between the rows of potted lilies. Her head lay against the man's brown and white serape. "Why did the Señora go?" the old Indian had mourned. "I told her that in times like these she should not go to the town for money."

"I am an American," she had said. "No one will dare touch me. I own this land for miles around. I am good to my Indians. What have the revolutionists to do with me?"

And what, James Buchanan thought, had they to do with him? He considered himself a Southern aristocrat. He believed in aristocracy and its ability to run a country. The American ambassador had proved that *noblesse oblige* paid. Since his coming the bitter controversy over the American-owned oil wells had been settled in favor of their American owners. Calles had dropped his order that owners of oil fields should exchange their titles for fifty-year leases, in accordance with the old Spanish law set aside by Díaz. Whatever these revolutionary-inclined Mexicans at the café might say, the ambassador by his gracious kindness had healed a breach growing constantly wider between the two countries. He had a gift for friendship. He had demonstrated it in his attitude to the Mexican people. He had won Calles by genuine interest in his plans for schools, road, and irrigation works. Now the ambassador and Calles were personal friends.

Following the example of the head of the Embassy, almost immediately on his arrival James Buchanan had reached out toward friendship with the Mexicans he met. He liked them, and they seemed to like him. Their never-failing graciousness had made any business he had with them a pleasant affair. But in the light of this afternoon's experience, he wondered if they really were friendly. When he had stumbled upon their attitude to his country, the avenues to friendship with all of them seemed suddenly closed. They were like turtles drawn within the smooth shell of their politeness. But what did it matter what such men thought? He was here in the interests of his own country, to gain advantages for it. With a gesture of finality, Buchanan threw away his cigarette. He took out his watch. It was time to meet Armstrong, one of his associates at the Embassy, for dinner. They were attending the first night of the opera together.

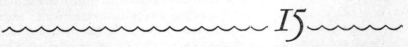

IGNACIO felt a pleasant glow of excitement as he and Pablo left the café. For the first time since he had come home he had been in touch with the "New Mexico," and Pablo charmed him. Just why he couldn't say. That was a part of the charm. He was not certain that he altogether trusted Pablo. He was too secretive about his work in the labor movement. Also it seemed to Ignacio that his half brother resented his inferior position in the family. To be sure, Vicente had done a good deal for his illegitimate son. He was a graduate of the National University—the university Ignacio's grandfather had wanted him to attend. But it was apparent that Pablo envied him the years abroad, whether because it emphasized their inequality or because he really coveted the European experience. As they walked along Pablo asked innumerable questions about Spain and France. And then, all at once, he declared, "I'd have gone to Russia, if I'd had your opportunity."

"You don't mean you're interested in Communism!" Ignacio exclaimed in shocked surprise.

"One doesn't have to accept a thing just because one wants to see how it works, does one?" Pablo, as they came out of the café, had put on dark, horn-rimmed spectacles which obscured his eyes, but there was a quizzical, half-amused expression lurking around the corners of his wide mouth as he spoke that Ignacio resented.

"To the men I was associated with in Europe, it seemed a somewhat naïve experiment. The Chinese, I believe, tried it a thousand years ago. Small groups everywhere have tried it. It's never worked." Ignacio spoke lightly, with the intention of erasing the impression in Pablo's mind that he belonged to Mexico's reactionaries.

"Not all Frenchmen, not all Spaniards agree with you," Pablo replied. "And it *is* working. If you'd seen Russia, you'd not be talking the way you are. Men here have gone over; they bring back word that the peasants and laborers have opportunities now."

"Is it true then, what I've heard since my return?"

"What have you heard? Lots of lies probably!"

"That Mexico's labor has gone Communist."

Suddenly Ignacio realized they were fast reaching the quarreling point where discussion was impossible. He had been baiting Pablo, and he was ashamed. He knew nothing about conditions in his own country. Not wanting to ruin the chance of friendship between them, he now made what for him was complete capitulation. "Why don't you show me what the labor movement is doing here?"

"If you are really interested, not just out to criticize——" Although Pablo detected sincerity in Ignacio's last remark, he was not certain that this elegant half brother of his was deeply in earnest about anything, but he, too, did not wish a quarrel to develop between them. He felt proud and happy in Ignacio's presence. "How would you like to go to a labor meeting with me sometime?"

"Fine," Ignacio answered absent-mindedly. They were nearing the

corner where he turned off to go home. To part there would emphasize to the oversensitive Pablo his illegitimacy. Glancing at his half
brother, Ignacio thought he saw that quizzical, amused smile again,
lurking at the corners of his mouth. He wished he could see the man's
eyes.

When they were within a few steps of the corner, Pablo broke the
silence. "How about going along with me to Villar's house—you know,
the man at the café whom we called Guadalupe. A lot of labor people
drop in there nearly every afternoon."

Graciously, but with some discomfiture, Ignacio accepted the invitation, realizing that Pablo had been as aware as he of the awkward
situation and had been quick to avoid embarrassment. He was annoyed
with himself for not being the one to solve their dilemma.

Silently they walked a few blocks until they came to a street Ignacio
did not know even by name. The one-story houses were flush with the
sidewalk. The iron window grilles, bowed a little in order to conform
to the rounded sills, encroached on the narrow space allotted to the
pedestrian. It was a poor street, and yet it had dignity, something
Ignacio associated only with his own part of the city. Pablo stopped
before a house lime-washed in pink. A young Indian girl slid back the
bar that locked the heavy door.

"Is the Señora at home?" asked Pablo.

"*Sí, Señor,*" answered the girl.

The gallery which surrounded the patio was narrow and empty
except for a chair in its farthest corner, where a woman was sitting.
As they entered she rose, walked toward them with quick, gliding step,
greeted Pablo affectionately.

"Soledad, I have brought a friend, Señor Ignacio Navarro, to see
you." Ignacio saw the exchange of glances between them—enigmatic,
unfathomable. And then in the woman's face came a look of recognition. After greeting him with a slight drawing together of her brows,
she turned, leading the way into a room Ignacio realized answered
for both sitting and drawing room.

To his eyes, it was an ill-furnished, bizarre place of meager furniture and brilliant decorations. A fresco filled the whole of one wall.
Ignacio had been well schooled in the technique of painting. Although
this work was entirely unorthodox in theme, he had to acknowledge
to himself that its execution was masterly. It was a picture of a village
fair, a scene typical of hundreds of Mexican villages. In the foreground
was the usual clutter of market day. The clay pots and dishes, fruits,

and vegetables spread out on straw mats gave the artist a chance for a gorgeous display of color, a riot of yellows and blues. Indian women, their hair braided with yellow and purple ribbons, and wearing bright blouses and full black skirts, knelt by their wares. In the foreground a child stood looking toward a group of women advancing from the portals of a gray stone building in the rear. Each carried tall stalks of corn. One woman was young, one middle-aged, one very old, but each was a portrait of Ignacio's hostess. Every mood expressed in the women's faces, whether somber brooding, laughter, tenderness, seemed to express an authentic Soledad. Was it this picture that impressed her personality on the room, or was it that her personality so dominated the place the artist had not been able to escape her influence when he was painting? Or had he not wanted to? Who was this Soledad?

"Pablo," she began impulsively, "if it weren't that my husband needs me, I should go right now into the country to teach in one of the villages still dominated by the great haciendas."

"And get malaria again?" he asked.

"You know I have done it before. Such forgotten ones are our neglected cousins. This is what I think when I walk along the street and see a group of Indians lost in this great city of theirs. Doesn't that ever occur to you, Señor Navarro?"

"Why should it?" Ignacio answered coolly.

"You see," she said, pin points of light leaping up in her black eyes, "I acknowledge my heritage. I am proud of it."

What reason had she to challenge him? What knowledge had she of his family?

"Let us sit down, if my wife is willing." Soledad's anger seemed to die away at the man's words. Turning to see who was speaking, Ignacio found himself face to face with a small, gentle-looking man.

"It is fine to see you here," he went on, holding out his hand.

With Soledad's challenge filling his mind, Ignacio had not until now recognized his host. It was Guadalupe Villar, the man who had gone out of the café with the North American. Then Ignacio's attention was caught by a great hulk of a man just entering the room. He had enormous feet and hands and a heavy body. This must be the painter Ignacio's class so hated, Diego Rivera. He it was, they felt, who had vulgarized the Mexican people throughout the world with his massive, heavy figures. Was he the creator of the fresco in this room?

"Walls!" the huge man was saying to the group in general, without stopping to greet any of them. "If we can only keep on, we could take painting out of its dilettante place in society. With plenty of walls, we'd make art into an instrument to serve the people. It wouldn't matter, then, whether they could read or not."

"You're more likely to lose the walls you've already covered than gain new ones," Soledad broke in. Her words were greeted with bitter laughter. Everyone knew of the effort there had been to have the Mexican frescoes erased from the walls of public buildings. Churchmen and aristocrats had urged their destruction. None knew this better than Ignacio. Some had been damaged.

"There is my fresco in Cuernavaca. If we could get individuals to donate walls all over the country, we'd not need the government to back us," the big man countered.

"But only the rich have that much money. I thought you didn't believe in rich men?" A thin-faced man who looked like Savonarola asked the question.

"It's a beautiful fresco. Have you seen it?" asked Guadalupe of Ignacio.

"I have heard of it," said Ignacio, in the same cold tone he had earlier used in answering Soledad. Guadalupe, finding him unresponsive, joined a group forming around the big man.

"There's news!" cried someone. "Diego has been asked to go to the States to paint on their walls!"

"There's other news, too," said Guadalupe quietly. "There's a rumor that Calles is urging that land distribution be stopped. He says it is not sound economically."

"Now that Calles is a hacienda owner, I suppose he wants to strut about in his borrowed plumage." Every eye in the room was on Soledad as she spoke. Her black eyes challenged them all. Then, with a little laugh, she patted her husband on the arm. "It's all right, Lupe, I'm not going to sing about the peacocks."

One by one the men left. A number were going to the opera—it was the opening night.

As Ignacio hailed a cab to take him home, he felt a sense of escape from a force that had rocked the cradle of his safety a little too violently. The burning eyes of Soledad haunted him. He would be glad to forget her. As for Pablo, he didn't think he wanted to see much of him.

16

JAMES BUCHANAN and his friend dined at the Majestic Hotel, where Jim had lived ever since his arrival in Mexico. From there they walked to the theater. These January evenings on the high plateau were like October nights in the northern United States, and both men felt almost unbounded energy. They passed along the street where the opera house built by Díaz stood. Its heavy marble walls had already sunk some distance into the spongy soil on which Mexico City is built. Tons of concrete would have to be pumped in before it could be used. They turned into a street congested with automobiles, the narrow walks filled with people.

"You always get a crowd for music," Buchanan's companion vouchsafed. "And the President is to be here tonight, I understand."

Already the lobby of the theater was crowded with men and women in evening dress. The stairs leading up to the lobby were lined with military cadets in pale blue uniforms holding back the poor and ill-dressed of the city come to catch a glimpse of their President. The official car, it was reported, had just left the President's house. But last arrivals were still being admitted to the theater. Coming up the stairs was a group of people, evidently a family, four couples in all. Their air of proud aloofness caught Jim's attention.

The elderly man at the head of the party was both distinguished and old-fashioned-looking. His forehead merged into the bald frontal part of his head. His white mustache almost touched his white sideburns that swept up to the line of white hair thick over his pronounced temples. He had the eyes of a zealot. The woman at his side eclipsed Jim's interest even in the man. From a peak on her forehead, her pepper-and-salt hair sprang away like the feathers of some majestic bird. Her eyes were piercing, not glowing as those of the man. The lift of her head was proud. A faint black mustache intensified the imperious set of her mouth. He knew the type. He had seen it in Paris. A matriarch who allows nothing to interfere with the traditional purposes of the family. A middle-aged couple brought up the rear.

Between the two couples walked four young people. One of the girls looked like the matriarch except that she had pale yellow hair. The other girl resembled only herself, he thought, she was so lovely, although not beautiful in the ordinary sense of the word. Her blue-black hair was drawn back in smooth bands over her ears. Only the tiny lobes, hung with delicately filigreed earrings, showed. Her face, although thin, was smoothly molded without any hint of the angular. Her black eyes had a wide-open, almost wondering look, which was enhanced by the position of her eyebrows, for they had an upward slant like small lifted wings. Her mouth tilted upward at the corners. She was smiling when he first observed her, but as her face settled into calm he was startled by its repose. It was a face you could not forget.

The young man walking beside her turned to speak to her. Why! He was the Spaniard who had been in the group at the café that afternoon!

"Who are they?" Jim asked his companion.

"The old man is Don Julián Navarro. That's his family, one of the oldest and most exclusive in Mexico. Counts back to the days of the Conquest and Spanish nobility. The old lady's family is as distinguished as his, I believe. The short young man belongs to a family who once owned as much land as there is in Rhode Island and Connecticut. A great deal of it was confiscated during the Revolution."

"Do you know them?" asked Jim.

"Do I know them? Did you know the old aristocracy of France when you were there?"

"No."

"Well, then, why should I know these people? They are said to be almost fanatically exclusive."

"It would be something to get past the impressive-looking matriarch, wouldn't it? She'd not let any of them break with tradition if she could help it." As Jim spoke, he wondered how it had been that the grandson was among the group of men at the café.

Drums sounded, Indian drums beating out a rhythm as old as the continent. Silence fell on the crowd. The President's party could be seen at the foot of the stairs. Slowly the President came, bowing to right and left. And with him was Calles, the former President, now called the Jefe Maximo because of his continued influence.

Don Julián and his family had taken their seats. Although they could be easily seen from the President's box, they did not rise and take part in the demonstration when the official party entered.

Louisa, sitting quietly at Mamá Grande's side, was laughing inwardly at the storm Ignacio's determination to come tonight had aroused in the family. Just how it had finally been arranged she did not know or care. It was enough that they were here and that Ramón was with them again. She had been frightened over the quarrel between him and Nacho, feeling guilty over the part she had played in their estrangement. She looked at Concha, sitting between her mother and father. Why doesn't she wake up? If she would only look at Ramón's eyes! She doesn't deserve him, the younger sister stormed to herself.

Ramón leaned over Concha's chair. "You will be a very beautiful wife," he whispered. "I have asked that our wedding take place this autumn."

17

THE next day Jim worked with the picture of Concha as clear in his mind as if he were still looking at her. Such an obsession, for obsession it must be, considering its tenacious hold on him, was an absurdity, he argued to himself. "There isn't even a chance that I shall ever meet her." He had always held his emotions well in hand; that they were strong, he knew, but he believed his will was stronger. He dismissed Concha's image but that same afternoon he found himself thinking of the girl's brother. He would like to solve the enigma of his presence in that group at the café. So although Jim had not intended to, once again he joined them. But the Spaniard did not come.

For several afternoons Jim walked over to the café, but as the Navarro heir did not appear he decided not to go any more. It was a strain to make the effort to understand these young men. He was always a little fearful of offending them. When Villar called up to say they had missed him, he was glad to have the tennis tournament at the club as an excuse.

It was a month before he went again. He was early. Only one man had come in—the Spaniard! Jim took the chair next to him. "I have become deeply interested in your Spanish colonial architecture," he said, thinking to start the conversation on some other note than the political.

"You have beautiful colonial in your own country," Ignacio replied, matching Jim in a polite exchange of compliments.

"Ours has a likeness to yours only in the restraint of the artist. But they are both good. You have seen some of our Southern homes?" Every line in young Navarro's face, Jim was thinking, indicated that the refining process had gone very far. His hands bore no mark of work, had none of the muscular bigness that labor brings. They were long and narrow with tapering fingers, hands that were firm, he imagined, and strong when they pulled the reins to control a spirited horse.

"No, I have never been in your country," Ignacio answered, "but I saw an exhibition of North American paintings in Paris. There were one or two of colonial houses. 'Southern colonial,' it was called, I believe."

"That is my part of the country." Jim wished they could go on talking together, but the table was filling up.

Pablo and a number of others just coming in were buying up the last copies of a *corrido* from a barefoot, ragged urchin wandering among the tables.

Jim had very early learned that the Mexican wit was something to enjoy but also to fear. Now, glancing at the paper Pablo handed him, he saw the first stanza of the *corrido* was a caustic and cynical lament over the proposed change in land distribution.

Laughter and ominous murmurs were mingled in the room. In a moment it was evident that there were antagonistic elements among the men. The soft gentleness of the city was gone. Jim thought he saw a flash of steel here and there.

Pablo, swinging the *corrido,* tapped it with his eyeglasses. "Hear! Hear!" He began to read the second stanza aloud in a mocking voice:

"Our Jefe Maximo and an Ambassador eat bacon and eggs
    together.
A privilege to us.
For it, we give the subsoil of our country,
Vital products, rich products.

They confer;
They decide
Land distribution is bad for an Ambassador and a President
    eating bacon and eggs together."

Jim was angry. He knew that the ambassador referred to was his own, and that Pablo had read the doggerel aloud for his benefit. This was unpardonable. He rose to leave, the only possible thing he could do under the circumstances.

He saw, to his surprise, that the Spaniard had risen, too. "It's an unforgivable breach of hospitality and taste," Jim heard him say in a low tone, looking straight at Pablo. The whole group was suddenly silent. They had gone deadpan, hiding their tender new self-respect from the fierce eyes of the Spaniard. But between Pablo and Ignacio there was no hiding of feeling. Their eyes interchanged glances as sharp as points of steel.

As Jim stood outside the café, angry over what he considered an insult to his ambassador and his country, he heard the young Spaniard behind him, saying, "We were talking of colonial architecture in the States. I have my car parked near here. If you would care to accompany me, it would give me pleasure to show you some houses we think are particularly fine examples of Spanish colonial."

"I should very much like to see them." Jim hoped his voice sounded as calm as Navarro's had. As they started off together, a gust of wind sent the winter dust whirling round them in cyclonic violence. Both were glad that talk, for the time, was impossible.

The politeness and graciousness of Ignacio's offer moved Jim deeply, a delicate, indirect way of expressing regret over the incident in the café.

As for Ignacio, he was silently ridiculing himself. So I imagined I'd find companionship in Pablo! he thought. Hereafter I'll stick to men of refinement and breeding.

Neither of them was aware that Villar had also come out. He watched them until they were lost in the clouds of dust, then turned to go home, the _corrido_ crushed in his hand. "I had thought to draw us all together for better understanding," he mourned. "If only the Spaniards and the North Americans would not stand aloof from our struggle, would lay aside their superiority and try to understand!"

Soledad heard Guadalupe come in and ran swiftly across the patio to greet him. Without a word he handed her the crumpled paper. When she read the couplets, her eyes shone with the light of combat. This was the kind of warfare she understood.

The full meaning of what the _corrido_ suggested was suddenly apparent to Villar. By any chance, was the division of land really to cease? His heart seemed to beat in his throat. He put up his hand, pulling at his collar. Jobs like his, then, would be done away with. Skating on the thin ice just above poverty as they were even now, it would be only a matter of days after his salary ceased before Soledad and he sank into its deep waters.

Profound discouragement took hold of him. Twenty years since the beginning of the Revolution, and yet so little had been accomplished! The reports in the archives here at the capitol were impressive: four thousand villages had received land; three-quarters of a million families had been benefited; much of this had been accomplished by Calles. But he knew what lay behind this façade of paper reform. The *hacendados* bought up many a state official; the state officials bought up the people's representatives, who sold the communal land back to the old and the new privileged class. But still he believed they could win, if the States would only leave them to work out their own problems. But the States always threw their powerful influence on the side of the rich. The first hatred young Villar had ever experienced arose in him now, and it was against the country which had given him his education.

18

AFTER some ten minutes, Ignacio stopped before a tall house, saying, "This is one of the oldest specimens of Spanish colonial."

The perfect balance of the windows on the two upper floors, the wide arched gateway on the street level, the restrained pattern of the wrought-iron railings before the windows, the rose-colored lava stone walls, all made the house one of dignity and beauty. To Jim's astonishment his companion said, "Perhaps you'd like to see the interior. It belongs to my grandfather. Francisco!" he called, ignoring the bell. His tone was full of authority. Almost immediately the gate swung open.

Ignacio had not intended, in the beginning, to take the young North American into his home—simply show him the exteriors of a few of the best houses in Mexico City, thus make amends for Pablo's rudeness. But as he stood before his grandfather's house, there flared in him a desire to defy his family openly. Except with defiance, Nacho did not know how to deal with his growing sense of frustration. Without consulting him, Mamá Grande had healed the breach made by his quarrel with Ramón. A larger dowry than at first intended for Concha had been arranged, he understood. The wedding was set for the autumn. Every afternoon Ramón was at the house, was there now, probably. Resolutely, Ignacio led the way through the high, arched gateway.

Across the spacious court Jim saw that two stairways curved to a landing from which a single flight led upward. On the newel posts stood alabaster urns. Their luminous surfaces gleamed softly in the half-light of the courtyard. The great waterspouts, jutting forth from the flat roof, were of carved stone. The iron railings of the galleries above were of exquisite workmanship.

"Beautiful!" exclaimed Jim.

Ignacio gave the customary polite answer of his people, "A *sus órdenes,* what is mine is yours."

They reached the turn, ascended the wide single flight, crossed the gallery to a glass door which the young Spaniard opened, saying, "Please enter." Jim had an impression of a high ceiling, high windows and doors, and over each, carved in relief, a shallow fluted shell which lent grace and lightness to an otherwise austere room. As they advanced over a rose and blue Aubusson rug that extended the length of the floor, he was conscious of a group of people standing at the far end of the room, the girl whom he had not been able to forget in the midst of them.

Concha thought, How does it come that Nacho is bringing a stranger—and a North American—home with him? For the man with Nacho *was* from the States. Of that she was instantly certain. She knew so well that unmistakable North American expression on the faces of men and women, as she saw them on the street, the knit-together effect of their features combined with an impatient, determined look, as if life were so short one must hurry to grasp it before it was gone. "The expression of people belonging to a Protestant country," her grandfather claimed.

There surged over her a feeling of indignation. None but the accepted and established were ever asked into the privacy of their home. That, Mamá Grande had taught them when she and Louisa were little girls attending the convent and had brought to see her, one day, an English girl as wellborn as they, but not known to the grandmother. Only Ignacio would break such a custom of the house. Ignacio who always did what he pleased. Ramón had told her that he associated with a revolutionary group. That was heresy. However, a man went his own way outside and a woman had little to say about it. But to break the ironclad rule of exclusiveness!

The two young men had almost reached them when Mamá Grande stepped forward, and with hauteur such as Concha had seen her use only once or twice in her life, greeted the stranger. And yet politeness was so cleverly combined with a cold aloofness that the man would neither trespass further nor go away offended, thought Concha.

Ignacio turned toward his sister and she saw pleading in his eyes. She suddenly realized that he was lonely in the very midst of his family. Her love rushed out to enfold him. Her approach to him, which had been closed ever since his return, might be open to her if she helped him now. She smiled and held out her hand to his friend. Nacho gave her a grateful look.

Then Mamá Grande said quietly, "We will excuse you, Concepción."

But as Concha turned to leave, she felt her hand grasped by her mother. Mamá seldom asserted herself where Mamá Grande was concerned. When she did drop her submissiveness, she had such regal bearing that not even Mamá Grande opposed her. She had that bearing now. Still clasping Concha's hand, she said to the stranger, "I am always glad to welcome Nacho's friends." She too had seen the imploring look in her son's eyes. Ever since his return from Europe Mamá had been deeply troubled over her son. Quietly she had waited for an opportunity to help him without intruding on the privacy of the spirit she held in respect. Kindness to his friend might open the way into Ignacio's confidence.

With an effort at casualness, Ignacio said, "Mamá, Señor Buchanan is interested in our colonial architecture. In Paris I saw paintings of the colonial buildings of his country. I wanted him to see the best of ours."

"Then I will show your friend about. Here, in the *sala* and in the dining room, are details of interest, Señor Buchanan, and someday Nacho must introduce you to his grandfather and let him take you to his library." Still holding her daughter's hand, Mamá led the way to the other end of the long room and opened the door into the music room. "Here is some particularly interesting ironwork. And here," she added, indicating the fluted shell over the doorway, "is a distinctive note seen only in the houses of those who have the right to display the pilgrim's begging shell."

"I noticed it as soon as I came into the room," Jim answered. "How cleverly the architect has used that detail to lighten a certain massive effect. You see, I was interested once in becoming an architect, and I did some studying."

"You found it unnecessary to go on?" Mamá asked. Jim realized she meant work was not a financial necessity.

Not willing to give any false impression, he answered, "Instead I took up diplomacy as a profession. I am connected with the Embassy here." He added the last remark, not wanting her to think he was simply passing through the city. He did not wish her to offer him such gracious hospitality only because she thought it involved no future commitments.

In this handsome mother of the young Spaniard he felt the warmth of a quickly responsive nature roused for some reason in his behalf. But he had an almost cruel realization of the exclusiveness of the family group—members of the wealthy and powerfully entrenched Spanish aristocracy. It had been conveyed to him through the ultra politeness of the matriarch. Perhaps, he thought, if I had not seen such exclusiveness evidenced in my Virginia relatives, I would not have been aware that her politeness is only a veneer.

Mamá released Concha's hand as they turned back into the *sala*. "Unlock the Chinese cabinet, Conchita. Perhaps Señor Buchanan would like to see what was brought over in the Manila galleons."

Jim watched the young girl in her moss-green dress as she walked across the room and knelt before a black lacquer cabinet. Grace characterized her every movement. "This is the best of all the pieces," she said, looking up at him, as he and Mamá joined her. "At least, I like it the best." Her delicately tapered fingers lay caressingly against the smooth surface of a hollow piece of yellow jade upright on a small pedestal of dark wood.

"How beautiful!" exclaimed Jim.

"A *sus órdenes*," answered Concha. "It is yours."

"It is yours to keep for me," he replied quickly, realizing that the formal politeness that necessitated the phrase sometimes led to the actual fulfillment of the words.

Concha was delighted with the quickness of his repartee—it was like that of her own people. She saw him all at once not only as a man from the States but as a man of refinement. She noticed his sensitive mouth, his intelligent blue eyes. He was a good friend for Nacho to have.

At that moment Louisa came into the room. A lively curiosity was expressed in her face as she looked from Mamá Grande to Mamá and Concha talking to the stranger, then at Ignacio, who was leaning against the fireplace. Undoubtedly it was he who had introduced this innovation in their lives. It pleased her. She was in league with Ignacio to bring about a change in the family's customs. Then she saw Ramón and how stormy his eyes were. Giving only a quick bow to Jim, she went and sat down beside Ramón.

When James Buchanan had gone, Concha, fearful that there was to be conflict between the old and the new matriarch, slipped quietly away to the roof—her haven since childhood. The sun had set behind the mountains, black against the luminous backdrop of the sky. To-night, as often at this time of the year at evening, the dry air drained all color from the city, leaving it but a skeleton of itself, unearthly, bone-white in the fading light, its vast expanse of empty roofs sunk in the hollowed plain. She was filled with apprehension over this afternoon's conflict between her grandmother and mother. Would there be open warfare now between them? How strong and beautiful her mother was without the cloak of her resignation! Why should there be so much resignation demanded of her mother? A small, startled sob escaped her. Resignation for herself too, in this marriage to Ramón.

The conversation which her mother had had with her on the day after her fifteenth birthday, long forgotten, drove itself forward now to the front of her mind. She remembered now how they had stood together outside the gates of the little hacienda to watch evening come down over the fields and how her mother had said, "I see in you, my daughter, many of the traits of your Aztec heritage. You have the Indians' capacity for profound abnegation. I hope you have, too, their proud independence." She was like Mamá! She, too, had strength, but how could she make it serve her?

James Buchanan woke the next morning to a moment of stillness between the night and the day noises of the great square outside his window. The thin, high air was devoid of sound; then into the silence came the hollow clang of bells. The bells' clappers beat quickly as if those who rang them would repeat their message as often as possible in the two minutes allotted to them. Abruptly they ceased. Again that strangely moving silence.

"Give me my shell of quiet." "Concha," the name of a shell.

Settling over Jim was the bitter sense of the impossibility of his desire. His friendship with Ignacio seemed to have come to an abrupt end. Whatever emotion had prompted the young Spaniard to take him into his home appeared to have spent itself by the time they came out of the house. Ignacio had left him at his hotel with a finality in his farewell that did not imply any further communication between them. But even if Ignacio had expressed a wish to see him again, he felt certain the matriarch would manage so that he did not know the family intimately.

~~~~~~~~~~~~~~~~~~~~~~~~~~~~ *19* ~~~~~

MAMÁ GRANDE knew it was idle to deal directly with resistance from her daughter-in-law. Once Vicente's wife took a position she held to it with complete stubbornness. She might even invite this North American to come again. It was the head of the family who must use his authority with Ignacio to see that such a thing did not happen.

Doña María had not heard her husband go out, as was his custom at this hour of the afternoon. Today she was glad. Ordinarily she would have been annoyed that he was still at home. Mamá Grande encouraged her men to have interests outside the family, although openly she deplored them. Her husband's absorption in the Church, and her son's in his second home, alike gave her greater opportunity to manage the household as she wished. But at times like this, angered and defeated, she found it convenient to place blame on the titular head of the house for not oftener exerting his authority.

She found Don Julián seated at his desk. A book lay open before him, but he was not reading. He was as still as an image, lost in profound meditation. Even when she stood close beside him, he did not stir. Even when she spoke to him, he evinced no knowledge of her presence.

"No wonder your family suffers," she said with bitterness.

He stirred, looked at her absent-mindedly. "What is it you have to say?" he asked.

"You sit here at the top of the house, and Vicente, your son, is only here in name. What have I done to deserve such calamity?" She lowered her eyes. "I who have never ceased to sacrifice myself for the family. The Holy Virgin alone knows the sorrows of women!"

"My wife," he said, stemming the tide of her words, "a man to you is unnecessary, once he has given you children. That I have done." And he turned to the book that lay open before him.

Mamá Grande, taken back, seemed uncertain for a moment. Then, setting her face in an exaggerated expression of martyrdom, she left him.

But whatever Don Julián might say to his wife, he could not remain indifferent to this act of his grandson when he learned of it the next day. The family was one organism. Let one member pull away, and the organism shuddered to its outer rim. An aunt in the house told an aunt in another household of Ignacio's act and of his mother's part in it. In the next few days cousins, aunts, and uncles found time to call. Nothing was said directly, but none in Don Julián's household except himself was unaware of the reason for the visits. In polite phrases they spoke of the changes that were coming to the city and how few were maintaining the fine old traditions. Even some of the best families were growing lax, did Julián not think so?

Don Julián was pleased at first that others were at last beginning to see as he did the grave nature of the changes taking place in the city. But when so many of them mentioned the fact, he began to wonder what was back of it all and demanded an explanation.

Doña María sighed heavily, saying, "I wished to tell you, but you would not listen. It is Nacho. He brought into the privacy of our home —into the very room where our precious Concha was sitting—a stranger. Furthermore, he was a North American."

"A North American! Send Ignacio to me immediately when he comes in," Don Julián commanded, and barricaded himself in his library against the remarks of any more of his relatives.

It was not necessary, he told Ignacio later, to bring his companions into the home. Politeness, yes, when he met these people from the States, even friendship with them if he wished it in his outside life. A man was free to follow his own whims there. But as future head of the house, surely he would not wish to destroy the exclusive position of the family. It was after this that Don Julián resolved to take Nacho in hand, show him by example what the life of a Spanish gentleman should be.

The week following, he asked Ignacio to accompany him to the small amphitheater where the tailing of the bull took place each Sunday morning during the winter season.

"At your age you should be able to exceed me, Nacho," said the old man.

"I haven't your prowess, sir," said Ignacio. "I'd rather watch your excellence."

"Times have changed." The old man gave a dramatic sigh. "At your age I excelled every other young *hacendado* in the state of Morelos. Many were the evenings, after a fiesta, my companions accompanied me back to my own hacienda chanting songs of my prowess."

Ignacio was delighted with this companionship. Heretofore he had known only the old man's sterner side. He felt comfortable and at ease sitting here in the sun among the handful of spectators. He was happy. For the moment, his act of rebellion in bringing a stranger unasked into his home had given him a kind of peace.

What a dandy his grandfather was, he thought affectionately. He had on a very handsome *charro* suit. The tight-fitting, soft, leather trousers showed to perfection Don Julián's slender legs and well-shaped hips. The silver buttons from hip to ankle gleamed in the sun, emphasizing his small, neat feet, as he strode into the arena. And the soft chamois jacket with its bold design embroidered on the back made his shoulders look broad. But as he turned his head in the cruelly revealing sunlight, Ignacio noticed the gray, old look of his grandfather's skin, and that his jowls were flabby. He'll never seem old to himself, thought his grandson, as long as he can compete with the younger men.

Ignacio's eyes narrowed. How well Don Julián's brain served him! The younger men relied too much on their strength. His grandfather relied on skill. Ignacio was an admirer of skill. How a thing was done was more important to him than the doing. There! Don Julián had seized the bull's tail. With an expert twist of his wrist he threw the animal.

"Bravo!" cried Ignacio, jumping over the rail enclosing the arena and embracing his grandfather. Ignacio was a Latin, now, to his fingertips, swept out of his uncertainties.

Don Julián made up a party to ride out to Xochimilco, the floating gardens of the Aztecs, where there was a restaurant famed for its good cooking. Ignacio lent gaiety to the gathering. He borrowed a guitar from one of the wandering group of musicians and sang to his own accompaniment. Don Julián had not been so happy about his grandson since his return. The boy would come out all right, he thought, looking across at him strumming on the guitar. The chicken, Veracruz-style, was excellent. It was a perfect day. Next Sunday he would take all the family to the bullfight. There was to be a very good matador, he understood.

When Ignacio was told of the plan, he wondered why he had not gone since his return. He had never missed a fight before he went abroad. Why, he had even wanted to be a bullfighter!

High and low, the people poured into the great tiers of the bull ring. By four o'clock thirty thousand people had quietly taken their seats. The bright day picked out bits of color in the great arena, splashes of red, yellow, and white on both the sunny and the shady side, making the circular tiers look like a mammoth bed of confetti. There were many family groups; even babies in arms could be seen where the poorer people sat in the sun. Don Julián led his party to reserved seats in the shade. The only member of his family not there was Mamá. She did not care for bullfights. Concha sat between Ignacio and her grandfather.

On the sunny side Soledad Villar had squeezed herself into a seat. Guadalupe was away in the country, and she could not resist coming. Each Sunday, from her house not far from the bull ring, she could hear the roar that went up when there was "excellence." Guadalupe would not want her to be here. She experienced a sense of guilt she would not have felt with her first husband. Then she forgot it. I like it very much here, she said to herself.

James Buchanan had come with a group of Americans. He wondered if the aristocratic Navarros were there. In the vast throng he failed to find them.

Into the arena was ridden a horse that set Jim's blood tingling. Jim, whose family came from the bluegrass country of Virginia, had been brought up to love good horseflesh. The band played, and the sleek, finely proportioned bay mare took the dance steps so long ago perfected in Austria for the Emperor's pleasure. Then she backed gracefully out. A little tune was carried across the arena from the band, a tune Jim was beginning to know, a jaunty little tune—the *diana* "*Salud!* Excellence!"

The matadors in their gold, blue, and pink costumes paraded across the pale yellow sand of the arena. A hush fell on the crowd. Opposite from where he sat, Jim saw the two halves of a door swing open, and a great black bull, excited and confused by the sudden sunlight after the darkness of his pen, plunged across the sand.

Jim leaned forward, caught by the scene, so brilliant and startling in its contrast of color and mood. The black bull, his hindquarters stained yellow with his own flap, tossing and lowering his thickset horns, seeking out his prey; the matador's attendants, agile, exquisite, dragging their red capes before the bull, then fleeing behind the barriers.

Men mounted on horses and with long spears in their hands entered the arena. "Let's not look. They're old hacks, but one might be gored," the middle-aged woman sitting next to Jim exclaimed.

"And yet you come often, don't you?" he asked in surprise.

"Yes, yes, I do. I think always I'll learn why my Mexican friends like to come. They are kindly people. It annoys them when we call the bull-fight cruel. They say to me, 'We think your wrestling is both cruel and ugly. A bullfight at least has beauty.'" She clutched Jim.

"Would you like to leave?" he asked.

"No, the Mexicans think it very rude if we get up and go out."

The bull, maddened by the picks caught in the fleshy part of his neck, was charging at his prey. Closer and closer to him the matador led the bull, cleverly manipulating his red *muleta*. From then until he drove his sword in between the bull's shoulders Jim had but one emotion, incredible surprise that a man would so futilely risk his life. Was there especial fascination in death to a Spaniard? Death like a black shadow constantly revolved around the ring.

Five of the six fights of the afternoon were over. Ignacio had watched with narrowing eyes, evaluating bull and matador. Studying each move, he had applauded only when there was excellence, but there was little of it today. All the fights were disappointingly mediocre. Now the last bull entered the ring. He was a brave bull! A clean fighter. So was his opponent! It was nothing now that the matador had bungled his first fight, for he was not bungling this.

"See, Concha, there is grace in every movement he makes. See how nobly he risks himself!" Ignacio responded to the classic portrayal of tragedy enacted before his eyes as a Greek in his age would have responded to tragedy in drama. It was like a catharsis cleansing him of the petty struggles of his idle, protected life. Ignacio rose, pulling Concha with him, adding his voice to the voice of the applauding crowd.

Don Julián, glancing at him, was satisfied. After all, Ignacio was like them. He, too, found release in this struggle between life and death. Death was met and conquered. Don Julián was an old man. It was good to see death conquered.

Vicente, sitting on the other side of Ignacio, was reveling in the sunlight over the arena, the dark blood that stained the pale sand, the dead bull dragged around the ring, the matador who was standing just below them holding up the ears and tail of his defeated adversary.

Vicente wished the woman of his little household was here to share this moment with him. He had meant to bring her until the crisis had arisen in the family and his help had been needed to keep Ignacio in line.

As one person the thirty thousand men and women rose, shouting approval. Had not the matador been so close to the bull that only by tightening of the muscles of his stomach had he escaped the horns!

Jim, going out with the great throng, thought he caught a glimpse of Ignacio, but he was not certain. The man gave no sign of recognition.

Ignacio, lost in the magnificence of the scene he had just witnessed, did not notice Jim.

Concha, walking by her brother's side, was very happy. She had been close in spirit to Nacho this afternoon.

20

ALL MEXICO was preparing for the first public observance of Holy Week since the closing of the churches. Don Julián insisted that Ignacio should take part in the return of the Church to its former position in the lives of the people.

At the end of the week the family was to visit their great sugar hacienda. Now that there was less agitation over the giving out of land, Don Julián felt it was safe to go. Both he and Mamá Grande were anxious to hold once more a celebration for Saint Mary of the hacienda, the patron saint. Mamá and Concha, taking some of the servants, were spending Holy Week there in order that everything should be in readiness for the great fiesta. They were planning for the days just after Easter. Every branch of the family was to be entertained. They would all gather in the beautiful Saint Mary's Chapel to celebrate the day of Annunciation. Don Julián loved this chapel with its copy of the famous picture of the young Virgin visited by the angel. On other days there would be dancing, a bullfight and many festivities.

Ignacio dutifully attended his family through Wednesday's Hour of Darkness. On Thursday evening he went with his grandfather and father on their pilgrimage to the seven churches, where high and low now joined in the democracy of devotion—barefoot poor and well-shod rich kneeling together, jostling one another as they passed in and out. Ignacio was scarcely conscious of the scene, his attention centered on his efforts to keep near to Don Julián and Vicente in the thickly packed throng. Once he heard his father say under his breath, "Only two more, and then we'll be through."

In the last church, on a side street and not so closely packed as the others, they found room to kneel in one of the back pews. There in the dark center of the church Ignacio could see the altar and, behind it, ascending tiers of white lilies and placed among them, enclosed in a golden custodial, the sacred Host.

It was nearing midnight. The altar bell rang, then ceased, not to be heard again until the Gloria on Saturday. Ignacio was swept back into his childhood, into its wonderment and awe. Why this disturbing emotion? He considered himself an agnostic.

On their return Ignacio followed his grandfather into his library. Standing by the desk, trembling a little at his own temerity, he said, "Grandfather, I feel I can no longer pretend to something I do not believe in. I am an agnostic."

Don Julián lowered himself slowly into his chair, his eyes fixed on his grandson. "You are what?" he said faintly.

"I do not believe in the Catholic Church. How can I believe in it? For four hundred years it has done nothing to educate the villagers or to lift them to a decent living. They exist in the utmost ignorance and poverty. The thousands of priests have kept them so."

"And when," asked his grandfather caustically, "did you become so interested in the Indian peasant?"

Ignacio flushed.

Sternly his grandfather went on, "I do not accept your statements. It is incredible to have a renegade from the faith in my family. My only grandson." Don Julián let the words fall as if too heavy for his voice to speak them. This was worse than he had suspected. Worse than it was with Vicente, who was only indifferent to the Church.

"And your mother?" The old man's voice broke.

"My mother is a saint," exclaimed Ignacio.

"In your world, the world of the agnostic, saints do not exist. If you consider your mother a saint, then you are not an agnostic. Consider, think how you will hurt your mother."

"My mother will respect my honesty."

"I at least can command you to say nothing of this to your sisters. Do I have your promise? Nor to your mother?"

"I promise to spare Mother as much as I can," Ignacio answered.

"And you'll promise to think the matter over?"

"Yes. I promise."

The next morning Ignacio left the house early, before anyone was awake. He felt an urgent necessity to escape the family with its undertow, pulling him slowly but surely back into its traditional life. To whom could he anchor himself to guard against submergence? Pablo he had offended in his quixotic defense of the North American. He stood alone except—except for the man from the States. Through Buchanan lay his escape. He remembered the groups of tourists the day before, urging themselves through the kneeling, worshiping crowds, whispering together, some even pointing. "Barbarous people," had been the comment of his grandfather. Now Ignacio, in his desire to strengthen himself against his grandfather's pleading, would join them, view the ritual of his people as a spectacle. He would seek out Buchanan and act as his guide. Thus he would gain the objective point of view he so coveted.

Jim was taken completely by surprise when Ignacio telephoned him, but he was delighted that the young Spaniard wanted to see him again. It might lead to friendship. But why should he have chosen this particular way of renewing the acquaintance?

For a time they stood in the Church of Guadalupe, crushed in with other sight-seers. The vast floor was carpeted with the brown kneeling throng—a moving carpet, for many were creeping forward toward the image of the crucified Christ within the transept. Candles held in their hands threw light down on the mosaic of their bronze faces caught in the moment of rapturous devotion. "There," said Ignacio, pointing to a man bleeding from a rosette of cactus thorns pressed to his chest, "you see the expiatory madness. Look over the crowd. You'll see plenty of it in these ignorant Indians." Jim did not know what to think. Was Señor Navarro not a Catholic then?

When they were outside once more and he saw the throng moving toward the booths where street vendors sold food, smelled the hot peppers and condiments reminiscent of the good things of his childhood, Jim would have stopped and eaten among the people, glad to bring life back into the ordinary channels; but when he suggested it, Ignacio drew him away, saying, "I think if we go immediately, we've time to visit a Spanish church before the three hours are over."

During the ride back into the city he continued to explain away the reverence of the Indians. "Now I will show you another phase of the same delusion," he ended as they got out of the car. All Jim was aware of at first, as he came into the church, was a kneeling crowd of well-dressed people, lost in sorrow. And then, as he lifted his eyes, he saw standing opposite him the life-size statue of the Mater Dolorosa. The gold balustrade that usually guarded her stood ajar and, clad in a black robe held by a knotted girdle, she seemed to have stepped beyond so that she might look across the transept into the sanctuary where men were lifting her Son from the Cross.

"She will be left alone to mourn through the dark hours of the night while her Son lies in the tomb," Ignacio whispered.

Jim had a sudden, startling vision of a real woman alone and sorrowing here in this vast church. The Mater Dolorosa was very human and very Spanish—the triangled face and mouth, the smooth black hair, the aristocratic bearing. He was reminded of Concha, a Concha grown older and trained in sorrow.

Outside, Ignacio began, "Of course you are only entertained by this realistic portrayal of suffering, something even the Catholics of your country no doubt would consider—shall I say, inelegant?"

"Quite the contrary," said Jim, nettled as he had often been today by Ignacio's determination to place him in the role of the scoffer. "I am deeply moved."

"I am alone, then, in my criticism. Make no mistake. These people we just left are not sorrowing for their sins. There was no expiatory madness there. It is simply that Mexico is never free from the knowledge of the continuity of its tragedy. It seeks the enactment of Christ's suffering to gain respite from its own suffering. We make this lifelike portrayal hoping to win for a time immunity for ourselves from the tragedy of death and strife, so constantly a part of our lives. We are not fooled by a few years of peace."

"You do not need to be a cynic to interpret the sorrow over Christ's death in that way," Jim said quietly, understanding Ignacio better now. For the time being he was necessary to the young Spaniard who was fighting a battle with himself; of its nature Jim could only guess. But surely such a destructive mood, such bitter repudiation of his people's faith was unfortunate for Ignacio, destroying more than it intended. Why such repudiation? Was it because of the periods in the country's history when the Church had been burdened with a dissolute priesthood which exploited the people? Or was it due to some personal frustration? "After all," he said, "your country has put up a magnificent struggle for freedom. Your suffering has been to a purpose."

Ignacio felt himself steadying under Jim's sympathetic understanding. Then he was swept with a new desire for revolt. He simply could not go down to the hacienda alone. Aunts, uncles, the whole clan were to be there, and the distant cousin Mamá Grande had decided he should marry.

"It is necessary for me to go down to our sugar hacienda tomorrow," he said, changing the subject abruptly. "Conditions have been such that we haven't held a celebration for Saint Mary, its patron saint, for several years. You might be interested in seeing it. I'll bring you back in time for work Tuesday morning."

"Wouldn't it be an intrusion?" Jim had not forgotten his impression of the exclusiveness of the family.

"Oh, no! There are others coming."

"But I'm due at the Embassy on Monday," Jim added, not entirely convinced.

"Perhaps you could arrange it." The arrogance in Ignacio's polite assumption that the matter could and would be arranged annoyed Jim.

"I rather think I'd better not go this time, but I appreciate your asking me," he replied.

"You must come." Ignacio was almost pleading now.

Jim knew he could manage it if he wished to. Hours were flexible with this regime of his government where friendship between two peoples was the goal. And then there was Concha.

Ignacio drove his car cleverly but recklessly. Gesturing to illustrate some point, often he used one or both hands, then let them fall gracefully again upon the wheel, maneuvering with dexterity his way down the narrow and congested streets of the old city through which they had to pass to get to the highway that led out of the valley. Then, at breath-taking speed, he covered the road across the open country and up the circling mountain drive. Part way, he stopped the car so they could view the city lying below them in the valley. The tiled domes of its churches shone in the sun; the smoke of its factories mingled with the departing mist.

"The maps of the old Aztec city are interesting," said Ignacio. "They show the city set in the midst of its three lakes. You probably know that all except one have been filled in. The spongy land makes a good base for a city shaken so often by earthquakes."

"The fruits of peace." Jim saw too late that his remark had been inopportune. A look of intense distaste came into the Spaniard's face.

In fact, the remark had turned Ignacio's dissatisfaction in his own people into bitterness against Buchanan's country. How glibly Jim spoke of peace. Fruits of peace indeed! How blandly he ignored the violence of his country toward Mexico! What about Texas? What about California? And here this representative of the Colossus of the North, sitting at his side, talked about peace in the scene below them. Why, in his estimation it was this man's country which had contributed so largely to Mexico's tragedy!

"You can't see from here," he said, "the place where the six cadets leaped from the tower of Chapultepec castle."

Jim was startled by the hidden reprimand in the words. It was in 1847 when the United States forces invaded Mexico City that the cadets had killed themselves in protest.

"Over there," Ignacio went on, "is the Star Hill. The first men to people this continent celebrated the coming of darkness there. It was a moment of anguish experienced once in a half-century, a terrible day belonging neither to the old year nor the new. With the fires in the city and in every village put out, they knelt on the mountaintop with dead torches, waiting for the spark, no certainty that two sticks rubbed together would give fire to kindle the bits of wood laid on the breast of the expiatory victim."

"But it always came," insisted Jim quietly. "The moment of joy and renewed faith as well as the anguished moment which preceded it."

"Down there in the city that looks so peaceful to you," Ignacio went on, determined to refute everything but tragedy, "the altars of my mother's people were destroyed to make room for those of my father's people. The long conflict of two races is still not ended—perhaps never will be. We are a tragic nation."

What was it Ignacio had said—"my mother's people"? So even in this exclusive Spanish family was the strain of the Indian. Was that the cause of this conflict in the grandson of the Spaniard, Don Julián?

As they drove on, Ignacio seemed sunk in moody thought. He scarcely spoke. Jim did not attempt to interrupt those broodings. After a time he became absorbed in his own reflections. Memories of his childhood awakened in him as he looked out over the country, now at the climax of the dry season parched and faded, the flanks of the hills bleached almost to bone-white. The land drew him into some relationship with it he had once had through his nurse, the houseman, the lowliest worker in his mother's fields. They had taught him that the earth was a man's true mother, that it nourished and renewed him.

He looked at his watch. They must be getting near their destination. "Just where are we?" he asked. There was no answer. He saw Ignacio had not heard him.

He began to feel uneasy. Perhaps the invitation after all had been given merely in politeness, just an elaboration of the over-polite salutation, "My house is yours," not meant to be taken literally.

Below lay a beautiful valley, irrigated evidently, for from edge to edge it was green. Each curve in the road brought the valley into greater detail. It was a tapestry of pale-green, broad-leafed banana, dark-green, fine-leafed coffee, and mile on mile of ash-green sugar cane.

Then finally, they turned from the main thoroughfare. The car rolled along through unbroken ranks of sugar cane. Ahead Jim could see the dome of a church, then a thick wall encircling some buildings, the watchtowers at the corners seeming to pit their strength against a village of huts clustered at the wall's base.

Ignacio roused himself. "That's our hacienda ahead," he said.

Jim felt intensely excited. Somewhere within that great house was Concha. And he was to spend two days under the same roof with her.

21

CONCHA walked along the gallery of the one-storied hacienda house until she came to a flight of steps that led to the flat roof. From this vantage place she could watch the road over which the cars from the city would come, and could look down also into the wide patio bounded by the house on three sides and by a vine-covered iron fence on its fourth. The rounded tops of the jacaranda trees in the patio were on a level with her eyes. The blue petals of their flowers had fallen upon the ground, making a carpet on the pebbled paths. A tangled mass of shrubbery filled the pie-shaped beds surrounding the fountain in the center. How everything had grown in the years they had been away! In the park that lay between the iron fence and the heavy masonry outer wall which enclosed all the hacienda buildings the trees had grown so high they obscured the near-by hills.

What a tremendous family they were! she thought, watching the members move about in the grounds below. Aunts and uncles and cousins once and twice removed had already arrived for the fiesta. Mamá Grande and a woman about the same age from another branch of the family were standing by the fountain in consultation. From where Concha stood they were foreshortened, and looked like the heavy sculptured figures so popular with native artists since the Revolution. A group of young men had just come in from riding. They lounged along the path that led to the wing of the house where they were quartered. Ramón was among them.

She turned, looking down on the Indian village to her right beyond the hacienda wall. She was thinking of her mother and these quiet days they had had alone here at the hacienda. She realized as never before the deep accord between them. Yesterday, when they had walked together in the park, her mother had said, "Now seems the time, while we are here alone, to speak to you again of your heritage.

"As I told you before, I see in you, my daughter, many Aztec traits. And now," she had said, "since our destiny and theirs is one, let us join the people in the village for the hours of Crucifixion. To share sorrow the Indians, as their ancestors before them, believe is fellowship." As she had gone out of the gate into the Indian village, all the urban expression seemed to have passed from her face.

In the church a crude hill of boards had been erected before the altar. There the villagers had raised a cross, with the dying Christ on it—a great man-sized figure made by the hands of their ancestors. It had not been hewn of stone or wood, but fashioned out of the substances of which all life for them partook—corn, ground into a pulp-like substance, reverently shaped into the image of the crucified Christ.

Quietly, one by one, the villagers had entered the church and with packs on their backs, and dust on their feet, had taken the path up the hill, stopping to kiss the crossed and nailed feet of the Christ. There were friendly faces among the pilgrims—Cleofas, Concha's maid whom they had brought down with them, was from the village, and Concha's old nurse, Francisco's wife, but there were other faces not so friendly. Pedro was there. It was said he had been one of Zapata's men during the violent Revolution. Concha wondered what her mother meant by saying her destiny was bound into that of the Indians. Ramón would scoff at the idea.

A car swung around the corner of the village, honking as it made its way up the street, scattering the children. It's Father! If he'd only not drive so fast! thought Concha. Another car followed. It was her grandfather's. She hurried down the steps to be in time to greet them. Ignacio was not with his grandfather, nor with his father! Louisa, sitting on the back seat of her grandfather's car with one of the aunts, looked upset. Concha saw there must have been some trouble. Don Julián's brooding countenance confirmed it.

"Vicente, where is Ignacio?" Mamá Grande demanded of her son as he came forward to embrace her. Why, Concha wondered, did her grandmother hold her father responsible for Ignacio? Hide it as she would from herself, she knew he was not one to assume responsibility for anyone—her handsome, spoiled, pleasure-loving father.

Hardly had Concha received her grandfather's embrace when Louisa took her arm and hurried her along the gallery to the room they had always shared. "Now we can talk!" she cried, closing the door. "But not about Nacho. I've heard nothing for two days except Ignacio! Ignacio!"

"But you must tell me what has happened," Concha insisted, immediately anxious about her brother.

"Oh, it's only that nobody has seen Nacho for two days. He went to the service with Grandfather Thursday night. Grandfather and he talked half the night shut up in the library, and then, well—he just hasn't been around since. He evidently isn't coming to the fiesta. If he does come, you can be certain he'll make trouble. He seems to want to make trouble," Louisa ended.

"What shall we do?" Concha was in despair. She had hoped that at this great fiesta, the first of its kind for so long, there would be no conflicts.

"Let's forget Nacho," Louisa answered impatiently. "I've brought you a frock for the dance, and I've one just like it for myself. I've been planning for a month that we should dress the same tonight. The dresses are white, so we can both wear them and look our best. Is Ramón here yet? I've picked just the right lines for you. You know—simple, the way you like it. The aunts are terribly cross with me, getting clothes in Holy Week."

As soon as she had shown Concha the dresses, she cried, "Now let's go and see everybody!" Down the gallery she moved with quickness and grace, but with that restless energy which seemed never to be satisfied. Cars were now arriving filled with old and young. Mamá Grande was bustling around, directing each family group to the rooms they were to occupy.

Louisa, quickly tiring of the spectacle, pulled Concha away again. "Let's dress for dinner. Everybody has arrived, I am sure."

"It will be hours before anyone else will be ready," protested Concha.

"I can't wait to see how you will look in the dress I brought. Do come."

As they reached the door of their room, Concha stopped, and stood listening to the hum of a single motor on the road, then the loud ringing of the gate bell. Around the circular drive shot Ignacio's runabout, a new possession he had had but a few weeks.

Louisa gave a squeal of excitement, and Concha a half-breathed prayer of mingled thanksgiving and petition. Now Mamá and Mamá Grande and Grandfather would be happy. No one need be angry if Nacho behaved himself.

Then out of the car stepped not only Nacho—but the North American! How had Ignacio dared to do it? He might better have stayed away than have done this! To repeat the same rebellion seemed stupid. He had made his stand for independence by bringing Señor Buchanan among them the first time.

Louisa, after one suppressed exclamation of astonishment, stood with her sister silently looking back up the corridor.

"I am here waiting," came Mamá Grande's voice from the main doorway of the house. The two young men walked toward her. Concha pulled Louisa within their room. "Don't let's listen."

Blandly ignoring the fact that she had met the North American before, Mamá Grande said, "Is this young man the one chosen to work with the overseer on the accounts? If so——"

"This is my friend. As such he is an honored guest." Ignacio's eyes and Mamá Grande's met in conflict. "Which room will you assign to him?"

"Now I recognize you," exclaimed Mamá Grande. "You must forgive me. I had seen you only once, and not expecting you today, I have made this unfortunate mistake. Indeed you must forgive me. Our house is yours."

"I'm sorry," said Ignacio as he showed Jim to a room off the second patio. "One cannot always tell what my grandmother may do. It would have been different if Mamá had been here. It was Mamá who wanted to see you again. You remember, she suggested you meet Grandfather, so that he might show you his library. It is unfortunate that Mamá has one of her headaches." Ignacio himself was shocked. He had never dreamed that within the frame of gracious hospitality Mamá Grande would find a way to insult his friend. He was trying with polite phrases to atone for her insult.

But to Jim, Ignacio's urbane words seemed unreal, merely the patter of surface courtesy. How much could he believe? Perhaps not even that the mother had a headache.

Alone, Jim tried to figure out how best to get through the next two days. He had no feeling now of elation because of his nearness to Concha. She seemed farther away from him than she had ever been.

At the dinner that evening he tried to make himself as inconspicuous as possible. That he should be so, Ignacio's grandmother had already seen to, he realized with a wry smile. She had placed him between two silent, black-clad, elderly women. Far down the table was Concha, sitting between the Spaniard they called Ramón and an elderly gentleman. She was dressed in white, with a high comb and a red flower in her black hair. He thought she seemed distressed, and once he imagined there were tears in her eyes at something Ramón said to her.

Often Concha looked toward the end of the table where Don Julián sat, moody and silent, drinking quantities of wine, eating little. His anger toward his grandson for this new defiance of the family's customs had not yet worn off.

Not once during the long meal did Concha glance in Jim's direction. Nor did Ignacio. Since that proud avowal of friendship and his profuse apologies just after they arrived, Ignacio appeared to have abandoned him. It was an outrageous position for the young Spaniard to place him in.

Later, as they moved toward the pavilion erected for the dance, Jim found himself the center and concern of many old and middle-aged ladies. They hovered around him, keeping him away from the young people. Well, he supposed it served him right for getting himself in such a situation. Then, as the music started, his mood changed.

I am as wellborn as they, he said to himself, and I am their guest. I refuse to be shepherded by a lot of old crones. With determination, he bowed to his elderly jailers and made his way over to the young people. He meant that they should either accept him or openly refuse him. No hiding this time behind polite attitudes.

He bowed before Concha and asked, "May I have this dance?"

There were bright spots of color in her cheeks. She hesitated only for a moment. In her heart she applauded the proud way Jim had walked across the floor.

He heard a mischievous laugh just behind him and then someone humming the gay little tune he had heard at the bullfight, a tune sung in recognition of excellence in any performance. It was Concha's sister. Did she recognize some excellence in his performance? Or was it sung to applaud Concha's bravery?

Jim felt excitement rising in him as Concha placed her narrow, delicately boned hand in his. A grave smile parted her lips as she thought, No one in the whole pavilion is more distinguished-looking than this tall stranger. Again, as on her first meeting, she was conscious of his finely molded lips, intelligent eyes. She was suddenly indignant with her family's attitude toward him. Something of Mamá's proud bearing in moments of crisis was Concha's as, after their dance together, she led Jim to a group of her girl cousins to introduce him. "Señor Buchanan is a beautiful dancer!" she exclaimed.

A new spirit swept through the room. The young people were in command. Why, many of their friends who belonged to less tradition-ridden families liked young men from the States. It was even rumored that they made excellent husbands.

Louisa walked over now to her grandmother and whispered, "The way to deal with Nacho is to accept the North American. Then he won't find it interesting any more to bring him among us."

Mamá Grande gave a savage grunt. "I won't have him dancing with Concha! Ramón doesn't like it." For once she felt powerless to manage her grandchildren and was secretly thankful Louisa had offered her a legitimate reason for taking no public stand against this intruder.

"I'll try to see that your wishes are obeyed," said Louisa with mock submission. But to herself she said, Concha is like Mamá tonight. She'll have her own way. I know I can't keep her from dancing with him.

"Is it never possible for a man in your country to see a girl alone?" Jim asked as he and Concha danced together a second time.

"No," she answered.

"It's tyranny on such a beautiful evening." The air was filled with the scent of orange blossoms overlaid with the heavy perfume of tuberoses. "In my country we could go for a walk, or even for a ride, and talk together."

"But not in my country," she answered, looking up at him. With a smile she added, "At least not in my family."

"Your country is partly mine. I was born here," Jim replied, ignoring her remark about the family.

"Then you are not a stranger. I should have known. You speak our language as one born to it."

"I have come back because it seemed home to me."

A light spread across her face.

Ramón danced with Concha next. He asked in a sarcastic tone, "Are you foolish enough to think that young man is interested in you?"

"Why should I?" asked Concha. "Certainly he is capable of enjoying a woman without letting his emotions enter in."

"Oh, is he?" Ramón did not believe this possible of any young man. "I simply want you to understand that if another man's lips so much as touched your hair, you would no longer be desirable to me."

"You are insufferable, Ramón. Señor Buchanan is Nacho's friend, and I mean to treat him with the courtesy supposed to be innate in our nation, although I am beginning to doubt it." Deliberately she left him and walked over to where Ignacio and Jim were standing. With mercurial quickness Ignacio's mood had changed. Gone was the feeling of frustration which had so bedeviled him on the drive down, and his humiliation over his family's reception of his friend. Caught up into the excitement of the evening, he was now the young lord of the house dispensing hospitality.

"You're taking part at the bullfight tomorrow, aren't you?" one of the cousins asked him. "We want to know so we can place our bets on you."

"I've done no training since my return," he reminded them.

"Ah, but a grandson of Don Julián would never refuse to be brave," a young girl standing near him cried.

With a careless gesture Ignacio signified his willingness. "And we must have one fight for the girls. There's a fine bull calf we can give them."

"Splendid!" Louisa, her cheeks flushed with excitement, embraced her brother.

The special dances were beginning. "Let's make Grandfather do the dance with the machetes. No one dances with more grace and abandon."

They found Don Julián sitting on the deep veranda with his overseer. He had forgotten for the time his anger at his grandson, forgotten everything except the sense of strength and gaiety returning to him here at the old hacienda where he had lived so much of his romantic youth. The moon hung, a pale disk, in the top of the trees in the park. The crowd of young men and girls pulled him along with them to the pavilion, and handed him two gleaming machetes.

"Where's Concha?" he asked. "I want her for my partner."

"Take me, Grandfather," begged Louisa, knowing that her sister and Jim were together, a little behind them. She had seen the look in Concha's eyes. It will do her good to flirt a little, Louisa thought, and it will do Ramón good, too.

Vicente left the pavilion, strolled along the gallery to where the hacienda overseer leaned against the wall smoking. "Have a drink?" he asked. Without waiting for an answer, he called to a house servant who stood in the doorway watching the dancing. The two took the glasses the servingman brought, then moved off toward the end of the house where they would be out of hearing.

"I heard you telling Father you hadn't had to use the ammunition. What did you use?"

The other gave a low chuckle. "Just put the fear of God in them."

"By what method?"

"Is that important to you? It's accomplished. Isn't that enough?"

Vicente looked at the middle-aged, solidly built Mexican overseer, at the broad spread of his hips and shoulders, at his heavy jaw and brutal mouth.

"Guess you could manage it all right, but I was just curious."

"For one thing, I had to spend a good deal of money. Doña María hasn't liked very much the amounts I reported to her in past years. And she didn't like any better the amounts I told her of this morning."

Vicente scowled. Undoubtedly the man had done well for himself. But the fellow had seen to it, through all these years of upheaval, that they kept their land and that it made money for them—years when he himself would not have risked his life here. He said, "Handouts to officers, big and little, to keep their mouths shut, I suppose?"

"That's about it."

"Any villagers killed?" asked Vicente.

"Now and then. But does that matter?"

Vicente did not answer for a little. "It won't be long," he said, "before I'll be the one to ask you *all* the questions."

"Meaning?"

"I shall want *all* the answers."

There was a long pause when both appeared to be listening to two blind men sitting outside the kitchen playing their guitars and singing repartee couplets in which there was an exchange of compliments. The singing was growing very animated.

"Getting the school closed helped," the overseer answered, apparently weighing Vicente's remark.

"That was several years ago, wasn't it?"

Ignoring Vicente's implication that he was telling of things past rather than present, the man went on. "She was a revolutionist, and she came and lived here with her kid. The Indians, especially the women, got to like her, and it wasn't doing them any good. It was she who got the villagers to send in that first petition for land. After that I told Soledad—that was her name—she better get out, but she didn't listen."

"Well?"

"I found out she was an infidel. After that, it was easy. You don't tamper with these Indians' God. When they found out she'd drawn a cross on the floor of the school and trampled on it——"

"They didn't kill her, did they? According to my recollection they didn't," Vicente added.

"No, but they would have, if I hadn't defended her!" The overseer went on with his tale, again ignoring the implication that these were matters of the past. "A couple of men got killed a few months ago. Thought they'd fight when they didn't get land as they expected. One of them was the son of that fellow over there who's singing. But you can see he's happy now."

"If you thought up the idea of a cross on the floor, I suppose you were the one who thought up the scheme about the villagers falsifying the number of heads of families."

"Who said I drew the cross? Who said I had anything to do with the fact that the report of the number of heads of families wasn't correct? You know Indians never tell the truth. Didn't, even about their own people." The man looked up, cunning and bravado expressed in his face.

"The fiesta tomorrow is a good thing," he added after a moment. "I've provided plenty of liquor. All we've got to do now is to show the villagers they get more by working for us than by owning their land. Doña María being upset about measles among the children is a good thing, too."

Even with this grudging acknowledgment of Mamá Grande's help, Vicente saw the man didn't intend to have any interference in his plans, now that the family had returned to the hacienda. One could hardly blame him. After all, he brought in the money, so the thing to do was to leave him alone. But Vicente didn't for a moment think Mamá Grande would take that attitude. His mother had been telling him this evening about the overseer's insufficient accounts and about his unwillingness to explain why something hadn't been done to stop the epidemic of measles.

"Better go slow while the family is here," Vicente advised him. "It will pay you in the end."

~~~~~~~~~~~~~~~~22~~~~~

THE two sisters in their room could hear the last guests moving along the gallery to their rooms, a soft shuffle of feet as the priest, here for tomorrow's celebration of Saint Mary's feast, passed on his way to his vigil in the chapel; then the *pat-pat* of Cleofas' bare feet on the stone floor outside their door.

"Go away, Cleofas, we don't want you," called Louisa, laughing as she helped Concha out of her dress. Standing off, she surveyed her sister. "So you are awake at last!" she cried.

A deep flush spread over Concha's silk-smooth skin, suffusing face and neck down to the curve of her bosom. "I—" she began and stopped. "I love him," she ended finally.

"Of course, but just for now, tonight, for the fiesta," said Louisa.

"No, not just for now. Always."

"But how impossible!" exclaimed Louisa, sitting down on the bed to study her sister with amazement. "There is Ramón, and there is Mamá Grande. Everything is arranged."

Concha set her lips stubbornly.

"You make a mistake if you take these episodes seriously," Louisa protested.

"No, not an episode." Concha shook her head in the fashion so familiar in their mother.

Louisa bit her lip, trying to think what to do. "But of course," she exclaimed, "you cannot decide yet. You know nothing about him, and after all he is a North American, even if he is a wellborn one. And you cannot tell what he intends so soon."

The stubborn determination deepened in Concha's eyes.

"You are certain of him?" exclaimed Louisa, lifting her brows.

"Yes," said Concha simply.

When they had gone to bed the two sisters lay side by side in rigid straightness, each hoping the other was asleep. Louisa was thinking, Then Ramón will be free. He had sought her out this evening time after time.

It had all happened so suddenly, Concha was thinking. At the end of the evening, as they danced, his hand had tightened on hers. She had looked up. Their eyes had met. His were eloquent with feeling. And she . . . she knew she loved him as she loved no other person on earth, that everything about him was dear to her, that she trusted him and believed in him. "I have seen you only twice, danced with you three times," she had said wonderingly.

"What does it matter," he had answered, "if we love each other?"

Whatever happened, she would obey that love. It meant breaking the bond with Ramón, opposing her grandmother, maybe her mother. She would have no one to help her, not even Louisa, perhaps. There was Ignacio. No, she could not depend on Nacho. It was something she would have to do alone. That deep stream of abnegation in her had its rapids, as Mamá had said. The imperative lay deep in her love. Yes, she would obey that. The clear morning light filtered through the crack between the drawn curtains. She turned over, lying spoon-fashion close to Louisa, and fell asleep.

Jim did not attempt to sleep that night. For the few hours that remained before day broke, he sat by the window in his room smoking cigarette after cigarette. The incredible had happened. He felt himself compounded of fire and ice. Heaven and earth fell away into cloudy nothingness, out of which their love rose. Then ice seemed to enter his veins; cold, hard reality asserted itself. He saw the cost to both of them. His experiences with the Navarro family had given him all too vivid an understanding of their pride and how powerfully entrenched they were, how bitterly opposed to change. It would be almost impossible for Concha to go against their wishes and marry him. Perhaps he had no right to ask it of her. Perhaps she would regret it later.

As for him, it meant he must give up the career he had planned for himself. In the Embassy there was little or no opportunity for a man married to a woman of another nationality, because, it was argued, it did not leave him single-minded in his work. He could not decide matters purely in the interests of his country. He would be a man with an emotional interest in two countries. According to all the goals Jim had set for himself, he knew he should give up this passion for Concha, marry discreetly—an American woman with money preferably, because money was very desirable in the diplomatic service. If he did marry Concha and did leave the service, what else was he fitted for? There was, of course, his interest in architecture, but he had not gone far enough in his studies to take it up as a profession. He had channeled all his life into preparation to be a good diplomat, an honored and important representative of his country. The icy hand of caution reached out, telling him it would be wise for both of them to give up their passion. Leave now before Concha had arranged the meeting with him which she had promised. Both of them would forget in time. It was safer to follow the pattern society had set for them. . . . Then again he was swept by his longing for Concha.

As soon as dawn came he changed into riding clothes, and asked the servant at the stables for a horse. The gates were opened. He rode out through the village. The paths across the valley were so narrow that as he put his horse into a canter its flying heels sent a rustle through the cornlike leaves of the sugar cane that grew on either side almost as tall as horse and rider. The thick-jointed stalks, with their polished purple markings and pale-green waving leaves, hemmed him in. The hacienda land was lush, fertile earth trenched to receive water let in by sluices from mountain streams; but as he came to the first hills vegetation almost ceased. The land was dry, rock-strewn, sterile, the once rich loam washed down onto the Navarro-owned valley. The villages among the spiny maguey were indescribably poor. He felt the hatred of the villagers as they surveyed him silently.

Not forever could the present truce exist between the upper and lower classes. There had been terror and suffering in the meeting so far; there were signs of more terror and suffering. He remembered the anger in the faces of the young Mexicans in the café when the *corrido* had been read implying land distribution was to cease. There was the unyielding desire in the Mexicans for land. In marrying Concha he saw he would be accepting her country. He had an almost uncanny realization of how completely she belonged to it. With her he would be drawn down into this struggle. He drew back. His decision the day he had first gone to the café with Villar came into his mind. He had decided then to stay clear of any part in the Revolution.

All at once he was swept by longing to see Concha again, just to hear her voice. There was a kind of emotional strength about her and in all she said that made the safe life he had envisioned for himself seem cowardly in the light of their love. He would marry her. He would accept the responsibility such a step involved. Turning his horse around, he rode back to the hacienda gates. He must arrange the matter with her family, take the burden from her.

He was in his room changing his riding clothes when he heard a tap on the door and an Indian maiden entered. "I bring you hot water for the shaving." Her voice was as gentle as a flowing stream. "And this!" Into his hand she thrust a note. "I am Cleofas. I will come again to arrange your room and for your answer." Then she was gone.

23

THAT night in a niche of the wall outside the hacienda grounds Concha and Jim had their first meeting. Indian lovers had met in this spot ever since the wall had been built. A great pepper tree hung its delicate trailing branches low over the wall, and the twisted trunk was hollowed as if meant for lovers. Mamá Grande long ago named it "the Place of the Vulgar." Once she had threatened to cut the tree down, but she had never quite dared to deprive the villagers of their trysting place.

Jim touched Concha wonderingly, ran his hand over her hair, which hung down her back. He buried his face in its black strangeness, so fine, so thick. She turned a little in his arms, and her lips met his.

"We have only a few minutes," she whispered, breaking the embrace.

"How shall we arrange matters?" asked Jim. "Shall I talk to your father?"

"My father!" Certainly this lover of hers did not understand her family if he hoped to win his cause through her father! "I myself will talk to Mamá Grande, tell her I will not marry Ramón and that I must marry you."

"Ramón!" exclaimed Jim. Had she cared for Ramón?

"It has been understood that Ramón and I would unite the two families."

"And you?" asked Jim.

She faltered. "It seemed the natural thing to do before you—before I met you."

"I hate to leave it all to you, Concha." He called her by her name for the first time, that lovely name—the name of a shell.

"It must be so," she answered. There was the sound of footsteps. "I must go now. Cleofas has come for me."

Out of the shadows Jim saw the Indian girl moving toward them, her *rebozo* close-drawn over her head. He watched the two disappear in the shadows of the hacienda wall.

IN SPITE of her brave determination to tell Mamá Grande she intended to marry James Buchanan, Concha waited from day to day, saying to herself, It is not yet the opportunity. The morning after the fiesta Jim and Ignacio had left for the city and most of the guests with them, but a few had lingered. I must wait until they have all gone, Concha told herself. The day the last guest departed, leaving the house to Mamá Grande, Mamá, Louisa, and herself, she still hesitated. Her grandmother was tired and irritable.

Then measles became a serious epidemic. Admonishing, directing, Doña María herself went along the streets of the village. The overseer shrugged his shoulders saying, "You can't do anything about it. If the children die, there are plenty more to come."

"I don't like to see them die, any more than I like to see kittens or puppies die. Besides, we lose workers. Some of these children are almost old enough to go into the fields," Doña María answered. It was a day with a cold wind, but she patrolled the village, sending inside every child with swollen eyes. There were many of them. "They should be kept in the dark," she commanded the women. But when she had passed, the children came out again into the sun.

"We are born to hardship," the women told each other. "Our children must learn to endure." Some of them had a faint remembrance that Soledad had taught them something like this—but then she had proved to be of the Devil!

Five children died the next day, and the sound of the *alabado* could be heard, hour after hour. The old psalm, with its plaintive note of sorrow, echoed through the rooms of the hacienda.

Concha at any other time would have been moved to pity by such distress, but today the song of mourning seemed only an accompaniment to her own troubled thoughts. She loved Jim, but the storm that would be created when she made known her determination to marry him would be greater than any upheaval that had ever come to the family. It wasn't only her fear of such a scene which kept her from speaking. She could not bear to hurt those she loved. There was her grandfather. She had not thought overmuch of him when she had made her decision. She had thought only of the battle with Mamá Grande.

Louisa had done everything she could think of to drown out the dreadful sound of mourning. She had ridden her horse over every path allowed to her. She had teased Mamá Grande to the point of exasperation to go back to the city.

"You have the ways of a child," Mamá Grande had said to her finally. "You will go to your embroidery and not leave it until evening. And remain silent," she added.

Louisa sat beside Concha, dutifully obeying except for the silence. "So it was only for the day after all," she said to her sister.

"I've just been waiting for the right moment," Concha countered.

"And you think there is a right moment?" asked Louisa. "Do you," she insisted, "do you think there is one?"

"No," Concha answered. Whatever she did, she would outrage loyalty. Loyalty to her family was set against the new loyalty born of her love. There was no use postponing the battle longer, she realized. She jumped up. Deep in her something had decided that loyalty to Jim was the most important. Without once looking back, she hurried along the gallery searching for Mamá Grande. But when she saw her grandmother sitting with Mamá, her hands for once folded in her lap, the enormity of her act frightened Concha. When she tried to speak, no sound came from her throat. She half turned to go back. Then she realized her mother was looking at her, and from the look, courage, dignity, and strength flowed into her.

"Mamá Grande," she began, "I have something I've wanted to tell you for several days, but you've been so busy. May I speak now?"

Doña María raised her hand in a gesture of consent and annoyance. "I suppose you want to go back to the city, like Louisa."

"It is more than that. I must tell you that I cannot marry Ramón, for I have pledged myself to Señor Buchanan."

Mamá Grande's face turned purple, a congestion of anger and speech choking her. Concha, the only submissive member of her family, standing before her saying, "I have decided to marry a North American!"

"You've decided nothing. The good God himself has arranged your marriage. You're out of your mind. A gringo! And you've only seen him twice. It's impossible! Go to your room," Doña María commanded. "Ignacio is at the bottom of all this. I'm going to settle with him once and for all."

Concha forgot everything except her need to protect her brother. "It's not Nacho, Mamá Grande. He will be on your side, I feel certain."

The old woman's heavy black eyebrows arched; the dark, strong hairs of her mustache quivered. "My side! What are you talking about? There is but one custom in this family, and you will obey it, Concepción."

Concha stood her ground. "I must marry the man I have chosen— without your consent, if you will not give consent, Mamá Grande."

To her astonishment, her grandmother began to plead in ingratiating tones. "Conchita, my little one, you are bewitched. Go pray to the sweet Virgin to release you, my little one, from the evil thought that you marry a man outside the faith."

"Not more outside the faith than Ignacio, who declares himself an unbeliever," argued Concha, forgetting she meant to protect him. "We have always had unbelievers in the family—and how do you know Señor Buchanan is not of our faith?"

"And your grandfather! Would you break your grandfather's heart?" Shamelessly Mamá Grande used that love of which she had always been so jealous, to get her way with Concha.

"I have pledged myself to Señor Buchanan." Concha spoke so low that Mamá Grande had to lean forward to hear her.

There was a note of ridicule in Doña María's voice as she answered. "So the naïve Concha thinks the young gringo is in earnest when it is only entertainment with him, someone for the little affairs. When he chooses a woman in marriage, it will be within the pattern of his own customs. And then the sweet little Concha will be——" She did not finish her sentence.

"The young man is honorable, and Concha is honorable," Mamá said quietly. "He came to me, asking for my daughter in marriage. I have given my consent."

"As if that meant anything!" scoffed the older woman. But her anger was transferred from Concha to her daughter-in-law, who stood before her now in silent reserve, accepting the flaying of angry words, the accumulation of bitterness over a lifetime of defeats with this quiet woman.

Concha could see her mother's fingers, clasped behind her, move over the beads of her rosary—small and perfect pearls.

As the accusations grew more personal, reaching back to the marriage of Vicente and Mamá, Mamá turned to Concha. "Go to your room," she said. Long after Concha had reached it, Louisa came in, white-lipped and silent. She would not tell what more she had heard their grandmother say.

25

WHEN several days passed, with nothing said of her marriage, and no preparations were made to return to Mexico City, Concha grew more and more apprehensive. Somehow she must get in touch with Jim.

She rang for her maid. "Cleofas," she said, "I need to send a message to the city. Could you see to it? I will pay well for a messenger, but—" she hesitated—"it must be done in secret."

Cleofas' eyes grew bright with understanding. "Ah, I know how it is," she murmured. "I, too, have to manage so your grandmother will not know when I wish to see a lover."

"But, Cleofas, this is different. I wish to marry the young North American."

With a small, soft laugh Cleofas took the note, saying, "It shall be delivered and an answer brought."

It was pleasing neither to Concha nor to Jim to carry on a clandestine love affair. After the third secret letter Concha wrote, "There is nothing for us to do but to run away. It is more honorable than what we are doing now."

But Jim, brought up as she had been with a sound respect for custom, hesitated. "It would violate deep instincts in us both," he wrote. "Let us wait a little longer and see if we can't win your family. It would cause less suffering if we can."

But as the days dragged on, it was Jim who began to break under the strain, he who at the end of the second week urged their elopement. But then Concha held back, suddenly, seeing too plainly how she would hurt her grandfather. "Let us be patient a little longer and see if Mamá cannot arrange our marriage," she wrote in answer.

A few nights later, when Cleofas came for the note at the time agreed on, she whispered, "If you are going to marry the gringo, as you say you are, it must be done quickly. Did you think your grandmother would not accomplish her purpose in anything she attempted?" The maid's quick ear caught the sound of a step on the stone floor of the gallery. She picked up a dress of Concha's. "I will press it immediately," she murmured. The door opened, but to the relief of both girls it was Mamá who entered.

"You may go now, Cleofas," she said, "but return later with the dress." When the door closed, she turned to Concha. "My daughter, I can do nothing to help you. In fact, we have only hurried your marriage to Ramón."

"Mamá, I can't marry him!" cried Concha.

"I have done all I could within the pattern of tradition. Beyond that, neither I nor you can go. I can offer you now only the comfort of the Church. Pray, Concha, for the submission demanded of you. Self-denial, renunciation are yours by heritage and training. Through my vow, you dedicated your womanhood to the Virgin Mother. Pray to her now to intercede for you, not for favors but for guidance."

"I think the Virgin Mother does not want me to marry Ramón," Concha answered, clinging stubbornly to her purpose to wed the man she loved.

After her mother had left her, she walked up and down the room, clasping and unclasping her hands. Somehow she must defeat Mamá Grande.

I must make it necessary, in her eyes, for me to marry Jim, she thought. If Ramón should refuse to have me—if he knew that I have met Jim secretly——!

A bold plan came into Concha's mind. She would see Jim again and in daylight. Arrange it so her grandmother would witness their greetings. Then if her grandmother opposed her any longer, she would threaten to let gossip of the affair reach Ramón. Mamá Grande's pride would never allow that. Nor would she let the knowledge of the, to her, disgraceful meeting reach Don Julián's ears. Concha depended on Mamá Grande's pride to keep it from him. If Mamá Grande saw she could no longer oppose the marriage, Concha believed she would contrive to win Don Julián to acceptance of it, too.

Driving his own car, Jim arrived at the tree by the hacienda wall a little before the hour Concha had specified. It was strange, he thought, to meet her there so openly. He looked at his watch. It was fifteen minutes after the hour. He felt a little foolish keeping such a tryst in broad daylight. Then the gate opened, and Concha came toward him. He forgot all the confused thoughts that had lain between them since their last meeting, all his perplexity over the family's opposition to him. He loved this beautiful girl. He moved forward, took her in his arms.

There was a strangled gasp of rage just behind him. A black-robed woman, a black veil over her head, pulled Concha away. It was the matriarch!

"Go before me so I may watch you," she commanded in a low, stern voice. "And you—" she said, turning on Jim—"wait here at the gatehouse until I send for you."

As the minutes passed, Jim despaired, seeing Concha as she had walked ahead of her grandmother, her shoulders bowed. Why had he ever thought he could override the traditions of this exclusive Spanish family? He heard a light step outside the gatehouse. Could it be Concha? But when he looked up, he saw Mamá standing in the doorway.

"Señor Buchanan, I cannot allow you to sit here. Please come," she said, smiling.

He walked with her across the patio and into the *sala*.

"As you know," she said, once they were seated, "I am not opposed to this idea of marriage between you and my daughter, if you can make her happy, and I believe you can. But you, I feel certain, will be the first to grant my right to ask you a few questions."

"Anything you may wish."

"You are a Catholic? I think not. Then it is most important that you understand the obligations placed on a Catholic by the Church.

Concha must be free to practice her religion. And children born to you must be reared in her faith. The responsibility is grave for her, and the Church, recognizing it, will ask you to sign a marital agreement."

Without waiting for an answer, she went on, "Concha is especially dedicated to the Virgin." Quite simply then she told him of her vow and its fulfillment. "I must know," she said at the end, "that you will respect that vow. Let her grow in an atmosphere of understanding. It is not necessary that you should be a Catholic to do this."

"For her sake and yours, I promise," he answered.

"There is one more matter that is important," she went on, accepting his promise at its true value. "It is right for you to know that in my family there is Aztec blood dating from the days of the Conquest. Concha bears many resemblances to the Aztecs, as do I. Is that acceptable to you?"

"I knew this before I asked Concha in marriage. Your son told me." Jim raised Mamá's hand to his lips.

Doña María, once within the privacy of her own room, spoke. "You have disgraced us all, Concepción. You, who because the good God spared you were especially consecrated to purity when you came to womanhood, have shamed us all. If Ramón hears of this, he will not wish to marry you. There is only one thing left to do. You must express a wish to enter a convent."

Concha had a sudden desire to laugh. Mamá Grande was certainly exaggerating the situation. After all, it was the year 1930, not 1880. "You could let me marry Señor Buchanan," she answered quietly.

Doña María's voice rose in anger. "Never!"

This was the moment Concha was waiting for. "If you do not let me marry Señor Buchanan, I shall see to it that Ramón knows that the North American embraced me. There are those in the village who saw us. I can arrange for some one of them to carry the gossip not only to Ramón, but to his mother. Then you will indeed be disgraced. You can save everyone, if you will. You have only to give Señor Buchanan the right to marry me. There will be a little flurry, some talk perhaps, but it will quickly die out once we are married."

"You are a wicked girl!" shouted Mamá Grande, beside herself now with anger.

The door opened. Mamá came into the room. "You will find Señor Buchanan in the *sala,* Concha," she said. "Wait there for your grandmother and me."

For an hour Concha and Jim sat side by side on a stiff-backed couch, but with a generous space between them, carrying on a desultory, impersonal conversation, for among the shadows at the end of the room sat one of the aunts like a blacker shadow, guarding them against any intimacy.

"I am sorry I made trouble for you. I thought there were only a few villagers to see me kiss you," Jim managed to whisper.

"I should have hated it, if you hadn't. Everything is going to work out very nicely," she told him.

What a surprising answer! He was more in the dark than ever.

At last Mamá Grande and Mamá entered the room. With flawless dignity Doña María greeted Jim. "Concepción's father will be here very soon. He will be pleased to arrange matters with you. He will explain to you our marriage customs." When Doña María had spoken, she turned and left.

For the first time, proud old Mamá Grande felt her age. Once in her own room she seated herself in her rocker, whispering to herself angry denunciations of her family. For work and sacrifice, she was repaid with rebellion and ingratitude. But after a little, as she rocked back and forth in the chair she had sat in so often, plotting and planning to enhance their prestige and wealth, she began again to plot and plan, seeking to weave anew the solidarity of the family. Neither Don Julián nor any of the aunts, uncles, or cousins of other Navarro or Salcedo households should know of this shameful meeting of Concha and her lover. They must be made to believe that the young man from the States had come to Mamá Grande herself, asking for the right to marry Concha, and she had given consent. But for what plausible reason would she give consent?

If she could have quiet to think, if she could only shut out the sounds of mourning that reached her from the village, she might be able to work out a plan. From one single hut near the hacienda wall the *alabado* rose. Submission spoke through the old psalm. Doña María closed the window. She must have quiet to think. How could she cover up Concha's rebellion and Mamá's triumph?

There was a stealthy step behind her, and someone's fingers stroked back her crest of white hair. Only Louisa would be guilty of such familiarity. Mamá Grande closed her eyes, the lines on her forehead relaxing a little.

"There is a way out," Louisa whispered.

Mamá Grande's eyes flew open. She sat erect. "How do you know
I want a way out?" she demanded.

Louisa's face was on a level with her own. It was a young replica
of hers, even to a faint line of down on the upper lip. Someday, except
for her coloring, she would look exactly like her grandmother. It
dawned on the old woman that to accomplish her purpose she never
should have chosen to work through Concha's deceptive submission;
rather through the lively willfulness of Louisa. Dangerous as she had
sometimes felt it to be, it could be more easily used for her purposes.
In this moment she understood that the young Louisa saw material
advancement as the most important thing in life. Concha never had.
Louisa was indeed the child of her heart. Louisa, named for Mamá
Grande's mother—French in temperament, French in name.

"Well, so you think you can undo the wrong your sister has wrought.
Why didn't you tell me before the harm was done?" Grudgingly
Mamá Grande opened the way for Louisa to speak.

A look between mischief and malice came into her granddaughter's
eyes. "It was not until Concha acted as she did today, that I felt free
to act. But if I tell you how things can be arranged you must promise
not to be shocked."

"What have you been doing?" demanded her grandmother, immediately suspicious.

"I can't give you the particulars, dear little Mamá Grande, but I
think you could arrange matters to satisfy Ramón if you offer me to
him in the place of Concha."

Doña María stiffened. It was effrontery on Louisa's part to accuse her
of making an offering of Concha. But Louisa and Ramón! Suddenly
she saw the value of such a marriage. Those two would go far together!
But would Ramón accept the substitute?

"He would like me for his bride," whispered Louisa.

When the old woman looked up, intending to learn by what im-
modest means Louisa had found this out, her granddaughter was gone.
Mamá Grande rose from her chair, her plans made. Tomorrow morning they would go back to Mexico City.

There was a knock on the door, and her son Vicente entered. "So
you have arrived," said his mother, motioning him to a seat.

"I have come to ask something of you," he said.

Her heart went soft within her. Whatever Vicente wanted she always
gave, closing her eyes to his self-indulgences.

"I want your promise that Concha's wedding shall be, in every particular, what it would have been if she were marrying Ramón."

His mother looked at him with half-concealed disgust. Never before had he been the mouthpiece of his wife. Never before had he asked for anything for anyone but himself. If he had come a half-hour earlier, for the first time in his life she would have refused him his wish. But now his request fitted her scheme.

"Yes," she answered curtly, "I intended to have it so. I am quite as capable as your wife of appreciating the necessity of thus covering up our chagrin." There was sarcasm in her tone as she went on: "And now that you have delivered your message, suppose you express your own disappointment."

Vicente swore under his breath. "It's Ignacio who is responsible!" Then he stopped. What had gone on between Mamá and him he intended to tell no one, but he was still angry over the necessity of giving his promise not to oppose the marriage of Concha and the man from the States and disappointed that Ramón was not to come into the family.

His mother watched him, angry because of the power his wife had over her son. "Sit down," she said, after she had given him time to stride about the room. "I'll tell you my plans."

Over Louisa's declaration Vicente slapped his knee, his good humor restored. So long as Ramón was in the family, what difference did it make to which of the daughters he was married?

The hacienda house seemed very still after the turmoil of the day as Mamá walked along the wide gallery toward the chapel. The shadow of the vines twining the pillars lay on the stone floor of the veranda. The air was sweet with the smell of honeysuckle and tuberoses. At this hour of quiet and beauty Mamá would give thanks that Concha had been saved from Ramón.

In a chair in the farthest corner of the gallery she saw Louisa curled up, her fair hair like gold against the brown leather thongs of the woven back of the chair. Her long, fringed eyelashes lay against her cheeks. Sleeping unperturbed by the happenings of the day, thought Mamá, as she stood looking down on her. She let her hand rest on her daughter's head.

Louisa's eyes flew open. "Grandmother has told you, Mamá, that I am to keep the family from disgrace? I am to marry Ramón."

"No, Louisa!"

"Yes, Mamá." Louisa's eyes looked straight into her mother's.

Now Mamá knew what she had always suspected. Louisa was in love with the wicked Ramón—so Mamá regarded him. He would have made Concha unhappy but he would not have changed her. He would make Louisa unhappy and he would change her into some likeness of himself . . . unless . . . oh, surely the all-compassionate Virgin would intercede and save her.

Once within the chapel door Mamá felt dismay leaving her. To the left of the altar stood the figure of the young Madonna in her pale blue robe, sweetly submissive, listening to the heavenly message brought her by the angel with spread wings hovering over her. Peace and purity hung in the air. Slowly Mamá turned facing the Mater Dolorosa at the other end of the altar, and went forward and knelt at her feet.

26

IT WAS late when Jim left the hacienda. As his car labored up the high pass through the mountains, the slow climb seemed to parallel his mind's effort to understand why Concha had gained such power by his kiss given openly. That she had broken some tradition of her family he understood—defying some fetish of purity, probably. The courage it had taken, he dimly guessed.

His interview with her father had been difficult, but the understanding of her mother had helped to carry him through. But that too was a mystery. Why was Concha's mother undisturbed by her daughter's act when the others were so greatly outraged? But what did it matter how they felt toward him? He was not marrying the family. He was marrying Concha. Incredible as it seemed, he was.

Her father in his talk had said, "We hope you will follow our ideal in your attitude toward our daughter. We feel a kind of worship for our wives because of their purity and beauty. For that reason we do not subject them to the grosser side of a man's life and struggle, as you, I believe, do in your country." Adore Concha Jim did, but he believed there was something more to marriage than adoration. He wanted companionship.

Jim had hoped to make his resignation from the Embassy a routine matter. But as soon as it was known among the staff it created a furor.

"Why are you leaving," one of his associates demanded, "when you are so successful with the Mexicans? We thought you wanted to live in Mexico."

"I do! In fact, I intend to live here always, go into some business. I am engaged to Don Julián Navarro's eldest granddaughter." By the expression on his friend's face, he comprehended how completely he was stepping out of his own world.

Armstrong, the member of the staff who had taken Jim to the opera, where he first saw Concha, refused to let the matter end there. "Look here," he said, coming over to Jim's desk, "I know the girl is a knock-out, but look, Jim, you'd better marry an American girl."

Jim stiffened. He resented the implied criticism of Concha.

The older man went on: "It's nothing against Señorita Navarro or her country. It's simply you've been reared in different ways. Understanding isn't going to be easy. You may think so now, but you don't half know the pull of tradition on the individual in families like hers. The Revolution hasn't changed them an iota."

"Oh, don't I understand?" exclaimed Jim, thinking of yesterday's experience. Just then their talk was interrupted by the ambassador's secretary calling Jim.

The ambassador was sitting at his desk watching the door through which Jim entered. Without speaking, he let him cross the room, motioned him to a seat facing him. "I've sent for you, Buchanan," he said, after a moment of further scrutiny, "to discuss the matter of your resignation. I dislike to see you resign, Buchanan. I think you have the qualities that would carry you far in the diplomatic world. On the other hand, you are right in realizing that a foreign marriage is a handicap. A man must not be swayed by personal emotions when it comes to decisions that have to do with his country's welfare. What I wonder is, have you fully considered the step you are about to take?"

"Yes." Jim's monosyllabic answer sounded stiffer than he meant, but he was finding it difficult to have people question the desirability of his engagement to Concha.

"Very well, Buchanan, I'll send in your resignation. But I dislike to see so promising a career ended." The ambassador looked at Jim curiously as if such a sacrifice of opportunity he considered to be a little off balance. "And I dislike to lose you from my staff," he added.

"Thank you for your interest." Jim rose to go.

"Just a moment!" The ambassador motioned him to be seated again. "If you've fully made up your mind, I thought perhaps you might like to join one of our oil companies down here. A man with your qualifications would be valuable to them. I should be glad to recommend you."

Waving Jim's thanks aside, he went on: "Our interests here can be an asset to Mexico as well as to ourselves. But we need to develop friendship if—" he paused, and his face seemed to take on guardedness —"if we wish to hold what we have established our right to. Here is my card introducing you to my friend Mr. Albright. As you no doubt know, he is in charge of all his company's business here in Mexico City. His company has long depended on his diplomacy to carry them through critical periods. He asked me the other day if I knew of a good man for the post of public relations. At the time I didn't. Now I find you are available. You are friendly. You speak the language like a native. Furthermore, you will be in a position to understand the old propertied class of Mexico. If the propertied groups of the two countries are friendly, there should be no difficulty in keeping the *status quo*."

Jim felt flattered that the ambassador thought him capable for such an important position. It was not going to be as difficult to get established as he had at first thought.

"As soon as you are formally released from your position here, I suggest you see Mr. Albright." The ambassador rose, holding out his hand. "In the meantime I'll telephone him and explain who you are. Good luck!"

27

BACK in Mexico City, Doña María went immediately to see Doña Leonora Fuentes. "I have come to you," she said, "over a matter of great import to both of us—come to you even before speaking to my husband, because of your wisdom and sagacity. I must make amends to you for a blunder made in my zeal to give you, my dearest friend, my dearest possession—my Concha."

The eyes of the two women met; in both, shrewdness was hidden behind the mask of politeness.

"I find that I have injured your son in my zeal, denying him the wife he really desires, my Louisa, who—as I now see—is the better fitted to be his wife. Because of her youth I had not recognized it before. I thank the Virgin Mother who watches over women that this has been revealed to me before it was too late."

Doña Leonora rose and rang the bell, asking that her son be sent to her. When Ramón came, she said, "Our good friend Doña María has come to repair a wrong done you and to give you the wife you desire. I understand that it is Louisa."

Doña Leonora, watching, thought she detected a flicker of surprise pass across her son's face when she first mentioned Louisa. If it was his wish to marry Louisa, of course he must have her, though Concha was the daughter-in-law she wanted.

"To you my eternal gratitude, Doña María!" Ramón raised the old woman's hand, kissing it with an elaborate gesture of homage. "I did not wish to harm anyone, least of all lovely Concha, so I have not declared how dear Louisa is to me."

For what reason was Concha being withdrawn and her sister put in her place? The substitution was not entirely unwelcome, Ramón was thinking. Ever since the fiesta, he had been angry with Concha. Though Louisa really was more to his liking, his pride was receiving a blow. But no one, least of all his mother, should know it.

When later Ramón learned that Concha was to marry Jim Buchanan, black hatred for both of them filled his heart. Someday he would have his revenge, but only when no one would guess how great was the humiliation of this hour.

28

ALL that day Concha waited for a call from her grandfather. Only when she saw him would she know whether he was angry with her or not. The hours passed. Night came. The noises of the house gradually died away. Finally the noises of the street died away, also, and still no word came from Don Julián. Miserably she crept into bed. The events of the last few days had left her exhausted, and she fell into a heavy sleep.

When she awoke, the sun was shining, and her sister was leaning over her. "Hurry, Concha, Grandfather has sent for you!" Louisa's eyes were shining.

Concha found him sitting at his desk as usual. "My little one," he began, looking at her with compassion. So she had not hurt him. Her plan had worked. Mamá Grande had not told. "My little one," he said again, "I have never wanted you to suffer, and I hope you will not now. But better now than later. Ramón is not worthy of you. I find it hard to explain to you. Louisa—Ramón. It seems it is better that they should marry."

Louisa and Ramón! So her grandfather had been led to think that Ramón had all along wished to marry Louisa, and that this was the reason for the change of plans. Suddenly Concha saw a great many things more clearly than she had ever seen them before. Her sister had always wanted Ramón. And Ramón? Had something been going on between the two? For a moment she felt humiliated. Then she dropped to her knees beside Don Julián. "Give me your blessing, Grandfather."

"You are not sorrowing?" Don Julián spoke with surprise. "I wish it were anyone else but this North American," he said as if thinking aloud. "He is not of our faith. I do not like his country. But he has asked for your hand." Don Julián rose and walked across the room, then came back. "In a time of emergency——" He broke off. "I have talked to him, and I find him to have his own culture. He will cherish you, Concha. But if I permit this marriage, you must give me your solemn promise, Concepción, that you will be faithful to the Church."

"I promise." Concha still knelt waiting for the old man's blessing.

"And you will go to Father Cristóbal with this man—" Don Julián could not yet bring himself to speak Jim's name—"and have him instructed in his duties to you and to your children?"

"Yes, Grandfather."

"And you will never relax your zeal in bringing up your children in the Catholic faith?"

At Concha's assent, Don Julián laid his hands on her head, blessing her, then left her without another word.

Concha was just coming out of the library when she saw Ignacio going down the stairs to the floor below. She ran after him, calling, "Nacho, Nacho!" Her grandfather had been spared the truth, so of course the story of her meeting with the North American had not been allowed to leak out. Her brother would not have liked it that Jim had embraced her openly, but he too would never know about it.

Ignacio turned at her call. That secret, careful expression which had hung like a veil over her old vivacity had been swept away. Her eyes shone, her lips seemed fuller, banishing the hint of asceticism he had detected there since his return. Instantly he realized the story that had been told him—that Louisa had undermined Concha's position with Ramón, and that poor Concha had been saved from humiliation only by Buchanan's opportune proposal—was false. She was marrying him because she wanted to!

"I've nothing to say to you, bringing a North American into our family," he burst out. His anger had risen now. He was jealous of Buchanan. He knew now he would rather have had her marry Ramón, for his own place in her heart would then have been secure. The American threatened it.

"Nacho," she said. "Jim's being from the States is nothing against him. I love him, and he is your friend."

"North Americans are always pretending to be our friends, and then taking things from us."

"If you knew all that, why did you bring him into our home?"

"I didn't expect him——" He checked himself. "I expected him to behave like a gentleman. It's just as I said, always taking what doesn't belong to them."

A look of understanding came into Concha's eyes. She perceived now what was the matter with Ignacio. From the step above she leaned down, placed her hand under his chin, raised his face to hers. "He hasn't taken anything from you, Nacho," she said gently.

Ignacio shook off her hand, ran down the last flight of steps and across the stone-flagged patio. Not waiting for Francisco, he pushed angrily on the bolt of the gate until it flew back, jamming his finger. Sucking at the torn place to ease the pain, he hurried down the street until he came to a café. He ordered coffee, sat drinking cup after cup, smoking one cigarette after another, drumming idly with his long fingers on the table. He did not see Pablo enter nor his expression of tolerant amusement touched with condescending pity as he looked at his spoiled half brother. Pablo was thinking that he would not criticize Ignacio so much if he enjoyed his idleness. But to be idle and unhappy —that was pure stupidity.

"May I share this table with you?" he asked.

"If you like." Ignacio called the waiter, ordering coffee for Pablo, not betraying how glad he was to see him. It had been too much to hope for—such a coincidence.

Pablo sat down, pleased at their meeting and reconciliation. Many times he had passed the Navarro house, hoping to see Ignacio. Today had been his first sight of him since the afternoon when he had angered Ignacio at the café. He felt a twisted pleasure in being with his half brother.

"Well, I must be off," he said after his second cup of coffee. "I should have been at my office an hour ago. Suppose we do something together this afternoon."

"No, thank you! I don't care for your friends," Ignacio replied, remembering how insecure he had felt after his afternoon at Guadalupe's.

"I, too, am my father's son," replied Pablo. It was the first time he had claimed the relationship. He read into Ignacio's refusal the implication that he, Pablo, the illegitimate, knew only the lowborn. It stung him to a declaration he never had intended to make for he wanted to appear proudly indifferent.

Ignacio was ashamed that he had spoken as he had. As the son of the big household, graciousness was demanded of him. "Of course I'll go with you. I was disgruntled over happenings at home. I have no opportunity like you to function in the new Mexico—if there is a new Mexico," he added. "What do you think now—will labor save Mexico? I understand that Calles, who built up the great labor organization, has smashed it. Only the leader has survived, he and his wealth."

Pablo ran his stout fingers through his heavy black hair, his mind filled again with the anxiety which his meeting with Ignacio had for the moment pushed out of it. He held only a clerk's position in the Department of Industry, but he had been able to better his condition by small services to Morones. He still was useful to the former leader. Whether Morones was or was not really out troubled Pablo. If he was out, then Pablo should be identifying himself with the new undercover leaders appearing among the labor class. But would these men be able to make labor powerful again, and would he become influential by joining them?

The men who had enjoyed the favor of Obregón and Calles had developed into a wealthy class and were beginning to regard labor and peasant movements as a threat to them as well as to the *hacen-*

dados and foreigners. If Calles' crowd had smashed one organization, couldn't they smash a new one?

Ignacio watched Pablo's self-absorption with some amusement. He's not going to involve himself by making any statement to me of where he stands, he thought. "What are you thinking about, Pablo?" he said aloud.

Pablo came to with a start. "I was thinking," he said quietly, "about myself. I was married last week. I was trying to decide whether to ask you to meet my wife this afternoon."

"And why not?"

Pablo shrugged.

Ignacio was a trifle taken back. Pablo's implication was that he did not trust his graciousness. "Let it be my invitation, Pablo. Both of you meet me for coffee." The café he named was one of the most fashionable ones. Pablo was pleased. Then Ignacio was not ashamed to be seen with him.

"This is the table I usually take. It's nice here by the window." With elaborate politeness Ignacio, forestalling the waiter, pulled out the chair for Pablo's wife—a pale, quiet, little thing with a sulky mouth and big earnest eyes. She had come directly from the school where she taught and carried a bundle of books and papers. She was a figure entirely without glamour or romance. What had made Pablo choose her? Ignacio was baffled. He felt he understood Pablo less than at any time since he had met him. He had thought him very ambitious. Why then had he married a woman like this?

29

Jim made use of his introduction to the oil company, but nothing seemed to come of it. Mr. Albright had said they might have a position for him a little later. If they did, they would let him know. Jim feared this was a polite way of getting rid of him. He was beginning to realize that it was not easy to enter business. Some days he would think he was on the track of a job, but it never materialized. Was it because he had no experience? He began to think seriously of going into business for himself, investing his money in real estate. Then he would remember what had happened to his mother's investments and draw back.

Early in the morning, just as day began to break, he would stir uneasily in his sleep, his sense of apprehension, unguarded during the night, stealing upon him in a wave of darkness, engulfing his happiness over his coming marriage. To rid himself of it, he would dress, walk the streets in the fresh May morning air. Only the workers were abroad so early and Indian vendors half buried under their loads of fruit and flowers, treading lightly, moving forward in a swift trot, their short, square feet hugging the ground like hands. Again, as on the first evening of his return, he would remember his childhood impressions of these people. Somehow they gave him confidence and the feeling that it was no mistake for him to identify himself with this country of his birth. Gradually the apprehension with which he had wakened would leave him, and he would give himself again with confidence to hunting a job.

One morning, when he went into Sanborn's for coffee a man slapped him on the shoulder. He looked up to see Armstrong from the Embassy. Jim had avoided his old friends of late—or had they avoided him? To his surprise he had found himself, since his resignation, somewhat isolated. For a few days his acquaintances at the Embassy enjoyed the excitement of his engagement, and then he had dropped out of their world. He no longer held a diplomatic post, and parties in the diplomatic world revolved around that status.

"You're just the person I've been wanting to see. If you aren't expecting anyone, may I sit down?" Armstrong asked.

Jim nodded his assent.

"It's a matter that came to my attention only yesterday. One of the mining companies is looking for a man for their office here in Mexico City. I thought you'd be just the one to help them out. Now that the government has honored the agreement on subsoil rights they are going into full production again. They want to build up understanding, cement their position with the Mexican people. In view of your coming marriage you, I thought, would be sympathetic to both sides—in short, would be just the person for them."

"It's something I'd like," said Jim. "And you think they'd take me?"

"I don't see why not."

Jim felt that curious disgrace slipping from him which an American always feels when he is unemployed. The morning sun was shining down on the table through the huge skylight that roofed the restaurant patio. The room was by that time full of men, for it was the hour when many businessmen came for coffee. He was happy to be here among them.

"Here's my card. This will introduce you." They had risen now and were going toward the door.

"We, as you know, are one of the old companies," said the manager into whose office Jim was ushered. "We've had a good deal of trouble, but things are better now. Native labor asked for fantastic raises in wages, control over our personnel, and so forth. That was the attitude of the revolutionary groups. There's a more conservative viewpoint now. A decided swing now that we have a property-conscious set of leaders. We consider your connection with a prominent Mexican family and your experience at the Embassy under the present ambassador good preparation for a place on our staff."

"I don't want to come into the organization under false pretenses," Jim answered. "I'm not at all certain that my connections will be of any value to you. The Navarro family has no influence that I know of with the present political setup, unless——" He hesitated a moment. "Well, come to think about it, a future relative of mine may have some influence." A chance remark of Ramón's had made him realize that, although scornful of the new regime, Ramón would probably co-operate with it. That Ramón was ambitious, he had no doubt; that he intended to recoup his family's fortune, much depleted by land confiscation during the Revolution, he had often declared. "There is nothing, though, you could count on. My greatest value to you, I imagine, would be a certain insight gained by being closely associated with a Mexican family, and my knowledge of diplomacy gained at the Embassy," Jim added.

"I understand perfectly," said the manager. "We simply want someone who will mingle easily with the Mexicans and can make friends with them. Suppose you visit our mines and some other outfits and see how we compare with them in our handling of the natives. Or, put it this way, see how you like us. Then you can decide if you want the position."

"I'd like to do that very much," said Jim. He wished to know more of the mining business before he decided. Furthermore, he was delighted at the prospect of getting away from Mexico City for a few days. The formality of his afternoon calls on Concha he was finding difficult. Seeing her only in the presence of some member of her family gave him no chance for intimacy. All the things he would like to talk over with her must wait until after their marriage.

As he entered the *sala* that afternoon, there were only Louisa and Ramón besides Concha. "If Concha won't ask you, I'll have to," Louisa cried the moment she saw him. "We've decided to have a double wedding, and we want our dresses to be just alike."

"Yes?" said Jim, not seeing why they needed him for this decision. If only he could get Concha away from the others for a little time so he could tell her his own important news!

"Yes?" mocked Louisa. "What are you going to do about it?"

"I?"

"He doesn't understand," cried Louisa, throwing up her hands in a gesture of despair. "In our country, it's the groom who provides the trousseau. So, you see, we have to consult you."

Concha smiled at the look of consternation on Jim's face. "Mamá was to explain, but my little sister can never wait," she told him.

Quickly Jim recovered himself. "I hadn't understood, but here, Ramón, if this is a matter for men, let us settle it between ourselves." He drew his future brother-in-law aside. "Give me full particulars so I won't make another slip." From the first he had been pleasantly surprised. He had expected Ramón would be unfriendly. Had Jim not taken Concha from him? But Ramón seemed satisfied with the new arrangement. It was puzzling. But perhaps, in these marriages of convenience, the men weren't necessarily in love with the women they married. He couldn't imagine not being in love with Concha, though.

"Oh, it's really a matter of form," said Ramón. "Usually you place in the mother's hands sufficient funds for the trousseau. Sometimes, if a man likes to take part in the selection, he arranges personally for his bride's garments. That is not done so much now. Louisa and Concha are quite capable, with Mamá Grande's help, of attending to everything."

As they were about to join the rest of the family—Doña María, Don Julián, and Mamá had now entered the room—Jim made a sudden decision. He told Ramón of the position offered him. It was evident that he immediately rose in Ramón's estimation. There was an expression close to respect in his eyes. He seemed to be measuring Jim as a worthy adversary. It gave Jim a glimpse of the real man—crafty, ambitious, with a cold judgment that would dissect every emotion, even of those most dear to him, making them serve his purpose. He realized that Ramón, in evaluating him, was deciding whether to use him as friend or foe. Which, Jim could not be certain. All Ramón said was, "I know something of the mining game. We might be of use to each other later on."

When at last Jim had an opportunity to draw Concha aside, her reception of his news was one of bewilderment. "Oh, I thought you were giving up your duties at the Embassy—" she hesitated—"because you were coming into the family . . . to be . . . you know, like Ignacio . . . to be quite free to do as you please."

"But I couldn't do that," protested Jim. "I have to work. You and I must rely on ourselves."

This seemed an entirely new idea to her, but he felt no opposition. Instead a kind of gentle submissiveness to any plan he might see fit to make, even to his absence from the city for a few days, although that, he saw now, went against the customs of her people. He realized in a household where men did not work, business that took a man away during the plans for his wedding indicated indifference on his part. He would have felt her acquiescence to his absence was too complete a submission on her part if he had not experienced her strength and determination in arranging her marriage to him.

As he went out into the late May afternoon and hailed a passing taxi, a plan was taking shape in his mind. He would send a check to Mamá in the morning for the trousseau but, besides, he would order some special garments sent down from New York. All the tender words he longed to say to Concha, all the embraces he longed to bestow on her, would be expressed in the fragile, lovely things he would send her. He'd wire his cousin and enlist her help.

The late afternoon sun shot patterns of light across the sky from behind a mass of rain clouds folding themselves back against the mountains. There had been a shower while Jim was at the Navarros', a forerunner of the coming rainy season. The air he now drew into his lungs was cool and inexpressibly fresh. Under the great trees of the Paseo de la Reforma, little girls like white moths passed him. A puff of wind lifted their veils, disclosing for a moment their childish faces. Moved by curiosity, he dismissed his taxi and followed them into a near-by church.

The place was all but empty, only here and there a kneeling figure, and within the sanctuary the little girls he had seen on the street, watched over by black-clad women, knelt, flowers clasped in their hands. The Virgin in her blue robe had been brought down from her accustomed niche to stand among them. They were not yet come to womanhood, for only in childhood might they wait thus on the Virgin in the month of Mary, he remembered now. Concha had explained it to him as a group of young cousins fluttered across the patio on their way to the church, one day as he came in.

Singing, the little girls now ascended the steps of the altar. Their childish voices drifted down to him. "The perfume of our flowers is the incense of our purity." Then, laying their offerings at the Virgin's feet, they knelt again, seven to the right, seven to the left.

At the end of the line was a child who, in a few months, would slip into womanhood. Already there were signs of its coming—or was it a trick of the dressmaker, that arrangement of folds of her dress, giving a little fullness over her childish breasts? As she knelt, with a conscious, pretty gesture she spread her skirts, covering the upturned soles of her shoes, and arranged her veil to fall in graceful folds over her slim shoulders. So Concha had probably knelt, a very few years ago, in the last such offering before coming to womanhood. He had a sense of the family's effort to guard her against any taint of worldliness. And yet those who had so cherished her would have offered her to Ramón's cold and calculating desires!

Chapultepec Park was not far away, and Jim sought the seclusion of its paths. Under the massive old trees he walked soberly, considering the task ahead of him and Concha. Out of their two civilizations they must weld together a partnership. He had only a dim knowledge of the forces that had shaped her, brief glimpses like the service in the church. She had even less knowledge of the forces which had shaped him. A man and a woman forged on different anvils. Catholic and Protestant. In her, proud Aztec had mated with proud Spaniard, making a new people. He, too, sprang from a new people, a proud people. His country, through the centuries, had encroached on hers. His had been greedy, hers fearful, envious. Their love would have to cross all these barriers.

30

THE NEXT week was full of interest for Jim. The mining concern had put at his disposal a car much higher powered than his own runabout. It took the steep mountain climbs without laboring. As he traveled, he marveled at the temerity of the Spanish invaders who had sought out such inaccessible spots in their devouring thirst for wealth. The land seemed tossed together in fantastic cubic masses, its planes and angles making a forbidding, uninhabitable land. And yet, wherever gold and silver had been discovered, cities had managed to fit themselves to the fantastic distortion.

Jim soon learned that the point of view among the foreign managers differed little. He was among men who talked the aggressive language of North American business. "It's our initiative," the manager for the mine belonging to the company he was interested in told him, "that has developed Mexico's resources. Now we've put in the money, the Mexicans are jealous and want to cash in on the results. If they didn't want us here, why did they let us come in the first place? It's been a hard period, but our position at last appears to be pretty good. As you know from your work at the Embassy, an agreement was reached after our present ambassador took over. That agreement, linking subsoil rights to surface rights, a thing not in the old Spanish law but in Díaz' agreement with foreign business, is now established permanently, we believe, with the new government. The ambassador's friendly approach seems to have accomplished the impossible and brought a permanent settlement fairly satisfactory to both sides."

Jim had too vivid a memory of the café and Pablo reading the doggerel couplets, ridiculing friendship with the American ambassador, to accept such a statement without reservations. And he saw with clarity the need to meet Mexico's emerging middle class halfway—or there would be trouble.

"As the products are being shipped out of the country, and the money payments for them go into your banking accounts in New York, San Francisco, or London, Mexico then, except by taxation— which I believe is not large—and what you pay to labor, is not benefit-

ing by its own industries. Would we not cement this advantage you
have gained," Jim asked, "by accepting a larger taxation? You would
still, as I understand it, be making more profits than you could in the
States. I had an opportunity, while I was in the Embassy, to know some
of the young Mexicans. There is a great deal of bitterness among them."

"Oh, those men! They are in the minority. I doubt if even their anger
is directed against the mining business. The bonanza years are over
for us. In other words, our property is not so desirable in their eyes
as the oil property, for instance. Then, too, the silver mines have been
in operation here for four hundred years, and in that time a lot of
problems have been settled. We've made a good many concessions to
labor. In the end it has paid to do it. Would you like to make a tour
of the mines?" the man ended.

Neither of them spoke as the elevator dropped down to the lower
galleries of the mine. The silence was complete, deep down there in
the earth, except for the intermittent rumble of a car loaded with ore-
infiltrated rock being pushed in spurts along the single track. In the
dim light of an electric globe that faintly illumined the tunnel passage
Jim saw the faces of the miners. He was used to the guarded gaze of
the Indians of the plantations, the men who lived close to the earth
they loved even if they did not possess it, but he was unprepared for
the dull eyes staring at him from the gaunt faces of men who had lived
underground since early childhood.

They came to an opening in the rock where the Virgin stood with
candles and small cups of burning oil before her. She was doll-like in
expression and proportion and dressed in French clothing of Carlotta's
time, and in her hand she held a broad-brimmed garden hat. Some
miner must have seen the French doll in a shop and mistaken her for
an image of the Virgin, so beautiful did she seem to him. Jim stopped,
going close to the little figure in order to observe it more carefully.

"Don't touch her!" exclaimed the manager nervously. "If she were
harmed in the slightest way, I believe the miners would kill us. Here's
the vein we're following. It's the richest we've struck for some time.
In fact we had begun to think this part of the mine was run out." He
picked up a piece of rock. The shining metal marked it here and there.
"If the vein holds up, this will be a big year for us."

As they left the shaft, a letter was handed to Jim. He opened it immediately. Mr. Albright wrote that the head offices of the oil company in the States had confirmed his appointment. Now he must
decide which of the two positions he would take—oil or silver.

On his ride back to Mexico City, he scarcely noticed the grandeur of the scene, so occupied was he with the decision he must make. The more he thought of it, the more convinced he was that his opportunity lay in the oil business. The mining problems, he believed, just as the mining man said, were probably pretty well settled, while the oil business was, as he knew from information he had acquired in his work at the Embassy, still in the beginning stages. It had hardly passed through its aggressive pioneering. There was a chance, then, to help shape policies. He would feel that he was not entirely giving up the work of diplomacy he had originally chosen for himself.

As the car reached the outskirts of the city, he had all but decided to accept the position with Albright. But before that decision was finally made, he wanted to talk to several people, among them Guadalupe Villar. Villar, although definitely in sympathy with all the reform movements, did not seem to have the bitterness toward the States the others had. Due probably to his greater knowledge of us, thought Jim. Whichever company Jim joined, he was to have charge of the public-relations department. Guadalupe would be a good friend to have. But now he just wanted to sound him out, get his general reaction to the States and to foreign business.

When Jim entered his room at the hotel, the first thing his eyes rested on was a pile of boxes from New York. He opened one after another. His cousin had not failed him. The garments were beautiful and fine, as he had wished them to be. There was a white negligee of chiffon and lace. He took it into his hands. It was like holding a cobweb. The last box, the largest of all, he only opened, not disturbing the shimmering lengths of the veil. With a note asking when he might come to see her, he sent the boxes to Concha.

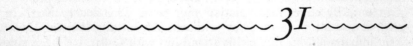

31

PASSING the building of the Board of Education on his way to Villar's office next morning, Jim had an impulse to see the murals so often discussed by the Navarros and their friends. "These so-called artists are making us, before the world, into a nation of Indian peons," Don

Julián had said only the evening before. "Rightly, a storm of protest is going up from the old families." The discussion which had followed had stirred in Jim a desire to see and judge for himself.

For a moment after he entered the building he was held by the magnificence of the scene. The walls of the galleries around the patio were aflame with color, deep blues and oranges that glowed with life. The figures were strong, well executed. The fresco of men going down into a mine seemed at first glance merely the everyday scene of labor. As he looked more closely, Jim became aware of something more in the picture. Although each man carried but one timber, a support to be placed in one of the galleries below, it was so carried on his shoulder that the heavy supports of the entrance to the mine formed uprights to the crossbars under which the miners were bowed, making a rhythmical procession of men bearing crosses. Wherever the cross was not complete, somehow the mind completed it. Inflaming propaganda of the most insidious kind, thought Jim, watching the steady stream of men and women with bare feet and solemn, inexpressive faces moving along the galleries and up the stairs, their black eyes lifted to the frescoes.

Jim saw the look of genuine pleasure which came into Villar's face when he greeted him. Seating himself on the window sill of his small and crowded office, Villar motioned him to take his vacated chair.

"We have missed you at the café," he said. "I have been concerned for fear you might have misunderstood the demonstration that day."

"As a matter of fact, it's over that demonstration and its meaning that I have come to talk to you. I am to be associated with a North American company here in Mexico, either mining or oil. Whichever company I join, I shall be there for the purpose of establishing good relations between your country and mine."

Villar had turned his head away and was looking out the window. Slowly he brought his gaze to rest on Jim. "Because of many happy memories of your country, I am going to tell you what is in my heart." He stopped, and then, as if it cost him considerable effort to speak, he went on: "By clever manipulation your country's influence has been used, as you know, to do away with one reform after another. Now your ambassador, because of his friendship with Calles, has been able to persuade him that it is unsound economically to give the villages their land. Sometimes we find your friendship more dangerous than your enmity."

"Are you just in making such a statement?" Jim asked, thinking,

So Villar's remark about the demonstration at the café was only for politeness' sake. He, too, feels bitterness toward the States.

"And why not?" asked Villar. "The giving up of our reforms has set us back years. We can make no great strides toward democracy so long as the United States sits in the saddle."

"Why do you say we sit in the saddle?"

"How can you say otherwise, when your businessmen deny us a chance to hold executive positions in some of the most important activities of our country—the ones they own—to say nothing of your ambassador's using his influence to hold our mines and oil wells permanently and now to check distribution of land among the Indian villages?"

"To answer your first complaint, have you men who are qualified to hold executive positions in these foreign companies?"

"I think we have. We shall never find out, if we have no chance to test our abilities. It is for your advantage that you hold us out of opportunity." Villar spoke with a kind of bitter resignation.

"Aren't you forgetting the vast amount of money we have poured into your country for the development of your resources?" Jim suggested.

"But who gets the benefit of those resources?" Villar asked.

"Certainly you get some of it," Jim insisted.

Villar lifted his hand in a gesture of futility.

Jim realized that in Villar's present mood if they went on talking he might alienate a man he respected, a man who might be of great value to him later on. "We are both right at least in part, I think, Villar." And he held out his hand.

For a moment the young Mexican hesitated. Then he held out his.

With an effort at casualness, Jim said, "You seem to be moving. Is Rivera going to do *your* walls, too?"

A stricken look crossed Villar's face. "I'd move gladly for that. The fact is, my work is done here. The government does not need surveyors of land, if no more land is to be divided."

"I'm sorry." There was genuine regret in Jim's voice. "But of course," he added, "there will be a place for a man of your abilities."

As Jim left Villar, he realized that his decision was almost if not quite made. The oil companies were the target of Mexico's bitterness in the past and would again be. The long struggle between foreign owners and the Mexican government he was now certain was not yet ended. It would be exciting, interesting work to help a great foreign industry establish itself in México's good graces. But before he decided whether to accept the position with the oil company, he wanted to make certain that he would have a fairly free hand in his work. He went directly to their offices.

"I shall be glad to have you in the organization," Mr. Albright said as he shook hands.

"I want to ask a few questions first."

"You mean you haven't accepted?"

"I have, if I can be of real service to you."

"Isn't that for us to decide?" There was a twinkle in the older man's eyes as he asked the question.

"Mr. Albright, to be perfectly frank, I want to know a little more of your policies. I don't want to get into anything I can't see through."

"Right. If I say I have urged your appointment because I want to meet Mexico halfway—and according to all I can learn about you, you do too—will that satisfy you?"

"Yes."

For an hour they discussed the means by which the company might build up good will for itself. Jim spoke of Villar and the other young men he had met at the café.

"Exactly," said Albright when Jim had finished his story. "It is in that class of Mexicans, the slowly emerging middle class, that I think the greatest bitterness lies. If we didn't exclude them from the executive positions, I believe we could win their confidence. You have a big job ahead of you, Buchanan. When can you begin work on it?"

"I am to be married next week."

"Naturally you want time for a honeymoon. Suppose we say three weeks from today."

32

Soon after Jim left him, Guadalupe, gathering his papers together, walked with them the many blocks to his home in order to save the few centavos it would cost to ride. He was hurrying, for he wanted to get home to Soledad. Soledad was never frightened. Soledad, whom he had protected since that day in the village, at the same time protected him.

He met her at their house door, carrying a basket brimming over with vegetables, a bunch of red poppies on the top. "See, Lupe, I scolded the man in the market today, and here is the result—two extra carrots besides the bunch and for the same price," she cried.

These bustling, housewifely ways she had acquired these last years, in which he had taken such deep satisfaction, hurt Guadalupe now, and he could not speak.

"But why are you here at this hour? Are you sick?" she asked. "I told the man at the market it would be so, on account of those wilted vegetables he gave our servant yesterday when I was too busy to go myself. He shall make me further recompense."

So interested had she become in the intricacies of future bargaining, that she almost forgot Guadalupe, the cause of her concern. But as he walked down the *corredor* ahead of her, she caught sight of his drooping shoulders. Dropping the basket, almost overturning it in her haste, she ran after him.

"What is it?" she asked, grasping him by the arm, swinging him around to face her, knowing before he spoke what he would say. Month by month, in the talk of the men who had gathered in this house, she had seen more clearly than any of them what the end would be.

"The hacienda program is to be given up. The order has gone out. There is no further need for my services." There was a stool standing just within the door of their *sala,* and Guadalupe sat down upon it. Suddenly he was very tired; he leaned against Soledad. Feeling the warmth of her thigh where his head rested, his fear subsided. Strange, he thought, it's because of Soledad I am afraid, and yet I am not afraid, now I am near her. Freed from fear, he felt his indignation mounting against the leaders who had let the structure of the new society collapse.

Soledad did not speak or move. A kind of Indian immobility had come over her. The Revolution, for her, was a fiery living thing. It was her people, her brother, the husband who had been killed, the *rebozo*-shrouded women like herself who had followed their men into battle. This behind-cover dictator, who had ended reform, had once been a soldier of the Revolution, lean, often hungry, now well fed, luxuriously housed. She felt burning shame creeping over her. It was as if she herself were the betrayer of the villages. But something gained from the years she had been a part of the ragged army made her compassionate of weakness. It was impossible for her completely to condemn. She knew the frailties of the men of the Revolution, the underdogs. She knew their longings, their hopes, their wild, uncontrolled desires. Abruptly she laughed. Then, with a shrug, she went back to her household tasks.

Guadalupe knew that laugh of Soledad's, the roots of its cynicism. He must find work somewhere, somehow give her security. Quietly he rose and left the house.

THE marriage of the Navarro sisters was one of the brilliant social affairs of the season. Mamá Grande indeed lived up to her promise to give Concha as splendid a wedding as if she were marrying Ramón. Jim was built up before the Spanish hierarchy as a member of the Southern States' aristocracy. Because he was a Protestant and the wedding could not take place at the center altar of the Church unless the Holy Eucharist was absent, Doña María made a bold move. It was in keeping with the family's exclusive tradition that the two sisters should be married in great privacy. The room used as a secret chapel in the years when the churches had been closed, made beautiful year by year as Don Julián had added to it paintings and golden vessels, and Mamá altar cloths of exquisite workmanship, Mamá Grande now turned to her own purposes. She made such a point of Don Julián's failing health, and the danger to him in attending a large public gathering that it was granted to her to have the wedding there.

She ordered the blocked-in doorway reopened, the wall which hid the room from view taken down, and the heavy masonry between the two stairways of the house cut through, to make a passageway leading directly into the former chapel.

As the place was small, only the members of the two families and a few of their closest friends could be invited. Photographers and reporters were excluded. At first Jim was pleased with the plans, for he wanted a quiet wedding and no publicity. Then, ruefully, he discovered that what Mamá Grande had done was to heighten the publicity. Invitations to the wedding were the prized possessions of society. A few of the bolder of his own friends hinted that they would like

invitations, something his reticence kept him from asking for. Mamá
Grande's first grudging acceptance of him had changed to a kind of
unwilling liking. He wished to do nothing to jeopardize this more
favorable position with her.

Of all the splendor and beauty of the ceremony nothing stood out
clearly in Jim's mind except the moment when the end of Concha's
veil was laid across his shoulders, a touch as light as her own, signifying union, and then the weight of the gold links of the bridal chain,
as the heavy loop was placed around his neck and the lighter one
around hers.

He remembered, too, Mamá's words. She put her hand within his
as they stood in the patio afterward and said, "I named her Concepción, and I have given her to you at the time when the maize has
burst again into life. Remember, if you are to make her happy, a man
according to the old Aztec law cultivated only as much land as he
needed."

What did she mean? he wondered. Did she not believe in their right
to the luxury that surrounded them?

34

For their wedding journey Louisa and Ramón were motoring to New
York. Concha, to Jim's delight, had chosen to spend their honeymoon
at the hacienda.

They were in the car, alone, the moment for which they had both
longed, but now that the time had come there was constraint between
them. Reared under Mamá Grande's strict regime, guarded all her life
by the elaborate rituals of separateness, Concha found herself bound by
established habits of reserve. She had boldly set aside custom and even
risked scandal courting the intimacy of Jim's presence in order to
force acceptance of him, but now she was shy.

Jim tried to keep his attention on his driving. He never drove with
Ignacio's nonchalance, since he felt a considerable respect for the
hazards of a road bordered by Indian villages. In Indian eyes a road
was a companionable stretch of country, an ancient expression of communal life where men stopped to talk, dogs sunned themselves, chil-

dren played. The automobiles that sped through his towns, their occupants ignoring the salutation of the road, "God go with you," the Indian resented. An accident, even a small one like the killing of a pig or chicken, sometimes roused a whole village to ugly protest. Jim wanted nothing of this sort to happen.

At last the road became less populated. He looked down at Concha. She was sitting with her hands lightly clasped, her eyes fixed on the distant mountains. He had an alarming remembrance of the withdrawal of this sensitive people at times when he had failed to understand them. He had forgotten of late how quickly contact could be lost. Was Concha in retreat from him?

The snow-topped mountains, Iztaccihuatl and Popocatepetl, the god mates of Aztec legend, lay bold against the sky. The sun came out from the clouds which had earlier threatened a shower and shone down upon the outstretched form of the woman mountain. Jim was impressed by the full and majestic sweep of the woman's form, her face forever turned to the sky, her hair streaming down the slope, her heroic breast and thighs outlined under the covering veil of shimmering snow—remote, mysterious, untouchable. His eyes turned again to Concha. She raised hers to him, and he saw they were eloquent with love, a love simple and fundamental. He felt a choking sense of gratitude.

The car swerved and again he was forced to give his full attention to his driving, for they were now climbing the mountain barrier.

"Tell me about you, when you were a little boy, Jeem." He loved to hear her speak his name. The Spanish "i" pronounced as long "e" seemed to give a special significance.

"Well, first I lived at a hacienda something like yours—only smaller —but when I went to the States, after my mother was killed in the Revolution, I was moved about from one member of the family to another. Sometimes I was in the North, sometimes in the South."

"You were lonely." She did not ask, rather stated it as a fact.

"I suppose I was, but I didn't realize it until I met you."

She laid her hand on his arm. "Not now, not ever again," she said softly.

It was night when they reached the hacienda. The gates were barred, but in answer to Jim's shout they were quickly opened. In the lights of the car he saw an old caretaker wrapped in a serape, standing aside to let the car pass. He had a sudden memory of another caretaker wrapped in a serape carrying his mother—— He put the memory from him. Up from the wooded park through which they drove came the chirp of insects and other earth sounds. They reached the second gate. Without command from him it swung back. Jim followed the drive which circled the central patio and stopped before the low steps which led to the pillared gallery of the house. He felt stillness and peace as he turned off the ignition and a curious sense of coming home.

There was a rush of bare feet down the steps. They were surrounded by the household servants. Conchita, the little girl they had helped to bring up, a woman now and ready for fertility, had come back to them. "May the good Lord bless our little Conchita!" cried Concha's old nurse, her wrinkled brown face alight. "It is a good year to marry. The corn is sprouting as it has not for years. Abundance has been granted by the good Lord." With soft, chattering words she led the two through the flower-framed doorway. Through an opposite door Jim caught a glimpse of a second patio, and the pool in its center.

"The fiesta meal will soon be ready," a tall, stately, brown woman told them. But it was long before they sat down to eat. Concha had first to take him over the house and into the chapel made fragrant for their coming with herbs. At the feet of the young Virgin, listening to the angel's annunciation, lay a great heap of red and white blossoms and a pile of yellow kernels of corn. Candles flickered in a soft breeze coming through the open door. Concha knelt and Jim, remembering his promise to Mamá to let her live in an atmosphere of understanding, knelt beside her.

At last they were ready to eat. The evening was warm, and their table stood on the gallery overlooking the second patio where they could see the moon reflected in the pool.

Jim had not tasted such *tortillas* since childhood, nor such hot chile. In the shadows around them he saw glowing Indian eyes resting on him. He began telling Concha of his childhood, of his nurse, of the old gatekeeper, of the stories they had told him.

"Why, it's just the same kind of thing I did when I was a little girl," Concha exclaimed, drawing nearer in spirit to the man beside her.

At last the house was still, the servants gone to their sleeping mats. She went to the edge of the gallery, leaned against one of the pilasters. In her close-fitting dress, her arms raised above her head, she looked taller and very slender. Joy in the symmetry of her body, the long thighs, the wide spread between the hips, filled Jim. With one stride he was beside her, mad with passion for this beautiful productive woman. He took her in his arms, buried his face in her neck, shaken with the scent of her body, the touch of her skin, her impassiveness. "Don't be afraid, sweetheart," he begged.

"But I am not." She relaxed in his arms with her head against his shoulder.

He carried her through the great silent rooms of the house to the room that had been hers since childhood. Desire could no longer wait.

Concha seemed always to have known that she would not be complete until she bore his body upon hers.

The next morning they walked out over the sun-filled valley lush with its growth of sugar cane. The clouds flowed down over the mountains.

And now Jim was able to talk to Concha as he had not in the days before their wedding. He poured out his longings for a home, conceding now how lonely he had been without close family ties. "I don't want just one child to grow up by himself as I did. And even if I have promised that they shall be brought up in your faith, you will be willing, won't you, to let them go to my country for part of their education? So they will know my way of life as well as yours?"

Jim is beautiful, thought Concha. The way his thick, soft, blond hair grows back from his temples, the firm, fine flesh of his cheeks freshly shaved.

She stopped, and took his face between her two hands. She felt the rough surface against her palms.

"My country is dear to me," she answered simply, "and I would not honor you if yours were not so to you. Our children shall do as you desire, but when they go to your country, I must go with them. Little things could not go alone. And you, too, not without me. I want never to be far from your arms."

"Concha, I have not mentioned it before—but Mamá Grande spoke the other day as if she expected us to live with your family. I—it seems to me we should have a home of our own."

"If it is your wish, my husband—all is as you wish." He saw that her love was as simple and natural as breathing to her.

Late in the afternoon there was a telephone call from Mamá. Don Julián was very ill. A few hours after they had left he had had a stroke from which he was not rallying. He was asking for Concha.

Night was settling down when they reached the city. The great lantern over the entrance of Don Julián's house had been lighted.

Hanging from an iron arm swung out and down from the first gallery, it threw its brilliance upward upon the stone waterspouts jutting out from the flat roof, making them look like down-tipped mouths.

The house was quiet, with none of the usual noises of a big household. Hand in hand, they ascended the first flight of stairs, reached the landing, turned, and followed the second flight. Still no sound. The *sala* was empty. Jim took Concha in his arms, pressing his lips hard upon hers. Then, as he released her, he said, "At last I've done what I have wanted to from the first day I met you—kissed you in this room."

"Wasn't it enough that you have kissed me so many times today?" she asked, smiling.

"No. In this room." And he took her again into his arms. Suddenly they drew apart hearing the swish of skirts behind them.

"Concha, your grandfather is waiting for you." It was Mamá Grande.

"I must go. Wait here, Jim, for me." Lightly Concha ran up the next flight of stairs. Jim could hear her hurrying steps on the floor of the gallery above and Mamá Grande's heavier, slower tread as she followed.

Through the library, where the light burned low before Don Julián's favorite image of the Virgin, Concha hurried—into the bedroom beyond. She saw her grandfather lying stretched out as quiet as in death, his arms above the coverlet parallel with his body. His eyes were closed. She knelt at his side. "My little Concha," he whispered. The words blurred. She put her hand over his. A smile more like a grimace passed over half of his face.

Jim waited alone in the silent room below, his thoughts shuttling back and forth between remembrance of the past hours with Concha and an almost superstitious feeling of the inevitability of this ending to their honeymoon. At last the silence of the house was broken. The outer gate creaked as it was swung back to let a car enter. There was a man's quick, running step, and Ignacio entered the room.

"Where's Concha?" he demanded.

"With her grandfather."

Pacing up and down, Nacho flung out the words as if they were a challenge to Jim: "This house is nothing without her."

Again the gate creaked. Another car rolled into the patio. Louisa and Ramón had arrived. Soon the room was filled with Louisa's excited questions.

Mamá entered. With quiet dignity she greeted them all, saying,

"Your grandfather has received the last Sacraments. He is waiting for you."

As they passed through the library Jim, even in this solemn moment, was impressed with its sense of tradition. He had never been in this room before. The tarnished gold of thousands of book bindings, the carved Spanish chairs enriched by cushions of ancient tapestry, and the dull gold frames of the pictures all created an impression of guarded seclusion.

At the door of Don Julián's room he stopped. Too lately come into the family, he thought, to enter. He could see Vicente standing in the shadows and Mamá Grande kneeling by the bed, her gray head bowed against the old man's hand. Concha was at the head of the bed; her young body supported her grandfather so that he could see the crucifix Father Cristóbal was holding before his eyes.

In the very early morning, as the church bells ceased their ringing, Don Julián died.

35

ACCORDING to a custom long observed in the Navarro family, Vicente inherited the estate, with the understanding that his mother should have what she wanted to spend. Concha and Louisa had been cared for in their dowries. Ignacio, like Mamá Grande, was not to be limited in his spending.

But although Vicente thus succeeded his father as head of the family, Doña María expected that headship to be only in name. She had been in control for many years now. Had she not, through wise management, guarded their riches and kept the Indians from open rebellion? She considered them lazy, immoral, and, given the chance, cruel, but she saw to it that they were well cared for, just as she saw to it that all the work animals on the estates were well cared for. And she was astute enough to realize that men must be kept reasonably happy. On fiesta days and Sundays there was plenty of *pulque* to drink, and she allowed the workers time to recover from its effects. She respected the Indians' devoutness. She paid the priests of the near-by town well so that there should be no personal charge for marriages, christenings, and funerals.

Always there were plenty of candles. Beyond that she allowed the over-seer to handle her Indians as he wished. This management she expected to continue until her death. She had made Vicente a playboy, and she meant him to remain so.

Vicente knew this, but he did not intend to acquiesce. Now that the government had given up the hacienda program, one need not be so careful of the Indians. The haciendas might yield a third more under his management, he thought, and with very little effort on his part. He wanted to gratify his tastes to the full before he was too old to enjoy them, to live in Europe as he had when he was a young man before the Revolution had curtailed his spending. It would take him a couple of years, probably, to get the return on the haciendas which he wanted, but after that he believed he would have his overseers trained so that he could manage the estate from Europe.

A few days after his father's death Vicente sought out his mother. He found her in the small room she used as office, standing in front of an old Spanish secretary, looking over some papers. He took her hand in his and raised it to his lips, saying, "I've not been a very helpful son to you. Father's death has brought me to a realization of my duties. As sole inheritor, I must stop being an idler and watch over you and the other members of the family. I shall need your help, of course, especially in the beginning. You will have to instruct me in hacienda matters."

"I understand your concern, and I appreciate your thoughtfulness, my son." Mamá Grande's old eyes were full of cynicism. "But you've not been trained for business. I've never wished to interfere with your pleasures, and I do not want to now."

"I know you have always spared me, wanting my happiness above all else." It was Vicente's eyes now that were cynical. "But it is for me to spare you, especially in these days of your deep mourning. I realize how valuable your careful records will be to me. They will help me in making my plans. Let us look over them together, Mamacita." The gentleness had gone out of his voice. His gaze was cold and calculating as he examined the papers, then carried them off to his own room.

My first step will be to cancel this order for farm machinery, he said to himself. The Indians are strong, cheaper than machinery. With the government's new attitude he felt safe from interference. It was the beginning of the dark period the Mexicans derisively called the era of the Millionaire Socialists. Calles, the former President, who more and more was dictating every move of the men, ostensibly in power, was himself now a *hacendado* and factory owner. He could be counted on not to press reform to any great extent.

Once Vicente had cut the estimate of expenses at the haciendas, he began to go over city expenditures. He should house his wife and mother in less expensive quarters, he decided, but he dared not suggest it openly. Perhaps he might manage it through Louisa. Now that she was married to Ramón she had great weight with Mamá Grande. When he talked to her about it, she clasped her hands, crying, "Father, it is just what Ramón and I want, but his mother will not hear of it. Perhaps if we can persuade Mamá Grande to take a smaller house, she will be willing, too. Many of the old families are doing it."

"Now don't spoil it all by too much haste," cautioned Vicente.

"Trust me, Father. I've learned to be discreet."

Since Vicente had taken over the management of the estate, Doña María had scarcely left her room. She had aged noticeably. Everyone said it was because of the loss of her husband. One morning Louisa, sitting on the low stool at the old woman's feet, said in her most beguiling tone, "This house is very lonely without Grandfather."

Mamá Grande roused herself. "If it is lonely here, we can do nothing but bear it, for the good Lord has decreed it so."

"Between us there need not be this meekness. Is it not so?" It was daring of Louisa to challenge her grandmother's devoutness, but she was often daring, now that she had become her grandmother's favorite, saving the family from disgrace by marrying Ramón.

"Tush, my child. I've brought you up to be reverent. What kind of wife will you make for Ramón?"

"The kind he likes." Louisa's yellow agate eyes looked for the moment as bold as her father's black ones.

"And what is it you want?"

"Not to wear black for three years, not to refrain from going out in society for all that time. Of course, right now I want to stay at home and honor Grandfather," she hastened to add, noticing the contraction of her grandmother's heavy eyebrows. "But later—Ramón, if I am to hold him, must be entertained. And I think it is best we have a small place of our own." She went on quite innocently, not giving her grandmother a chance to speak: "Why don't we all move into new houses? Why live here, Mamá Grande, with forty rooms to take your time and money? Father will be absent at the haciendas a good deal. When he is not——" She decided not to say where he would be the rest of the time; instead hastened to add, "You and Mamá could have a small, comfortable house in the fashionable part of the city for much less expense. Let Concha and Jim shift for themselves. Ignacio, of course, until he is married, you would want with you."

Doña María sat erect, all lassitude gone from her. "What!" she exclaimed. "The Navarros live elsewhere than in this mansion they have occupied with such distinction! You may tell your father, Louisa, next time he has a proposal like this to come straight to me. As for you, my child, I shall ask Ramón that for the first period of mourning you remain here as members of my household. I am certain Doña Leonora will grant me this boon in my bereavement. I want the strictest observance of all our customs. Only if you are here shall I know they are observed. Of Concha and Jim, too, I shall request it. Now send for the cook, Louisa. I've been idle long enough."

After that with a strong and heavy hand Doña María ruled her family. No more of her authority should be taken from her. It was a tyrannical rule, from which very soon Louisa and Ramón escaped. Ramón wanted to have a free hand; he wished to neglect no opportunity to ingratiate himself with the leaders of the new regime. In this era of the Millionaire Socialists and lavish expenditures on the part of many officials, it was easy to buy privileges and concessions. Ramón placed his money adroitly, gaining for himself immunity from all manner of half-enforced social reforms. And he mingled with the men in power no matter how much he despised them. He had not Don Julián's proud aloofness, nor Ignacio's fastidiousness. He believed the Spaniard could get back his position if he discarded such niceties.

36

BEFORE Concha had recovered from the shock of her grandfather's death, Vicente's and Louisa's rebellion had channeled all Doña María's energy into the subjugating of those left her. In spite of his deference, she felt her husband had escaped her; in spite of the shaping she had given to her son, he had mastered her. Louisa had duped her, pretending she was marrying Ramón to save the family from disgrace, when she had done it only to further her own willful desires. Concha had chosen against her grandmother's will. Mamá Grande meant now to control Nacho. She believed she had found just the right woman for him. She was older than he; she was handsome, as perfect a Spanish type as Ignacio. Once she became his wife she would curb his waywardness, for she was stubborn, forceful, and devout.

Concha was fully aware of her grandmother's intention. At all costs Nacho must be rescued. But even as Concha threw herself into the battle, she was filled with pity for her grandmother. She soon learned that nothing is so binding as pity. It was a tyranny which Mamá Grande shrewdly turned to her own advantage.

Concha's need to help Nacho and her love for Jim were now brought into a conflict she could not resolve. Why, after sacrificing the family to her wishes in the matter of her marriage, must she now sacrifice her young husband to the family? She feared that the retreat from the world demanded by their mourning was difficult and unnatural for Jim. The house was gloomy and devoid of gaiety. And often in the evening she had to leave him alone when Mamá Grande called her for personal services which at times kept her away from Jim the whole evening. Brought up as she had been in the atmosphere of the double household, she was troubled that sometimes Jim did not come home until very late. It never occurred to her that business kept him.

But when she was with him, the conflict ended. She was the product of two peoples of warm and passionate nature. In surrender to her love, she gave herself so completely that for days afterward she retained the sense of oneness with her husband and identification with his world. That God had granted her such happiness filled her with wonder.

To Jim, who had had no close ties since early childhood, possessing a woman like Concha was to have all his unexpressed emotions suddenly thrown into one stream. He had thought they would have their own home, but he gave up the idea gladly when he found that it distressed Concha to have him speak of it just now. To have her snatched up by her family so quickly after their marriage was difficult and disappointing. But those silent moments of their union offset this sense of frustration.

And there was his work to occupy his mind and keep him from thinking overmuch of the place he held in the Navarro establishment. Mamá Grande treated him with the barest courtesy. He realized he had not succeeded in making her like him as he had once thought he had. Ignacio and Vicente ignored him. Strangely enough, Ramón was the only man in the family who seemed interested in him. He even offered to introduce Jim to certain officials he thought might be of help to him. But after Ramón and Louisa left, Jim, treading the long stairs and balconies in the early morning when all the others were asleep, felt often like a ghost inhabiting the Navarro house without their knowledge. Once he was at work identity came back to him.

His first morning in the office Albright explained to him that the present big objective of their company and a British one with wells in the same region was to get the lease of some land adjoining their highest-producing wells. "We don't want to develop it," said Albright, "but we want to control it—see that no one else starts drilling there and draws off our supply. It's government-owned, and we feel that now, while the government is not pressing the theme of 'Mexico for Mexicans,' is probably the best chance we'll ever have to get a long-term lease on this offset land. However, we've got to go carefully. We have one or two officials interested already." He named them. "We expect you to get us in touch with others.

"We have one other bit of land we must get hold of if our big well is to be really protected." He took from a drawer a map which he spread out on his desk, saying, "That we are going to handle alone, as it doesn't affect the British wells. You see this corner of land up here. Well, that piece is owned by a group of small villages. We want to buy it."

It seemed to Jim in these first months as he worked on those two projects that his mind was like a sensitive instrument registering a new Mexico. The preconceived idea of the country of his childhood faded. In its place was a Mexico neither peon nor aristocrat. A country made up of men, sometimes corrupt, sometimes idealistic to the point of fanaticism, but all volatile with sudden enthusiasms and as sudden indifferences. He came to the conclusion that their chance of getting the lease on government property would be due to one of those slumps into lassitude. Just now the ardor to own and control their own riches was at a low ebb in Mexico.

Ramón introduced him to several men in the office of government lands, always arranging the meetings at cafés or restaurants, giving the affair a purely social aspect. But usually before the evening was over Ramón found the opportunity to speak of Jim's position with the oil company, and Jim was able to get in a few words about this offset land they needed.

One evening Ramón asked him to a small party—two men besides themselves. Ramón chose the most notorious cabaret in the city, frequented mostly by the new, rich officialdom. Jim had never been there before. He was astounded at its vulgar ostentation. It had the frescoes so popular now in Mexico, but they were not frescoes of miners and laborers nor the great nudes of Rivera depicting Mother Mexico fertile again. The central figure was of a woman clad only in scarlet gloves stepping forth from a sea of mauve, plumelike feathers.

The two men Ramón had invited were rich Spaniards. One of them had once owned a hacienda, he said, near the oil fields of Jim's company. Casually he mentioned the group of villages to the north of the oil fields. Later, when Ramón and the other men were talking together, he said, "It is rumored your company would like to buy the land recently appropriated to those villages."

Jim was startled. How had the man learned their plans? "Such matters," he said aloud, "are in the hands of the manager, Mr. Albright. I can speak only for myself, but I should hardly think he would be negotiating for more land."

"I understand," said the man, twirling his wineglass. "Naturally you would know nothing of it, but in case you ever do learn of the matter, you might wish—" he paused a moment, adding—"connections. There are ways of coercing these villagers if they don't wish to sell. Here is my card." He made a pretense of slipping it to Jim secretly, but, glancing up, Jim saw Ramón was watching them intently.

What was Ramón after? Was he making money by such illegal proceedings? Then suddenly a disturbing thought crossed Jim's mind. Was Ramón for some reason trying to get him in wrong with the government? Suppose he had fallen for this illegal procedure? "Ways of getting hold of these villagers if they don't wish to sell!" Had Ramón intended to use the transaction to upset the deal with the government? To gain the little pocket owned by the villages and lose the large government tract would indeed put Jim in a bad position with his company. He decided to see less of Ramón.

When he told Albright of the incident at the cabaret, Albright sat for some time thinking. "I don't know where the leak came," he said finally. "There is a memo in my private files of the lay of the villages but nothing more. You should start immediately on that deal before anyone else gets ahead of us, Jim."

On the first hours of his journey Jim could not divorce his thoughts from Concha. Why had she looked so disturbed when he told her he must be away for a few days? But after a little he gave himself over to planning. He was to pick up a young lawyer at a near-by town who knew the Indian dialect of the villagers and who had gone on ahead to talk to them.

"I haven't had any success," he told Jim as soon as they met. "They say they don't want to sell their land. The government gave it back to them, and why should they want to part with it?"

Jim, too, wondered a little why they should, but it was his job to get hold of it. He tried to think of some argument he could use, but there was none. Anyway, he decided he'd talk to them himself.

The villages he found strung out along the flat earth of the coastal plain. Almost at the center was the "mother" village, where the market was held weekly, under the shadow of a great Spanish church built there evidently soon after the Conquest. The church was disintegrating due to lack of repairs but not lack of care. It was scrupulously clean. The houses in the village were mere groups of hovels, each with its patch of corn. Emaciated dogs and unkempt children roamed the plaza, untidy with the refuse of the market held the day before. Men sat idly in doorways, and from the dark interior came the ever-present sound of the women's stone rolling pins grinding the day's supply of corn.

In front of one of the houses the Mexican lawyer stopped and asked to see the headman of the village. A child went to call him. From the expression of the man's face when he came, Jim sensed that he was frightened. It flashed through his mind that Ramón's friend he had met at the cabaret might have been here before him. Jim did some quick thinking. Why not outwit any such attempt by leasing the villagers' land?

The headman of the village, huddled in a heavy serape although the sun was intolerably hot, was squatting before the bench on which he and the lawyer were sitting. "Can you explain to him, Señor Romero," he asked the lawyer, "what it means to lease land and that we would like to lease theirs?"

"And where would my village and my family go?" asked the old man shivering with a malarial chill which made his teeth chatter. His black eyes were still filled with apprehension when the matter had been explained to him. "This is our land, our *tierra*. Where else would we go?"

"Ask him, Señor Romero—" Jim's plan grew in his mind as he talked—"if he would lease the land to us, provided he and his village and the people of the other villages were allowed to stay here and raise their own corn as before."

The old man seemed more troubled than ever. Surely for no good purpose would men pay money and gain nothing from it.

"Explain to him," Jim went on, "that we want them to guard the wells at this point."

"And why?"

Despite the squalor of his surroundings, there was a quiet dignity about the man as he spoke. Jim was reminded of the gatekeeper tending his mother's hacienda in his childhood. Leaning forward, he spoke to the headman directly now, knowing that he would not understand the Spanish words but hoping he would grasp the sincerity behind them.

"I cannot explain that to you," he said. "You have customs which you do not share with outsiders. I have mine. Why I wish the wells guarded I cannot tell you, but I will make you a promise on paper that you can take to the official who gave you the land. Let him judge whether my promise is good—fifty centavos a year for each *hectárea* you own, and you may live here and raise your crops in peace." Jim paused and let the lawyer translate his words.

"I will talk to my people," answered the headman.

Not until they were back in the near-by town where they were to wait for the villagers' decision did Jim, on sober thought, realize he had exceeded his authority in promising to sign a lease. He had been instructed by Albright to buy the land, not lease it. Immediately he sent a wire to Albright and then paced his room, awaiting the reply which seemed a very long time in coming. Suppose his chief should not agree? He had made a promise, accepted by the old man in good faith.

There was a knock at his door. "The message, Señor."

Albright was on the telephone. After a little discussion he told Jim to go ahead.

There proved to be two weeks of tedious negotiation before Jim won his point. Day after day he sat on the bench in front of the headman's hut, talking to a group of men gathered from all the villages, answering questions, bargaining, waiting. The brilliant tropical sun stabbed at his eyes; the hot, humid air made him dizzy. His mind ached with the effort to penetrate the fog of suspicion that hid the minds of the villagers.

Then came the day when he watched the men put crosses opposite their names. Then he stacked the little pile of pesos constituting the initial payment on the table. He had won.

As he drove away, he saw again the men's horny hands as they grasped the pen. Their fingernails were as thick as toenails, made so by heavy toil, the dirt of their fields ground into them.

"What do you suppose they'll do with the money?" Jim asked the lawyer.

"Buy drink, probably."

Some of it, of course, but not all of it, Jim thought, remembering the faces of the men as they signed.

37

LITTLE by little, Concha and Jim gained more time to be alone. Jim suspected that it was Mamá who managed it. Concha would be sent on errands at five o'clock just as he was leaving the office.

"Mamá said there is a good concert tonight," Concha told him one evening as they met. "She thought it would not break the custom of our mourning if we sat in the gallery where no one would know us."

They went to a quiet, out-of-the-way place for dinner. At the concert they shared for the first time their delight in music. Their own deep love for each other seemed to be poured into their hearts through the beautiful sounds filling the opera house. Chavez was conducting that evening, and was playing Sibelius' *Symphony No. 2 in D major.* "See what his friend says about the symphony in the program notes—that it's an expression of Finland's national feeling," Concha whispered to Jim. "It's as if he spoke for Mexico as well as Finland." She was lost in the love of the land expressed in its first movement, and then filled with emotion at the mounting intensity of the music that seemed to call a nation's spirit into life. She reached out, clasping Jim's hand. "Finland is a small country, too. We are alike."

She insisted that they walk home. "I want just to feel Mexico. Don't you feel it, Jim, this beautiful earth we are treading? *Tierra,* land, the only word we have for home. You love it, too, Jim, don't you? You were born here."

Jim realized she was caught up into one of the swift emotional tides of patriotism that swept her people.

"I care for two lands," he answered, "yours and mine."

"And so will our child," she urged.

His hand tightened on hers. To some men it would have been a disappointment to have children so early in marriage. To Jim it was incredibly wonderful. Something starved in him welcomed the responsibility.

"You have another wish, Jim," Concha said after a moment's pause. "It is a home of our own."

"Are you certain you want it, too, Concha?"

"I always have, but on account of Nacho and Mamá Grande——"

"Nacho must save himself as you did," he said gently.

They were standing in front of the Navarro house now. "Yes, Nacho must save himself. And I must save you," she said as if speaking to herself.

"From what?" he asked in astonishment.

"From this house," she replied gravely.

Jim found a piece of land to his liking in a new real-estate development. He believed Concha would like it. On the drive through the city and up to the heights, he did not speak. He was staking so much on her first impression. Finally he drew up his car. "How would this suit you?"

"Oh, Jim," she exclaimed, "I had not thought of anything so lovely!" The splendid view of valley and city held her entranced. Up and down and across the open space she walked, as if she must press her foot upon each inch of land. "I feel close to the earth here. I've felt like this only at the hacienda. You know, as if the earth were my mother. Mamá would say it is my Aztec blood."

Jim was impatient to have the house finished, but Concha knew Mexican workers could not be hurried, and she was in no hurry herself. She liked this slow growth of the house, in keeping with the growth of her child. Standing in the strong sunlight, she would watch the stone carver chiseling the soft gray volcanic rock of lintel and doorpost. As the exquisite carving, part Spanish, part Indian in feeling, grew under his hand, his splendid baritone voice would ring out in one operatic aria after another. Soon the iron *rejas* would be put in place in the windows. Soon her child and Jim's would be born.

The winter of continued sunlight was nearing an end. An occasional sharp flurry of rain marked the coming of spring. Jim often drove his car in the early morning up to the new house, with an idea of hastening the workers. He had hoped to move in before their baby was born. He was beginning to see that this would be impossible.

Maybe it was better to have Concha with her family just now, he was thinking this morning, for he foresaw he would have to be away for a while. He planned to propose to Albright that he go down to the wells at Tampico and see if the labor situation couldn't be smoothed out. Mitchell, in charge there, was putting in an unusually stiff policy with labor, now while labor was weak. The ruling clique in the government had used the rival unions to wreck the once powerful government-supported union. But now that it was wrecked, they were destroying the rival unions. There were rumors that some of the labor representatives had been murdered and some deported to the penal colony. Mitchell, he understood, was co-operating with this policy.

"Of course I know all this," said Albright when Jim took the matter up with him. "And you know I don't like that way of doing things. But Mitchell is in charge down there. Maybe it's best for us not to interfere."

"What makes me disagree with you, Mr. Albright, is that from pretty reliable sources I have it that a new labor group is forming which may prove to be very influential. Don't we need to be on friendly terms with them if they become so?"

"If that is going to happen," Albright answered, "see Mitchell by all means, tell him about the movement, and emphasize especially that we don't want anything to jeopardize our getting that lease of government property."

At first the road to Tampico wound through hilly cattle country and high mountains, then it turned east and dropped to the coastal plain. Oil fields had already been developed over an area of ten thousand square miles. Jim's first vivid impression of the blackened region was that oil blasted a country. He had the same impression of what it did to cities when he saw Tampico, center of the oil interests. It was a city where men made vast fortunes, but where vice and crime flourished. Every conversation held its undertone and overtone of avarice and lawlessness.

Jim found Mitchell to be a bland, benevolent-looking man—the kind you might be tempted to pour out your troubles to, if you didn't know his reputation. He had come here as a youth when men killed to get leases and fought to get pipe lines down. This was the school in which he had learned his business ethics. Jim soon realized that to introduce a policy of consideration for labor to such a man was to insult him.

"The upper-class Mexicans," he told Jim, "are elaborately polite, but don't let that fool you. They are filled with jealousies and suspicions like overcharged electric wires. As for labor—— Only those who are marked for defeat by their own weakness let themselves be weighted down with the weak masses, and that goes for this new crowd you're telling me about, too. I've got along because I use the Mexicans as it serves my purpose. When it helps me, I support the ruling group; when it tries to stop me, I join the revolutionists and shout for a change. Just now I'm not crying for a change." Mitchell's voice took on a sudden harshness. "I wish you could make Albright understand this.

"The men in the camps are ignorant, superstitious, and they're cunning. It's no Ladies' Aid Society I have to deal with. To see the oil is got out of the wells, transported to our sea terminal, and shipped, I need a free hand. Albright can offer as much palaver as he feels is necessary to officials in Mexico City, but not down here. It's up to him to get that lease through."

But after Jim had seen the camps he knew he had to try to win Mitchell to some concession for labor. There was enough reason here for any group to rise and cause trouble. Bad drinking water, huts worse than dog kennels, malaria and typhoid on the scale of epidemics but never treated as epidemics. No playgrounds, no anything. The workers might seem to Mitchell like a weak, inarticulate mass, but let leaders come among them and there might be such organized publicity that the whole of Mexico would be roused to protest.

He'd meet Mitchell on his own ground. He'd talk his own language, leave humanitarian reasons out of it. Put the thing on a business basis. "I've been over your camps," he told him when he entered Mitchell's office the next morning. "They stink."

Mitchell smiled benevolently. "What did you expect?"

"You are taking me too literally." Jim's voice was hard and cold. "I mean they could be made to stink to high heaven politically, once a good publicity fellow got into them. He could start the whole of Mexico talking. They'd drive you out."

"How do you think a Mexican would run a camp like this? My camp would look like the Waldorf-Astoria beside the kind he'd run."

"You can't shoot your way out with the sort of labor party I see emerging," Jim answered. "They'd ruin you and us."

Mitchell, concerned at last over the possible power of a very active and strong labor group, determined more than ever to root out any suspect. A man who made a protest over anything, he'd fire immediately, he thought to himself. A labor agitator he'd turn over to the authorities who just at present were as much against organization of the workers as he was.

"How they are treated down here isn't the real gripe," he said aloud. "The Mexicans use conditions in a camp for a red herring across the trail. What they want is to get into our offices, snoop around in there, know all we're doing. Be executives, my eye! That's what Albright's always talking about, too."

"That's not what I'm talking about," Jim answered. "Your camps lend themselves to agitators as they are now.

"Suppose," Jim went on, "Albright waived the point of Mexicans in your office which he has been advocating, couldn't you meet him on a few concessions to labor—do it now while they're weak and get their good will—do it yourself, not wait for them to force your hand?"

"First you see if Albright agrees. Then I'll think about it."

On his way back Jim, as he was very near the offset land leased from the villages, felt a curiosity to see if they had done anything useful with their money.

He found the village sleeping in the noonday sun. There was nobody about. He left his car and started along the space between the huts which did duty for a street. In the treeless expanse the light dazzled his eyes. His head began to ache. It was foolish to do this in the middle of the day. The church was just ahead of him, and he stepped in to get out of the glare. The transept was a mass of scaffolding. High up he saw two men at work painting the ceiling in an intricate pattern—blues, yellows, and browns—very Indian in its feeling.

"Señor—" one of the men had recognized him and was bowing to him over the edge of the scaffolding—"it is you who gave us this beautiful ceiling." He spoke in broken Spanish. As Jim went back along the street he saw a new, shining plow standing by the headman's house. So these Indian villages did want to improve their conditions! He was more than ever convinced that their settlements around the oil wells should be improved.

When Jim talked Mitchell's answer over with Albright, his response was at first indirect. "I think that either Bob Mitchell's ideas or mine will survive in the company, but not both," he said. "It's a fight between Mitchell and me on policy. If he wins, they'll put a man of his views in my place." Jim looked at Albright, contrasting him with the black-haired, bland Mitchell. Albright was the clean-cut type of American. His blue eyes were direct and honest in their gaze. His light-colored hair and mustache and clear skin seemed to contribute to a kind of sanitary cleanliness of spirit so lacking in Mitchell.

"I should not find such a situation very much to my liking." Jim was indeed disturbed at the thought of Albright's being out. He had a genuine affection for him and, besides, he would not find it easy to work with a man who had Mitchell's slant.

"Why don't we compromise with Mitchell now, before it is too late?" Jim asked. "See if he won't clean up down at the camp if we stop urging that the policy of the company be changed to let Mexicans into executive positions. That's the thing that makes him see red."

For some time Albright sat thinking. Then he said, "Yes. I'll surrender that point for the time being if you can get Mitchell to advocate decent houses and some kind of a dispensary."

"I can at least try," said Jim.

~~~~~~~~~~~~~~~~~~~~~~~~~~*38*~~~~~~

More and more Ignacio was becoming an onlooker in his own country. He had no faith in race or class—Spanish, Mexican, or Indian; neither conservative nor liberal. Like a remote, elegant god, he surveyed a world from which his superiority set him apart to judge the weaknesses of all. He had no more faith in Pablo and Guadalupe, representing free Mexico, than he had in Ramón, offshoot of old Mexico. With cynical detachment he watched all three and gathered pleasure from their individual weaknesses. As for the leaders of the new Mexico—! The noble-sounding phrases of the Revolution were as hollow as drums. Hacienda reform! Why, these social reformers had become *hacendados* themselves.

This afternoon he thought he would look in on Guadalupe. He had had an argument with his grandmother, and before his mother he had spoken ill of the Church. How he could have done so he could scarcely understand. In all his rebellions against the family, his mother had been exempt. He held her in reverence, and although he maintained his aloofness from the Church, before her—until today—he had always shown it respect.

His grandmother had been pressing him again to marry. "A man without any filial emotion!" she had taunted him.

"Perhaps it is time, if Mexico ever knows peace, to let the defeated swallow the victorious," he had answered. "If I do not marry it means one less Spanish family for the Indians to absorb."

"You are a traitor to your Spanish blood," cried Mamá Grande.

"If we disappear it will be an atonement for our sins of aggression in this country." Ignacio only half believed what he was saying, but when Mamá Grande pressed him as she was now doing, he had an insane desire to throw over every tradition.

Mamá, who had been sitting at her embroidery frame, said quietly, "If you wish to make atonement, my son, that could and should be done within the Church."

"The Church!" Nacho had thrown back his head and laughed. "That despoiler!"

"It is true," his mother had answered, "the Church has erred in temporal matters here in Mexico, but its spiritual benefits remain unchallenged. Refuse not the comforts of the Church, my son!"

He had risen at her words and hurried toward the door, angry with his grandmother for causing such a betrayal of his feelings in his mother's presence. The profound sadness of her eyes told him how deeply he had hurt her. He wanted to get away before he surrendered to both his grandmother's and mother's demands upon him. But his mother had followed him out and walked with him along the gallery. "I see, my son, that you have for the time lost your faith," she had said in a somber voice freighted with sorrow. "I thought until now you were only indifferent. I shall ask the Holy Ghost to show you the difference between the Church as a spiritual body and a temporal one."

His mother's words had cut deep. He wanted to make whole again his cynical armor. Guadalupe Villar might furnish him with the means. He had had up to the last few months a humble devotion to his work

which Ignacio respected, but now Guadalupe talked no more of
agrarian reform and evidently he had given up working for it. That
was the way with these reformers of Mexico. No stability.

It was long past the siesta hour, but Guadalupe still dozed in his
chair. Today he felt dull and listless; some days he felt restless. He
was beginning to court lethargy, for it blocked off his feeling of use-
lessness and the chasm of poverty which yawned just below his feet.
The only position he had been able to secure, since the government
had dropped him, was that of guide for one of the tourist bureaus
when there was a sudden rush of business. For many days now there
had been no call for his services.

"There is the bell, my husband. Discouragement is a luxury, isn't it,
allowed only to such as this Ignacio who so often comes to see us? It
is probably he, waiting impatiently outside. Hurry! Open the door
that such an important man shall not be delayed. It is odd, isn't it, that
of all who used to gather here to talk of the fruits of the Revolution,
only this rich one who did not believe there were any such fruits should
still come to see us?"

"You are not just, Cholita." Guadalupe roused himself in answer
to her torrent of bitter words. "You know that the others are poor
like ourselves, and many of them have gone back to their towns, hoping there to make a living. Remember, we haven't the money now to
take the bus even to the edge of the city where some of our friends still
live. The important thing at present is to pay the rent on this house.
We must not step down into poverty."

"Do not keep the rich young man waiting!" cried Soledad.

But when Guadalupe opened the door, it was not Ignacio but a
stranger who stood there. Half filling the street was a large touring
car with two women in it. "Are you the Guadalupe Villar I was told is
a good guide and interpreter?" the man asked.

"I am that one," said Guadalupe.

"We'd like you to come with us right away. Our regular guide has
failed us."

As they drove away, Soledad saw Ignacio's car turn into their street.
"My husband is not here," she called from the doorway as he drew
up in front of the house and got out.

Ignacio, not accustomed to being excluded from any place he wished
to enter, gave the slowly closing door a sudden push and stepped
within. "Yes, his car passed me. He must be in the service of the Mil-

lionaire Socialists to be riding about in such grandeur." There was a mocking note in his voice which Soledad resented.

Her black, slightly prominent eyes smoldered. "He is supporting us by acting as guide to tourists when he can get the chance. Of his struggle you have not cared to learn. I shall now say to you what I have long wanted to say. I am not like my husband. I have not his gentleness. Let there be no patronizing today, my rich one."

"Why should I patronize you?"

"Why you do is your own affair. I am only concerned with the fact that you have come here time after time, strutting about like a gaudy peacock, surveying us as though we were barn fowls."

Ignacio laughed, highly amused by Soledad's anger. He liked her spirit. He liked her. He liked her round, full figure. She was older than he. He wondered what it would be like to know her intimately. "You'd make a very nice peahen. Since your husband is away——"

"Get out!" Soledad gasped.

But Ignacio made no move to go. With sudden interest he noticed she showed signs of strain. For the moment he understood the pride and the fear she and Guadalupe were living under. "You are a teacher. Can't you get into the public schools and help until things look up for Guadalupe?" he asked with rare gentleness.

"I have tried, but I am not a Catholic, and it is difficult."

"As governess then?"

"To the rich?" Soledad was immediately on her guard.

"I'm thinking of my sister. She is soon to have a child. I have been advocating that he should hear only the pure Spanish from the very start—no Indian nurse from whom he will learn that dreadful sing-song of the illiterate."

"From whom he will gain Indian strength," Soledad answered.

"The Indian cult so popular among your friends," he corrected.

Soledad laughed, but not bitterly. Tragedy and gaiety lay close together in her, and her anger had spent itself. "If you are our friend, you may stay and we can talk about the teaching. Of course you mean a nursemaid." From under her lowered lids slyly she glanced up at him. Her red lips were parted, showing her even white teeth.

Again, as so often in her presence, Ignacio felt a definite attraction. "I'll let you know about my sister."

Later, when he rose to go, he hesitated a moment wondering if she would let him kiss her, decided not to risk it. He had already forgotten his promise to speak to Concha about her.

~~~~~~~~~~~~~~~~~~~~~~~~~~*39*~~~~~~

GUADALUPE VILLAR found his work as guide particularly onerous during this trip. He was sleeping in the poorest hotels, eating almost nothing in order to save all he earned to pay the rent. He felt tired and unable to be interesting.

Today he had taken his party to a fair. "They seem to have so little to sell," said the North American he was serving. "Why, there is nothing here but corn, women's *rebozos,* and sleeping mats. What are their homes like? Don't they have furniture in them?"

"No." Guadalupe knew many of these villages. He had surveyed the land around them although none of it had been given to them. He thought of the dark windowless huts, the earth floors where they spread their sleeping mats at night. Sometimes there was a table lent from house to house for the festival of a wedding or birth. The only bit of color in the drab interiors was a crude picture of the Virgin of Guadalupe. He thought of the shallow saucers Soledad had of deep blue and brown, no two alike in their freehand decoration of green cactus, bursting yellow and red flowers, little brown men and browner and very humorous burros. To Guadalupe these saucers were a spontaneous expression of his people, the upflung fire of the Indian personality breaking the mold of misery in which their lives were cast. "There is some interesting pottery over here," he said, thinking to distract the tourists' curiosity from the plight of his people.

That night he could not sleep, his own insecurity pressing in upon him. He and his country, what had they to hope for? He felt desperate, alone, and faint with hunger, for he had not dined the evening before, with the idea of saving every centavo for the rent.

Very early in the morning he went out, entered the first restaurant he found open, and ate until he was satisfied. Now that he had eaten, he could think clearly and quietly. Somewhere there must be a position for him, a piece of work he could do. Despite this backward step in the agrarian reform, the country in many ways was advancing. Mexico City was growing. Roads were being built to connect his country with other countries. He was well trained. There must be a place where he could earn a living commensurate with his abilities. He straightened his shoulders with renewed self-respect and determination.

He thought of his last conversation with James Buchanan. Guadalupe realized now he had been too bitter that day over the defeat of the agrarian reform to meet Buchanan halfway. But they had parted friends. Now Buchanan's last words came back to him: "You are too good a man to be long out of employment." He would go to see his friend when he returned to the city. Perhaps Buchanan could give him a job.

That day the tourists found Guadalupe a fascinating guide. He took them to the village where the pottery they had seen at the fair was made. In a courtyard littered with yellow corn husks Rosa the potter knelt on the ground and fashioned with no other instrument than her deft hands a water jug of a strange gray earth which turned jet-black in its firing. The women of Guadalupe's party were enchanted by Rosa with her delicate brown skin. In her hair were twined bright woolen bands of yellow and purple. She wore a pink blouse and black woolen skirt, its fluted white top bunched like a spread accordion at her waist in the back.

Guadalupe told them of the long history of this black pottery and a little of Rosa, a descendant of the first potter of the village.

At the restaurant that evening he borrowed a guitar and played for his patrons. He did not sing the words, but he played the tune about Soledad that began with a lullaby and ended with a soldier's song, the one he had improvised when his hope for a Mexican middle class seemed certain to be realized—farmhouses like those he had seen in America, silos close by red barns, and long village streets with comfortable houses on either side, one of them his and Soledad's.

On their return to the city, the tip the tourists gave him was good, and Guadalupe pocketed it without too much humiliation. He was thinking of his visit to Buchanan. He and Soledad celebrated that evening. After all, if everything was to be all right from now on, should they not be merry after so much despair?

Jim was genuinely glad to see Guadalupe. "I've meant to call you up and see how things were going with you, but I've been busy. A new job and lots to learn. How is everything?"

"Of course I want most to hear of your work," Guadalupe answered, following the polite formula of his people.

At last the greetings were over, but Guadalupe found it hard to state the reason for his call. It seemed so evident Buchanan thought he had come in a purely social capacity. Finally he plunged desperately into his need for a job. "I thought perhaps you could use me in some small executive position, either here or at the wells. I believe I could really help in bringing about a harmonious relationship with your labor."

Jim leaned back in his swivel chair, his gaze wandering from Villar to the ceiling. He did not know what to say to this young Mexican. He did not like to turn him away, but "no executive positions for Mexicans" was the very crux of the compromise he hoped to bring about between Mitchell and Albright.

And now here was Guadalupe, a man he deeply respected, in need of just such a position as he had agreed should not be given to Mexicans! He could not go back on the arrangements, much as he would have liked to help his friend, fully as he believed Villar was fitted for an executive job. For one moment he let himself dream of what he could do with Guadalupe if the oil business were in his hands. He'd put him in charge of those camps of Mitchell's and give him the go-ahead signal to make a model settlement of them.

"I am sorry," he said, putting the idea aside, knowing it was impossible. "Personally I should like to have you associated with me. I believe we could work together, but I must abide by the policy of my company." He did not need to say what that policy was. Villar knew.

Guadalupe rose. His manner was so formal, so remote, that Jim had difficulty in realizing they had ever been friends. Friendship between them seemed brought to an abrupt end.

Soledad, too, had been thinking how Guadalupe could find a place befitting his abilities. There was Pablo. And yet she did not entirely trust Pablo. But when Villar came back from his interview with Buchanan, she saw she must act.

"Why not try to get in the labor department? That is where the struggle will come when we free ourselves from these new rich. Why not go to Pablo?"

"Pablo!" exclaimed Guadalupe. "Who knows where Pablo stands? Perhaps he belongs to the remnants of the old outfit. If he does, he's hanging around the Millionaire Socialists."

"And perhaps he doesn't!" snapped Soledad. "There's a new movement starting up. Labor isn't going to be downed forever. Perhaps Pablo is working with them. Perhaps he's working with both," she added with that cynicism she never completely lost. "How do you know unless you talk to him?"

With a shrewd, penetrating glance Pablo looked Guadalupe over. "What's the matter, Lupe? Out, I suppose, like a lot of the other idealists?"

"Out, yes," Guadalupe answered. "About the idealist, I'm not so certain."

With some indirectness Pablo suggested that Villar come over to them. "Them," he indicated, was no longer the defunct labor group, but something new growing up.

"I'll certainly consider it."

"Come along with me, then, where we can talk. My car is just around the corner." When they were well out of the city Pablo began, "I believe I can trust you. It's a job for an idealist."

Guadalupe felt more than a little irritation at this harping on idealism. His recent encounter with Buchanan had shattered his last idealistic dream. All he wanted was to cling to a rung of the ladder that would hold him up from submergence in poverty. He glanced over the car. "I thought from the look of things, you were attached to the millionaire labor official. Just where do you stand, Pablo?"

"My left hand," said Pablo with a smile, "doesn't know what my right hand does. That's one of your favorite sayings, isn't it? I think I've heard you use it. I've come to believe it's a very good saying."

Guadalupe searched Pablo's face. It had changed somewhat since he had last seen him. The muscles had tightened; the expression of his eyes was shrewder. "For which hand am I to work?"

"You can decide that for yourself. The government is trying to attract more foreign capital, as you may know. The reactionaries have petitioned the government, asking that new foreign capital be promised exemption from taxation for five to ten years. We want to stop that. And we want to get some active militant unions started. How would you like to be our representative at one of the oil wells? We want the workers to stand for Mexican labor—ninety percent must be Mexican, not only unskilled but technical; better wages, too, of course, and better living conditions. It's a long job; we've only just started. I think I can manage to get you in as a stillman. Then it's up to you to get your organization going."

So here was his chance, thought Guadalupe, to organize against foreign-owned concerns like Buchanan's outfit. "Yes, I'll accept," he said slowly.

"Can't I go with you?" asked Soledad when he told her of his new position.

"It is secret business. I must go alone, but each week my salary will be delivered to you." Guadalupe felt a glow of pride—he was able again to speak of a salary! "You are to keep this house against my return. The Revolution is not dead. Whatever happens, you will remember that, won't you, Cholita?"

40

EACH morning with the other men Guadalupe went to his work, although each day it seemed more difficult to rise. The dampness coming up through the thin mat on which he slept had set his bones to aching, and the long hours of toil left him exhausted. Jim Buchanan's refusal had seemed the final frustration, closing the way forever to professional achievement. His dream of an ever-increasing middle class, of which he was to be a modest member, no longer attended him. Nor could he any more get pleasure from reciting statistics about a million serfs freed and given land in the hacienda program, when he saw these serfs, not in alluring figures of six naughts, but poverty-stricken and ignorant like the men around him—men like himself, men clinging to a raft against drowning, one by one dropping back into poverty.

He had taken the job Pablo offered, mainly that he might hide himself away. At the wells he was unknown. The heavy work and his hopeless companions gave him a sense of crawling deep into obscurity. First with despair and then with stoicism he accepted his fate.

Too conscientious to shirk the task for which he had come, after a time he began to talk to the men of a new organization. At first he met with nothing but suspicion. What had unions ever brought them? What could you expect of any leader? So often since the Revolution the leaders had made promises and failed to fulfill them. Many who worked at the wells were here because the land to which they belonged had not been given to them as the Revolution had promised.

In bitterness they remembered how they had believed first in Obregón, then Calles, and, of course, Morones—and at this very moment Morones possessed a ring with a diamond as big as a centavo and a great car. What had they but toil and hardship?

"But are not your wages higher?" Guadalupe asked.

"Yes."

"And you have many privileges you did not once have."

"Yes. But bit by bit they are being taken from us. If it serves our masters, we shall lose all we have gained."

The spirit of the crusader was aroused again in Guadalupe. These men must not lose their faith. Some way, somehow, he must give it back to them. Gradually they came to trust him because of his goodness. One day he asked them if they would join an independent union in order to protest against the universal minimum wage of forty centavos a day, just made law. One after another gave his consent. Guadalupe felt a warm singing inside him. These men were beginning again to have faith.

He did not know that the government had declared unions illegal.

41

Jim wanted Concha to enter the American hospital for the birth of their child, but Mamá Grande was outraged at the idea. This first great-grandchild of hers must be born under the Navarro roof, as her children and grandchildren had been.

"I'd feel safer about her if she were at the hospital," he had said to Mamá, hoping to win his point through her.

"It would be a great disappointment to Mamá Grande—and maybe to me," she had added. "And I think really Concha would like to be here in her home, although she wants to do whatever will make you happiest."

Reluctantly he yielded. But as the time drew near, he began to wish he had not. Suppose something should happen! They were much better equipped at the hospital for emergencies. The family doctor made light of his anxiety, saying, "Most of the exclusive members of society prefer the accouchement to take place at home."

One afternoon in early May as Jim returned from his office he found the house in unusual stir. The doors were opened into the once secret chapel, tapers alight before the statue of the Virgin. Maids were hurrying about. Mamá Grande's voice could be heard giving commands. He hastened up the stairs to his wife's room. She was lying with her eyes closed. As he bent over her she whispered, "I think it will be soon." His heart seemed caught and squeezed.

"My son," said Mamá as she walked with him to the door, "this is something Concha must do for herself. You're not to worry. The doctor says he's not expecting a difficult birth."

As he went back along the gallery, he heard a light step behind him and turned to see Louisa. Taking his arm, she paced back and forth with him. "You don't need to act as if you were giving birth to the baby yourself. That's for Concha to do. Ramón, at a time like this, would be off having a good time. He'd come home only to see the results, and he'd expect the results to be what he wished them to be—a son."

There was something in Louisa's tone that made Jim look at her more closely. Was she unhappy with Ramón, or was it that she envied Concha the prospect of the child? "I'd be just as pleased to have a little girl," he answered, "if she looked like Concha."

"Concha, Concha," Louisa mocked. "I wouldn't know what to do with a man like you." She dropped his arm and moved about with irritated energy. Jim had never seen her like this. Her eyes were as bright as the stone they resembled. "I must go now, but I'll be back later. Please take me to my car."

After she had gone he wandered through the great house, often taking out his watch. An hour, two, passed. Louisa had come back and Ramón with her. Ignacio joined them. The two men went into the dining room for a drink.

At last Mamá called down from the gallery above. "You may see Concha now, Jim. You have a son."

Louisa turned away. He heard her say with a little laugh, "How pleased Ramón will be!"

Jim had an uneasy certainty that Louisa believed Ramón still cared for Concha. Then, as he entered his wife's room, he forgot all about it. Mamá Grande met him at the door. "It's been a very easy birth," she told him. "You see there was no need to take her away."

Indeed when he first looked at Concha she seemed only a little pale, touched with a new beauty. Around her shoulders had been laid a light blue robe. The masses of her hair formed a soft halo around her head. She was looking down at the baby held in her arms, and her face was alight. "See what we have, my husband!" With a hand that trembled he pulled the blanket away from the little bundle in her arms.

Then the family tiptoed into the room, in subdued voices offering their congratulations. He heard Vicente say to Mamá Grande, "I've never seen a lovelier mother. Almost the Madonna seems to have come down to us." Vicente's words spoken to him before he was married came back to Jim. "We worship our wives, something quite different from your feeling for them." Everything had been done, he realized, to induce that feeling in him. He had a great longing to bring their life down out of the clouds. Concha and he had still to learn to be close companions. She knew so little of his work. Gently he lifted his son from her arms. The baby was fair-haired like himself.

"He looks just like Louisa!" one of the aunts exclaimed as the family crowded round.

"He looks like me," said Mamá Grande.

"Whoever it is he resembles, he's an imperious little soul," said Jim. "Listen to that cry of his."

"He must be named for his great-grandfather and grandfather." Mamá Grande announced, "Julián Vicente Buchanan y Navarro."

At last they had all gone, and Jim sat by the bed holding his son. Concha had fallen asleep. The room was very still. Pulling back the flap of the blanket, he examined the baby's face, lifted one of his hands. It's shaped like Vicente's, he thought, and Ignacio's. He is more Spanish than Concha, with his long skull, and narrow face. How had they two begot him?

"My dear!"

Concha had wakened. He grasped her hand with his free one.

"It is a long name, isn't it? We'll call him Vicentito—Tito for short. He is like you, Jim."

The next night, Jim was awakened. Someone was shaking him. Then he realized it was Mamá's voice saying, "Concha is very sick. She is asking for you."

"What has happened?" He threw back the covers, was on his feet in an instant. "She was resting quietly when I left her."

"She had a chill about midnight. There is an infection. I am sorry, my son, that we did not do as you asked. This might not have happened in the hospital. But it is too late now. The doctor is here."

When Jim entered the room, he found him just leaving. Taking Jim outside, he told him to send for the priest.

"You despair of her, then?"

"Yes."

"If you feel you have done all you can, are you willing I should send for my doctor?" In a crisis Jim involuntarily reached out for his own people. This Mexican physician had a good reputation, but Jim wanted someone who did not so easily interpret failure as divine will. He wanted someone who would fight. "I do not believe my wife needs to die. I take it you have given up the case." Jim pressed for an answer.

"It will be useless to call another. The office of the physician ends where the priest's begins. But it is as you wish." The man bowed himself down the stairs.

Jim hurried to the telephone, and then, incredible as it seemed to him, he had to urge his doctor to come.

"I do not like to take the case from a Mexican. I do not wish to lay myself open to the charge of taking his practice away from him."

"My God," Jim almost shouted into the telephone, "my wife is dying! Surely you'll not stand on professional etiquette now."

"I must have the consent of one member of the family, or her own," came the voice over the telephone.

Jim raced up the stairs to find Mamá Grande in charge in the sickroom. "Are you willing I should have my doctor?" he asked her in a low tone.

"We will leave her in the good God's care. I have sent for Father Cristóbal," she answered.

Jim leaned over his wife. She must help him now. He could see that the fever which had followed the chill was high. Her cheeks were a deep red. When he spoke to her, her eyes as she opened them were glazed and lifeless. "Concha, listen!" He tried with all his will to fix her attention. "I want Prescott. He can save you I am certain, but you must tell me you want him—or else he will not come."

Slowly her eyes cleared, and as if making some effort to come back from a far-off place, she regarded him intently. "No, I must not die. My baby——"

"You consent?"

"Yes." Her eyelids fell back over her eyes as if without her volition.

Hour after hour they fought for her life. Never for one moment did Jim acknowledge they could be defeated in their struggle to save her. On the third night the nurse and the doctor stood at the foot of the bed consulting. Jim saw they were about to give up. He leaned over Concha, whispering, "You must help us fight, Concha."

From somewhere deep in a soft oblivion free from the pain closing over her, she roused herself. Jim's words had reached her. Out of the mist, clearing, death stood by her bed, but there stood also her husband, the man she loved, and his face was set with purpose. Her frail, drifting spirit and his strong one were forged together. She had strength now to fight that figure of death—drawing back a little more, a little more. Out of the dark shadows a light began to glow, growing brighter and brighter. Oh, the ineffable sweetness of the figure in the midst of the light—the all-understanding Virgin Mother! "Do not try to escape pain and suffering, my child." Concha tried to hold out her arms, but they fell weakly upon the bed.

Jim saw her smile. No doubting, there was a change for the better. The doctor stepped forward and took her pulse. He beckoned Jim out of the room. "We've won. You'd better get some sleep."

42

Jim was away from the office a couple of weeks. The morning he went back, Albright called him and handed him a flat, legal-looking envelope bearing the stamp of the Mexican government.

"You don't mean we've secured the lease of that offset land?" Jim could scarcely believe it even though he was looking at papers with the proper signature affixed. Both he and Albright had despaired of ever getting it. Why, two weeks ago on his last day at the office before Concha's illness, the official in the department of government land had told him flatly they would not grant the request. And Jim felt certain he meant it. He was not one of the new, eager-to-get-rich officials, but a man left over from the revolutionary regime, and possessed of a sincere nationalism.

"Grand!" said Jim. "But I don't understand it."

"Strangely enough, it's nothing to be very happy about, at least not too happy." Jim noticed now that Albright looked anxious. "I doubt if it's been done because we've overcome their suspicion," Albright went on. "Quite the opposite. Almost as soon as I received the papers I had a call from the British company, and they are as mad as hatters over the deal. They didn't get their share. They accuse me of double-crossing them."

"Trouble between us?—that's bad!"

"I think that is just what it was done for. To divide us. What do you know, Jim, of the new labor group forming? My opinion is it's pretty strong under cover and that it's just waiting for an opportunity to revive the oil controversy. In such a case they don't want the two big oil interests—England and the States—standing together."

"I suppose our next job," Jim answered, "is to do what we can to smooth things over with the British company."

"Whatever you can do, Jim, do. I am not in a position to say much. There is no way to prove I didn't maneuver to keep them out. They know me to be friendly with the Mexicans. They think I used that friendliness to double-cross them."

~~~~~~~~~~~*43*~~~~~

CONCHA'S convalescence was a slow, hard struggle, extending over months. Sometimes it seemed to her family that Concha would be a permanent invalid, but Jim never accepted such a fate for her. During the long weeks that she lay in bed each evening he took over the care of her. He would bring the baby in to her, putting him in her arms, but placing his hand beneath so that she was not bearing the child's full weight, for her arms had little strength. He talked to her of the new house, finished now, simply waiting for her to furnish it. Especially he dwelt on Tito's nursery. He sent to New York for samples of wallpaper, insisted she choose between nursery rhymes or funny animals for a dado. He brought her lovely ornaments picked up at antique shops, things to be put in the new house.

During the day Concha's sick body asserted itself over her mind and kept her floundering in a chaotic world of apprehension and fears—she would die and Tito would be motherless and grow up to be bad. Tito was marked by her sickness. But when she heard Jim's car drive into the patio, everything that had been difficult while he was away seemed to be taken into his hands and put in order. When he entered her room, her sick self found itself transplanted into his well one. Sometimes when he was not there, her need of Jim became so great that she would cling to an old coat he liked to slip on in the evening. She would wrap it around her, giving the excuse that she was cold.

Then, as she grew better, her apprehensions over Tito gave place to the fear that she was spoiling Jim's life. One night she could bear it no longer. "I know, Jim, I am wrecking your life. Tell me what to do."

"Listen, dearest," he said, drawing her close, "I'd rather be married to you sick than any other woman well."

"Oh, my dear," she cried and sobbed out her relief on his shoulder.

Gradually strength and interest came back to her; but secluded so long from everything that might worry her, she scarcely touched Jim's world now.

It was a world, Jim realized, growing increasingly more complex. Relations were still strained between them and the British over the lease. Conditions were strained, too, between the Mexico City and Tampico offices. Mitchell had never met Albright even halfway on the labor question. The treatment of labor at the wells had become an embarrassment to Albright and Jim when they were negotiating for the offset land. It was an increasing embarrassment to them when there were small differences with government officials over distribution centers in cities and towns, the use of tank cars on the new roads, and numerous other matters which constantly needed smoothing out. Jim found that more and more the company's treatment of labor was dragged into the discussion.

This was only one of many indications that new leaders were coming up among the working class who were going to demand return to the reforms of the Revolution. There was great discontent with the present regime. The rim of poverty around the city had deepened again. None of the newspapers dared mention the growing number of suicides, the swarms of prostitutes, but by popular ballad and anecdote anger was being expressed. The street in Cuernavaca where the Jefe Maximo had built his house was now called "the Street of Ali Baba and His Forty Thieves." Jim did not believe the people would be denied the fruits of the Revolution much longer. Then subsoil rights would again become an issue.

If American business and Mexico were pitted against each other in bitter controversy, a controversy that would fill the papers, what would Concha think of his part in maintaining the position of the United States? That he would have to do as a representative of the company. The only thing he could hope for was that some compromise could be reached with labor. With Mitchell's stand, it looked doubtful. He remembered uneasily the night of the concert when Concha had revealed how deep within her lay the love of her country. Well, perhaps they would be in their own house by then. Together and alone, they might find a common ground. Concha would soon be well enough now.

Everything seemed incredibly beautiful to Concha as the year moved toward the rainy season. She loved the first mounting of the clouds over the mountains. Then the rainy season was upon them with its heavy fall of shining rain. Daily now she walked out along the gallery and down first one, then two, flights of stairs to meet Jim on his return from his office.

They had been married two years now and Tito had had his first birthday, was two months into his second year. He was learning to walk. Often the two of them would go slowly along the gallery and wait at the top of the stairs for Jim to come bounding toward them, take his son in his arms, then kiss them both.

Today they were hiding behind one of the newel posts at the foot of the stairs planning to surprise him. They had never before come this far to meet him. As Jim got out of his car, Concha noticed the tense, driving expression in his face—the North American look her grandfather used to call Protestant. She had the odd feeling she did not know the man she was married to. Then Tito, unable to wait until his father reached the foot of the stairs, came out from his hiding place, and Jim's face took on its customary smile of welcome.

44

SOLEDAD was very lonely after Guadalupe left for the oil wells. One day on her way home from market, a ragged urchin insisted on carrying her basket.

"But I carry my own," she told him. "See, I am strong like an Indian woman!"

"But I wish to eat," was his plaintive response.

"When did you eat last?" she asked.

"I do not remember."

Impulsively Soledad took the boy by the shoulder, meaning to give him food.

"Please, Señora, do not take me to the police," he begged. "If I carry your basket every morning, I shall not need to steal ever again." Then, as he saw they were approaching a shop that sold bread, he relaxed in her grasp.

After he had eaten, Soledad made him take her to his home, which was in an old mansion divided into sections for the families of the poor. Still holding him by the shoulder, she made him lead her across the patio, around babies, dogs, and piles of refuse, between lines of clothes flapping in their faces. In the dark cubicle he called home, a woman knelt over her grinding stone. Her upper garment was open to the waist, her body wet with sweat. A baby was slung on her back; another sat on the damp stone floor at her side. As the woman reached for the boy, Soledad stepped in front of him. "He has done no harm. I have come to see if he may take a small position in my home."

The matter was soon arranged. The boy's father long ago had left her. The father of her other children did not like this extra mouth to feed.

Soledad was happier now. The house wasn't so silent. Guadalupe's going had been a terrible thing. To have his protection taken away brought back the cruel memory of those days before he had come into her life. But now, caring for someone else, she was able to forget the frightening past.

But after a few months Guadalupe's letters ceased to come. Had something happened to him? And how was she to pay the rent and care for Tony? She bethought herself of what Ignacio had said the last time he had come to see them. He had spoken about a position, caring for his sister's child. She counted back and realized it had been over a year since then. For Soledad, to think was to act. She sent a note to Ignacio's sister, stating her qualifications and asking if she might come to see her.

Concha, realizing that during her long illness Tito had been spoiled by his Indian *nana,* and in fact by all the family, thought a nurse who had been a teacher might be very good for him. Soledad had given

Ignacio as a reference, saying he had known her husband. What Ignacio said about Soledad when Concha talked to him made her decide to interview the woman.

Soledad glanced scornfully about as she passed through the gate and stood in the patio of the Navarro house, waiting for consent to see Señora Buchanan. Space enough here for many families to live in decency and comfort. The old man at the gate was about to lead her around to the servants' entrance when Concha spoke to him from the balcony above.

"You are to go up those stairs," he told Soledad, pointing to one of the two stairways across the patio. As she reached the turn she looked up and saw standing at the top a tall young woman. In the upward climb she kept her eyes on that waiting figure, for the purpose of deciding whether she liked Señora Buchanan enough to serve her. With characteristic realism, Soledad was not fooled as to the nature of the work. She was going out to service in this rich Spanish household. Nevertheless, the decision to accept that service would have to be an emotional matter. If she did not like Ignacio's sister, she would find some other way of caring for Tony and keeping the house against Guadalupe's return.

By the time she arrived at the top step, she had decided that Concha bore no resemblance to Ignacio. Had she done so, Soledad believed she would have refused to serve her. Nor did Ignacio's sister have his arrogant bearing. That she was beautiful pleased Soledad; that she was unassuming pleased her more. Her defenses were already weakening.

Concha studied the advancing woman for the purpose of deciding whether the precious Tito should be committed to her care.

For a moment neither woman spoke. Then Soledad said, "I find us *simpáticas.*"

Concha smiled, letting it pass that Soledad appeared to be making the decision. "I will show you my son." She led the way along the gallery to a large, high-ceilinged room. But the room was empty. "Tito, Tito, where are you?" she called.

He rules her, Soledad thought, listening to the sound of alarm in Concha's voice.

There was a tiny, mischievous laugh. Following it, they came upon a sturdy child about a year and a half old trying to make his way up the stairs leading to the next floor. His hair was red-gold in the shaft of sunshine which shone down upon him. His small, long-fingered hand clasped the rail of the stairs as he tried to pull himself up. He gave one glance over his shoulder and sat down.

"What are you waiting for?" his mother asked.

He held out his arms to be carried.

"No, I will not carry you," Soledad answered him. Tito stared at her. Never before had anyone, not even Mamá Grande, refused to do his bidding. Still he surveyed her. Then, seeing there was no help, with great difficulty he crawled from stair to stair, Soledad pushing his fat little bottom from behind. As she leaned over him for a last push, he turned around and put his arm around her neck.

"I think Tito has decided it," said Concha.

When they stood on the wide space of the roof, Concha's gaze went immediately to the surrounding mountains, their contour clearly marked against the sky. Soledad looked at the city. She had never seen it from such a vantage point. From here miles of straight streets angled out like spokes of a wheel. The low, flat roofs were cut here and there by tall modern buildings. In the light-drenched, still air, the smoke from factory chimneys rose in gray, straight columns. No blurring haze or mist made their outlines waver.

"It's always beautiful," said Concha.

Soledad gave a short, quick laugh. "For people like you, maybe."

Concha was startled, the aristocrat in her offended. For a moment she drew back. Just then Tito pulled on Soledad's hand. As she stooped to lift him, his mother saw an expression of tenderness pass over Soledad's face. It will be good for Tito to be with this woman, she thought. He must not grow up to be self-willed as Nacho is.

"I can stay only until five each day. I have a boy of my own to look after." Soledad continued to take the initiative in the bargaining.

As they went down the stairs Mamá Grande met them. "This is Soledad Villar, who has consented to be Tito's governess," said Concha.

"*Consented!*" With vehemence Doña María spat the word out, then turned and walked away.

A satisfied smile passed over Soledad's face.

A few days later, at the end of the siesta hour as Jim was going down the last flight of steps to the patio where his car stood, he came upon Tito laboriously making his way up the stairs, the new nurse encouraging, pushing. "I am glad to see you are making my son work," he told her.

"I believe I have heard my husband speak of you in the past—Guadalupe Villar—no doubt you remember him?" Guadalupe had told her of Jim's refusal to employ him. She had been hoping for just such an opportunity.

"I hope your husband is well," Jim said a little stiffly.

"I do not know. He went away many months ago to find work. I have not heard from him of late. The last word I had was from Tampico."

For some time after Guadalupe Villar had visited him Jim had not been able to forget the look of hopelessness which had settled over Villar's face and his quick withdrawal from friendship. All the charm and politeness which Villar possessed to so marked a degree had vanished. However much Jim might try to accept the prevailing idea that Mexicans were not efficient, he knew in his heart that he had identified himself with Mexico fundamentally because he liked and believed in its people. He knew Villar was capable of filling a small executive position, as were many other Mexicans. He believed they could accomplish certain things in their country that an American never could. He was bothered, too, by the fact that he had lost Villar as a friend.

But in the months that followed, what with the multiplicity of his problems at the office and Concha's sickness, he had forgotten Villar. Now Soledad's presence brought him vividly to mind. He was genuinely disturbed at the bad fortune which had evidently overtaken him, for why else would his wife be in need of this position as nurse in his family? After he was back in the office Soledad's last words came into his mind. Tampico! She had spoken of letters sent her from Tampico. She had also said she had not heard from Guadalupe for a long time. Could he have been the man Mitchell had had arrested at their wells for labor agitation? But the idea was fantastic.

Up to the time she had met Jim on the stairs, Soledad had determined only to finish out the day. She had had two encounters during the morning with Mamá Grande, from which Mamá Grande had come off victor. Now she decided she would not leave. The irony of her position amused her. Two men of the household would find it convenient to avoid her. Ignacio did not want his grandmother to know of his friendship with her, and Tito's father very evidently did not wish to be reminded of Guadalupe. The situation gave her bitter happiness.

~~~~~~~~~~~~~~~~~~~~~~~~~~~~~~~~~~~~~~ *45* ~~~~~~~~

CONCHA was almost well now, and the doctor had promised that next week she might begin to furnish her house. This afternoon she was going to Louisa's to meet some relatives of Ramón's newly arrived from Spain. Jim had come home early to accompany her. Ignacio was joining them. When they entered the Fuentes' apartment, Louisa stood at the farther end of the *sala* with a group of strangers.

"Those are the relatives. They belong to the old Monarchist party," Ignacio said to Jim. "I saw something of them when Ramón and I were in Spain."

After they had been introduced, Ramón drew Jim aside. "There's a German here I'd like to have you talk to. Herr von Brenen came over on the ship with our Spanish relatives. It seems he is interested in the oil output of Mexico. Do you speak German?"

"I'm sorry, I don't."

"Then I'll translate for you."

The man sitting by the window in the room the three entered was middle-aged, with keen, cold eyes. "Pardon me for this intrusion at a family gathering," he said, bowing with great politeness, "but my business is urgent. As you belong to this noble family of Spain, I should be happy if you could arrange for me to have a talk with the head of your organization. The endorsement of this family will give me the prestige I need." He bowed elaborately in Ramón's direction. "I am in a position to offer them a very attractive price for the oil."

"I shall be glad to arrange the interview, Herr von Brenen," Jim replied, ignoring his remark about the family. "But I don't want to raise any false hopes in your mind. We have no surplus at present. I doubt if there will be any available for foreign export in the near future, if ever."

The man's brows drew together as if surprised that anyone would refuse what he asked. Jim wondered what his position was in Germany. "Where can I reach you?" he asked to soften his last statement.

"If you will tell this friend of mine, he will know where to find me." Herr von Brenen inclined his head toward Ramón.

As they returned to the *sala,* Ramón said, "Spain and Germany might be profitable customers for you. I should suggest you give Herr von Brenen all the encouragement you can."

"Do you think the market is going to fail here or in the States?" Jim asked, hoping Ramón would give some explanation for his interest in where they sold their oil. A faint sense of concern crossed his mind. There was rumor that Germany was secretly rearming. Was Ramón in any way connected with that movement, and if so, why?

"No failure of markets here, of course. It's only I believe in a rich class in Mexico, foreign and native. If this government stays in power, as I hope it will, you'll be putting down a lot more wells." Ramón lowered his hate-filled eyes. "Markets——" He waved his hand. His tone was light almost to the point of carelessness. "I think we had better get Ignacio to translate for you at the office. His English is better than mine. I'll arrange it with him right now."

Jim, watching Ramón move about among his guests, tried to figure out what was behind his sudden interest in the oil business. Ramón had changed considerably in the last year. Change was hardly the word—it was rather an intensification. His small, black eyes had grown more cunning in expression, while his body and face, always a little too plump, had grown plumper. He's living by his wits, was Jim's conclusion, and it's a very comfortable existence. He knew that Ramón had to a considerable extent recouped his family's fortune since he had taken over management. Just how, Jim did not know, except that this brother-in-law of Concha's owned two factories that were doing extremely well, and that he used his money lavishly to buy protection from all manner of official regulations. "Papá Ramón" was the name given him around the city. It sounded as if he were benign, but Jim doubted that this was the meaning of the nickname. There was subtlety in Mexican epithets.

Louisa had definitely changed. Her light, careless manner had given place to studied calm. She looked very Spanish. No woman in the room, not even those lately come from Spain, seemed more Spanish than she. It had become a cult with her of late. Too, she had recently assumed a devoutness that Jim doubted had any spiritual basis. Her yellow eyes held a shrewdness which belied the spiritual. To be in the same household with Mamá, as he now called his mother-in-law, was to have a yardstick to measure the things of the spirit. Louisa did not meet that standard.

The sisters were standing together, a little apart from the roomful of people. Louisa wanted something of Concha. Of that Jim was reasonably certain. A restless, unsatisfied look had come into her face. Concha, as he could see, was uneasy under whatever attack her sister was making on her. She looked grave and a little stubborn.

Silently Jim was cheering for his wife. The family used her so often for its purposes, but there was a point past which they could not go. There was a quality in Concha not unlike her mother. He noticed that Ramón was watching the two, and Jim had a definite suspicion that he was using Louisa to influence Concha. He wondered if it had something to do with the German.

That evening Concha seemed restless. He feared the afternoon had been too much for her strength. He kept watching her as she wandered about their sitting room. Finally she came and sat down on a low stool beside him. "Louisa wants me to do something about Nacho. Ramón says he is going with a group who are wholly at variance with the Spanish ideals."

"What does she want you to do about it?"

"She thinks he should marry the woman Mamá Grande has chosen for him."

"You mean that Mercedes person who was at Louisa's this afternoon?" He remembered the woman's thin, unfriendly mouth.

"Ramón says it's necessary if the family is to keep its position among the most exclusive." Concha seemed to be talking more to herself than to him, not really asking for an answer. All at once she turned directly toward him. "Of course I wouldn't want Nacho to marry such a woman." She smiled. "But Nacho will take care of that. He'd never give in to Mamá Grande on that point. It's something else I really wanted to tell you. Louisa said Ramón was giving you an opportunity to show your devotion to the family, a chance for loyalty. Jim, I wouldn't listen to what she said. I didn't want to know what she was talking about. There isn't anything you could do that wouldn't be right. In all these months that I've been ill, I—I could almost stoop and unlace your shoes."

Gently Jim drew her to him and kissed her. "Don't, Concha. Please don't say things like that. I am bound to make mistakes. Difficult problems are arising at the office. My advice will be asked. Maybe it won't all be the kind Ramón would say was loyal."

"What has that to do with our love, Jim?"

"Nothing," he assured her, "nothing. But don't ever doubt me— don't ever think I mean to fail you."

46

UNDER Soledad's care Tito was becoming strong and resourceful. She did something for a child and for all those she loved, and she was beginning to love Concha. For the first time in Soledad's life she found herself entering into friendship with a woman. At first she had been on the defensive, holding herself in reserve, watching that her mistress did not ask extra service or extra time of her as Doña María tried to. Gradually she had come to trust Concha. It was nice, this friendship with Concha. She began telling her about the lime-washed pink house, how proud she and Guadalupe were of it, of its orchid-filled patio, of Guadalupe's work in the Bureau of Haciendas of the government, even of the men who used to gather in the little *sala* to talk. At first she did not speak of Guadalupe's absence. Those happy years with him were what she wanted to remember, forgetting the present uncertainty and his absence.

Every morning with Tito they went to the roof. Up there the sun and Soledad's talk were performing the final curative phases of Concha's recovery.

"Where is your husband now?" asked Concha one day. She had come to have a deep interest in Guadalupe; so well had Soledad described him that she could see his slender brown fingers picking the harp, his gentle, quiet face lighting with the splendor of his thoughts.

"He has had to go away and leave his work since the hacienda program has been given up. The Revolution has been betrayed." Soledad stretched her hand out in a gesture which included everything to the horizon. "This city was to be freed of poverty. There were to be workingmen's houses, and no one was to go barefoot. And we would take the land from the rich *hacendados* and divide it among the villages. Guadalupe says in the States all farmers own their land and live in white houses and have big barns in which to store their corn." Soledad's idea of Jim's country was little short of a paradise.

"Do you think it right to take property from people who own it?" Concha asked her. "That would be stealing."

"Stealing? To take back what was stolen from them? I've taught in an Indian village. I know how these rich men nibble, nibble away the land of the villages, bring unjust lawsuits. . . ." Soledad remembered she was speaking to the granddaughter of the very *hacendado* she was describing. But having spoken so, she was glad. She felt the thrill of battle. "What right have you rich to have everything?"

"You talk the way my brother does," said Concha, not letting herself be drawn into Soledad's anger.

"*I* talk like Señor Ignacio!" Soledad was too indignant to refute the charge.

"Where did you know my brother, Soledad?"

"He was one of the young men I told you about, who used to come to my *sala*. But he was not a doer, just a talker. And so is Señor Buchanan. Guadalupe asked a position of him, but he didn't give him any because he was a Mexican."

"Nonsense!" Concha answered. "You are overwrought, Soledad. If my husband did not give Guadalupe work, it was because there was none."

Soledad did not attempt to explain. She was sorry now for her outburst. She wanted to say so. Instead she darted across the roof after Tito. He was making a dark pattern of footprints on one of the sheets the laundress had laid on the roof to dry.

"For shame, Tito!" Soledad knelt and looked into the child's eyes. "Show Leona you are sorry."

"He will do no such thing!" Mamá Grande had come quietly to the roof, and she was angry. "No member of my family apologizes to a common Indian. I have heard enough of your revolutionary talk. You are to go now and not come back into my house."

As Soledad's anger rose, words of condemnation, vindictive, mean words tumbled about in her mind. Then it was almost as if Guadalupe's arm had been laid across her shoulder, the way he used to lay it there. She saw Tito gazing trustingly up at her. She must not frighten him, she must not lose Concha's respect. These two were dear to her.

"Mamá Grande, if you do not want Soledad here I have no right to insist, but I want you to know I do not share your opinion. I believe Tito is sorry." Concha turned to her son. "Tito, show Mother you are sorry. Give Leona's hand a little pat."

The child looked at the three women standing around him. Then he shook his head and held out his arms to his grandmother. In triumph, Mamá Grande lifted him and carried him down the stairs.

Concha and Soledad for a moment could not hide their discomfiture. Then they both laughed. It was so like Tito to seize the opportunity to be carried. It eased the tension between them, and Concha was able to say, quite naturally, "Until I have my own home, I shall have to let you go. But will you come to me then? Tito needs you." She added quite without intending to, "And I need you."

Soledad tried to hide her consternation at leaving. She needed this work—and she needed her friends, Concha and Tito.

47

HERR VON BRENEN arrived at the offices of the oil company on the minute of the hour set for the interview, but there was a wait for Nacho. When he finally entered, it was with distaste for the task and disgust with himself that, in a moment of social graciousness at Louisa's party, he had agreed to serve in such a capacity. It offended him to be the mouthpiece for men of two other countries, bargaining over his head for the resources of his own. The German and the American discussed Mexico's oil as if it were something which they could freely barter away. The German wanted to get hold of the product for a new Germany, and the American talked in terms of what would promote the interests of the United States. Ignacio felt that Mexico was but a tool in their hands. In tight-lipped anger he translated their words.

Then suddenly a shaft of light illuminated the dark rebellion of his mind. His country with its tossed-up mountains, its hot plains, its broken volcanic land held products so precious that it could affect the future of the whole world, if it wished to. For oil, men would fight, would sell their souls. Mexico controlling her resources, controlling herself, might be the savior of the world. He did not realize that during this revelation he had been sitting silent while everyone waited for him to translate Albright's statement that at present they could promise Germany nothing. Perhaps later.

"Shall I repeat, Señor Navarro?" Albright asked, a little sharply for him.

"If you will, do so, kindly; the import of your words is not entirely clear to me." As Ignacio spoke, the penetrating vision left him. But later he caught glimpses of it again. That evening he began to question Jim about the oil problem.

"Why don't you make a study of Mexico's resources, Nacho?" Jim did not think, as Ramón did, that Ignacio was a mere waster. He simply had not found anything into which he could wholeheartedly throw himself. French by training, French in many of his mental characteristics, he was plagued by the Frenchman's incisive mind that saw defects in every cause, while his Spanish temperament demanded blind devotion to a cause.

The idea apparently appealed to Ignacio. He went the next day to libraries and bookstores, hunted out every book and pamphlet he could find on the subject, went to Pablo to get what labor men had written. He took over his grandfather's library and immersed himself in his studies. Often, in the evening, he asked Jim to join him. More and more Ignacio depended on these discussions with Jim to clear up debatable points.

Jim began to realize that Ignacio's attitude toward him was changing to one of genuine friendliness. He knew Concha's brother had resented his marriage, but he had found it hard to believe that Nacho would hold that resentment indefinitely. This growing friendship was helping Jim to get through the last weeks in the Navarro house, which he was finding daily more difficult. Mamá Grande had never forgiven him for taking matters out of her hands the night Concha had come so near death, and now she laid on him the full blame for the separate home.

Jim was throwing himself into their talks with enthusiasm, delighted with the three-cornered companionship that was growing up among Ignacio, Concha, and himself, for Concha often joined them. Afterward she would ask him questions. Her reactions were clear-cut and very much her own. She had not known before of the extent of her country's wealth. It made her proud and happy.

The history of the mineral wealth of Mexico they all found fascinating. The Aztecs had done little more than gather gold and silver from the surface of the ground or sift it out of the sands of the rivers. They used the two precious metals in chains, bracelets, and nose rings. They never discovered the riches of iron. It was the Spaniards who dug the mines. The Spanish Crown was the owner by law, but once the miners had given the royal fifth, they were free to enrich themselves.

In Don Julián's library Concha found a book containing a legend of the Spaniard's discovery of silver in Mexico. A Spaniard went hunting in lonely mountains. To keep off the wild animals he had built a great fire against some rocks so full of the precious metal that in the morning he found a stream of molten silver pouring down into his fire. There was another story of a Spaniard so rich that he built a path of silver over which his daughter walked on her marriage day from his house to the church.

Ignacio studied the long history of the part the rich mines had played in the political life of the country and its struggle for independence from Spain down to the later period when Díaz set aside the old Spanish law and sold to foreigners not only the surface land of his country but the rich deposits under the ground which before could only be leased.

This brought Ignacio to the drilling of Mexico's first oil well, and the scramble for concessions. Don Julián's library was now lighted far into the night. More and more often, like his grandfather, Ignacio paced the room. His eyes glowed as Don Julián's had and as the eyes of the young man did in the portrait over the mantel. His mind jumped ahead to the present and to his meeting with the German in the offices of the American oil company. Forces both good and evil wanted to control the oil of Mexico. Ignacio believed he understood why the Germans wanted this precious product. Memories of conversations which had taken place among his French companions in France came back to him. "Secretly Germany is preparing." It was up to Mexico to keep her oil from going to Germany! But how could she when someone else owned it?

The next evening when Jim came in Ignacio introduced the subject of subsoil rights, arguing that it was only just that Mexico should take possession of this wealth of hers. Jim felt Nacho was going too far in such a statement. "Isn't it too late for Mexico to control her subsoil products?" he asked. "Your government sold them and received its price. How can it go back on its word?"

"How can you say that? The old Spanish law stated that all such wealth belonged to the nation and could never be sold. The Spanish law is patterned after the Roman which all Europe accepts. What right have you to set it aside in favor of common law used only by you and Great Britain?"

"All right," said Jim, "but your government under Díaz—and if I am not mistaken your family has always been a supporter of the Díaz regime—passed a law linking subsoil and surface ownership. Then it was that my people bought in good faith."

"Good faith? A country that sends its ships into a foreign port— Veracruz is a Mexican port, isn't it?—and orders them to fire. Dollar diplomacy!" snapped Ignacio.

His words bit deep into Jim's pride and love of his own country. "There are things I think you should take into consideration about your own country before you condemn mine completely," he answered.

"What? The way you have deprived our northern states of water because the rivers happen to rise in the country you took from us?"

Jim, feeling that Ignacio was taking an unfair advantage, dodging the real issue in bringing up border rivers and that perennial sore point—Veracruz—said, "Let us stick to our point. We were discussing the rights of foreign ownership. I say my people bought your oil land in good faith and developed it. You can't go back on a legal transaction whenever you feel like it!"

"The Constitution of 1917 only reasserted the old Spanish law that the nation must be the owner of its subsoil," Ignacio answered, clinging stubbornly to that point. "Díaz was a dictator, and we're not obligated for all time to honor his bargains. You forget there has been a Revolution in this country, and by your unwillingness to co-operate you are hindering the new democracy from achieving its purposes."

"With leaders like your Millionaire Socialists, controlled by a dictator in power for a decade—and for God knows how much longer—you call yourself a democracy! A country like yours!" Jim laughed.

Ignacio jumped to his feet. "That's an insult!"

Suddenly Concha, sitting until now in the shadows clasping and unclasping her hands, rose and left the room. Jim felt himself arrested in mid-flight, his interest in maintaining his end of the argument gone. Without a word he hurried after his wife. In the heat of the discussion he had forgotten her presence. She would be distressed, thinking this was a real quarrel between her brother and himself. He and Nacho would shake hands tomorrow, probably, and start in again each to prove his point. But for her sake he was genuinely sorry he had spoken as he had. He had no real explanation why he had, except that after being careful never to offend the Mexicans with whom he was constantly negotiating and showing the same care at home, it had seemed good for once to speak out.

He found her in their sitting room standing by the window, her back to the room. "I'm sorry," he said, walking over to her and putting his hand on her shoulder. "I didn't mean to quarrel with Nacho."

For a moment she made no response. When she did speak, her voice sounded unnatural. "Then it's not so that you care for Mexico. You've only pretended to."

"Why, of course, I care. What I said to Nacho doesn't change that, does it?"

"I think so." She walked away from him, pacing back and forth with quick, agitated steps. In his heart her husband despised her country. Why had she not seen it before? There were the remarks Mamá Grande had often made about how North Americans scorned Mexico. There were the things Soledad had said to her about Jim's not taking Guadalupe into his employ because he was a Mexican. There was this work of Jim's about which he had told her so little. Now she understood why. It was not with Mexicans that he was working, but with men from the States who owned rights in Mexico they shouldn't. Nacho had said so tonight.

She picked up a toy of Tito's from the table—a rabbit with pink ears that Jim had ordered from the States for his Easter. Everything for Tito Jim wanted sent from the States. His father was teaching him to look down on Mexico! In a flash she was certain of it. All the terrible apprehensions which had tormented her during her sickness, vague ominous fears for Tito's safety, leaped forward in her mind, justified now. They were warnings to be on her guard against the insidious influence of his father!

"It's bitter enough that Tito will not love Mexico," she cried. "You won't let him."

"Concha, this is foolishness! Tito isn't going to be brought up that way. You said once that outside things like business had nothing to do with our love." Jim walked over to her, took her hands in his. "Look at me, Concha," he begged. "Surely you can't doubt me. You know yourself the government you have now is rotten."

"I am a Mexican, the way Mamá is," Concha said in a low tone, not raising her eyes to his. "I have come from the very pores of this earth. Nacho is like that, too. When we go away, we take a pot of earth with us. When we are lonely, when we are sick, we let it run through our fingers, we gather it into our hands. You don't understand. You can't. No, I must have no more children. You know what that means as I am a Catholic." There was a stubborn finality in her tone.

Jim dropped her hands, stunned for a moment by her words. After months of continence, a discipline he had gladly accepted during her long illness, he was now faced with what might be a lifetime of celibacy forced upon him by Concha, claiming her right to demand this of him because of a fancied reflection on her country. It was unfair, preposterous. All the disappointment and resentment he had long held under broke through his control. "I married you to have a wife, children, and a home. What have I had?" he cried. "We had one day alone together for a honeymoon. Ever since your family has absorbed you. Why, we hardly see each other except at night when we go to bed. And now—!"

"You mean you have not been satisfied with our marriage?" Concha in white-hot anger snatched her dressing gown from the wardrobe and started for the door. Then she remembered the family and returned. She would not want to meet her mother's eyes, would not want her mother to know that she had refused to keep her marriage vows, denying her husband children, denying him, too, the physical means of expressing their union. Only with her husband's consent had she the right as a Catholic not to have children. But she closed her mind to what Mamá would think, hardened her heart against Jim.

Jim could not sleep. A dripping faucet in their bathroom maddened him. "What inefficiency!" he stormed.

"Isn't efficiency a little dull sometimes?" Concha laughed lightly as she spoke.

"Oh, I *am* sorry. I did not mean to annoy you." Jim's tone was sharp.

A feeling of superiority came to Concha. "It is nothing," she answered. "It's just that we Mexicans do not look at things that way. If you knew Spanish literature—

"Sister Water, let us praise the Lord,
  A thread of water gentle and transparent
  That chirrups all night and every night by my chamber,
  A thin stream of water—what is so artless?
  The soul of water spoke to me in the dark."

She repeated the little poem twice, adding the second time, "Of course you wouldn't like it."

"I'll see that the faucet is fixed tomorrow." Jim's tone had an edge to it.

"But that's for Mamá Grande to decide." Concha's tone had an edge to it too.

In the morning they were like strangers to each other.

Ignacio no longer asked Jim to join him in the library. When the two met at mealtime, he was elaborately polite, too polite for Jim to make any advance toward the old friendliness. He would often turn to Jim, seeking corroboration for some point in international law. At such times, around his thin, fine mouth lurked a sardonic smile, as if he enjoyed the position in which he was placing his brother-in-law. For Jim to answer truthfully might renew the quarrel, a thing he would have welcomed if it were not for Concha. He felt that in some subtle way Ignacio and Concha had joined forces against him. Emotions they themselves did not fully understand, he in all fairness had to acknowledge, swept them together, leaving him in a backwater.

It had been an especially difficult evening. Nacho had made rapier-like thrusts, ridiculing international relations. Mamá Grande, sitting at the head of the table, showed evident enjoyment of the scene. Concha was amused, too. Only by a great effort had Jim held himself from open conflict with Ignacio. Now he and Concha and Mamá were alone in the *sala*. With exaggerated politeness Nacho had excused himself to go to his studies. "I know I tire you with my constant insistence on serious matters, is it not so, my brother?" he asked in a tone of mock solicitude. "But I ask your tolerance and your patience. I, like my country, have so much to learn, is it not so?"

"Nacho does not know whether he is ridiculing you or himself," Mamá said as the door closed behind him.

"Does he ever ridicule himself?"

"Certainly," Concha answered. "When his skepticism reaches its ultimate logical conclusion, he becomes skeptical then of himself."

Jim looked at his wife. Did he lack subtlety in her eyes? He had thought of himself as forthright. He felt at a disadvantage among people whose strength so often lay in skepticism. He stood up, longing to escape to his own people. He could no longer follow down blind alley after blind alley, always coming in the end to the barrier Concha had now erected against him. She was silent when they were alone, elaborately polite to him at other times, and she was doing nothing toward furnishing their house. Forgetting even to make polite withdrawal, Jim strode toward the door.

"My son, I have been wanting for some days to talk to you. Will you honor me with your attention?" Mamá's calm and lovely voice brought him to a standstill. For a moment he paused, indecision gripping him, not wanting to enter again the labyrinth of the family. Then, remembering the real affection existing between his mother-in-law and himself, he went and sat down beside her.

"And you, too, Concha." Mamá motioned to a chair opposite Jim. "I know you want your family to yourself, Jim, and it is right you should have it. Concha is well enough now."

From the floor above suddenly came Tito's faint wail, and Concha, instantly alert, half rose to go to him.

"I'll see what's wrong," said Jim, welcoming the opportunity to get away. He did not want even Mamá to try to settle the difference between him and his wife.

As the door closed behind him, Mamá turned to Concha. "Of late I do not think you have been fulfilling your promises, your solemn vows, my daughter, taken with Jim. When you came to womanhood, I placed in your hands your full heritage. Cherish it, bring it to full life and productivity, Concepción."

Concha stood up, saying, "I shall of course respect your wishes, Mamá, in regard to Jim and Tito having a home of their own."

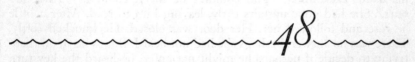

THERE was every chance for reconciliation between them, Jim felt, when a few weeks later they were settled in their own home. He relaxed in the quiet atmosphere of the privacy and comfort of their well-run establishment. Concha had been trained by her mother and grandmother in every art of housekeeping. He could see she was taking a housewife's pride in having each detail brought to perfection. She seemed happier than she had the last weeks in the Navarro house. Certainly time would mend the break between them. Undoubtedly Concha's long illness had played its part in her not wanting to have any more children. As she grew stronger, she would naturally want them. Surely her love for him expressed so often during the long year of her sickness was bound to reassert itself. One derogatory statement about her country could not change a relationship grown increasingly close as together they had fought for her recovery, a relationship far transcending the physical. Such a fight as they had made surely had welded their spirits together.

But as the weeks went on and Concha still maintained her aloofness, he began to despair. Was there something in her race which never forgave? Were things once said between two people never forgotten? He was filled with remorse for the harsh and false things he had said about their marriage the night of their quarrel. He would like to set himself right, but she had given him no opportunity to do so.

Their lives still conformed to the habits that existed before their estrangement. Concha was at the door to welcome him when he returned at noon for dinner and the siesta hour. She met him downtown at the end of the day, and together they hunted in the antique shops for pieces of furniture they wanted for their house. They planned to attend the summer opera. Nights when they were at home they sent away the nurse and put Tito to bed. But it was all shadow-boxing. There was no reality in their companionship.

And then one evening he began to wonder if, perhaps, Concha did not know how to break the impasse grown up between them. He had been holding Tito while his mother undressed him. The child had put up his arms, pulled their heads together and tried to kiss them both at once. Afterward, going downstairs, Concha had impulsively taken his hand, exclaiming, "Tito couldn't be nicer, could he? And he's ours." She had gone upstairs early, leaving him to read. After a little he rose and followed her. Her door was closed. He knocked softly. There was no answer. Perhaps she had not heard. But as he stood there trying to decide if perhaps he might not enter, he heard the key turn very softly in the lock.

The sun shone through the four big windows of the nursery. Concha watched Tito, who was playing with some tin soldiers Jim had brought him the evening before. Was Jim gaining too much influence with their child? Tito adored him. It was she who must care for Tito, guide him in his spiritual life, make up for her sin in bringing him into a household divided as it was, and as it must now remain.

With relief she heard Louisa's voice in the hall below. "I'm up here," she called.

Louisa came in, threw off her coat, and sat down on the floor by Tito. Concha noticed how often Louisa let her fingers linger over

Tito's small hand, how often she touched his soft curls. She felt a longing to end this tortured desire of her sister's for a child.

Louisa, looking up, caught the expression in Concha's eyes. For a moment she was angry that her secret had been discovered. Then she laid her head on Concha's knee. "I can't bear it. Ramón—there's another family! They have a son."

Concha stroked the thick mass of gold hair so like Tito's. There was nothing to say that would be any comfort to Louisa. All at once fear took hold of her. Suppose she should lose Jim as Louisa had lost Ramón!

That night she slipped quietly out of her room. It was brilliant moonlight, and the rooms were flooded with it even as they were filled with sunlight in the daytime. She and Jim had planned the house together, combining the best their two countries had to offer. "The patio must be kept," Jim had insisted, "but let's do away with the galleries which act only as passageways. It's cold in this high altitude going outside in the evening every time we want to get from one room to another." He had brought the walls out flush with the patio. A huge skylight had made it an integral part of the house.

She stood in the wide door of the living room looking at the fountain in the center of the patio, at paths set in intricate Indian patterns of blue and yellow tile. A shaft of moonlight touched the broad leaves of banana palms. The air was as warm here as at the hacienda, for Jim had insisted on a central heating system. Everywhere were the signs of Jim's thought and ingenuity and, yes, his love of the things of her country.

And she had condemned him simply because he criticized her country! And yet even now a quivering sense of pain passed over her when she remembered his laugh when he said, "A country like yours!"

As the night wore on, step by step she worked foward to a clearsighted conception of her marriage. There must be compromise and knowledge on her part. If she asked Jim to understand and respect her way of life, she must give understanding and respect to his. She had never let him explain his position that evening of their quarrel. She loved him, and in her heart she knew she trusted him.

Slowly she turned and walked up the stairs. She was wearing a long white robe of wool. A heavy cord knotted around her waist had slipped its knot and trailed on either side, making an accompaniment of soft thuds as she ascended. She turned the knob of Jim's door. She could hear his quiet breathing. She went over to the bed, looked down on him. He was lying on his back. In sleep his mouth looked stern and he remote, withdrawn.

She slipped off the robe, crept in beside him. He did not move. She felt insecure in the narrow space left for her. And then in his sleep Jim turned, throwing his arm across her. It was heavy, pinning her down, but the warmth of his body passed into hers, and she slept.

Summer merged into autumn. Concha found herself given over to a kind of brooding peace. In the quietness and solitude of her house she made the delicate adjustment to her marriage. In moments of passion, companionship, even strife, the shaping to Jim went on! She began to study English. That evening of their quarrel, some of the time she had not understood what he was saying. If at times of crisis he went back to his own language, then she must be able to speak it, too, if she wished to share his life completely.

By LATE fall Soledad's slender resources had dwindled to nothing. She had paid the rent one month in advance. But now she had not enough left to send the mere pittance she owed Tony's mother. She asked the woman to wait a few days. "The payment from my husband will come soon."

"I cannot wait," said the woman sullenly. "I'll put him again into the market."

"He can't go back to that," Soledad pleaded. "I'll soon be able to pay for his services. There's been a delay. Here are two pesos."

The woman looked at Tony's good shoes and stockings, his school suit. They would sell for more than that. Soledad heard the child's weeping as he was dragged away. Tomorrow she would go to the pawnshop and see if she could not get them to take Guadalupe's harp, and then she would bring Tony back. But today she was too tired.

She took a chair into the patio, and sat very still as Indians sit. She tried to think back to the days of her girlhood before the Revolution, to the morning her mother had said, "You can join the girls in the weekly promenade at the square tonight. You are old enough." Her father had sat in the bandstand, looking down on the promenade, and her mother on one of the benches that bordered the square, correctly garbed in black, gossiping with her old friends. Soledad had walked with the girls in the space between the bandstand and the benches, while the boys walked around and around in the opposite direction. One had thrown flowers which had fallen at her feet. How light her spirit had been then!

But after that there had been the Revolution, and her spirit was never light again until Guadalupe had come and made her his wife. And now Guadalupe was dead. Soledad was as certain of it as if she had witnessed his death. Tragic by nature, tragic by experience, she accepted tragedy, admitted no hope of his return. That night she wakened, sobbing, slept only to awaken to sob again. Her very flesh suffered as the part of her that was Guadalupe was torn from her.

The next day she looked at him from a distance in critical judgment, saying to herself, If he had been more self-assertive, he might have won through, hung on here until the hacienda program came to life again. Ironically it now gave promise of doing just that. But then, if her husband had had that self-assertion, she argued, feeling guilty in her criticism, he would not have been Guadalupe who had given her shelter, Guadalupe whose very feet she would have kissed in adoration of his gentleness. Again he and she were one. Whether he was strong and she weak, or he weak and she strong, she had no knowledge. They were the indivisible one, now forced into this hideous separation. Finally she came to the place where she could suffer no more. Body, mind, and spirit were bludgeoned into numb acceptance of her fate.

She had only one wish left—to see Pablo and accuse him of Guadalupe's death. At the entrance of the building where the Department of Labor was housed a man told her she could not see Pablo, but he made no effort to stop her when she walked up to the door and turned the handle. She found Pablo sitting alone before his desk.

He rose, exclaiming, "My little one, I had meant to come to you today."

"With me, you do not need to pretend. I have always understood you, Pablo, so let us dispense with flattery. Guadalupe is dead. This I know, but how he came to die—that I expect you to tell me."

Pablo moistened his lips. "We have had no report that he is dead."

"A report! I need no report to tell me when Guadalupe is dead."

For a moment Pablo's face lost color. Then he recovered himself. "If he is dead—and I do not say that he is—we Mexicans look lightly upon death. If we do not die today, we die tomorrow. Was it not spoken so among the soldiers of the Revolution? And Guadalupe died for the Revolution."

"I think," said Soledad, "he died for you."

"Not for me!" There was a hysterical note in Pablo's voice. "I said for the Revolution. He was protecting me in a way, yes. He realized my importance to the organization, and he preferred that they send him to the penal colony. He could have bought his freedom by giving my name. Brave Guadalupe!"

"Islas Marias!" Soledad spoke the words scarcely above a whisper.

Pablo turned away from the gaze of her somber eyes. "You must understand, Soledad, the labor movement has been fighting for its life. All along the line there has been betrayal. The very man who has imprisoned our men without trial was once a prominent labor man. We could not guess that he would turn traitor to the cause." Gradually Pablo's arguments became smoother. "It means nothing that Guadalupe is in prison. He will come back to us. There is work for him, important work ahead. You are overwrought, my little one."

"Stop talking so much, Pablo," she cried. "You are not worthy to kiss the ground Guadalupe walked on, and you know it. But because you have plotted and schemed, sometimes betraying labor, sometimes serving it, you will come to power. The organization is full of men like you. And yet it is good. This is a mystery I do not understand, but I think Guadalupe did. So he saved a rotten little politician by the name of Pablo." She turned and went out.

Day after day Soledad sat in the house, with hunger and insecurity, as in the days of the Revolution, stalking through her mind. All the stark scenes of fighting and camp life, and the orgies in the towns after victory stalked her, too. Guadalupe's gentle hands had pushed them away for a time, but not destroyed them. Deep in her mind behind the curtain of Guadalupe's gentleness they had lain, waiting for just such a moment as this.

The face of the man she had called husband now came to take the place of Guadalupe's serene countenance. She remembered Ramiro's flashing black eyes, his lightheartedness, and his bravado. In the long line of the marching troops, her *rebozo* drawn over her head, her feet bare, her stomach often empty, she had followed him, carrying his guitar. And later there had been the child to carry in her *rebozo*. She could feel now the warm weight against her back. Her lover had been shot in one of those terrible nights after victory. Then there had been his child to care for. She had not mourned overmuch the passing of the little girl. Life was too hard for a woman caught in the terrors of the Revolution.

And then had come Guadalupe, showing her the beautiful fruits of Revolution: blueprints of little villages, each man owning his land, a school at the center, men and women eagerly talking in her *sala,* great murals honoring labor, and newspapers saying anything they wished— and this little house, orchids growing in the patio, and Guadalupe playing his harp.

She clung desperately to her home. "Here we are hidden away among the quiet, everyday people to whom Mexico belongs," Guadalupe had said. Soledad watched a teacher who lived down the street start every morning for the School of the Revolution where she taught; she watched for her return in the afternoon. The teacher was trim-looking, and walked with a quick, alert step. On the lapel of her jacket was fastened a silver pin shaped like a vase. From it three violets rose, and they were as fresh in the evening as in the morning. The tiny silver vase must hold a drop of water. The never-drooping violets and the woman's sincere, hazel eyes stood to Soledad for all she would like to be.

"I'd steal to keep this house," she whispered. "Oh, no, Guadalupe, really I wouldn't!" But there were only three pesos now left in her purse.

Late in the afternoon Ignacio, passing the house, noticed that the door stood ajar. Had they moved away? He'd take a look around. And then he came upon Soledad sitting in the *sala,* not noticing him even when he stood before her.

Only when he put his hand on her shoulder did she stir. "There is no need to come here, Guadalupe is dead."

It was the first time Soledad had spoken her husband's name aloud since her visit to Pablo. But it eased her to talk of him now, and Ignacio found it good to listen. The tenderness in her voice was for Guadalupe, but somehow it seemed to include him. Like Pablo and his friends, in those days when they used to come here, to be near Soledad when tired or frightened was to feel cared for. Ignacio was bewildered and groping. It was nearly four years now since he had returned to his own country, and he had found no way to be a part of it. The vision he had had of his country's wealth in subsoil products benefiting the world had seemed at last to lead to something, but his brother-in-law from the States had made it plain to him that he was tilting at windmills. He wished he could rest his head against Soledad, but he feared to bring down her wrath upon him as he had done once before.

As she went on with her tale, he began to be aware of an urgency in her voice. "This is Guadalupe's home," she kept saying. "I must see to it that nothing ever happens to it."

"I thought you said he was dead. You speak as if you were waiting for his return."

"Yes, he is dead," Soledad answered in a flat tone, "so I do not wait for him, but the house—Guadalupe said the fruits of the Revolution were homes like this. This house he would wish me to keep."

Ignacio, who never had wanted for money, at last understood her predicament. She was about to be evicted. He did not want that to happen. He wanted to come here and talk to her. It was the easiest thing in the world to keep the house, a mere matter of money. When he picked up his hat to go, he left a roll of bills where it had lain.

As Soledad closed the door behind Ignacio and walked back along the gallery, her footsteps sounded hollow and frightening. Ignacio's coming had scarcely interrupted the anxiety pressing in upon her. In expressing Guadalupe's pride in this house, she had only strengthened her anxiety. She had but one recourse, as she saw it. She could keep the house for a few days longer if she pawned everything she had of value, or found work. But where could she find work? The city was full of idle men and women. What had she of value? Looking over the *sala,* furnished at such effort, she saw nothing that would bring money except Guadalupe's harp. It was old, but perhaps the pawnbroker would take it. As she stood off to survey it, her hand rested on the table and on Ignacio's pile of bills. She looked at them wonderingly. A miracle! Soledad's childhood held miracles. Often for long hours she had studied the paintings in the cloister next to the church. The history of life was portrayed in the rows on rows of miracle paintings— escape from death, sickness, earthquakes, plagues, all fateful destinies. So did man express gratitude for answer to his prayer. But she had not prayed. With that money she could pay the rent and bring Tony back.

Slowly she grasped the truth. Ignacio had left the money. She threw the roll of bills across the room. It struck the strings of the harp, and they sent out a brief twanging. So this rich one thought she could be bought! Grimly she waited for his return. He would come in a day or two. Of that she was certain.

When he came she opened the heavy outside door for him and led him along the gallery, without a word. Once within the *sala,* she burst out, "There is your money, there in the corner! Pick it up!"

Ignacio with a quick movement grasped Soledad's shoulder, pushed her down into a chair. His feeling for her was now fully in keeping with what his father had taught him—all women of this class could be bought. "You'll listen to me, Soledad. Your interpretation of my generosity puts matters on a different plane, one not there in the beginning. I am making you an offer. You can be the mistress of this small house that you so desire to keep. Despite my dislike for you, I find you desirable. And you, there is no need for you to deny it, you also——"

Laughter filled with the bitterness which Guadalupe had for a time exorcised from it, burst from her. "Let us make this arrangement, if you wish," she said. "It is only, you must understand, so that I may continue to live here where Guadalupe wished me to live. But I warn you, what the Revolution has taught me I shall teach you. It will enter into you, and when you leave me—which you will when it suits you—you will no longer be able to draw your cloak around you and stand apart. I shall see that you learn to suffer in the Mexican way."

Ignacio's lips curved in a scornful smile. "If it makes you happier to base our arrangements on heroics, do so. I should like you to be happy. It would make it pleasanter for me. But suppose you leave the word Revolution out of our conversation. I am tired of the sound of it, and even you must know it is over. Of all people, you should know that. Living with me you will forget it."

"There is but one touchstone to Revolution, my friend, and you don't hold it. You can't wrest it from me. I *am* the Revolution!"

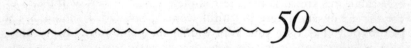

50

IGNACIO had not counted on Soledad's tenacity, or she on his. For weeks the struggle between them, except for blindly passionate moments, was never surrendered by either. Ignacio's long effort to root out the tormenting, uneasy guilt which he had suffered ever since his return from Europe was reaching its climax. He had never ceased to be haunted by the demand on him to go down into the struggle of his country. But now he intended to give himself over to every sensation that would bring forgetfulness. In this mood, with cold and clear intent, he went about the seduction of Soledad. Ever since he first met her, she had threatened his proud aloofness from the people. "They belong to *us*," she had said when speaking of the ignorant, poverty-stricken villagers. And he knew she meant that royal as was the Aztec blood that flowed in his veins, it did not absolve him from his relationship with the downtrodden Indian of the present day.

Even now she lifted her head proudly and said, "I shall see that you learn to suffer in the Mexican way." If he recognized her invincible spirit, he must indeed dip down into the struggle of the people. If he could make her surrender to comfort and luxury, then he felt he could maintain his cynical sense of superiority.

Bit by bit he changed the quality of Guadalupe's home. The meagerly furnished *sala* he made into a place of comfort for himself. Gradually he increased the luxuries which he considered necessary to his own living.

Soledad continued to sit in a straight chair and talk of the Revolution. She had the gift of the storyteller. Often, in spite of himself, his attention would be given to some tale she was telling. He had not known until now that she had actively participated in the Revolution, marched as a *soldadera*. Vividly she sketched for him the long trainloads of soldiers, the women setting up housekeeping on the flat roofs of freight cars, grinding their corn, patting out the *tortillas*, hanging flowerpots on the sides of the cars. "It was easy for men to die for the Revolution. Dying was nothing. They used to play a game. Thirteen men sat around a table. I saw it once. They put a revolver in the middle, spun it around. Bang! It went off. Then they called in another man." But she did not tell him that the one who had slumped in his chair was Ramiro, whom she had called husband.

"I think this fresco is not the complete you," he said at the end of the tale. "You are a very beautiful woman, Soledad. I should like a picture of you as I see you. Will you let me paint you?" Every Mexican, whether high or low, was in part an artist, expressing his emotions in music, poetry, or painting. Ignacio was talented in all three.

"As you may wish," Soledad answered absently.

The next afternoon the sittings for the portrait began. Soledad felt a childlike sense of dressing up when she put on the bright red Spanish gown of heavy satin he had found at the hacienda the last time he had visited his father. Sitting quietly, her hands folded on the satin skirt, she felt a sensuous pleasure in its rich surface. She had never before had opportunity to experience feminine delight in beautiful clothes.

When the picture was finished, it was hung opposite the fresco. I am indeed beautiful, she thought. When Ignacio brought a piece of tapestry and suggested they hang it over the fresco, she did not object. She was a little ashamed of those other Soledads, forever carrying their banners of cornstalks. She ceased to tell him stories of the Revolution; and when a note came from Concha saying she was now in her own home and would like to have her care for Tito, she thought, I don't have to serve anyone now. She tore the note in two.

One day in the late summer she went to a large store in search of some material for a new dress. It was exciting business, buying clothes to please Ignacio. She was beginning to want his approval and admiration. She was trying to decide between two lengths of silk when she heard a familiar voice close beside her, saying, "It's here, Louisa! This is the silk I thought you would like." It was Concha! Suddenly the desire to please Ignacio was gone. He was not taking her into his world, the beautiful world Concha lived in. It was an ugly thing he was doing to her!

She fled along the aisle and out the door of the store to the Zócalo, the ancient Aztec square. Here she could take a streetcar. If I go quickly, I can get away from the house before Nacho comes. This I must do, she thought. She saw the car coming along the track was the one she wanted. She walked fast, not noticing the people coming toward her. Usually she was watching, not wishing to meet anyone from her old world. A man stepped before her, saying, "And so it is our little Soledad, the fiery exponent of Revolution!" It was Pablo. He looked her over. There had been some gossip about her of late. In his ironic gaze, Soledad saw he recognized both her beauty and her present way of life.

"I take it you have not followed the news, my little one. It would not interest you, now that you are rich, to know there is a new educational program. You would not, I suppose, care to teach in a rural school in the mountains—just room for a man to squeeze between the boulders to enter the village?"

There was irony in his voice, too, but Soledad ignored it. "Where is it, Pablo? I am in a hurry. Tell me quickly. Where do I go to get that school?"

"You should know where to go. You have not forgotten the Bureau of Education, have you? But there is no hurry. There have not been many applicants for such a school."

Once within the little pink house, Soledad dressed in the simplest, most inconspicuous dress she owned and packed a few things in a bag. She was ready now. Only one more thing she had to do—leave her message for Ignacio.

As she crossed the patio to the *sala,* she snatched up the knife she used in pruning. Quickly she cut down the hanging which hid the fresco. For a moment she stared at the young maiden wearing a yellow blouse and full skirt, the costume of the people, walking with two older women, carrying the beautiful product of the land. With a sob she turned to leave. But there across the room, mocking her, was the portrait of Ignacio's creation: herself clad in rich satin. The knife was in her hand. She would now forever destroy that Soledad. But as she raised the knife and touched the canvas, her wrist was caught, and a strong arm swung her around. Ignacio's angry face confronted her.

"So this is the way you mean to repay me! I have trained you, but not for another."

Soledad wrested herself free. "Stay where you are. I am leaving you, but not for the reason you think. What have you done to me, Ignacio?" There was both anguish and pleading in her voice. She turned away from him and walked from the room and out of the door.

Ignacio made no move to stop her—she would come back when her money was gone. He examined the portrait to see whether she had harmed it. Yes, there in the corner her knife had done a little damage. Evidently she meant to destroy the painting. He went in search of his paints with the idea of repairing the blemish. When he returned, he noticed for the first time that the hanging was gone from in front of the fresco. His attention was held by the vigor of the painting. The fresco is far greater than my portrait, he thought. The man who did that is a real artist, and I—I am only a dabbler. He looked again at his work. How odd! What I've done is to copy the face in the fresco. Only the dress and the setting are changed. I came under its power without knowing it.

He paced about the room. The thought that the clumsy, heavy man he had met once, in this very room, should be superior to him in any way was humiliating. It's outrageous, he thought. But that's not Soledad, that woman he created. I know the real woman, and I'll paint her. I'll show her for what she is, soft and vain, without integrity.

All night, half waking, half sleeping, he thought about his picture. He'd do a nude. But in the morning he had another idea. He'd repaint the face of the young woman in the fresco, make her a satyr among decent women. He painted rapidly, so clear in his mind was the image he wished to put on the canvas. It was almost as if his hands had nothing to do with it. Hour after hour he worked. The food the servant brought him he pushed impatiently away. He felt power and strength. This time he was no dabbler. The woman with her banner of cornstalk, he would show to be a fraud.

It was done. The light had almost gone from the room. Now he would rest. He sank down in a near-by chair. Almost before he relinquished his hold on the brush he was asleep.

It was late morning. The sun stood high in the sky, throwing its light straight down into the patio where the servant was watering Soledad's flowers. The wet soil threw off a clean, earthy smell. The pungent odor reached Ignacio, wakened him. The patio and Soledad were associated in his mind. Then he remembered.

He rose, walked across the room, and wheeled quickly, to face his work. No copy this time. Here was a living, breathing Soledad indeed! But it was the Soledad he had last seen—grieving, bewildered, frightened. Her last words rang in his ears, "What have you done to me, Ignacio?"

He hurried from the room. He wanted only to get out of this house, never to return. He would lock the doors and send his own personal servant to dispose of the things. But at the door he turned back. He wanted a keepsake of Soledad.

No man in the Navarro family ever gives up a "small house" without some keepsake, he said to himself, justifying his need to remember. Turning over the contents of a chest of drawers where Soledad kept her most personal possessions, he came upon a faded photograph of a girl in an old military coat which reached to her feet. A *rebozo* was wrapped around her head. A bandoleer all but covered her small, narrow chest. A heavy pistol in a holster hung at her waist. A rifle almost touching the ground was clutched in one hand. Why had she kept this photograph of a stray child? But when he looked closer, he saw it was Soledad herself.

He studied the pinched, sober little face. A ragged bang of hair hung down over the child's forehead, almost into her eyes which looked steadily, solemnly at him. The mouth drooped a little, but the chin that was pressed down into the folds of the *rebozo* was firm and determined. His heart went out to the small Soledad. Those children of the Revolution! The Revolution! Never would he be able to forget the stark scenes Soledad had drawn of those days.

~~~~~~~~~~~~~~~~~~~~~~ *51* ~~~~~

LEAVING the pink-walled house behind forever, Soledad went immediately to the Ministry of Education and asked for the position as teacher in the most backward village. Two villages were named. Soledad chose the one situated in the hills above the Navarro land. There were few applicants for such places, and with Pablo's card matters were soon arranged. The bus would take her as far as Cuernavaca. After that she could probably hire a burro the rest of the way, or she could walk.

For the two hours on the bus she sat with her eyes straight ahead of her, staring at a small image of the Virgin of Guadalupe fastened above the driver's head, a light burning beneath. In reality Soledad's gaze was turned inward. She was seeing her husband returning for the last time from his office at the Bureau of Haciendas telling her in a hopeless, dead voice that the program of reform had been declared at an end. Again she was standing beside Guadalupe, and he was leaning against her. Gradually she had felt his despair leaving him, some strength rendered from her to him, because of her belief in the ultimate triumph of the Revolution, because she had been at the Revolution's fiery, living center and had seen men die for land and liberty. And now she herself had failed him.

Restless and troubled, she walked the streets of Cuernavaca—those where poverty dwelt in all its ugliness and then along the Street of Ali Baba and the Forty Thieves. A gate was open. She stepped within. A stone mansion more like a castle than a house shone white in the brilliant sun. Four towers adorned its four corners, each tower embellished with four smaller towers. On the low wall surrounding the fountain in the center of the garden colored globes were mounted on crouched lions; giant porcelain peacocks, their tails studded with imitation jewels sparkling in the sunshine, stood at intervals on the smooth, clipped lawn.

Farther up the street, standing out on a hill cleared of any tree or shrub that would serve for ambush, stood the palace of the Jefe Maximo himself. Once he had not been afraid to die, but that was when he was poor and belonged to the people. Soledad felt a burning shame, a sickening guilt. Indivisible in spirit, those who had been joined in the fight; indivisible in spirit those who had betrayed the Revolution. The new Mexico, like the old, had not been able to resist luxury and ease; softness had consumed its fire and its purpose.

Her one idea now was to get away from this city, even as earlier it had been to get away from Mexico City. Get back to the land whence the Revolution sprang. She spent no time hunting a burro; she would walk. She slept along the way, trudged on the next day. After a time she realized that the road was familiar. She must cross the Navarro land to reach the village she sought. Late that afternoon she came to the hills.

Hour after hour she followed the mountain footpath, walking rapidly with the short, quick steps of the Indians who so often trod this way. She was hardly recognizable now for the woman who but a few days ago lived with Ignacio. Over her hair lay dust like fine ash. Her clothes were whitened too by the same powdery substance. It was as if she had taken upon herself the guilt of all the betrayers of the Revolution.

Gradually fresh hope came to her. There was this renewed movement for schools, of which she was now a part. Was some indestructible spark of the Revolution igniting the lush growth so long fastened upon the good roots of democratic effort? Guadalupe seemed to be walking at her side. With him near she felt her turbulent nature controlled and shaped into strength.

That evening she passed between the two great stones which guarded the entrance to the village high on the mountainsides above the rich hacienda of the Navarros.

52

A few days after Pablo met Soledad, Ignacio dropped into his office. He had not seen his half brother for weeks. What brought him now? Pablo wondered. "Come in, come in, Nacho, my office is yours." With a quickness that belied his thickening body Pablo got up and placed a chair for Ignacio. "What can I do for you?" he asked in his most gracious tone, as he seated himself once more behind his desk.

"Nothing. I was passing and thought I'd look in on you."

So the gossip is correct, thought Pablo; now he's at loose ends. Soledad has left him. "You're not interested any longer in subsoil rights, I judge," he said. "Too bad, for the whole question may be revived. The tide has been running against us for a very long time. But indications are that the labor group will be stronger again, as it was the first two years you were abroad. Then there will be action."

Ignacio had only half heard what Pablo was saying about labor's revival. His mind was busy with Pablo's remark—"the first two years you were abroad." Had Pablo always followed his movements, even dating events by them? Suavely he answered, "My activities hardly seem important enough to date national events by, Pablo."

For a moment Pablo looked a little discomfited. He had not meant to betray his lifelong interest in his half brother. "We have the same father, haven't we?" he said. "Wouldn't it be natural that he would sometimes mention you? But, speaking of Father, if you want to live as you are living now, I would suggest you look into his situation. He isn't doing so well at the hacienda."

"What are you insinuating?" Ignacio was immediately on the defensive. "The old threat, I suppose, about taking away land. So that idea isn't dead?"

"I was simply giving you information that might prove useful. Father is squandering money at a terrific rate. But it means nothing to me." Pablo shrugged.

After Ignacio left, Pablo made a sudden resolve to go down and see what really was going on at the hacienda. He was the stronger of Vicente's two sons, the more useful, he the man who by his own efforts could become rich. The last months had been encouraging. He was gaining influence in the new labor movement.

It was time Vicente knew how powerful he might become and respect that power. Why, he could see to it, if the movement to distribute land was again taken up, that the Navarro land was confiscated. Then where would these two precious idlers, father and son, be? Pablo did not intend to hurt Ignacio, and he did not wish anyone else to do so. Least of all Vicente. He was squandering the Navarro fortune, and Pablo meant to stop him if he could. He would frighten Vicente into a more discreet way of living.

53

IN REALITY Vicente had not done so well as he expected at the hacienda. There had been trouble among the villagers ever since he had let the overseer go and taken over the supervision himself. An unusual number of breakdowns in the sugar-mill machinery had necessitated several large outlays of money. Some of his new plantings of sugar cane were not doing well. His personal expenses were heavy. He had not been able to hold himself in check until he reached the Riviera. Interest in a very beautiful young woman in a near-by town had cost him a great deal of money of late.

If he maintained the family's traditional elegance, he must borrow heavily this year. He wished he dared propose to his mother that she show a little economy in the running of the household. Forty rooms kept with the elegance of the days of Díaz was a tremendous drain on his dwindling cash. But Vicente dared not insist on curtailment. He had tried to suggest it through Louisa and had been worsted. He feared, too, that if he mentioned it now Mamá Grande might investigate and learn what deep inroads he had made into the family fortune.

Since he had taken over, she never had visited the hacienda. To all outward appearances she ignored its very existence. That had made it possible for him to entertain whomever he pleased. His parties had become notorious. That she knew a good deal of hacienda affairs he had no doubt, for occasionally she let slip some word which showed special knowledge of conditions. The old gateman Francisco, Vicente believed, was her special envoy, although Vicente rarely saw him in the village. He came and went secretly. It was nearing the time for the festival of the dead, and to that festival Vicente felt certain he would come. He meant to watch for his arrival and frighten him into silence.

Francisco was a little earlier than usual in reaching the village this year. The Old One was more lenient in substituting someone at the gate now that on his return he brought her news. The sun still stood high over his head as he reached the outlying fields of the hacienda. Leaving the road, he walked deep into the cane. The yield was not good, he noted with satisfaction. The village had managed the revenge well. Francisco's face darkened.

As he returned to the road the *hacendado,* looking like the Evil One himself, as he sat on his great black horse, blocked the way. "What are you doing on my land? Who gave you the right to enter my field?"

"This is a short way to my village which perhaps the *patrón* is ignorant of."

"You think you can give me that kind of flimsy excuse?" Vicente swung his whip so that it flicked Francisco's cheek. "I want this spying to cease."

Francisco stood silent. He did not need to answer. His black eyes were eloquent with hate, before which Vicente drew back. He had gone farther than he meant to. Using the voice of benign paternalism, the tone which he had heard his father use when he disciplined his Indians, he addressed the old man. "I could have you arrested and thrown into prison for your trespassing. Fenced land—you know that fenced land is private property. Instead I have taken this kinder way of reminding you of your lawless act. You are free now to go to the village. I intend to be very kind to you, Francisco, for you have been long in service to my family. I pay well for the carrying of right messages. Come to my office before you return tomorrow."

But the next day Francisco did not come, and when Vicente rode through the village there was no sign of life. All the doors of the huts stood closed There were a few petals of marigolds half buried in the dust of the churchyard and along the street—a reminder of yesterday's celebration. But why were they acting as if today were a fiesta day too? The sugar mill was empty; no one had reported for work. Vicente rode out to the fields. No sound of the swish of knives as the stalks of sugar cane were cut through and fell with a brushing noise against the uncut cane. Only the soft rustle of the thin leaves blowing against each other.

Vicente turned his horse about. He was reluctant to pass through the village again, but there was no other way of reaching the main hacienda gate. As he rode through the empty street his skin prickled with fear. Through the closed doorways he felt many black, malevolent eyes watching him. When he reached his house he poured himself a glass of whisky and downed it with one gulp. After that he was able to laugh off his fear. He even swaggered a little before himself. Francisco might hate him, but he believed he would obey him and carry no more reports.

Nevertheless it was with relief that he heard a car moving up the village street toward his gate. To his great surprise and pleasure Pablo got out of the car. Then his pleasure was dimmed. Had he come in behalf of his mother? Vicente had not thought of her for a good while. Certainly Pablo would not have the time to make him a long visit. He did not wish him here for the great fiesta he had planned for the end of the week. If he witnessed such a display, it would be difficult to ask him to continue the support of his mother which he had assumed of late. Display it was to be, with bullfighting in the family's bull ring, a rodeo, and the last evening a dance for all the countryside. And yet it relieved his nerves to have Pablo here, gave him renewed assurance.

"It is good to have company. My family does not honor me often with a visit," he exclaimed, giving his son the accustomed embrace.

"Nacho sent you his felicitations," Pablo replied. "I saw him just before leaving the city."

"I suppose business won't let you remain long, but a short visit is better than nothing."

"I'm here only for an hour or two. I will not mince words with you, Father. I came today because you *are* my father, and I want to give you a fair chance. Beneath the surface the country is again stirring with the old revolutionary cry."

"Is the cry by any chance that the new rich shall rob the old rich?" Vicente sneeringly asked.

"There is an older saying," said Pablo quietly, "about the land belonging to him who works it. You will be a marked man if the government should ever revive the hacienda program, unless you are better to your Indians. If they ask for land, and they surely will under your treatment of them, they are bound to get it."

"The present crowd of exploiters reinstate such a program! You are crazy, Pablo."

"Dictators do not last forever. You know that well if you let yourself think of Díaz' end," Pablo answered. "There are new leaders springing up among the working people. They will be heard someday."

"By any chance are you one of them?" Vicente had uttered the words purely in jest, but looking at Pablo he suddenly realized it might be so. He knew nothing of Pablo's position. "So you *are!*" Vicente settled back more comfortably in his easy chair. "As your father I am safe then. My land will be left untouched, is it not so, my son? Is it not so?" he urged, leaning forward. He wished now he had done more for this son of his, more for his mother Elena. He had better do something for her, show some interest in her. He must see her and insist, too, that she direct their son's course with more care.

Returning to the city, Pablo drove with as splendid a disregard for the restrictions of the road as Ignacio himself could have displayed. Faster and faster the car moved, keeping pace with his thoughts—the need to get away from his father, the need to get away from himself mounting as the miles accumulated behind him. In spite of everything, he had until of late looked upon his father with a son's dutiful respect— an attitude carefully fostered by his mother. His feelings had now run the gamut from tempered respect to doubt, and now revulsion. It was the crafty, selfish look in his father's face when he had said, "Is it not so, my son?" So his father would pull him down to keep himself safe. The resentment which had lain hidden in Pablo's heart all his life against his father, held under until now, became a live, stinging hatred whipping him on. Faster and faster he drove, away from the hacienda.

But as the distance from his father became greater the vision of himself grew clearer, too. Down in his heart he knew, even if he could not be used as his father had wanted to use him, he could be used if it were for his own benefit. Soledad's stinging words when she had accused him of causing Guadalupe's death still lashed at his self-esteem. They were not entirely true, but they held enough truth to make him wince. He had taken no stand to help Guadalupe, waiting to see whether the new labor group could win. In the meantime he had been a frequent participator in the elaborate celebrations of the old labor leader; now quietly he was sitting in on some of the discussions of the new labor group. It was with these men, he believed, that the salvation of his country lay. Under leadership of the man Toledano an organization called the Confederation of Workers and Peasants had been formed. The best interests of his country would be served by identifying himself with them openly.

He was drawing near the city now. He would get Guadalupe back from the penal island. The resolve to do so eased him back to his old self-esteem.

54

EARLY in December, Jim, Concha, and Tito spent a week end with Vicente at the hacienda. In the high altitude of the valley of Mexico the harvest was long over; but here where the land stepped down toward sea level it was just beginning. Every Indian field of corn along the way was in the process of being reaped. On the road they met men and burros laden with sacks of corn. In the fields men moved along the rows, picking the ears from the stalks.

At the hacienda there was such a bustle of harvest that Jim felt as if he were about to celebrate Thanksgiving Day in his own country. Vicente had respected the time-honored custom and given the villagers a day in which to reap the small plots of corn behind their huts. Women passed them going to the church with baskets of golden maize. The men were coming home with sacks of corn and the children with bundles of the husks to be used later to wrap tamales in. Francisco's wife, Concha's old nurse, was sitting in the sun outside her door, and Concha got out of the car to carry her son over for the old woman's blessing. Cleofas came hurrying from a hut farther down the street, bringing her son for her former mistress to admire.

Vicente welcomed them with unexpected warmth. Sitting with him that evening on the wide veranda overlooking the patio and the hacienda park beyond, Concha caught a glimpse of another man than the self-indulgent one she had known all her life. Her father was in a nostalgic mood which took him back to his young manhood the first years after his marriage. "Nacho was about the size of Tito, and we were living here. I was young then and looked at things a great deal as Nacho does now. I, too, was full of grand ideas. It was before the Revolution. Díaz was in power. It was a day like this. I had been reading a book by a fiery-headed patriot who wanted hacienda reform. Your grandmother was here and when she saw what I was reading she whisked me right off to France."

"Did Mamá go with you?" asked Concha.

"No, Mamá Grande had some sort of idea that your mother was responsible for my high ideals." There was a note close to pain in Vicente's voice as he said this. "The Matriarch will see that Nacho learns how to enjoy himself, too," he added with a laugh.

So Father was like that once. Suddenly the purposes of Mamá Grande were plain to Concha. As she had separated Vicente, weaned him away from Mamá, so she would have separated Concha from Jim. Mamá Grande's child, her grandchildren, were hers to be broken to her will. These others, these extras in her family were excluded, cast aside as soon as they had perpetuated the line of descent. Only Ramón of those added by marriage to the family was acceptable to her. He was so because he furthered her insatiable craving for wealth and position.

Her father's words rang in her ears. "She'll see that Nacho learns how to enjoy himself, too." Would he become like his father? He mustn't. Surely Mamá, who had rescued her, would rescue Nacho.

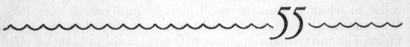

55

THE first of the nine *posadas* ushering in the Christmas celebrations was to be held at Concha's and Jim's house, and all the kinfolk, as Jim's Southern relatives would have put it, were to come. And what a family it was, with uncles and aunts, grandmothers and grandfathers, mothers and fathers and children! Jim thought, as the candle-lit procession circled the house. They were singing the traditional Christmas song, begging for admittance.

Jim joined Concha in the response. "Who are you and why do you come?"

"There is a child about to be born, and there is no room in the inn." Jim opened his house door to the family.

Vicente and Nacho, leading the procession, entered, bearing a litter between them. On it were the wax figures of the Holy Family. Crossing the patio, they placed it behind high candles at the far end where the long windows gave back the light of the tapers from their dark surfaces.

"Please, will you show me the *piñata?*" asked a little girl with large black eyes and black curls reaching to her waist, as she slipped her hand into Jim's. He didn't remember he had ever seen her before, but evidently she belonged to the family. He led her into the spacious living room where a great jar, hidden under the red and white skirts of a doll in a *china poblana* costume, hung suspended from the ceiling. All the children had trooped after them followed by their elders. The room was full to capacity when Jim blindfolded the little girl, put a stick in her hand with which to strike the swinging jar. There was a babble of voices and a cry of "Excellence!" when the jar broke at her first stroke and candy and toys fell in a shower. Jim, reading the names attached to the packages, hunting out the owners, had a happy sensation of being an accepted member of the clan.

Before the evening was over he felt he had all but reached friendship even with Mamá Grande. She took an almost childish delight in every innovation in the house. Until tonight she had refused to visit them. She insisted he show her the central heating plant and the perfectly appointed American kitchen, explain how the skylight over the patio worked to let in air and rain. She patted him on the arm, praising him for what in his country would have been called "gumption." "I heard men from the States made good husbands. That is why I allowed you to have Concha," she said, glancing slyly at Louisa.

As Jim turned from closing his house door behind the last guest, his face was alight with happiness. "I've always wanted to be the head of a big family, Concha. Patriarchal, perhaps, in my desires. I was tonight and liked it."

Concha put her hands on his shoulders, looking deep into his eyes. There was no trace of that baffled look they had held during their estrangement. She must see to it that it never came back.

Some time after Christmas Concha felt tension arising in Jim. First she thought it was due to the fact that a director of the company had come down from the States to make changes at the office. Jim had told her that he was not in sympathy with the new plans. But gradually she came to see that what was troubling Jim was connected with her. Did she fail him in some way?

They had come home from an evening spent with Mamá Grande and were standing at the entrance of their house, looking out over the valley. The moon was shining over the rim of the mountains, lighting up the plain and the city. High against the sky, blue even at night, the two tall mountains, Popocatepetl and Iztaccihuatl, shimmered and sparkled under their snow-white covering.

Concha laid her hand on her husband's shoulder. "Something is wrong. I fear somehow it is due to me, and I am troubled."

"Not really due to you. It is only that the company is preparing to fight if the struggle between our two countries over oil is to be revived as they think it is."

"Am I in some way connected with that?"

"It's hard to explain. It's the fear I may disappoint you," he said.

"I thought all that was settled between us."

"We never talked things out. I knew you were willing to bear my children, but we didn't talk things over. Something is happening in Mexico. I'll be torn between the interests of our two countries. I want to be fair to both."

"Jim, why don't you really explain things to me? Tell me exactly what you think is going to happen."

He hesitated a moment. Should he risk telling her just what he thought? He decided he would; he must if they were fully to understand each other.

"Of course, if the ideals of the Revolution come to life again," he began, pulling her arm through his and pacing up and down in the moonlight, "there will undoubtedly be the old question of subsoil rights. That means the business I am in will be affected. I know you don't like the foreign companies holding onto your oil wells. On the other hand, my company suspects the motives of your country in trying to confiscate them. To put it frankly, they think the men coming into power in Mexico, like those in the past, see a way to get possession of developed wells without much labor or expense, and so to gain prestige for themselves among the common people. In seeing my country's side, do I seem unfair to your country?"

"I doubt if I'd ever think that again, but I might have to disagree with you," said Concha, and after a pause she added, "Maybe we'll always be a little strange and foreign to each other, but that does not matter." They stood facing each other but not touching, approaching some deeper understanding. His eyes, held to hers by the intensity of her gaze, seemed to see into the innermost recesses of her heart. He was safe there. His uncertainty was gone.

56

THAT winter and spring of 1934, Calles, the Jefe Maximo, sitting in luxury and fear on his hill in Cuernavaca, knew he could no longer ignore the stir within the body politic. But sure of his own ability to rule, if concessions were made to the younger men of his party, the Jefe Maximo suggested a six-year plan and a president who would stand for reform: Lázaro Cárdenas, who while he was governor of the state of Michoacán, had gained a reputation for devotion to reform. But the Jefe Maximo believed he could shape him as he had other men. The election would be but a show of democracy. Afterward Cárdenas would obey him as the others had in the past.

But by summer Calles grew uneasy. His candidate was taking it on himself to draw near to the people. He was not content to make a pretense of stumping the country in the usual way, traveling in the "Olive Train," the President's car, to certain large centers. Often he would leave the long green train and go by foot, visiting forgotten villages in the high mountains, making promises to the people that the Jefe Maximo did not wish to see fulfilled. But he saw he had no alternative; he could not now draw back. Lázaro Cárdenas would have to be the next President.

Despite the fact that the man in the street knew that Cárdenas was the Jefe Maximo's choice and would be elected whether they wished him to be or not, there was growing enthusiasm for him. His name was scrawled on walls and public buildings, spoken in the markets all over Mexico. Zapata's words were again on men's lips, "The land belongs to him who works it." Cárdenas used them. The men of the mountain village where Soledad had gone as teacher told her about him when they returned from their journey to the nearest market town. "Go and hunt him out," she urged them. "Ask him to visit your village and see how poor you are, while down in the valley is the great hacienda of the Navarros which once your ancestors in part owned."

In March, four months after his election, Cárdenas visited the village, passing his great body between the two stones that marked the entrance to their all but sterile mountain valley. Soledad, not feeling worthy to talk to a soldier of the Revolution—for so she considered him because he had fought as a young boy and now was speaking the words of Zapata—stood far back in the darkness of her hut which did duty for school and house. So she watched him through the long day as he sat behind a table in the town's dusty plaza patiently listening to the villagers telling him they needed land, they needed water.

Pedro, in the hacienda village of the Navarros, was growing very old. If Zapata's words were to come true before Pedro's death, the miracle of land for his people must happen soon. Yesterday the children of Pedro's daughter, gathered around her in the early morning as she warmed over the *tortillas* of the day before, had cried suddenly, "We hear hoofbeats!" The woman had settled back on her heels to peer through the doorway, and there, half hidden in the smoke of the morning fire, she had seen Zapata riding swiftly on his white horse. He had come back to help them! That evening as Cárdenas came down from the town in the mountains, Pedro met him along the road and told him of Zapata's visit. Would not he who spoke Zapata's words see that the village was given back their land before he, Pedro, died?

Pedro spat when he saw Don Vicente driving his car through the village in the clear March morning. That the dust kicked up settled over the inert Pedro did not trouble Vicente. He was in a hurry. He must make Mexico City by evening. Mamá Grande had sent him word to come to the city for the celebration of Ignacio's Saint's day. Of late Vicente had been more and more bold in ignoring any such summons, but this time it suited him to comply with his mother's wishes. He had heard rumors that there was to be more hacienda land distributed than in any previous administration and that his was included. Ramón would know if it were so. Meeting him casually at dinner, he might learn whether Ramón would use his influence to block such a catastrophe in the family.

Vicente's son-in-law had fulfilled all his hopes for him and more. He was almost as rich and influential now as his father had been before the Revolution, made so by his own adroit handling of the men in power, whom he despised but did not despise to use. Yet he had never broken with the proud Hispanic Mexicans—the remnant of the once powerful Creole aristocracy. And he worked always for the return of temporal power to the Church. But, unfortunately for Vicente, Ramón had not only evaluated the new Mexico, shrewdly

estimating weaknesses and profiting by them, he had also appraised
the weaknesses of his father-in-law. On their last meeting Vicente had
hinted that he was in need of money. Ramón had given him to understand that he did not share the prevailing sentiment that members of
a family contribute to a member in need; he played a lone hand,
trusted no one but himself, worked only for himself. If he refused to
give money, would he also refuse to give his influence? That Vicente
must know. If he did refuse, then Vicente must humble himself before
his son Pablo, gain his help. It did not occur to Vicente that in the
end Pablo would not help him.

Everyone was already gathered in the *sala* when Vicente drove his
car into the patio. He was tired and felt dirty and unkempt after the
long ride, but he went directly to the *sala,* took his mother's pudgy
old hand in his and raised it to his lips in honorable salutation. "I did
not get your message until last evening, my mother, so you will forgive
the lateness of my arrival and my appearance."

"My message should have reached you earlier. But your time is so
occupied with the duties of the hacienda you naturally cannot bother
about a message from me. I have waited patiently since early afternoon
for your arrival. I can wait yet a little longer until you are rested from
the journey and have had time to dress for the celebration in honor of
your son. Your father would have wished it so."

Doña María's undue patience, her reference to Don Julián, thus
calling attention to her widowhood, were cunningly used, he understood, to express her displeasure of him. There had been growing hostility between them ever since he had taken over the hacienda management, her once indulgent love turning acid under opposition. All
such indulgence—now that neither her son nor her grandson complied
with her wishes—was lavished upon her great-grandson Tito. He stood
at her side now, her jeweled fingers covering his small right hand resting on her knee. Concha feared that any moment the child might
grow irritable under the enforced quiet. The room was very still after
Vicente left. Everyone sensed that Mamá Grande had called them together this evening for some purpose other than celebration.

Since the death of her husband Mamá Grande's pepper-and-salt
crest of hair had turned white and taken on a soft, downy texture.
Although brushed back from the peak on her forehead in the usual
fashion, it no longer sprang away like the feathers of some majestic
bird as it had when Jim first saw her. It looked more like the crest of a
little white cockatoo topping her head, lending, Jim thought as he

watched her, a kind of eerie nonchalance to her face that belied her piercing black eyes. Was she bent this evening on mischief to her family—or on discipline? He saw all the members were now waiting with varying degrees of apprehension. Each knew in lesser or greater degree her cruel striking power.

Tito, sensing the tension, looked from his great-grandmother to his mother as if about to make a break for liberty. But as Mamá Grande's hand tightened on his, he straightened his shoulders and stood still. Mamá seemed aloof. Nacho sat silently alert. Louisa was nervous. Ramón, sitting next to her, stroked the nape of her neck in sensuous enjoyment of her nearness.

In their concentration no one had noticed that clouds were rolling up from the mountains, that lightning ran in spearheads of blinding light along the circle of the hills, black and terrible against the massed clouds, and that in the northwest mountains and clouds were already bound together by sheets of falling rain. Suddenly a clap of thunder broke over their heads.

Tito tore his hand loose from Mamá Grande's and fled to his mother's protecting arms. His action seemed to loosen the statuesque figures in the room. Jim and Ignacio moved quickly to close the long windows. In the flashes of lightning they saw the streets rapidly emptying, people huddling in doorways, caught by surprise, for it was very early in the year for such a storm. Mamá moved to close the doors just as Vicente dashed in from the rain-swept gallery. Louisa laughed.

The storm subsiding as quickly as it had come, Doña María rose and led the way to the dining room. As they passed along the balcony Concha and Ignacio simultaneously leaned over the rail to listen to the sound of water gushing down from the great waterspouts to the cobblestones in the patio below. Their eyes met, each remembering the stolen moments of delight when as children, escaping detection, they had darted out to stand under the water falling from the spouts. Concha noticed how spent Nacho looked. What has happened to him, she thought in alarm, and is it he whom Mamá Grande means to punish?

Throughout dinner, as the servants moved about the dining room, the conversation held to a light note, but there was ill-concealed tension in all of them, Jim thought, except Mamá Grande. She appeared to be enjoying herself, her attention centered entirely on Tito, who she had insisted should sit on her lap so that she could feed him. She was noted for the rich and delicious food she always served, but no one knew better than she that the highly spiced Mexican dishes were

not what a child should eat. "Ah," she cried when he demanded more
of the richest dish of all, "he is indeed a stallion! Is it not so, my
Vicente and my Nacho?" Jim longed to rescue his little son, the victim
of her kindness, but he feared if he opposed her he might bring her
anger down on the luckless member of the family who was the cause
of this gathering. He whispered to Concha sitting next him, "He'll be
all right, and I don't think we'd better interfere."

"Say you have had enough, Tito," Mamá Grande said in answer
to the anxious look in Concha's eyes, "and I will release you." But when
she saw he already was asleep, his long lashes resting on his cheeks,
she said, "Take him. His weight is too great."

As Jim lifted his son in his arms, for a moment all eyes were on him.
Louisa spoke out of the silence that engulfed them. "Oh, I forgot: I
turned little girl this afternoon."

"You?" asked Ignacio with lifted eyebrows, looking at the sophis-
ticated Louisa.

"For you, Nacho." She motioned to a servant. Taking the plate
brought her, she placed it in front of him. "Here is the roll you and
I always divided between us when we were children. The 'gossip'—
that's its name, Jim," she said, turning to him. "See, it's a horrid long
tongue." She handed it to Ignacio. "The 'kiss' I keep entirely for
myself." There was a teasing note in her voice, and she looked at her
husband.

"Don't be silly, Louisa." Ramón's voice was edged with anger.

Louisa's agate eyes sparkled. "I stopped to get them on my way
here this afternoon. I had fun choosing them. I bought a 'nun' for
Concha. Remember how I used to tease you, slipping it onto your
plate and whispering that you were born to dress the saints?"

"You are no longer children," Mamá Grande interrupted sharply
as the last servant left the room. "It is not only to celebrate Ignacio's
Saint's day that I have called you together. News has reached me that
I feel I should pass on, for it is important to you all. For me, who long
to join my beloved husband, it is not so important. I am only the
unworthy channel through which information of such import reaches
you."

After waiting a moment to emphasize her widowhood, she went on:
"I believe, Vicente, you felt it took a man to manage the hacienda.
Well, it takes a woman to smell out danger. Again there is a threat to
all *hacendados*. Their land is to be taken from them, ours among the
rest."

Vicente did not answer, did not even lift his eyes from the table. He seemed to be studying his beautiful hands, spread out before him, one on each side of his coffee cup.

"Through old friends I have learned that a group of influential *hacendados* mean to act to stop such vandalism. This common person called Cárdenas come up from the people can, like all the rest, of course, be bought. They are rushing a fund to him. I have no authority, of course, but knowing the disaster that faces us, I am going to call on you to join them. To save the Navarro estate let us give our share to the fund, Vicente."

"Who gave you this information?" he asked, not raising his eyes.

"I am not at liberty to say."

That had been Ramón's stipulation when he brought the news to her. It had been his plan also to bring up the matter in a family gathering, thus flushing his prey into the open. Vicente, he knew, was headed toward bankruptcy. Now was the time to lend money to him for the fund and in payment exact Vicente's promise to abdicate in his favor. Ramón believed he could make money enough to keep Louisa's family in a position of prestige and at the same time increase his own wealth. If the matter were handled privately, he feared his father-in-law might go back on the bargain.

"I, too, am an owner. I'll match any sum you put up," he said.

Vicente sprang to his feet. "This is no place for such a discussion. You and I are the only owners of haciendas. Let us discuss this matter in private."

"We are one family. Why not here?" Ramón wanted—and so did Mamá Grande—from Vicente a public acknowledgment of his failure and his promise to relinquish his control.

"How much money can you with safety give to the chest and not cramp yourself for working capital?" Ramón urged.

"The return has not been good of late——" Vicente began.

Ramón tapped impatiently. "Tell us, exactly how much can you place in my hands tomorrow morning?"

"None."

The enormity of the disclosure left Doña María speechless for a moment. "And so my son," she said at last, "rewards me for the years when I saw to it that he lived the life of a gentleman. To my son-in-law alone can I turn for help in this hour of our need."

Ramón's beady, black eyes rested on Vicente. The fool! he thought. He deserves to lose his wealth, but this time the safety of one *hacen-*

dado is the safety of all, so I must see that Vicente's land is saved for him.

"I think I can tide you over," he said. His gaze traveled to Ignacio. He's a fool, too; he looks as proud as if he were the one, not I, who has the money, Ramón thought. "If I put up a suitable sum for both of us," he went on, speaking directly to Vicente, "I want a written assurance that neither you nor your son, who is to inherit from you, will have anything to do with the handling of the estate from now on. I will attend to it and make a report to Doña María." This report was the price Mamá Grande had exacted of Ramón for bringing Vicente's financial condition into the open.

"I refuse my consent." It was Ignacio speaking. "I do not wish this fund sent to buy up the President. I am on the side of the villagers. Let them have the land. My whole life has been colored with the struggle to keep it."

"And you would like to go to work?" Ramón's tone was silky-smooth.

Ignacio half rose from his chair, his hand reaching instinctively for a weapon of defense. "That has nothing to do with the present issue," he replied, settling back in his chair, haughty disdain in his voice, and his hands like his father's quietly resting on the table.

"I fear it has a great deal to do with it," Ramón replied. "Poverty is inelegant. You are a very elegant person, Nacho. But, of course, I would not force riches upon you, or your father." Ramón rose and with elaborate politeness raised Mamá Grande's hand to his lips, then turned to his wife. "Come, Louisa," he said, and walked ahead of her out of the room.

"Wait one moment!" cried Vicente, but Ramón did not turn.

As the door closed behind them, Ignacio spoke. "Mamá Grande, I am not altogether without knowledge myself. In this matter I have later information than either you or Ramón. Even now it is too late to offer money. This new regime is proudly honorable—at least for the time being," he added with a return to his habitual skepticism. "Tomorrow morning we shall receive a summons to appear at the hacienda and sign papers dividing our land with the villagers. Let us do it with the dignity that befits our heritage."

"I turn over rich sugar-cane fields to my Indians!" Suddenly there burst from Mamá Grande satirical, high-pitched laughter. Then she too rose and left the room.

"I'd like to talk to Father alone. Take Mamá away from this," Ignacio whispered to Concha, with a glance at Vicente, who had bowed his head on his hands.

"Father," Ignacio began, once the door had closed on Concha and her mother, "I have a message for you from Pablo."

"Pablo!" Vicente's head came up with a jerk. "He will get me out of this?"

"Pablo said to tell you that two hundred acres will probably be your allotment. But the government means to finance a few co-operative organizations, and he thinks he might get them to set up one between you and the villagers. By hard work we could soon make it pay."

"I'd see myself in the grave before I'd stoop to such a plan. You can tell Pablo that for me."

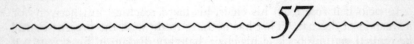

Concha was in tears when she came into the room where Jim sat with Tito asleep on his lap. "We are going to lose the hacienda," she told him. "Nacho says they won't accept money."

"So a bribe won't work this time?"

"I had not thought of it as a bribe. The land is ours. Surely Mamá Grande would not——" She stopped. Yes, her grandmother would consider bribery honorable if necessary to save the family's wealth. But there was no wealth left, according to her father. Concha's mind was a jumble of half-understood statements made this evening.

"Did you know about Father, Jim?"

"I didn't until Ramón told me a few days ago."

"Ramón!" exclaimed Concha. "Do you suppose——" She broke off. "Could he be Mamá Grande's source of information?"

Tito stirred and cried out in his sleep. Concha, forgetting everything else, leaned over him and put her hand on his forehead. "His head is hot."

"He's all right," Jim assured her. "He's thrown up everything that could possibly hurt him."

"My poor darling!" Concha murmured, putting his coat over him. "We must get him home at once."

For a long time after Tito was in bed and sleeping quietly, Concha sat by his crib watching him and thinking of the painful events of the evening. Every emotional strain which had ever existed between any of them, it seemed to her, had shown up this evening. This Revolution, which had always before stood outside the family, a pressure uniting them in struggle, seemed tonight to have forced a wedge between the members. Nacho had even upheld the taking of their property by the government. No longer own the hacienda! She put her head down on the crib rail, crying quietly.

Jim had come to the door frequently to see how things were going with her. Now, seeing her bent head, he came and laid his hand on her shoulder, saying gently, "Try not to think about it tonight, dear. It may not be so bad as you suppose." But in his heart he knew it was worse even than she realized. He feared that both the hacienda and the house in town were threatened. Anything the government paid for machinery or buildings would be required to settle the debts Vicente had incurred, if the things Ramón had told him were true, and he had no reason to doubt they were.

Back in his own room Jim began going over the events of the day crowded out until now by the happenings of the evening. Early in the afternoon Albright had called him into his office and told him he was resigning and leaving soon.

"But why?" demanded Jim. "We need you here as never before. Cárdenas is making labor stronger every day. There is going to be a showdown at Tampico soon as sure as I am sitting here. That demand for a wage increase they made last week indicates how the wind is blowing. We need you," he reiterated.

"The company doesn't think so." Albright was looking away, out the window, and Jim could see something had happened to change him from a successful to a defeated man. Sandy-complexioned, sandy-haired, he had not shown his age until now. But under defeat his skin had turned yellow and old-looking and his heretofore fine-drawn features had lost their clear contours.

Perhaps he is too old for the job, thought Jim. Then he brought himself up standing, blaming himself for disloyalty. He knew Albright was a wise administrator.

"It is this way," Albright went on. "They're going to put in a stiff labor policy. For that I am not fitted. I'm willing to acknowledge that I don't stomach that sort of thing. What I do resent is being held accountable for the break between the British and ourselves."

"Then they mean to work with the British and present a solid, uncompromising front against all labor's demands?" asked Jim.

"My successor will be here tomorrow," was Albright's only answer.

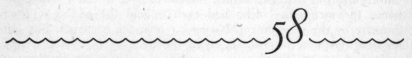

IGNACIO left the house in search of Pablo. He knew Pablo was to be at a labor meeting this evening, to be held in an abandoned theater in one of the poorer sections of the city. He parked his car on a well-lighted business street a few blocks away, having heard that hubcaps and tires and anything else removable from a car were often stolen in this district. Then he walked through the narrow cobblestone streets to the address Pablo had given him. The place was full almost to capacity, but he found a seat toward the back on the aisle. His sensitive nostrils drew in with every breath the odor of garlic and sweat, both fresh and stale. He turned in his seat, almost facing the aisle to avoid it, but it hung in each fragment of air. It gave him a new and vivid sense of the meaning of toil, of its effort, its exhaustion. What would it mean to be born into it? he wondered. He studied the individuals around him. They were all poorly clad, all showed the effect of unending work.

He had to smile when he thought of how dangerous these labor movements were pictured in his own set. There was an almost domestic appearance to the crowd. The women had brought their children and even their babies. Breasts were bared for their nourishment. There were groups of young working girls, very pretty in their cheap clothes. Ahead of him sat two boys of perhaps sixteen. The usher touched the shoulder of one of them, telling him to take off his hat. Such sense of decorum surprised Ignacio. Used as he was to the politeness of all classes of Mexicans, he had not expected it at this labor meeting.

On the platform among the labor leaders was Pablo!

A young woman dressed in pale-blue evening dress had come onto the platform and was singing a song entitled "My Beautiful Mexico." A small girl sitting in the row in front of Ignacio stood up in her seat, clapping her diminutive hands, crying, "The lovely lady!"

When the song was finished, the labor leader Toledano rose. Ignacio wished he were sitting nearer the front so he could study him more closely. A hushed silence fell on the crowd. As the man began to speak, it was as if he gathered these people into the hollow of his hand, squeezing them tight into one massed emotion. That sense of superiority to all human beings except those of his own class left Ignacio. It was a queer, not altogether pleasant feeling to be thus stripped of superiority. Yet, though he felt smaller, he felt greater than he had ever felt before, his shoulder touching the shoulder of the man next to him, touching the shoulders of men of labor all over the country, all over the continent of North America, for the labor leader was talking of the continental solidarity of all workingmen.

Toledano stopped speaking. Ignacio felt his mind released from the massed mind. Quickly he rose to go. All around him suddenly he felt hatred. Those sitting near him stood up, too, hemming him in. He saw Pablo elbowing his way through the throng. "It's all right, boys," he said.

"What did you do a thing like that for?" he asked, when they were outside. "They thought you didn't like the speech. This is a tough neighborhood. They'd just as soon pull their knives on you as not."

"Anyway it got you down off that platform." Ignacio gave a little laugh. "Father won't have anything to do with your plan."

⁓⁓⁓⁓⁓⁓⁓⁓⁓⁓*59*⁓⁓⁓

The next morning Concha was awakened very early by the ringing of the telephone. It was her father calling to say that he wanted her to go down to the hacienda with the rest of the family. "I want you all to see I am not responsible for the loss of our land. The officials are giving it to the Indians today."

When the car stopped for Concha, Louisa was not in it. Ramón had been summoned to his own hacienda, and she had gone with him. Vicente was driving. His mother was sitting beside him. Concha took her place with Mamá and Ignacio on the back seat. Concha was relieved that Jim had not come, for she did not want him to witness her family's humiliation. She believed Jim sensed this. That there was another reason for his absence she did not guess, for he did not tell her of the crisis at the office, fearing it would worry her.

As the car entered the unpaved street of the hacienda village, the villagers did not as usual stand aside to let them pass. Several times they were obliged to stop to await a pedestrian's slow crossing of the street. Close to the gates of the hacienda two men were preparing an arch of flowers, through which the officials were to pass on their way to the hacienda offices.

Doña María went there directly, sending for the Indian men she knew were at the bottom of this. She felt even now she could settle with them. They would not dare to assert their claims now that she was again here, might not even wish to. But no one came in answer to her imperious ringing of the bell which for centuries had called the Navarro peons to church and to work.

Later Concha found her sitting in the old rocker in her room. "Mamá Grande," she said gently, "the government's representatives are here, and Father has asked you to meet them."

As they entered, the officials rose, and Vicente placed a chair for his mother. Vicente had gained a new dignity. Whatever he may have done in the past to tear down the Navarro name, whatever anger and humiliation he may have felt in the present situation, whatever fright over the future, he bore himself now as one worthy of his proud heritage. Not by look or gesture did he show that he was being stripped of his wealth. Once when the division of land was being discussed, Mamá Grande cried out in protest. He gently laid his hand over hers. "It is nothing," he said, turning to the men. "My mother finds change difficult."

"The sugar mill, if you wish, we will buy from you," said the President's representative. "The valuation we have set upon it is low, for it is in bad condition."

"I prefer not to sell it," Vicente answered. "I believe you are making my allotment two hundred acres. I think I can use the mill to advantage."

Ignacio, watching his father, for the time held him in respect.

Late in the afternoon, in the bull ring, the ceremony of division took place. The arena was crowded with people from the hacienda village and the near-by mountain villages who were to receive a portion of the valley. The slavelike submission so long accepted that the very bone structure of their faces seemed to have set in passivity, was overlaid today with a strange look of undisciplined and wild hope. Into the grandstand filed the officials, the President in their midst. "Ah, he is truly a stallion!" they murmured. One after another the heads of families, clad in clean white trousers and overblouses of pinks and blues, took the unaccustomed pen into their hands and put a cross by their names. When this was done the bulk of the rich fields of the Navarros had gone out of their hands, back to the Indians.

As evening settled down, musicians arrived from a near-by town. One man plucked at the strings of a great harp; another kneeling on the ground beat with the flat of his hand on the base. As the night advanced, the music grew wilder, shriller, more nervous. One violinist, then another and another, raised his instrument to his mouth, wailing into its hollow center. Great jars of liquor were brought out. The drinking began. Men and women danced on the planks fitted over a sunken place in the earth. The beat of their feet made the platform a great drum accompanying the harp. The men sang, shouting their couplets vilifying their enemy Vicente, then other enemies, men from the other villages. Machetes flashed in the lights.

Mamá stood at the door of the *sala* listening. An old serving woman of Mamá Grande who had come to cook that evening knelt beside Mamá. "I am frightened," she said. "I am afraid. What do my people know about anything except serving the *hacendados?* Hear them now."

"Out of the depths of four centuries of servitude we rise," Mamá answered. "Such a release frees lusts and hates too long stagnating."

Vicente drank himself into a stupor, which dulled his anger and sense of loss.

Mamá Grande sat erect in her old rocking chair until dawn. What she was thinking no one knew.

Concha, as the night wore on, sought a quieter place in the second patio, but the only quietness was the still pool with the moon reflected in its depths. She longed for Jim. She had thrown over her dress the white woolen dressing gown he had given her when she was ill. It seemed to offer her a kind of protection.

Suddenly skyrockets burst into burning stars, then as suddenly went out. Concha felt her self-possession cracking under the sound of harp, Indian drums, violins, pounding horses' hoofs. She fled back toward the more inhabited part of the hacienda, intending to seek sanctuary in the chapel, and all but stumbled over a man stretched out in the shadow of one of the great colonnades. She gave a little cry.

"What do you fear?" It was Nacho's voice. "None but a member of the family would be here, but I suppose like the rest of them you see only violence in tonight's demonstration."

"What else should I see in it?" Concha leaned against the pillar waiting for her heart to steady itself.

"I mean you're all alike. You think if the villagers have half a chance they'll go to the bad. Haven't they a right to a fiesta? Do you think Father's fiestas here have been any less wild just because they were less noisy?" Nacho demanded bitterly.

"What should I know of Father's celebrations? And I do not necessarily share his viewpoint toward the villagers." Concha quietly answered both questions at once. "But I do share Mamá's. She is not against the Indians, and she said . . ." Concha's words trailed away. Just what had Mamá said as she stood in the doorway earlier in the evening?

"Yes," Nacho answered with cynical inflection. "Tell me. You can't even remember. You don't understand Mamá, and you don't understand me. You don't know how to suffer with your country."

"Are you certain you do?"

The slight note of disdain in Concha's voice Ignacio was quick to catch. He raised himself on one elbow, turning his face away from her toward the pool. Then with surprising honesty he answered. "Yes, but to no purpose. I can't do it, Concha. I can't make myself enter into the struggle. I——" He raised his eyes to his sister. This man looking at her was not the Ignacio Concha was used to seeing, often a little angry, always a little arrogant. His eyes were as if the spirit within looked out between prison bars.

She dropped on her knees beside him. "Can I help, Nacho?"

"Perhaps—if you will let me talk."

"Put your head in my lap as you used to when we talked hidden behind the wash on the roof." Concha tried to speak naturally, not show how unexpected such confidence was from him after all these years.

Slowly, haltingly at first, then with his sentences tumbling over one another, Nacho told her of his life since he returned from Europe; his first beautiful impression of the country, his effort to identify himself with the new Mexico, how he had met Guadalupe, how he had met Pablo—but not who Pablo was. She sensed he scorned Pablo for his opportunism and yet envied him his place in the midst of the struggle. The word "futility" was often on Nacho's tongue, and "separateness."

When he had finished she did not speak, except through the tender motion of her hand as she smoothed back the blue-black strands of hair from his forehead. His eyes were closed, and without their troubled gaze she was suddenly aware his face was still that of a youth.

Nacho was not yet thirty. He had his life before him, and she was young. Why did they all hark back to a past that was gone forever? Her mind picked up things her grandfather had said to her long ago. The old man's fear over the change which had taken place in Mexico in his lifetime had been transmitted to them all. Disillusionment and fear were for the old. Suddenly in a flash of understanding as deeply realized as a vision, Concha saw that a new people was being born from the union of Spaniard and Indian, neither downtrodden like the Indian from whom Nacho's fastidious nature made him withdraw or overprivileged like the Spaniard he had so long sought to be.

"Nacho, you are not a Spaniard, although always from the time you were a little boy you have tried to think you were. You are a Mexican. If you accept that, can you not then take your part in the new Mexico and help me to? You said I didn't understand what is happening tonight. I don't. I can't bear for us to lose the land. I hate the government for taking it. And yet Jim seems to think they have the right. If we don't understand, what is going to happen to us? If we took our part, you and I——"

Nacho sprang to his feet. "I've told you I cannot do it!"

The first pale light of dawn had touched the sky. The air was sharp with the chill that comes when day and night meet. "We'd better get some rest before the ride back." Nacho spoke with entire detachment, establishing a barrier between them once more. But he took her hand as they walked along the gallery of the main part of the house. As they passed the open door of the chapel, they saw Mamá kneeling before the Mater Dolorosa.

Later that morning when the family left for the city Vicente refused to go. "I've some land left and the house. I'll manage things my own way. Now they've had their debauch, the Indians will come whining, wanting me to lend them money to pay for the celebration and for their next planting. Then's when I can begin to bear down upon them. I'm willing to wait."

Concha, looking back, saw her father standing at the hacienda gate, his fedora rakishly tipped over his brooding but still bold right eve.

There is a momentum to riches not immediately lost. Mamá Grande continued to run the establishment as the Navarro household should be run. Ignacio still lived his life as a rich gentleman. Mamá still gave generously to the Church. The habits of luxury and ease had so long been the structure of their lives that they did not yet realize the structure had been shattered. Their credit seemed inexhaustible. Vicente, by a supreme effort, secured another loan, this time heavily mortgaging the city house.

Jim put from his mind the collapse he knew must in time of necessity come to the Navarro fortune. He had more pressing matters to think of. Albright had left, and a man named Tompkins had taken his place. He knew nothing of Mexico and leaned upon Jim for a thousand details Albright had at his finger tips. At first, the change had seemed an entirely stupid one to Jim, but as the weeks went by he could see a pattern emerging.

Tompkins, although he knew nothing of Mexican affairs, knew a great deal about oil as an international commodity, and he knew the British and their oil interests all over the world. He was an adroit businessman. Before many weeks he had established an entirely friendly position with the British firm offended over the so-called double-crossing by Albright. It made Jim wince to see how Albright had been made responsible for that business of the separate lease.

As to labor, Tompkins did not commit himself these first weeks. Jim had hopes of making him see that a compromise would be valuable.

Very early Jim was distressed to note that the new manager was accepting the traditional position of many foreign businessmen: Mexico was easy to exploit.

60

On the day the village had received its land a member of the official party sat in conference with the elders. "The government has no money now to give you for machinery," he said to them. "Look to the *hacendado,* co-operate with him and get in return the use of his tools."

The faces of the villagers darkened, but they did not say what was in their hearts: that they were suspicious of Don Vicente Navarro; that he would outwit them if they dealt with him; that it was better to work for themselves. They would turn the land back to its ancient use. Each man would raise enough corn for his family, cultivate and harvest it with the tool each possessed—his machete. That would please the old gods, too—let a man cultivate only as much of the earth as he could use. The rest belonged to the god of fertility. Thus would they gain security for themselves and their children.

Vicente planned to follow Ramón's example, buy from the villages the sugar cane they produced in their fields and hire the men as day laborers to cultivate his two hundred acres and to work in the mill. But from the beginning there was bad blood between Vicente and the village. On the morning after his return from the business of arranging a loan Vicente, mounted on his horse, paused at the gate of the hacienda, struck by the fact that the Indian men, some of the women and children following, were walking along the ancient footpath which led across his acres to their newly acquired fields. Out of the gates he dashed. Like peas from a pod, the men, women, and children scattered before the flying feet of the horse. When Vicente reached the man leading the little procession, he drew rein. "I have given you no permission to cross my land," he shouted. "Make your own path, and make it on your ground."

In sullen silence the villagers retraced their steps, setting out again on the longer journey which was necessary if they skirted the Navarro property.

With his fedora pulled low over his eyes, Vicente watched with grim satisfaction until the last man was out of sight. Then he rode back to his house. He had sent word to them the night before that he was ready to hire men for work in the mill and in the sugar cane. He sat all morning in the quiet house waiting for laborers. They'll come. They'll need money. The terms will be hard, grimly he told himself.

At noon the elders of the village, Francisco leading—he had left the employment of Mamá Grande now that he had fields of his own —entered the office. Now, now, thought Vicente, I shall get what I want. The swine couldn't hold out a day.

"We have come," Francisco said, "to inform the *patrón* that the road from the hacienda which leads through our village we find dan-

gerous for our women and children. For this reason we have closed
it. There is a longer one which we know you will consent to use."

"I shall use the main road as I see fit. And now, until you have a
desire to work, do not come again to see me."

It was after dark when a knock came on the barred gate. When
Vicente opened, two of the ne'er-do-wells of the village stood there.
Holding their broad-brimmed hats respectfully over their chests, they
addressed him: "Señor, you have always helped us in the past."

Affable as he had never been before and friendly, Vicente invited
them to sit and drink. When the *pulque* had done its work, he began
his negotiation. "I'll give you money in exchange for those slips of
paper given you by the government. Then you won't have to work
even for me."

The two men looked at each other. Never before had money come
to them so easily. Always they had been made to sweat bitter toil in
return for money. Now all they had to do was to turn over to him
their land. When the transaction was done and a few pesos were hidden safely in the belt of each of them, Vicente saw them to the gate.
Softly, without noise, they skirted the sleeping village. By morning
they would be in the great city of Mexico. They were free men! Then
suddenly the old man Pedro, a gun raised, blocked their way. "What
have you been doing?" he asked. "It has been agreed among us that
there should be no communication between us and the *hacendado*."

There was no answer.

"Speak or I shoot."

Then did they confess their sin against the village. Pedro marched
them ahead of him back to Francisco's house for punishment.

From then on two forces were locked in bitter struggle: ignorance
and fierce desire for the land on the side of the villagers; outraged
privilege and fierce desire for the land on Vicente's side. For the families of the two men who had sold their birthright the village sought
to get back the deeds. Taking their meager funds, they hired a lawyer.
Vicente hired one, too. His lawyer was more clever.

And over and over the men of the village attempted to cross
Vicente's fields, but Vicente hired men from distant towns to watch,
with the order to shoot if necessary. Over and over Vicente tried to
use the front gate of the hacienda. The villagers mounted guard day
and night, taking turns sitting outside with rifles across their knees.

One morning in the early summer Vicente determined to break the deadlock. He could no longer endure the ignominious exit from the back gate of the hacienda. At any cost he would ride down the road. He mounted his horse and rode to the gate, pointed the mare toward the street where the children were at play, and gave a cut of his whip to the horse's flank. The thoroughbred, nervous under the unexpected sting of the lash, leaped forward. Pedro stepped out from the shelter of the church. There was a sudden sound of a shot. Vicente reeled in his saddle, then fell, sprawled in the dust of the road. When the men of the village lifted him, he was unconscious but still breathing.

Old Francisco brought the news up to Mexico City, telling the new gateman at the Navarro dwelling to report to his mistress what had happened.

Problems at the office that morning had taken all Jim's attention, so much so that he did not immediately leave after Concha's telephone message to come to the Navarro house was given to him by his secretary. It was a half hour before he went out to his car, and even then he stopped on the way to do an important errand.

As he drove into the patio of the Navarro house, the gatekeeper spoke to him chidingly. "Señor, you have been needed here for some time by the women of your household."

Across the court and up the stone steps, their treads a little too high for the ascent ever to have become effortless to him, Jim hurried. As he reached the top of the first flight he looked up and saw Concha's white face as she leaned over the balcony railing of the floor above. The sun standing directly over the tall house—for it was noon—threw a shadow of the iron grille in a pattern on the white skirt of her dress. With one slender hand she clasped the edge of the railing. She was leaning forward, and the sun touched her hair. He could see by the set of her sensitive lips and her eyes that something terrible had happened. He sprang forward, running up the next flight.

As he reached her she swayed a little. He put his arm around her to steady her.

"My father has been shot. The villagers—" she began in a half-drowned tone—"he tried to get ahead of them. We must go at once to him."

"How did you hear?"

"Word came through at the gate. I don't know who brought it."

"Perhaps it is not so; perhaps they are only trying to frighten you," said Jim. But he knew in his heart that undoubtedly the news was true. He felt now that ever since the land had been handed over to the village he had feared something like this would happen.

"We can't find Nacho," said Concha.

"I'll have to go down then. We can't wait for him. Send him along as soon as you get hold of him."

"Mamá Grande and Mamá are ready, and I must accompany them," she answered.

"None of you must go. It's too dangerous." Jim knew that it might be dangerous for him but far more so for Doña María, as the villagers would link her to the long debt-enslaved years and to Vicente's unjust rule.

"It's no use trying to stop them, and as they are going, I must too. I am not afraid. There is my old *nana*. I can talk to her. And Francisco is there, and Cleofas. They will see that I am not hurt."

The memory of his own childhood and the understanding between him and his mother's Indians made Jim realize that Concha was right. He said no more against her decision. When Mamá Grande and Mamá came down the stairs they were dressed in black with black veils shrouding them, as if they knew Vicente was dead. The word brought was only that he had been hurt. Jim saw with a start that the black-draped figure with them was Concha.

"Please order the big car," Mamá Grande commanded. "You are to drive, Jim. Mamá will sit beside you. Concha and Father Cristóbal will sit with me." As she spoke, Father Cristóbal came through the doorway from the small patio. He was dressed in street clothes according to the law of the country. In a bundle he carried his priestly garments and the Holy Sacraments.

As they neared the village Jim started to take the longer way to the hacienda, obeying the villagers' decree. But Doña María stopped him, saying, "I will enter only by the front gate."

"Then we must halt here. We must ask their permission," said Concha. "I will speak to them."

"As you will," said Mamá Grande. "However, it is not necessary. These Indians fear and respect me."

Jim saw that there was nothing to do except let Concha go, but he felt the goose flesh on his arms and legs as he watched her walk from the car to the entrance of the village street and down it to Francisco's hut. She knocked at the closed door and was admitted. It seemed to Jim she would never come out. But at last he saw her framed in the doorway. turning to speak to someone before she left. Then with bent head she came back to the car. "We may pass," she said, "but very slowly, lest we injure some child."

"In an empty street." A wry laugh escaped Mamá Grande, but she made no further protest. From open doors faces peered sullenly out. When they reached the gate leading into the hacienda, Pedro stepped from the shelter of the wall. He placed his hat over his chest, bowing. "Enter," he said.

When they were within the hacienda grounds and the car had stopped before the deep, pillared veranda Concha leaned over, laying her hand on Mamá Grande's clasped ones. "I must prepare you. He died an hour ago."

When later the cortege was ready to leave and the gates of the hacienda swung back, the entire village was lined up along the desolate street.

The old Spanish church, the one to which Ignacio had first taken Jim for the Easter celebration, was filled with the rich and the poor for the High Requiem Mass. Poverty and wealth mingled always in the churches, whether for a wedding or funeral or the daily Mass. Far to the back, jostled by the crowd, Pablo and his mother knelt.

In the weeks that followed many times Mass was celebrated here at the Spanish church and also at the private chapel of the Navarros for Vicente's soul. Mamá bought many tapers and placed them in the church and chapel.

61

Ignacio did not bother himself over the settlement of the estate. He was glad to leave such matters to his grandmother. Seemingly he was not concerned over the loss of his fortune. "I shall be little affected by the change. I do not believe in wealth," he told Mamá Grande. "All I ask is that my grandfather's books are left to me."

In truth he had lived almost a monastic life since Soledad had left him. His rooms he had stripped of all their luxurious accessories. That comfort and privacy were possible to him because of his rich surroundings—the great house with his room hidden deep in its center, the library where he could shut himself off, servants to wait on him—he seemed not to realize.

He was working, if fitfully, assisting Pablo. Pablo, knowing that Ignacio would have need now of employment, had offered him a position in the new and struggling People's University to teach subsoil problems. It pleased him to put Ignacio to work and also under obligation to him. Ignacio had consented but only on the condition he was not to be paid. Pablo was annoyed. There was no obligation if no money was given for the work. In fact, the obligation was thus transferred to him.

But Ignacio held firmly to his point. The People's University was an instrument of the more radical element in the labor movement. Unthinkable for the once wealthy and still proud Ignacio to be under hire to a people's group. No, he would accept no money for his services. This was a gift to the institution. But he had no time left, he claimed, to go through his father's muddled affairs.

Thus to Doña María fell the task of saving enough of the fortune for them to live with a semblance of their old grandeur. At first she was gratified again to hold the reins, but soon she knew she was too old to manage all the details.

She appealed to Ramón to help her. But quietly Ramón found business demanding his presence in the States. He already had two households to support. He wished to have nothing to do with an impoverished third. It was Nacho who must work for the replenishment of the Navarro family fortune as he, Ramón, had in his family after his return from Europe.

Then Mamá Grande appealed to Jim.

When out of the chaos of Vicente's accounts Jim established order, he found little left. The haciendas, the city property, everything that could be mortgaged, Vicente had mortgaged in a last effort to rehabilitate himself. After gaining Ignacio's consent, Jim sold what hacienda property he could, paying off as many creditors as possible. For the two hundred acres surrounding the house of the big hacienda he found no buyer. No one wished to risk living there after Vicente's death.

Next he proposed to Mamá Grande that she let Ignacio dispose of the great mansion. Business in the years since the Revolution had crept close to the Navarro dwelling. Jim believed they could sell it for a sum considerably over the mortgage placed on it. Many of the old families had moved into smaller dwellings. "There would be no loss of position attached to such a move," he assured her. Mamá Grande flatly refused. With some hesitation, Jim then proposed they make the great house into apartments for the rising middle class.

She saw that the plan was sound. The rental ought to pay more than the interest on the mortgage. By this means she need not leave the home that had been hers ever since her marriage. A semblance of the old grandeur could be kept. The top floor could be adapted to their needs; the library left for Nacho's use—and hers when she entertained—the music room off it for Nacho's sleeping quarters. Julián's bedroom suite could be arranged for her. Mamá, if she cared to remain with them, could have a little room at the back. Or perhaps her daughter-in-law would prefer to enter one of the hidden convents. From now on her part in the family might well be to make constant intercession for Vicente's soul.

All these plans passed quickly through her mind. "This can be done," she said aloud. "Hard as it is, I must stay here for the sake of my dead husband, loyal to him to the end of my life, preserving his memory."

"The antiques with which your house is filled would pay for the remodeling and should leave a considerable sum for running expenses until you begin to get an income from the apartments," Jim told her.

"Sell my furniture! What a dishonor to Don Julián!" exclaimed Doña María.

"But Mamá Grande, what will you do with so many things?" Concha asked, trying to help Jim out.

"They can be stored for Nacho. When he marries, he'll need them. No, it's enough to ask me to give up the house. I can borrow. I'll see the bank tomorrow."

The next evening she sent for Jim again. She was sitting with her head thrown back, defiantly watching the door as he entered. "I want you to change banks for me. I have never experienced such impoliteness."

"I'll arrange it," Jim promised. "And now have you considered my proposal of last evening?"

"I suppose you'll have to have your way. Sell the things. I don't want them." Angrily she wiped her eyes.

The morning the sale began Jim found Mamá Grande, Mamá, and Concha standing in a nervous group awaiting the first buyers. "Concha and I will take care of this," he said. Quietly, without a word, walking proudly, Mamá Grande went up the great stairway, Mamá following. Concha gave him a grateful look, thankful for his understanding action which had come not a minute too soon. The antique dealers, those rapacious hunters who watched for the downfall of old families in order to buy their heirlooms, and women of other countries hunting the old and beautiful were crowding through the gates just opened by the servants.

The great candelabrum with its three thousand crystal drops went first. Jim knew the woman who bought it. She was the wife of one of the men of the American community, a woman of great wealth in her own name. She did not recognize him. How, he wondered, was she going to get it out of the country? There was a law that antiques could not be taken out, and this surely came under that head. She must be counting on the belief among many foreigners that money rightly placed made it possible to avoid any law in Mexico.

The house was a maelstrom now of eager, excited women. In the mass Jim noticed another woman whose husband belonged to the American Embassy. Quiet and dignified, she was moving about the rooms, touching a hanging, an old vase, almost with reverence. She turned to Concha. "It is a privilege to look at such beautiful objects. What exquisite taste these old families had! We owe them much."

He saw her attitude was going to make it easier for Concha. In fact, he realized that for the moment his wife had forgotten the real import of this morning's events and was leading the woman around showing her inconspicuous but beautiful heirlooms scattered about. That Concha could forget like this was a great relief to him, and yet somehow he had not spared her as he had the two older women. That she should share this hard day with him seemed in the mingling of their two selves right.

Late in the afternoon Jim came upon her standing in the patio, superintending the last alabaster vase as it was taken from its place on the newel post. And then as the gates were closed, the sale over, and the house left to its habitual seclusion, Concha put her head on his shoulder and wept.

"My dear," he begged, "I can't bear to have you feel like this."

If I could only stop, thought Concha. I've been brave all day. But now I am spoiling it all by crying, and Jim will think I'm more unhappy than I really am.

But it was good though to share with Jim emotions she knew no other way of expressing: mingled relief that this great house which demanded so much of them all was no longer their master, the sense of loss for the beautiful objects which had surrounded her all her life, and pity for old Mamá Grande hidden away in the great library above.

"It's only that I'm tired," she managed to say at last. "It really isn't half so bad with me as you probably imagine it is."

62

A FEW evenings later Jim and Concha took the plans for the new apartments to Mamá Grande. They found her sitting in the library. Jim spread out the blueprints. He was justly proud of them. Because of his American desire for air, light, and efficiency, he had spent a great deal of effort to make these small apartments attractive places in which to live. "You see," he said, "each one has light and plenty of air. There are no dark, ill-ventilated rooms."

"It is immaterial to me about the light and air. For the kind of people who live in little spaces, what does it matter?" Mamá Grande answered.

Jim in his astonishment said nothing for a moment. "I am puzzled," he said at last. "Isn't it important to you *who* should live here with you?"

"Was it important that my servants were common people?" she asked. "They, too, were in the house with me. I shall make rules, and those who live here will keep them."

"Very well," said Jim, folding up the blueprints. "I'll go ahead and arrange for the work, if you are satisfied."

"I am satisfied if you spend as little money as possible."

"I can, of course, see that they cost less, but then I cannot use these plans." Jim was about to slip the rubber band around the roll when Ignacio entered the library. "Would you by any chance care to see these?" Jim asked him.

Ignacio held out a languid hand, took the bundle, slowly unrolled it. Suddenly his languor was gone. For some time he studied the drawings, asking an occasional question. Jim watched him, realizing that he had not seen Ignacio so interested in anything since his study of

Mexico's subsoil resources, puzzled over what it was in these blueprints that had appealed to his fleeting fancy.

"I had not dreamed you were doing anything like this!" Ignacio exclaimed, finally looking up. Jim could see he was excited. "I had thought Mamá Grande would insist on two or three elegant apartments for—well, for her friends."

"And just where would there be revenue in such elegance?" asked his grandmother, a caustic note in her voice. "I am not in a position to give charity."

Ignacio again turned to Jim. "This is exactly what we need in this city—accommodations for the growing middle class." He had a sudden, vivid vision of Soledad standing before him saying, "This little house, I can't give up. In the new Mexico there were to be thousands of little homes, clean and sunny . . . for workers . . . apartments that teachers and engineers could afford."

"Do you need any help in getting these plans executed?" Ignacio asked.

"Concha does," answered Jim. "I'm too busy to oversee the work properly. I hoped to direct it through Concha. I have no right just now to spend time for things outside the office."

"I'll take it over from here on."

Mamá Grande did not often oppose Ignacio, and she did not now. Jim was secretly elated. Nacho's timely entrance had saved the plans and also brought him an assistant.

As the two men stepped out on the balcony outside the library, Ignacio said, "The sun is setting. I should like to see the view from the roof before we go down." Was this a move on Nacho's part toward a renewal of friendship? Jim wondered.

As soon as they were out of hearing Ignacio said, "I am fearful of conditions growing out of the civil war in Spain. We'd not like to have the Monarchist group controlling things here. It's going to be important for us to have great solidarity in this hemisphere. Labor is getting very strong under Cárdenas. It would be a pity if the foreign companies let it come to an issue between them and labor. That might lead, as it did in Calles' administration, to definite trouble between the two countries."

"We have a new manager, as you no doubt have heard. Just what his stand on labor will be I don't yet know," Jim answered, taken a little aback by this sudden resurrection of the subject of foreign ownership in Mexico, a subject never mentioned between them since that disastrous quarrel they had had over subsoil rights. Had Ignacio's position changed on this question, and if so why?

Just then Concha joined them, and Nacho dropped the subject. He turned to his sister, saying, "Have you noticed how the city is changing since we used to play here and I used to brag I could throw my ball to the edge of the city?"

"Yes, it's much bigger," she answered. Looking closely at her brother, she realized he was less arrogant in manner than he had been. Out of all the pain and suffering of the last year, she perceived, something good was emerging. Already their lives were shaping to a unity they had never had before. Mamá Grande trusted Jim, although grudgingly, and now here was Nacho at last being really friendly with him and offering to help with the apartments.

"This is a city that is going to influence the world." Nacho's eyes were aglow as he spoke. She felt a tightening of her happiness back almost into pain. Was Nacho simply carried away with a new idea? Would he perhaps in the middle of the work on the apartments suddenly lose interest? Was his friendship for Jim only a passing whim?

63

THE work on the apartments went forward slowly, for it was a long, tedious process extending over months to turn the old house with its solid masonry walls, its intricate passageways, into modern apartments such as Jim had worked out in the blueprints. Both Ignacio and Concha were inexperienced, and Jim was busy. Mamá Grande would have been a valuable helper with her practical bent, but she refused to take any part once the top floor was arranged to her satisfaction. "I am old and tired and need my last years for the Church. It is time I considered my future," she said with a somber look in her eyes. "Surely after my sacrifices I am entitled to such considerations. My husband——"

"Let us go on as we have done," Nacho answered quickly. When Mamá Grande retired like this into her widowhood no member of her family ever opposed her. "That is, if you are satisfied, Mamá Grande, with what we are doing," he added.

Mamá Grande grudgingly granted she was. "Only the elite are shabby these days. It is a distinction."

One possible humiliation worried her: that Ignacio might have to earn his own living. To avoid this she was trying to spend as little as she could, hiding her poverty behind proud gentility. Never had a man in the family worked in an office, except Concha's husband, and after all he was an outsider—not born into their exclusive coterie nor into the Church. Neither institution, therefore, expected much of him.

Mamá did not wish Ignacio to be forced to take a position either, but for another reason. She felt that at last he was beginning to come into harmony with himself. She did not know how, but she did not wish the process to be interrupted. But she knew what Mamá Grande did not—that Jim was paying some of their bills. The old woman's little economies did not make up for her extravagances. Someone must earn money if Ignacio was to be left free.

Quietly Mamá made her plans. There was a way in which she could earn enough money, she believed, so that Ignacio need not take regular employment. She knew of a small building not far away that was vacant. Antique shops flourished all over Mexico City. She would start one, begin by selling some of the precious heirlooms handed down to her from her own family, and she would sell the possessions of people like the Navarros who were having to give up their big houses. She would not mind a great deal being a shopkeeper.

"Do you wish to do it?" Ignacio asked, when later she told him her arrangements.

"Yes, I wish to do it," she answered simply.

Mamá Grande was angry at first—a shopkeeper in the family! It was then that Mamá told her she must choose—either Ignacio or she must work.

"It shall not be Ignacio." Thus Doña María indirectly gave consent to Mamá's proposal.

In a few weeks the antique shop seemed to have become a part of the city. It did not look new with such ancient objects in its windows, and dust accumulated quickly in the showroom, settling over the innumerable articles brought Mamá to sell. And Mamá herself, sitting at an old Spanish desk, pushed close to the entrance so that she could see any customers when they entered, seemed always to have been there. The working people passing along the street soon accepted her as one of themselves.

Six months after they were started, the apartments were finished.
Concha and Nacho had experienced real companionship in the work
they shared. But there was discussion between them when it came to
the renting. "I want only working people to live here, Concha. I am too
busy to interview them, so you will have to do it, but I must give final
approval."

"What do you mean by working people?" Concha demanded.

Ignacio began explaining to her the tenets of the labor party.

Finally Concha cut him short, saying, "You're full of theories, Nacho,
that I can never remember. I would like simple people to live here,
you know, and kindly, but I shall not care what they do for a living.
You can be certain that no rich ones will be housed here, if that is what
you wish to avoid. You and Jim saw to that in the planning."

With meticulous care, Concha investigated every applicant. She
weeded out those who thought to bring to themselves special distinction by living in the old Navarro mansion. The tenants she chose finally
were unobtrusive, kindly folk who she thought would make good
neighbors for her grandmother and Mamá. Nacho approved her selec-
tions, admiring her for her liberalism, thinking she had decided as he
had on the theory that they were from the middle class.

At last all the apartments but one were rented. It was the smallest
of them all, not large enough for a family with children. Concha was
wondering if they would have to reduce the rent on it when into the
office made from the gatekeeper's former room a young woman came
to ask about it. Immediately she caught Concha's attention. She was
undoubtedly Mexican, and yet there was something about her that
reminded Concha of a woman from the States, something indefinable.
Whether it was in her expression or her manner Concha could not
decide. Something direct and determined.

"I have just heard of these apartments," she began. "And I came to
see if, by any chance, there is still one vacant."

As Concha did not answer, she went on quickly: "I can give you
references. My father and I have recently come here from the States,
where I have been studying to be a doctor. He formerly held a position
in the government."

"We have one apartment left, but I doubt if it would suit you, for
it is very small." Concha was uncertain whether this young woman
would be willing to accept the restrictions Mamá Grande had insisted
on for all occupants, rules about the hour for the closing of the gate,
rules about not using the galleries except to pass along them to their

apartments, and many others. Concha did not wish to bring friction into the house.

"I want a small apartment." The young woman was looking at the floor plan as she spoke. "This little one not marked rented I see is on the south, and it is large enough for my father and me."

"I shall have to speak to my brother about it. He is renting only to working people." As much as she wanted to rent the apartment, Concha still hung back.

"I am working," the woman answered quietly. "I am attached to the children's hospital."

Just then Ignacio entered the room. He frowned. So he, too, thought she wouldn't do. Then suddenly his face seemed lighted from within. "Why, Berta, it's you!" he exclaimed. "Where have you been? I hunted everywhere for you when I came back from Europe!"

It was the young woman's turn to look puzzled.

"Remember," Ignacio said. "I used to walk home with you from the preparatory school. I didn't know you for a minute. You were such a little, wiry thing then. You're so softly rounded now." He was looking into her eyes. The lively eyes of a boy, he had thought once, because of their intelligence. They held depth and understanding now.

"Ignacio Navarro! Nachito, how beautiful to see you again! And to think it is to your house I come." She grasped his shoulders, looked up into his face, and laughed. "And I hear you accept only working people. You, Nachito, who always were such an aristocrat. Now we can indeed be friends—and may I have the flat?"

She was all Mexican now. Concha no longer had any doubt of her as a tenant, but it was startling to find Nacho welcoming her quite so warmly.

"Yes, of course you can have it!" he exclaimed. "Come, I'll show it to you myself!"

Concha watched them cross the patio in the bright sunlight, disappear in the long curve of the stairs.

Tomorrow the tenants were to move into the apartments. Late in the afternoon Concha walked slowly from floor to floor, making her final inspection. At first she did not notice how quiet the place was now that the workmen had gone. But slowly the stillness penetrated her consciousness, and with it came the knowledge of how changed would be the life of her old home from now on. Only a ghostly sense of grandeur clung to the marble stairways, the galleries. Looking down into the patio, she saw Jim hurrying across it and was thankful. There were too many reminders of the past to face alone.

"I wanted to have a look before the people move in," he said as he joined her. "It's nice, isn't it?" He took her hand, leading her from apartment to apartment. "A man with a moderate income can live comfortably here. I'm proud of what we've done."

As they came out again onto the gallery, after looking at the last apartment, they met Mamá coming in from her shop. "Tomorrow?" she asked. Jim realized then that both Concha and Mamá dreaded tomorrow. He wished he could get off to be with them, but Nacho would be here.

Early the next morning, as he and Concha drove down into the city and along the Paseo de la Reforma the clear light of the November morning threw patterns of the great trees down onto the pavement. From all the side streets cars were coming into the great avenue; and at each *glorieta* at the quarter, the half circle, more of them joined the ever-thickening stream. Concha knew the noon crowd when shoppers and businessmen streamed down the streets going home for dinner and the siesta, but this morning's procession of moving cars gave her a new impression. As they came closer to the heart of the city, men with brief cases sprang lightly from cars, disappeared into buildings along the way. Office workers filled the narrow sidewalks.

The whole aspect of the city had changed, she suddenly realized, since her childhood. The French architecture of the days of Maximilian and Carlotta, even the dignified Spanish colonial architecture, seemed dwarfed by the towering square buildings set solidly like the old Aztec pyramids. In the recessed corners of the Monument to the Revolution stood massive stone figures of laborer and peasant. This was an outpushing, vigorous, new world that frightened her a little, a world consuming her world.

As Jim turned into the street where the Navarro mansion stood, they saw the gate was congested with furniture and people. In the midst of the melee of men, women, and children thronging the patio was Nacho. He hurried forward. "It's terrible," he exclaimed, throwing his hands up in a gesture of despair, "all these people!"

I can't leave them like this, thought Jim. The office will have to wait. "I'll call the office, Concha, and arrange to come in a little later. I'll help you out here first."

"If you would, Jim!" Concha gave him a grateful look.

But when he came back from the telephone, he said, "I can't stay after all, Concha. I'm needed at the office. The Oil Workers' Union has sent in a demand for a new contract. Mr. Tompkins wants to talk over some of the details with me. Nacho will have to attend to things."

~~~~~~~~~~ *64* ~~~~

LOUISA and Ramón were at home again after their long visit in the States and had asked Concha and Jim to come in for cocktails in the afternoon. The first thing that Jim noticed when they walked into the smart apartment was that Ramón's Spanish relatives were standing at the far end of the room with Louisa.

Jim had an uncanny feeling of time running backward. Then the scene shifted, bringing the incident out of the past into the present. When he talked to them, the Spaniards did not seem like the same people who had been there two years ago. They had lost their self-assurance, shaken from complacency into fear.

"The civil war in Spain is terrible," one of the women exclaimed to a knot of people gathered around them. "Even our old servants turned against us. Why, even the nurse who had helped when our daughter was born deserted us, went over to the republicans. None of us was safe."

"But you are now," said Ramón. "Here in Mexico you can make your home until Spain puts down this *canaille.*"

"We had thought so," said the man standing next to Jim, raising his beautifully manicured hand to his forehead in a gesture of despair. "But is it not true that here in Mexico this President of yours has declared in favor of the rabble?"

No one spoke for a moment. Then Louisa broke the silence with her light, tinkling laughter. "That is nothing but a play for popularity with the common people." At her words the tension in the room seemed to crack like surface ice over a pool. Beneath was the old self-confidence these people had always had. Their aristocratic assurance was again established.

When they left Nacho walked with Concha and Jim to their car. "These relatives of Ramón's are here for a purpose. They and their kind have made a bid for German aid to kill the liberal tendencies in Spain. They want to throw us, too, on the side of Germany." Ignacio spoke in low tones scarcely above a whisper. "Herr von Brenen is back again. He is here to get oil at any cost. He intends to make trouble with your labor, bring about enough friction if possible to stir up the old question of Mexico's resources. Can't your company do something about that contract your labor is asking for?"

Jim looked at his brother-in-law, trying to decide what his motive was in trying to help the oil companies out—a direct reversal of his earlier position. Was Nacho speaking for some part of the labor organization? Tompkins had ignored the Oil Workers' Union's demand for a better contract. Was this a way to frighten him into acceptance of their terms? But if so, how on earth had the unions secured the elegant Ignacio for their spokesman?

"I don't know whether I should ask you, Jim, but this is no time for polite speech." Ignacio seemed anything but the dilettante now. His tone was earnest, direct. "Why did your office put aside the wise Señor Albright who so long managed diplomatic matters for your company, and bring in this man Tompkins, who knows nothing of Mexico and cares less?" he demanded.

Jim hardly knew how to reply. He had no right to divulge the policies of his company, and yet he wanted to meet Nacho halfway. "Probably because they thought he understood the international problem. The change was made at the head office in the States."

Anger flared for a moment in Ignacio's eyes, but he answered quietly. "I've changed my mind, not about our right to own our subsoil, but about the advisability of struggling for those rights at present. I've come to the conclusion that for us to take the oil wells over now would be bad. Mexican oil should stay in this hemisphere. If there is a quarrel between Mexico and the States, as there would be if we took the wells back, it might give Germany and Spain their opportunity to get hold of the oil while we are divided."

"And do you think there is a determination on the part of the President to take over the wells?" asked Jim.

"If you can do anything to make the head of your office see how important it is to stay on good terms with us just now, you will be serving—" he paused—"well, maybe the whole world," was Ignacio's somewhat evasive answer.

"What is your authority for saying so?" asked Jim, hoping to flush Nacho into the open and learn what his connections were.

"I cannot tell you. I am exceeding my authority to say what I am going to. The railroads," Ignacio went on, "are bound to be taken over by Mexico under the new expropriation laws proposed by the President. The oil wells, too, unless there's a change of policy. But do away with bad blood between yourselves and the laborers, and you don't need to lose your wells any more than the silver companies their mines. They have managed to come to agreement with labor. But this policy of ignoring their demands—you can't handle labor that way. Only by coming to terms can you possibly save your wells from confiscation. There will be demands, and they may seem severe, but I beg of you, try to get your company and the others to meet them. You must understand that I am saying this because the time has come when we Mexicans must choose between fear of the States' domination and fear of being drawn into the quarrels of old Europe."

"Why do you say that with liberal Spain now winning?"

"But what does it do to us?" asked Ignacio. "The aristocrats are the refugees over here, is it not so? That is a danger to us—old Spain again settling itself in here. And there is Germany. . . . We cannot afford to get into trouble with your country at a time like this. Confiscation of the wells would raise hell between us, as you know."

Concha stood a little apart listening to Ignacio's urgent plea. She saw that Jim was deeply affected, too.

When they were in their car Jim's concern did not leave him. Ignacio had succeeded in communicating to him his own strong conviction that the oil controversy was more than a matter of business; it was a matter perhaps of war or peace in the world eventually. It was not necessarily with any authority that Ignacio spoke. Jim's former suspicion that labor was making use of Ignacio left him. It might well be Nacho's study and his Spanish connections had given him a deeper grasp of the struggle than any of those more directly connected with it. If Tompkins could come to know a man like Ignacio, it might change his attitude toward Mexican people and eventually toward the Mexican government. He might come to see that friendship was of paramount importance in the delicate negotiations which lay ahead.

Tompkins was more and more accepting the prevailing attitude among foreign businessmen, which seemed stupid to Jim—that all Mexicans were a cross between highway robbers and guitar-twanging *caballeros*. For that reason there was no need to negotiate with them on labor problems or any other matter. The American efficiency was to be preserved, and offices run strictly by Americans.

As an opening wedge Jim decided to ask Mr. Tompkins to a dinner

party at their house to meet Mexicans socially. He had met Tompkins' wife at the office and had found her both intelligent and kindly, a
woman who might help her husband to see the Mexicans in a different
light.

Carefully he and Concha chose their guests: Mamá, Ignacio, Señor
Mendoza and his daughter, an editor of one of the Mexican papers
and a sensitive young Mexican lawyer, and their wives.

When they gathered in the patio for cocktails, Jim sensed a faint air
of condescension in Mr. Tompkins, and Ignacio was definitely on the
defensive. It was too bad of Nacho, who knew how much was at stake.
The situation was exaggerated by the fact that the Mendozas, on
whom Jim counted because of their fluent English, had not yet arrived. Mr. Tompkins spoke very little Spanish, and, with the exception
of Concha, the women spoke very little English.

Concha was standing between Mr. and Mrs. Tompkins quietly
sipping her cocktail, answering their polite, conventional remarks. But
she was her most aloof self. Jim knew what a private kind of person
she was, and that this quality had been enhanced in her during the
years of mourning for her grandfather and father when rigid restrictions had set her apart. Perhaps it was asking too much of her to meet
strangers within the mourning period for her father.

All at once Concha seemed to sense the situation and Jim's distress.
She smiled assurance, and then took over the party, drawing first one
and then another into the conversation. "It is a great pleasure to me to
hear you say you find my country beautiful, Señor Tompkins. And you
have seen Cuernavaca and Acapulco?"

He fell into the trap. "Yes, yes."

"Oh, but you should see all of my country—Mt. Orizaba, Fortín,
and Veracruz, and of course Tampico and Puebla. You have much yet
to see." Her eyes were dancing now, but she appeared innocent in
introducing Tampico. Jim saw a gleam of malice come into the news-
paperman's eyes, but Concha went innocently on. "And here are
friends who know your country and love it. Señor Tompkins, let me
introduce Señorita Mendoza and her father."

"Indeed I know it," exclaimed Señor Mendoza, "and its glorious
history. I owe much to your countrymen's kindness."

Jim saw, as they took their seats at the table, that Tompkins was
enjoying himself. He was seated on Concha's right with Berta Mendoza next to him and Señor Mendoza directly across. Ignacio was a
little farther down the table. "My husband tells me," Jim heard

Concha say, "you are a collector of old manuscripts and books. My brother—" she nodded toward Ignacio—"and Señor Mendoza share your passion. 'Passion'? Is 'passion' the word, Señor Tompkins?"

A look of keen pleasure passed over Tompkins' face. He was indeed enjoying himself, both because of finding others in this group who shared his "passion" and because of his pleasure in the beautiful woman at his side. He had not known until now that his subordinate had made such a notable marriage. These all seemed to be distinguished people.

Mamá, quietly observing Mrs. Tompkins who sat nearly opposite her, had noticed that her eyes wandered over the room from one antique to another. In her slow but correct English learned since she had opened her shop, Mamá said, "Beautiful old things touch you deeply—is it not so, Señora Tompkins?"

Jim saw that there was real accord between these two and he drew them into conversation over the *objets d'art* to be found in Mexico, Spanish, French, and Chinese.

"It's like our New England—" Mrs. Tompkins turned to Jim— "with Chinese things hidden away in the houses. Clipper ships there and Spanish galleons here bringing them in."

"There was more wealth in Mexico," Jim answered, "so I think you'll find articles here you never saw in New England."

Everyone talked now of subjects cultivated people over the world talk about—of books and music and even a little of politics, although Jim led them away from that subject. He did not want Tompkins to feel the evening had been planned to influence him in favor of the Mexican government. Ignacio described some of the old books in his grandfather's library.

Mr. Tompkins listened intently. "Such fine old books are priceless," he exclaimed.

"My house is yours," Ignacio replied.

The next morning Tompkins stopped at Jim's desk as he came in, rubbing his hands together. "We are indebted to you for an exceptionally pleasant evening. Your brother-in-law seems to know a great deal about old manuscripts. I thought perhaps we could have lunch together someday."

"Fine," said Jim; "but I warn you, Mr. Tompkins, he will probably want to talk about the labor situation in Mexico. He is almost as interested in it as he is in books."

"Indeed. And is he as good an authority on it as on books?"

"Something more useful than that to us just now, I think," Jim answered quietly; "a touchstone, shall I say, to Mexico?"

"Well, let's have the luncheon," was Tompkins' reply. Immediately he strode off to his private office.

The luncheon was highly successful, the kind you have when enthusiasts meet, thought Jim. He was inclined to think Ignacio was almost ready to invite Tompkins to the house to see his grandfather's books.

At the end Jim introduced the subject both he and Ignacio had been waiting to bring up—the present demands of labor.

"I suppose, like the rest of your countrymen," Mr. Tompkins began, "you think the government has a right to take over the wells at any time."

"Yes, a right, but I do not think they should exercise it now."

Mr. Tompkins leaned forward, his attention definitely caught. "And why do you say that?"

"Because of a larger issue."

"And that is?"

"That the oil should stay in this hemisphere. You no doubt know as well as I that in the last war Mexico was the second biggest producer of oil in the world. It would not be good for it to fall into the enemy's hands, if there is to be war with Germany. And it would if our two countries quarreled."

"Let us waive the question of war. How do you suggest we avoid a quarrel between our countries?"

"By reconciling yourself with labor."

"Ah, I see. Very clever!"

On the way back to the office Tompkins said to Jim, "I have the feeling, Buchanan, that someone in the government is making your very charming brother-in-law his mouthpiece."

"Perhaps that increases the value of what he said," Jim answered. He was disappointed that Tompkins had missed Ignacio's sincerity and evident conviction and had taken his analysis of the matter as a clever trick to frighten the foreign companies into compliance with labor demands.

65

A few days later Tompkins called Jim into his office and told him that he had about decided to join with the oil companies of foreign countries in a protest against labor's sudden new demands. "The general consensus is that what they ask for is fantastic—hospitalization, vacations with pay, old-age pensions, higher wages, and a large percentage of executive positions open to them. How do you feel about it, Buchanan? Wouldn't we gain strength and probably win out by joining them?"

"You mean with no concessions to labor?"

"Yes, we are going to make some concession on wages."

"What I think is that the group has chosen the wrong item on which to compromise. If you'd open up office jobs, I think they'd give way on other things. At least compromise with you."

"Why do you say this?" Tompkins tilted his swivel chair back, put his feet on the desk, his hands under his head, indicating he was ready to listen.

"You've met my brother-in-law. He is bitter against your exclusion of his countrymen from all important positions."

"Isn't he an exception? Certainly he's of a different class from most of the Mexicans I have met."

"In his knowledge of books, yes, but not in his matter of pride. I believe you will find the same feeling all through the growing middle class as well as in the old aristocracy." Jim was thinking of Guadalupe's withdrawal when he refused him a job.

"I see." Tompkins brought his feet down to the floor, turned again to the pile of papers on his desk.

"Suppose I could persuade the other companies to make this concession——"

"I doubt if you could ever convince the more conservative oil companies that yielding to the Mexicans on the question of office personnel would be to their advantage," Jim answered. "Especially the British companies. You've worked with them. You know they have almost a caste system when it comes to executive positions. The only hope, I think, is for us to act independently."

"I was sent here to make peace between us and the British. Now you propose I break it all up."

"I think, if I understand what's going on, you'd save our wells for us."

When a week later the unions threatened to strike if their demands were not met, Tompkins told Jim that he was joining with the British. "We mean as a solid bloc to show the unions and the country that a threat will get them nowhere."

Jim was sorely disappointed, and he hated to think what Nacho would say when he learned the unyielding attitude of foreign business. Ignacio had believed after his talk with Tompkins that the North American saw the issues and would act for the larger good. Jim could imagine the bitter expression on Ignacio's face when he heard the news.

As the months dragged on and no agreement was reached with labor, Jim realized that the whole country was turning against the foreigners, especially against the States. Why was it Tompkins and the other oil men did not realize what was happening? Nothing he could say influenced any of them. In every contact he had with Mexican officials he sensed their withdrawal. The very atmosphere seemed charged with emotion.

Even in his own house Jim found he was not exempt from the country's disapproval. The servants, friendly until now, withdrew behind a blank wall of reserve. And even Concha, although she did not let it affect their relationship, was deeply disturbed. She read the papers avidly. Often afterward she would pace the room with quick, agitated steps, or sit for a long time in brooding silence. It was as if they had suddenly turned a corner and had entered a dark, unknown world where antagonism between their two countries threatened their happiness.

As the days and the weeks passed, this other world seemed to have made out of Jim a man she scarcely knew. Always before she had felt that she was Jim's paramount interest, but now she realized that his work held that place. And yet he seemed to need her as he had never needed her before. Sometimes all evening he appeared not to know that she was there, preoccupied with his own thoughts, but if she left the room he would soon follow. This new strange relationship wherein she played such a secondary part in his life seemed oddly enough to be deepening Jim's need of her.

Although the inner core of Jim's being was rooted in Concha, all the rest of him was concentrated on the delicate task he had set himself. He was trying to keep some good will between himself and men he knew in the government in order that he might be a middleman later between them and the oil companies. At luncheons, dinners, and at the cafés in the afternoons Jim tried to make these men see both sides of the question.

In May, when the winter of brilliant sky and brown parched earth slipped into spring, with the plateau valley touched with the green of sprouting corn, Tito celebrated his fifth birthday. Jim planned to stay home, for Tito had begged to have his father all day. Very early the little boy crept quietly in from the nursery. Giggling with delight, he kissed his father's nose, his closed eyes. "Little mosquitoes pestering you," he whispered.

"You're disturbing your mother," Jim whispered back. Then he picked his son up and carried him back to the nursery.

"I get a cake today, and I get another on my Saint's day and presents. Do I get presents, Daddy?"

"Not until Mother is up." Jim helped him into his clothes, and together they went out into the garden.

At half past eight Tito wanted his breakfast. As they walked through the patio, the telephone rang. "Just a minute, son." Jim picked up the receiver. "Really? I'll be down immediately."

Tito clung to his hand, crying, "You can't go! You promised! And I haven't seen my presents."

"I'll stay home on your Saint's day," Jim assured him.

"What is it, Jim?" He had not heard Concha coming down the stairs.

"The Oil Workers' Union. Seventeen thousand of them and affiliated unions have struck. They are tired of the delay over their demands, they say. I've got to get down to the office as quickly as I can."

The quiet seemed ominous as Jim drove through the city. Not a streetcar or bus was moving. Surely now the oil men would see the need for conciliation. But when he entered, an angry Tompkins met him. "We'll never surrender to such a threat," he said, "even if we close the wells down. Let 'em starve for a while. Then they'll see what a benefit we are to the country."

Jim forgot that the man before him was his chief. "Look here,

Tompkins. I warned you that you were pressing the Mexicans past forbearance, that they'd turn on you. Can't you see you won't be able to do anything if you make them hate you? People starve sometimes —as irrational as it may seem—rather than give up their national pride."

Mr. Tompkins looked angrier than ever for a moment, then changed suddenly. "I want you to come with me to this meeting. Tell the others what you've said to me."

The telephone was ringing. "Yes, yes, that's what I think. I'll be right over."

The meeting dragged on and on. All of the men were angry, all of them certain, as one said, that the Mexicans needed to be taught a lesson.

Then there was the meeting with the labor representatives. Jim was translating, and he tried to soften the refusal, a little, couching it in polite Spanish words. But he knew he had not succeeded, when every Mexican face went deadpan.

66

IGNACIO, standing on the balcony outside the window of his room and looking down on the dead city, felt resentment burning in him against these highhanded foreigners who neither saw Mexican rights nor respected Mexican laws. Well, labor would teach them.

He went in and down to the apartment of Berta Mendoza. She had left long ago for the hospital, but Ignacio knew he would find a welcome from Señor Mendoza. The old man was sitting by the French window in the sun. On the balcony outside pots of flowers were blooming. He had been reading the morning paper. It lay now spread out on his knees. As Ignacio entered, he looked up. His smile held great sweetness. Ignacio felt his anger quieting.

"You mustn't take this too hard, Nacho. I know the people of the States well. They were kind to me when I was an exile there before the Revolution. The Good Neighbor Policy is pretty young yet. Give it time. Business is always the laggard in any country."

"Time!" exclaimed Ignacio. "It isn't time they need to find out that we are not an inferior people. It's a change of their natures. We'd better join the European bloc and be done with it. We are acceptable to them."

"Berta asked that you meet her at the hospital tonight," said Señor Mendoza, shifting the subject. "It wouldn't be possible for her to get home in time to dress for the concert, she said, with the streetcars tied up."

It was a beautiful May evening. Nacho parked his car outside the hospital and waited. After a little Berta came out to him, but she was still in the uniform she wore at the hospital. "You'll have to go without me, Nacho. I'm terribly sorry. There's a mother having a bad time. I don't know whether we can save the baby."

"Why do you let them use you like this?" cried Ignacio.

"We've had this all out before, Nacho. Please go and enjoy yourself." Berta leaned wearily against the car door.

"As a matter of fact, the concert has been called off, but I thought we'd have dinner together and then I'd take you for a ride."

Seeing how disappointed he was, Berta yielded a little. "Get your dinner, Nacho, and then come back for me. I'll try to be through."

Berta glanced out the hospital window from time to time. Ignacio still sat there slumped down in his car. Then at last she was free, and she hurried into her street clothes and out to the car. Swiftly Ignacio drove through the city, empty of the usual traffic. Silent, almost as if it slumbered, the old city lay under its canopy of stars. Berta, tired from the day's work and the long walk to the hospital that morning, sank back with a sigh. And then as they drove on, her strong body gathered new force and exhilaration. Both the day and the evening seemed good to her. Ignacio could feel her lassitude giving way to exuberant joy in the evening.

"Berta, you've got to marry me. Days like this without you are intolerable. I need you more than those people do at the hospital. Why do you keep putting me off? I adore you, Berta."

"Nachito." There was reproach in the way she spoke his name. "This we have agreed we would not talk more about."

"But you never have told me why. I know you love me. I've seen it in your eyes."

"Nachito, I shall tell you here tonight under these stars I do love you, but I will not marry you—not until you learn to work." Now she had said it, and she was almost sorry. And yet—no, she was not. His body, thin and elegant but never exhausted with effort, sometimes, as tonight, affronted her.

"You know I am teaching a class at the People's University. I have spent a couple of years in the study of my country's resources."

"When you feel like it. Men like you, Nacho, have been idle too long in Mexico. Go to the States, study to be a lawyer—or a doctor or anything. Come back and help your country. Then I'll marry you."

"The States! After what is happening in Mexico right now!"

"When you have learned what it is to exhaust yourself for your country, then you will have the right to be bitter against the States, as you are today. In the States men work. Now take me home."

That night Berta turned and tossed in her narrow bed. Here she lay under the very roof that housed the man she loved and yet she was separated from him by a gulf too wide perhaps ever to be spanned. She knew herself strong, vital, and inclined to manage. To marry Nacho as he was now would be to destroy him. He must have force and purpose to meet her force, or else in marriage he would indeed be destroyed.

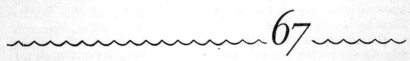

67

TWELVE days passed, tense with emotional violence, but there was no rioting in the city, none at the wells. Stubborn men sat quietly waiting in the labor offices; stubborn men sat quietly waiting in the offices of the oil companies. Then the Federal Commission on Conciliation took the matter in their hands and the strike was ended pending their decision.

The summer of 1937 with the whole of Mexico under the tension of waiting had its effect on the Navarro family in divers ways. Jim saw little of Concha and Tito. Many mornings he left his house before Tito was up; often he came home after he was in bed. After a time the little boy ceased to ask for him. Several times he was out of town for a week or ten days. In gas stations in the city and in towns throughout the country unpleasant incidents kept occurring. It seemed to Jim he scarcely smoothed out a wildcat strike in one place before trouble broke out in another. His one objective was to keep the men representing the company from being drawn into any lawless act which might embarrass the company.

Ignacio, when Jim saw him, which was not often, had retired within a shell of politeness. As far as Jim could learn from Concha, Nacho spent a great deal of time with Ramón. Had he cast in his lot with those who were trying to have the wells confiscated? Strange bedfellows, those working for confiscation—the ultranationalists and the ultra-Europhiles who wished to withdraw as far as possible from the States. Surely Ignacio had not joined them.

It was Mamá Grande's moment. She would see that Ignacio under Ramón's tutelage became the gentleman he was meant to be. His former constant attendance on a woman like Berta Mendoza seemed to be over. Good! She would see that the chance of such a self-seeking, ordinary woman to worm her way into the Navarro family was ended once and for all. Her influence removed, Nacho would forget these crazy ideas of study and reform he had been indulging in so much of late.

One evening after Ignacio had left the house she sent for Berta. "If the *doctora* will be seated, we can discuss a matter delicate indeed, but one I must take up with you."

Berta took the chair designated, on guard lest she betray some small knowledge of Ignacio that this predatory old woman might use to harm him.

"It has been brought to my attention," said Mamá Grande, "that you in your kindheartedness have been doctoring the small ailments of the people who live in my house. Is it not so?"

"Yes," answered Berta, unaware of the trap that was being laid for her, relieved that the talk was not to be about Ignacio.

"And you sell to them medicines?"

"Not really sell, just let them pay what they cost me. Many of them often go without what they need because of the expense."

Doña María's jeweled hand tapped the arm of the chair. "And you have a license to sell?"

"No, of course not. I am not running a pharmacy."

"Ah, *doctora,* I am afraid you avoid the point. If this should be reported . . ."

"I think you are overalarmed, but if it bothers you——"

"There is only one way to put myself right with the authorities. I dislike to lose a *doctora* who has been so kind to my tenants, but I think I must ask you to find another house in which to carry on your . . . pharmacy."

"I understand." Berta rose, and left the room. She walked along the gallery, fear in her heart now for Ignacio, understanding him now as never before. Every wile the old grandmother had would be used to keep him from achieving anything. Had she been right to refuse him?

"You are perplexed?"

Berta turned, to look into Mamá's understanding eyes.

"I must move from here at the order of Doña María, because I have occasionally doctored a sick tenant." It was characteristic of Berta Mendoza that she answer Mamá's question in this forthright fashion. And yet, as she spoke, she knew she was not giving the real reason for her going.

"I think I understand. It would be pleasant to have you come to see me at my shop. I think we have much in common." Mamá smiled and passed on into the room where Mamá Grande was sitting.

Often late in the afternoon that summer Berta stopped at the shop. She got into the way of helping Mamá with her accounts. Mamá found bookkeeping difficult. One woman or the other always led the conversation round to Ignacio. Both loved him; both were grieved over his present way of life. Berta felt it was her fault. Mamá prayed and waited.

As his father before him, Ignacio gave himself over to easy pleasure and to Mamá Grande's soft care. His cause was gone. Neither the Mexicans nor the North Americans had the idealism to put self-interest aside and work for unity. Why then should he try to save them?

One evening he discovered that Ramón was the member of a secret movement meant primarily to divide the Americas at the Rio Grande. Ramón, a little drunk, gave the salute. A Spaniard lately come from home thought it meant Ignacio was a member of their organization. "Good to welcome a man of your standing," he whispered. "The old Mexico restored. Church and state one. Landowners holding the power and the riches. Union with Spain."

Many things about Ramón which had puzzled Ignacio now fell into place. The coming of the rich relatives, and always with them Herr von Brenen. Mexico helping Spain, Germany. They in turn helping Ramón and his friends back into power.

The spark of endeavor burning so low in Ignacio kindled again into purpose. More passionately than ever he now desired unity between the States and Mexico. He lived out his days on the surface as idly as ever. He slept until noon. In the evening he was the gayest member of the café crowd. But under his gaiety, under his lazy, indolent eyes, his mind was alert, missing no possible clue. It was an exciting, all-absorbing task. Carefully, sometimes by brilliant flashes of understanding, he pieced bits of information together. The most ignorant, dissatisfied Indian villages, those which had received no land, were to be inflamed with a doctrine of hate toward the States and toward their government which planned to take their God and their saints from them.

Now it was that Ignacio was seen most frequently with Ramón. But often Ignacio went to a small house on a side street—Pablo's house.

At the very end of the summer he learned the name of the secret organization—Sinarquistas. It meant order—military order! A military organization, then!

68

THE grapevine service in all political centers of the world sends its messages out ahead of the event. In August a few days before the findings of the Arbitration Board were to be given out, it was noised about that the report would be sensational. No concession whatever was to be made to the oil companies. They would have to accept labor's demands. As soon as Ignacio heard it, he hurried over to see Pablo. He found him excited and elated over the news.

"The oil companies will never comply. You know what that means, Pablo," said Nacho.

"The President will expropriate the property, I suppose. And should."

"Expropriation!" exclaimed Ignacio. "It's no time for that. What that will mean you know, Pablo."

"The patriotic Nacho!" scoffed Pablo. "Is your interest perhaps with the North American in your family? You have been hard hit of late. Too bad to have another source of income jeopardized."

Ignacio's hand moved instinctively toward his pistol. Then he controlled himself. "Pablo, you know from the information I've brought you that peace between the two countries is a desperate need just now unless the reactionary Europe you have been at so much effort to keep out of our country is to control us."

"Oh, I don't know." Pablo was a little ashamed of himself for such an unwarranted attack on Nacho. Entangled beyond his understanding were the strands of envy and love for this brother better favored than he, who always somehow remained superior. He wanted to think of him as a dilettante and a waster. It would add further to his envy of him if Nacho should become an effective factor in Mexico's struggle. For this reason he had never introduced Nacho to the close labor group around the President of which he was a member. Pablo feared his half brother would outstrip him in the political world if he set himself to the task. And yet deep in Pablo was a pride in this brother of his.

Nacho leaned forward. "Suppose we should confiscate the wells? You know the German who twice has come here for the oil, and you know that he is here now. And you know the reactionaries in this country who intend we shall sell to him. We might have to if we no longer had the States for a market. We can't afford to anger the States now. In normal times, of course, I'd be for confiscation, too, but not now. Not now."

Pablo was moved, shaken out of his bad temper by the emotion in Nacho. "If you feel this way," he said, "why don't you do something about it?"

"What could I do?"

"You and——" he hesitated, malice again arising in him. It would be amusing to send Nacho on a thoroughly quixotic errand. "You might go and ask the American ambassador what to do." It was said half in jest, half in earnest. Even to cynical Mexicans like Pablo, the elderly American ambassador who for the last two years had walked among them with such simple friendliness was becoming a symbol of understanding between the two countries. Men could not dismiss him lightly from their minds. He had won out here in Mexico by the sheer weight of friendliness. When he had first come, he had had to be guarded on his ride to the Embassy, because all Mexico remembered him as the Secretary of Navy who had once ordered American ships into Veracruz. Mexico would never forget it, but they had respect for genuine friendship, and the ambassador's brand could not be doubted.

"I'd simply be a Don Quixote tilting at windmills," Nacho answered.

Pablo flushed, realizing now he couldn't outwit Ignacio. Ignacio had guessed his thought.

Later, as Nacho went toward his home, he began to think. Jim still might influence the oil people. There was just a chance.

He found Jim sitting at dinner with Concha, lost in anxiety, for he too had heard what the verdict was to be. He had eaten little, and now sat absent-mindedly crumbling a piece of bread.

Into this perplexity Ignacio plunged. Refusing to sit down, he paced the room in a way Concha knew so well indicated some project burned within him. At last he burst out: "Why doesn't your office do something, Jim? You're headed straight for trouble. Don't you know it?"

"Yes, I know it." Jim's tone was dull and hopeless.

"Why don't you do something about it, then?"

"I've done everything I know how to do," Jim replied in that same flat tone. Then he raised his head to look at Nacho, his brows drawn together. "I haven't noticed that you've been doing much of late to help."

Concha watched the two men, fearful that there was to be a battle between them. One she understood because she loved him, and through that love had developed tentacles of understanding; the other instinctively because she was united to him by the racial strands of character. If only they could come to trust each other fully; if only each could cross over into the other's mental territory; if only she could spin a bridge for them on which to cross—together they might act to some purpose.

"If you two—" she said, choosing her words carefully, then all at once forgetting caution, like Nacho, afire with her intention—"if you two," she repeated, "should go together to the American ambassador, you two who represent two countries' interests but who want the same solution, might he not, hearing your arguments, be able to influence somebody somewhere?"

Concha's inspiration ended in vagueness. She really had no idea of the business details. She expected both men to ignore her remarks, for now that she had spoken they seemed futile. Why she had thought of the ambassador she did not know, except that he was a symbol of the Good Neighbor to Mexican people.

"I had the idea suggested to me at my office," said Jim at last. It was the memory of that talk which had so oppressed him this evening.

"Perhaps now you won't be so much in favor of these Mexicans," Tompkins had said.

Jim had winced at the opprobrium put into the word "Mexicans," but he held himself in control.

"This is what the Good Neighbor Policy is doing to business," Tompkins had gone on. "The ambassador who talks so much about it ought to help his own countrymen for a change. You might tell him that it would be wiser for Mexico not to present any such terms, for to a man we won't accept them."

"It seems a risky thing to defy the findings. This will be a government report. You know the threat of confiscation which always hangs over us," Jim reminded him.

"They won't dare. Haven't we staved it off ever since 1917? Our troops could be used as before. It's not beyond possibility, you know. Of course we will consult our lawyer at every step."

Jim had no intention of carrying his chief's message to the ambassador. Nor did he think Tompkins meant him to. Tompkins, he realized, was only blowing off steam. But now—it gave him an excuse for carrying out Concha's idea.

"A labor man suggested it to me," Nacho answered, breaking into Jim's thought. "But neither your suggester nor mine, I imagine, thought of our going together."

In an odd respectful way they both looked at Concha. Seeing she had gained an advantage, she asked, "Why not do it now?"

"In the evening!" Jim exclaimed. "Business isn't done that way. He's probably giving a dinner or something. It's only at his office——"

"They say he lives very quietly," Concha persisted. "This is not exactly business. It's . . . it's—" she paused for just the right word— "it's people talking things over in a friendly way, isn't it?"

"If it's a hunch," said Jim, smiling now on Concha, "perhaps we'd better act on it. Only a hunch will work now. It's about his style to see us informally."

"Meet his good neighbors to talk over a neighborhood problem?" Nacho's eyes held a wry merriment.

"Do call him," urged Concha.

When Jim and Nacho entered the reception room at the Embassy, they were struck with the quiet homeliness of the scene. The ambassador was alone and had evidently been reading. His finger still marked the place in the book.

They had some hope, they told him, that before the report came out he might, through his government, bring some pressure to bear on the American companies not to refuse the findings, but offer a settlement beforehand.

"And you—" the ambassador turned to Ignacio—"would rather see a settlement than confiscation?"

"As matters stand in Europe, yes," Ignacio answered quietly. Then he told him the hazards ahead as he saw them if the wells were taken over at this time.

"I'm tremendously interested in what you've both told me, and I'll of course do everything in my power to bring about peace," the ambassador said when Ignacio had finished. "It is most unusual," he added, "to have the two countries so ably represented in the same delegation. Such accord is one of the most encouraging signs I have seen."

Both of them felt encouraged. Although the ambassador had not committed himself, Jim felt he intended to do what he could. Even before they left, he had rung the bell and asked the servant to have his secretary called.

As they left the Embassy, Nacho asked, "Would you be willing to meet a friend of mine, a labor man?"

"Perhaps I'd better not. I have no authority. It might be interpreted as a commitment of some sort. Do you mind?"

"I doubt if you need to worry about that. Suppose you consider it— well, a family affair. The man is my half brother."

For the moment Jim was taken back. As intimately as he was connected with the Navarros, he hadn't expected any of them to speak of Vicente's other family. It was only in the final settlement of Vicente's affairs that he had learned about it. That Nacho would speak so casually of his illegitimate brother surprised Jim, but he knew now that to hold back would condemn him. And something might even come of this casual visit to a labor man. It was the Mexican way to bring important things about through unofficial channels. Always the personal relationship. Maybe this was an overture from a higher source. "Of course I'd like to meet your half brother." Jim tried to say it casually as a Mexican would say it.

Ignacio had proposed the meeting feeling that it was time for Pablo and Jim to know each other. Both would be needed in the coming struggle.

The whole atmosphere of Pablo's house was middle-class, carefully harvested comfort maintained only by vigorous denial of indulgences and acceptance of work. Ignacio never came here that he did not wonder about it. Pablo had access to a great deal of money. Or did he? Just where did Pablo stand in the government?

Pablo's wife was sitting in her accustomed place in the *sala*, correcting papers for her school. She had always been a person without glamour or romance for Ignacio. Why had Pablo, obviously ambitious, married her? Ignacio asked himself for the hundredth time.

"My brother-in-law." Ignacio turned slightly toward Jim after he had greeted her.

"We welcome you to our humble house. It is yours." The woman spoke mechanically. Turning toward Jim and then back to Nacho, she said, "But here is Pablo."

Jim hid his astonishment. The man entering the room was the same one who in the café so long ago had read aloud the *corrido* condemning the former American ambassador. So he was Nacho's half brother! He was oddly like Vicente in build and in the shape of his face; his round, wide-open, prominent black eyes were like Vicente's, too, except for their expression. They are the eyes of a man who knows power, he thought. Who is this Pablo? Where does he stand in labor's hierarchy? Odd that I've never met him when I've conferred with labor men.

"So at last you've remembered to come and see us, Nachito. Perhaps seeing me at my office at the University today reminded you of us." Pablo threw his arm affectionately over Nacho's shoulder. But Jim sensed that Pablo was not at ease with his more aristocratic brother.

For a moment there was only the scratching of the woman's vigorously driven pen and the sharp sound of rain on the foliage in the patio. Then, hoping to draw Pablo out, Nacho remarked, "Cárdenas is putting heart into the Revolution."

"Cárdenas will go down in our history along with Juárez," exclaimed Pablo. "I traveled with him when he was campaigning and afterward," he said, turning to Jim. "There is a stallion for you! He is fearless."

For an hour he talked of Cárdenas and his reforms, but in all his talk no mention was made of the oil controversy.

Once they were outside, Jim asked, "Nacho, what position does your brother hold in the government?"

"A very small position in the labor department, but in the labor party he has tremendous power. Just how much even I don't know. He holds

some undercover position. But I do know that he is a personal friend
of the President, and can always get his ear."

So this Pablo was Ignacio's source of information, thought Jim.

69

THE papers carried the findings of the Arbitration Board in great headlines and commented on them in biting editorials. In cafés and
pulquerías hastily written *corridos* appeared—couplets bitingly scoffing
at Dollar Diplomacy masquerading under the guise of the Good
Neighbor.

The investigation declared the labor increases offered by the companies were far below what they were able to pay. Even if the wages
asked by the oil workers were tripled, the production of Mexican oil
would not cost the companies what it did to produce it in their home
countries. Therefore, the Arbitration Board upheld the findings of the
experts and awarded labor an increase of wages which to all the companies would amount to twenty-six million pesos. To Jim's surprise
the Board had sided against labor in the matter of executive positions
for Mexicans in foreign firms.

When the foreign oil companies met together to discuss their answer,
most of the local men agreed with the higher executives sent to Mexico
to handle this crisis, that they would not give in to the demands of
Mexican labor.

Jim had accompanied Tompkins to the meeting. Now he leaned
forward, saying quietly, "Gentlemen, I was asked to come into the
organization of which I am now a part because it was thought I was
in a position to know the Mexican people intimately and estimate the
sincerity of their reactions. From my years of close association with
them, I believe that if you don't accept the Arbitration Board's findings, you will lose out entirely. Emotion is running high among all
classes. The Mexican people with few exceptions want confiscation—
would welcome it in fact."

"You fail to remember we have big and powerful governments behind us," said the spokesman for one of the English companies. "It
would be a steal, and we'd put it right up to our governments to take

action. This is not an individual matter. It sets a precedent in all countries. A statement should be made to the papers immediately."

Jim looked on hopelessly as the statement was given out. Suddenly he was electrified. What was the spokesman for the foreign companies saying? "We cannot and *will not* pay the amount asked for extra wages and safeguards to labor." *Will not!* Those words were addressed to the government of the country in which they were guests! Jim could already see the screaming headlines in the evening papers, and he could see Concha's face when she read the words, "We will not pay." She would flush with humiliation. And Nacho—— Jim dreaded to go home.

When later he went into his house he found Concha standing by the long window at the farther end of the patio. She was silhouetted against the magnificent panorama of the valley and the mountains, the two great snow-covered peaks glittering white against the blue Mexican sky.

At his step she turned. "How could they do such a thing?" she cried. "We are a free people. How would you like us to act like that to your country?"

Jim felt his heart go dead within him. He was very tired. For months he had worked with every bit of energy he possessed to prevent this from happening. He sat down in the nearest chair, putting his head against the back, shutting his eyes.

He felt her fingers lightly touching his forehead.

There was no merrymaking in Jim's house at Christmastime. The temper in Concha's family was such that Jim could hardly play host to them this year. Neither Mamá Grande nor Ramón would come. Even Nacho might not. Concha avoided an awkward situation by saying she was not well enough to entertain them all.

On the first day of March the Supreme Court gave its decision. It upheld the findings of the Arbitration Board.

The oil companies refused to accept the decision.

Late that afternoon Jim was getting ready to leave his office. He had stayed on a little after the others to tend to a few last details. He felt some extra tension in the city. I'm foolish, he said to himself; this business has got on my nerves. He went to the window, and gazed down on the street. The office was very still. A door banged. He turned to see Ignacio walking across the room.

"The fools!" said Ignacio, laying his soft felt hat on the desk and lighting a cigarette. "No one in his right senses would defy the verdict of a country's Supreme Court."

Jim did not answer.

Nacho's tone was cold, even dispassionate as he went on speaking. "I have just seen Pablo. The President is done with your outfit and all the others. He means to take over the oil wells tonight. You have just one chance left. If within the next hour we can persuade the oil companies to accept the Supreme Court's decision, you may save yourselves. You understand I'm not interested in saving the companies for their own sakes. I don't give a damn what happens to them, but I do care what happens here."

Even in the midst of Jim's consternation he felt a little thrill of satisfaction. Nacho had said, "If *we* can reach them."

"I can try. Tell me definitely, Nacho. Give me some evidence that the President means to act."

"He is meeting now in secret conference with some of the senators. There are labor men there, too. Pablo sent word to me that if you could see the look of mingled anger and stubborn determination on the President's face, you'd know he would act as he has said he will."

Jim seized his hat. He knew where Tompkins would be, where all foreign businessmen gathered at this hour of the day. Although he knew he held the last card in his hand and every minute was precious, he schooled himself to walk with casual indifference into the cocktail room of a downtown hotel and order a drink. Then, when it was brought to him, he rose as if he had not before noticed that his boss was there, went over to him and under cover of their casual greetings murmured, "May I speak to you a moment on important business?"

"It cannot wait until morning?"

"It cannot wait an hour."

"I'll get away from the crowd. Be up in my apartment in a few minutes. Here is the key."

The moment Tompkins joined him, Jim said, "I have word, reliable word, that the President means to issue instructions tonight to take over the oil lands. He is in conference with his most trusted senators right now. I can tell you no more. You have to take my word that he is through with us. He considers our attitude insulting."

"My God!" gasped Tompkins. "He wouldn't dare. Why, he knows what the United States and England together could do to his little country."

"He does not think they will interfere," Jim answered. "Here is his statement which will be released to the press tomorrow morning. It says, 'This means no international conflict. America has a chance to prove her friendship for a smaller country by not interfering in our internal affairs.' We've just one chance, and it may be too late even now."

"What is it?"

"Meet their demands. Abide by the court's decision."

"If you're right, and somehow I believe you are, I'll see what I can do." Tompkins walked across the room to the telephone. "I'll have to get hold of our lawyer first. He is downstairs. Ask him to come up. Then we must get in touch with the others."

As Jim listened to the harangue going on over the telephone, he paced the room, knowing that each minute lessened their chances. A half-hour later, he left with the compliance of the companies, a hastily written slip Green, the lawyer, handed him. He gave it to Ignacio, who had waited in the lobby, went with him as far as the entrance to the palace, watched him cross the great patio, disappear in the shadows of a stairway. Then he went back to the hotel to wait.

When Nacho came, defeat was written in the lines of his face, his whole body. "It was too late," he said briefly. Tompkins swore.

Jim wanted now only to get home. For days he had hardly sensed Concha's presence; now he was in urgent need of her. But when he reached home and had told her his news, he realized that she did not share his disappointment.

Watching him, Concha wondered just how she could help him out of that closed world into which he had entered. It was the kind of world Ignacio dwelt in so often. She had not thought it would ever be so for Jim. Ignacio's world would always be within himself. Jim's had seemed until recently an objective world of affairs. But now his hand, lying inert on the arm of his chair, said more eloquently even than his eyes that he was defeated and shut off. And yet there was a wild, tumultuous crying in her heart. Mexico, her country, was freed of its long humiliation.

70

IT IS entirely in keeping with the Mexican temperament to hold a fiesta to celebrate the confiscation of the oil wells while the whole earth echoes to the astounding act, thought Jim. He was standing at his office window watching the parade of Mexican soldiers, cavalry, and labor battalions. Trotting along the narrow walks at the side were sombrero-crowned men from the country, dark-faced women with their *rebozos* drawn about their heads or across their backs as cradles for their babies. From the variety of costumes, every faraway village must have heard that the oil wells had been returned to the nation. With startling clarity his impression on the evening of his return to Mexico eight years ago came back to him—the Indians of Mexico were like an old, half-buried river, its source hidden deep in the earth.

Later, standing in the Alameda under its tall trees which threw patterns of light and shade across the waters of ancient Spanish fountains, Jim watched the people with their offerings moving silently into the Palace of Fine Arts. So they would pay for the expropriated wells! On the side of the government it was only a spectacular gesture to ask for these offerings. It would take vast funds from the treasury to pay for the confiscated property, but this stream of dark-faced Mexicans moving upon the temple of art, giving a chicken or a bit of pottery, believed they were buying back their country. Jim saw a familiar figure in the line. It was Concha!

That morning Tompkins had informed him that a skeleton organization was to be kept here in Mexico by the oil company for the purpose of coming to a settlement with the government on the price to be paid for the properties. They did not believe they could use Jim in it. It was a bitter disappointment to him. He had hoped he would be chosen to help in this difficult task because of his understanding of Mexico's point of view.

Tompkins had offered him a position in another Latin-American country where the company owned wells. But did he want to take it? He believed, now that the battle had been fought and he could stand back and get the perspective, that Mexico was entitled to control of her own property. Suppose a like situation should occur in another country?

Financial security was all on the side of accepting the position. His surplus since helping the Navarros was very small, not large enough, in fact, to warrant waiting for a position here in Mexico to turn up. The alternative was to go back home to the States and start over. But to move to another Latin-American country or to move to the States would be equally unacceptable to Concha. He knew well that transplanting would be almost impossible for her. Not only were her family ties too strong, she had to a remarkable degree the Indian feeling for place. Whichever alternative he chose, he might leave her here and go alone . . . hold onto security for a few years until his resources were built up.

Weary of the effort to decide what to do, he left the crowded streets, got into his car, and drove home.

The house seemed without occupants when he entered it. He went to the dining room and poured out some dry Spanish wine, sat down before the empty table. After a little he heard Concha, Louisa, and Tito talking together in the hall. "Let me have Tito for a while," Louisa was begging. "You and Jim should be free for a little."

"Well, just for a day or two," Concha answered reluctantly, "if Jim wants to go away for a little rest."

He rose and went to meet them. Tito rushed toward him. What a big boy he was! Jim's eyes seemed to come suddenly into focus as if he were seeing his son at closer range than for a long time.

"Jim," cried Concha, "I've tried all afternoon to find you. Mamá has asked us to come see her. Are you too tired?"

He smiled. "I'm never too tired to see your mother."

It was after closing hours when they arrived at the antique shop. Mamá led them to the back, where one small electric bulb burned, placed for them two delicate French chairs. "They're lovely, aren't they? They were brought to me just today by an old man whose family had furnished their house after the French style in the days of Maximilian and Carlotta. Those days are gone." As she spoke, Mamá seated herself opposite them in a high Spanish chair upholstered on back and seat in cardinal red.

How handsome she is! thought Jim, glad to forget his perplexities in her presence. The brilliant red emphasized her iron-gray hair piled on the top of her head, her clear olive skin, her great black eyes, her high cheekbones and well-modeled temples.

Silence brooded over the little shop, and Mamá's voice seemed scarcely to break it. "I am not unaware of the struggle you are facing," she said, addressing Jim. "North Americans are not popular in Mexico just now. You have been thinking of going away."

Jim started. He had told nobody of his intention.

"There is a real place for you here." She paused a moment, rested her head against the royal red velvet of the chair's back. Her large dark eyes seemed to glow in the faintly lighted room. "It has been revealed to me what that place is. Your people, Jim, and Concha's have always belonged to the land. There is the abandoned hacienda, two hundred acres of sugar cane under cultivation and a village in need of guidance. It is in our villages—" she looked toward Concha now— "that the final salvation of the country lies."

The plan was so preposterous that Jim had a desire to laugh. But he controlled himself, saying quite soberly, "But I'm no farmer, Mamá."

"You don't need to be," she answered, "at least to begin the task. You need to be a good businessman and humane enough to co-operate with the village."

Was the plan so preposterous after all? As Mamá said, he came of landowning people in the States. And what did his father do when he came to Mexico but repeat the pattern? His mother, too. And what other way lay open to him? He saw now that he had made an almost irrevocable choice when he entered business outside his country. Then a few years here seemed of little importance in the long stretch of his manhood. Now he realized with clarity that the years between twenty-five and thirty-five are precious beyond belief to a man, the kernel of his life. Most of these he had spent in Mexico. It would be difficult to go home.

And yet success at the hacienda seemed almost insurmountable. He would have to depend on the village for labor. Was it possible to work out some co-operative effort with men of a village that had killed a member of his family? He knew his fellow countrymen would laugh at the idea, consider it fantastic. He knew all the various branches of the great Spanish-American clan to which he belonged would smile in superior fashion at the idea. They'd say that no Indian in that village could ever be trusted. There was even real danger in the attempt. Opening up the hacienda would look to the villagers like the very evil they had killed Vicente to rid themselves of. Even if he convinced them that he was a different kind of man and they allowed him among them, could he change passive acceptance into active co-operation? Finally, where was he to get the capital?

"Suppose," he said at last, "all that you say is so, it is not safe for Concha and Tito."

"You mean," said Mamá, voicing what Jim evidently hesitated to say, "because my husband was killed there, they might be killed?"

"Yes, his murderer has never been punished. Why wouldn't the villagers feel they might get away with something like that again?"

"Perhaps it is better the murderer has not been found," Mamá went on. "The villagers might feel then they had to be avenged on our family, since they would consider us responsible for the apprehension of the slayer."

"I couldn't risk it." Jim looked at Concha as he spoke.

"I am not afraid, Jim," she said. "I would like to live at the hacienda. Tito could stay with Louisa until we were settled."

"I must think about it." Jim rose. "First I must be assured it is a sound business proposition. Such a venture needs to be backed by several men. And I must talk to Nacho. After all it is his land."

~~~~~~~~~~~~~~~~~~ *71* ~~~~~

ONE morning a month later Concha and Jim drove out of the city of Mexico toward the barricade of mountains. At the highest point from which they could view the valley Jim stopped the car so that they could look back at the city spread out in the valley beneath them. Neither spoke. Still silent, they drove on to the top of the pass. It was cold and bleak up there, a kind of no man's land eleven thousand feet above the sea.

Tito's absence raised in Jim's mind his earlier doubts over the project. It revived vividly an incident of his own childhood. He was sitting securely between his father and mother, that sense of security so soon to be shattered by the death of his father and the killing of his mother. Was he offering Tito some such future? He threw off the moment of doubt. Everything pointed to reasonable success in the undertaking. Through Pablo he had met one of the hacienda experts who knew that part of the country well. The expert had assured him he could start harvesting the cane as soon as the rainy season, soon to begin, was over. In the rich bottom land of the hacienda the sugar cane, though neglected and the yield lighter than under care, would be salable.

Ramón had bought the house in town. He had even offered to put up some capital, but Jim had not accepted. He wanted a free hand. He did not wish to be placed where he would have to carry out policies of which he only half approved. He was through with that kind of business. At the hacienda Concha and he could be their own masters.

Concha was caught in a wave of homesickness. Giving up her home had been a much greater wrench than she had expected. When Jim had first told her they must sell the house in order to free his capital for their new undertaking, it had seemed possible, even interesting. But when they began to dismantle the house, and bedroom, nursery, *sala* were emptied—places created for certain purposes—it seemed almost that the whole intricate, delicate process of their marriage was being destroyed. She had a curious sense of her own roots twined around the house, as she had once seen a tree's roots around an old shrine. In time the roots had grown into every crevice until shrine and tree were one indestructible entity.

She roused herself to talk brightly to Jim, but only for a little; the words and the brightness were soon expended. Jim, engrossed in plans, did not notice.

The air was hazy with the smoke of many burning fields. This was the Indian's way of treating his land, burning last year's stubble. They could see many exhausted fields lying fallow, the Indian having moved his little corn patch to ground not yet robbed of its life-giving powers.

Gradually the land shelved down in small and large valleylike steps. On the hills the grass was dry, shining yellow in the sunlight, but in the valley wherever there was a stream there were trees in blossom, some with white starry flowers, some with long violet clusters. Some had deep red flowers. All were waxy and glistening.

At last they came to the old hacienda grounds that now belonged to the villagers. Sugar cane had been uprooted to make room for corn. Here and there a man was plowing with a primitive plow pulled by another man. The land seemed empty and unused.

"They do a better job than they are credited with doing. What land they use is well cultivated," said Jim.

Then they came to the hacienda's cane fields. They showed neglect. Jim's lips set. Here was a task. It would test all his powers.

Concha was thinking, How shall I approach the villagers? Jim and she had decided that the best chance to win them over lay in showing them in the very beginning that they would not override their rights. They would consider the road through the village a private one and so naturally consult its owners about using it. For this reason they had sent no baggage ahead, intending to win the villagers before letting them know they had come to stay. They had brought plenty of food with them, and of course the great house had plenty of furniture. "I want us to come as friends. Our chances of success lie in establishing that relationship," Concha had insisted. "The villagers are both violent and polite. We must appeal to the politeness."

Nearer they came. From a slight elevation in the road they could see the hacienda walls, broken in places, entirely gone at one corner. Then the car dipped quickly into a little hollow, and there was the village, the great colonial church dominating the huts.

"We had better stop here," said Concha. "Let me go first and talk to them."

"You're sure it's all right?" There was anxiety in Jim's voice. "If you don't come back in half an hour, nothing will keep me here."

"Please trust me, Jim. So much depends on it." With these words Concha, as on the occasion of Vicente's death, went alone down the road, but she did not stop as then at the first hut. The danger was not so great today. She knew that bravery was an asset among these villagers. She meant they should admire her courage. But it faltered a little in the emptiness and silence, for no one was in sight. She realized now that she should have known the village would be prepared for their coming. It shows, she thought, how unaware of primitive ways of obtaining information one becomes in the city.

Indeed the village, by that primitive process lost to the city man, had by its own means of communication learned that members of the Navarro family were arriving today. As the hacienda appeared to have been given up after Vicente's death, they had encroached a little here and there on hacienda land. They had used the stones in the wall, and in other ways too they had encroached. They could explain, of course, the matter of the Virgin coming to dwell among them. The Mater Dolorosa preferred a niche in the village church to the hacienda chapel. That of course the señor and his lady would understand was beyond their control. The Virgin of Sorrows had told them she wished to dwell among them.

What was to happen now? Was it all to come to nothing, this gaining of the land? Was today not to be better than yesterday? Despair held off by a kind of resigned skepticism possessed the villagers. They hated all *gachupines.* And there was a gringo coming, too. Since Vicente's treatment of the village even Francisco and Cleofas had joined in suspicion of the Navarro family.

Pedro, Zapata's man, had already left for his wild, hidden haunts in the mountain ravines. The hunt was on again, he supposed, to kill him for killing the *hacendado,* and never did he intend to be taken alive. His gun was his only companion. The desire to kill rose in a great wave in Pedro. He shrugged. He would come back at night and avenge his death before it took place, he decided with the grim humor of his people.

Concha went on until she came to the house of Francisco. At first no one answered her knock. "I have come," she said in a quiet tone, speaking into the silence, "as a friend, knowing I shall receive the courtesy of you who value courtesy."

There was a pause, then a rustling within. At last the door was opened, and before her stood Francisco's wife, her old nurse.

"*Nana,* you nursed me and reared me, and now I am come to dwell near you. Please let there be peace between us."

"My little *niña!*" cried the old woman. Then she drew back. "I do not know. Francisco is now in the fields, but the sun is setting. He should be here to sit in his door soon."

Concha replied, "Then I will sit here at the door looking toward the west and wait." Evidently her plan was working, for Francisco appeared so soon it might seem that he had heard the whole conversation.

The two sat at the door gravely talking. It was a very long, slow talk, but in the end there was accord between them. "We have no wish to disturb the life of the village," Concha explained.

"Go in peace, *niña.* It is your land," he answered. He used the polite words of his former servitude. In those long subject to others a semblance of acquiescence is worn like a shield. So was it now with Francisco.

That night when Pedro crept in close to the broken place in the hacienda wall, Francisco was sitting there. "Put away your gun,

Pedro," he said. "Our Concepción has come back. She is to be safe here if things are as she says. Do you understand, Pedro?"

"And the gringo will take our lands. And that is to be allowed?"

"Until we know they mean to harm us they must be safe," Francisco answered.

Pedro grunted. "My gun and its sweet message can wait."

Concha had been lying awake, and she heard the voices and the fall of a stone at the break in the wall. She raised herself on one elbow, fear gripping her in its tight-closed fist. She wanted to scream, but that grip on her heart had taken her breath. Before she could breathe again the voices had died away, and the night was still except for the rustle of the banana leaves in the patio, a dog barking in the village, the braying of a burro. She lay down, her body pressed close against Jim's. At last she slept.

72

WHEN daylight came, although Concha forgot her fear, it was not replaced with joy for the task ahead. The uprooted feeling that had been with her on the journey down was still a tangible, physical sensation. And the hacienda house in the glaring light of morning, with its dusty, unoccupied rooms filled with a faded elegance, depressed her. There were the pitiful signs of Vicente's last efforts to look after himself when the village refused to serve him. Concha's instinct to care for the men of her family reached out to him in the grave.

Mechanically she went about closing off the distant patios and surrounding buildings, centering their life around the main patio, leaving Jim to work out the hacienda problem by himself. She had no surplus energy, no surplus will to grapple with his difficulties. Cleofas was the only woman in the village who seemed to have the time to help her. The work was hard and Concha was not used to it.

Jim found the sugar mill was not only in bad condition, but much of the machinery for extracting juice from the cane had disappeared. The refining rooms were left, but everything was in a state of neglect. Among the villagers there was neither friendliness nor unfriendliness.

With polite expressions of their regret, they told him they could not work for him, pleading their need of time for their own fields. They made a great show of their industry. No man or boy could be found loitering along the street in the daylight hours. Day after day the silent opposition continued.

Toward ten o'clock one morning Concha came into the dining room. If she could only have slept until noon, then the day would have been shortened and perhaps made bearable. She was startled as she entered to see Jim still seated at the table. "Why are you here?" she asked.

"I should have known I couldn't do it. I was a fool to try."

The instant he had spoken Concha knew that her husband's discouragement was not only because he was beset with seemingly insurmountable difficulties. He might not be conscious of it, but the flagging of his spirit had been partially in response to the flagging of hers. There was a danger in a man and a woman growing as deeply into each other's lives as she and Jim had grown. If she gave Jim the sheltering warmth he needed, she felt certain he would be able to battle with his problems. If she withheld it as she had been doing, she would maim Jim, bring defeat down upon them both. Something more she realized. It was not enough to offer him that shelter. She must be an active partner in this undertaking, understand all the intricacies of the sugar industry, as Mamá Grande would if she were here. But the effort to perform this creative act seemed too great. Then suddenly she seemed to draw on some heretofore untouched reservoir of energy. "Why do you say we can't succeed?" she asked.

"What can I do without laborers? And they won't work for me. They say they are too busy. I imagine they're loafing off in the hills."

"How did you approach them?"

"Well, I've offered them good pay. When that didn't go over, I tried suggesting we pool our resources. I'd supply seed and tools, plows and hoes for use in their fields, and they'd supply the work for mine."

"Father probably offered them the same things and then—" Concha hesitated—"and then he did not keep his promise."

"That might explain it, but it wouldn't help us much, would it? There's too much for us to live down here, Concha."

"It would help," she answered, "if we could find some way that would satisfy them that we meant really to share. Think, Jim! Isn't there something that would prove to them you were not here to exploit them, that you shared a common need with them?"

"And what would that be?"

"To make a living for your family as they for theirs. It isn't like the old days when we were so wealthy and they so poor."

"Only to ourselves do we seem poor. What we have must seem like untold riches to them. I see no common ground."

Concha realized she had blundered here in knowledge of her own people, too far removed from their dark history of centuries of poverty.

"I haven't been over the hacienda yet. Perhaps we could go together to see it. We haven't yet ridden the horses you had sent down. I'll be ready in a minute," Concha said, rising from the table.

It was a half-hour before she returned dressed for riding, her eyes sparkling.

"See," she cried, "it's Louisa's gift. She wanted me to feel that our life here was the return to the old *hacendado* ways."

Concha was wearing a woman's *charro* suit. The chamois-soft beauty of the leather jacket with its silver embroidery and the wide brimmed hat which she had turned up at one side in the manner affected by the old Spanish grandees gave a dash to her personality Jim had never glimpsed before. Her piquant beauty stirred him anew and changed his own stale mood of the morning into zest for their joint undertaking.

Together they rode slowly down the drive. As Jim had said, there were no men about. Concha, who like all her countrymen reacted quickly to new stimuli, felt their barren beginnings slipping away. In the park the bright waxy green leaves of lemon and orange trees shone in the sun. The morning was hauntingly beautiful. The rays of sunlight seemed as tangible as bands of rain falling across the first green sprouts of corn in the villagers' fields. They passed through a thicket of coffee bushes shaded by the broad, light-green leaves of the banana and then out into the wide cane fields; the cane, uncut, unirrigated since Vicente's death, grew in neglected tangles.

"How terribly uncared for!" exclaimed Concha. "This part of the land used to be the best in all the countryside. I can just remember Grandfather taking me to ride, seated in front of him on a great black mare. He was wearing a *charro* suit, and the silver buttons shone in the sunlight. He looked very happy and handsome. It must have been just before Zapata's men overran this part of the country. Grandfather was so proud of this particular field."

"It's the great problem that we have to face, bringing the yield back. I had planned to see first what irrigation would do. If that failed, root up the old plants and start new. That would be expensive. If I could only get men to help me get the irrigation ditches into shape!"

Concha noted that Jim no longer spoke as if he were through.

Suddenly he drew in his horse. "Concha, I think I know what is the trouble. It's come to me like an inspiration. Let's ride up into the hills. According to the maps I have we'll come on the stream that feeds this land. If it is low, I think we'll have the answer to the villagers' opposition."

"I don't understand." Concha was ahead and she half turned in her saddle.

"If my hunch is right, we'll find the water has been diverted from our ditches. Some of the villagers' cane fields look surprisingly good. Am I not right? If the villagers thought they were stealing water, they would try to thwart me by not helping me get the system working so I wouldn't find out where the water was going. Wouldn't they do something like that?"

"Yes, and furthermore this ride of ours would be a dangerous thing."

As she spoke Jim sensed that they were being followed. It might indeed be dangerous to take Concha to the hills, but she already had put her horse to a gallop. There was nothing to do but follow. Jim caught up with her just as she neared the stream. It was too late now to reconsider.

They dismounted and Concha knelt, dipping up the clear water in her two hands, letting it dribble away between her fingers.

"It is low. There is about the amount of water here there would be after irrigation."

Jim knelt beside her, examining the primitive sluices leading to the cane fields. They had been blocked as cleverly as if nature had done it, but he could find no new channels. Finally, he rolled up his sleeve and reached deep into the stream. His hand touched the boards of another sluice carefully hidden under dirt and sod. "Yes, I'm right," he said, as he stood up.

"You mean they've stolen the water?"

"They think they have. As a matter of fact, they have a right to it according to the law, but perhaps they don't realize it and think, as you say, that they have stolen it. What I imagine has happened is that your father made them believe that, as the source of the stream was on his part of the land, he owned the water. According to the law, as the greater share of the property went to the villages the irrigation water belongs to them. We have only a lien on them. But there are many ways of evading the law. Your father probably paid lawyers to find a loophole for him. It's being done over and over by many of the former owners of haciendas."

"If we could take away their fear!" Concha sat back on her heels as an Indian woman would sit at the washing pool.

"I believe," said Jim, "that if we can handle it right, we've hit on the way to get co-operation. I've got to do some thinking and estimating. I must act immediately. I am certain someone followed us. The news will spread that I've found out what they've been doing."

In the early afternoon he came to Concha with a paper in his hands. "This is the way I see it. The whole irrigation system here is a very old affair—dates back to the early Spanish Conquest. If we went to work and put in a proper system, we could, I believe, bring all the old hacienda lands into full production, theirs and ours. This I could afford to do, if they would give their labor. We could have a contract drawn up, which would be legal, that we would own the irrigation system jointly. In time we might come to run the mill under the same scheme. I would only have a vote like the rest of them. If they had a part in the management, maybe they'd get over their suspicion that we are here to take their freedom from them. Do you think they'd do it? And if they agreed and we drew up the papers, could we trust them, Concha? Something I learned in my childhood makes me think we could, if we could establish their faith in us. It's the only way I see to do anything down here," he ended.

"I've been brought up to believe that you can't trust any of them." As she spoke, Concha looked out of the window at the row of little children from the village perched like crows on the top of the hacienda wall. With a kind of downward swoop not unlike a crow, one of them dropped into the patio, darted toward a bright handkerchief lying there, hid it under a diminutive shirt that reached to his navel. Then, clambering up the strong vines which clung to the wall, he resumed his perch among the others. Bringing her attention back to the room, Concha answered, "But something out of my childhood tells me, too, that it can be done."

"Good," said Jim. "But where do we go from here?"

"I expect you should go to the headman to talk the matter over, and the headman is Francisco. But you mustn't be in too much of a hurry to drive a bargain," she cautioned.

"I know." Jim was thinking of the time it had taken to get the villages farther north to lease their land to the oil company. It might take even longer here where suspicion against the Navarro family was so deep-rooted.

"Tell Francisco in the beginning that the major part of the water rights belongs to them and the other villages in the mountains," Concha suggested.

"Would you? Won't they think then that there's no need for co-operation? Won't they take advantage of us, supposing we can't help ourselves?"

"We'll have to take that chance, Jim. It's our only way out, isn't it?"

After he had gone Concha paced the patio waiting and fearing. Perhaps her advice was wrong; perhaps Jim would lose everything by this move.

"The papers will be like the papers you hold which gave you land," Jim explained at the end of his talk with Francisco. "You own the water rights, I the irrigation works, and a joint committee will control the water. We will send for the same officials who allotted the land to you, if you decide you want such papers."

"I will talk to the village," said Francisco. "We will have to decide together."

From long memory the villagers were afraid to trust aliens. The old irrigation system would do. In fact, cane would grow without irrigation. Not so plentifully, but enough. Yet in them was a fear that if they did not comply, somehow these people, richer and stronger than they, would turn the law in their own favor. Better to acquiesce. And, too, Francisco and his wife and Cleofas had known Señora Concepción from a child. They trusted her. She had said communal ownership. Communal ownership was the way of their forefathers before the Spaniards came. It was the way they held the land now. There had been trouble among the three villages over the water. In reprisal, the other villages had stolen corn and animals. If all of them could agree, it would be good for all!

73

AT THE end of the village street close to the hacienda gate, arches covered with flowers led to the platform erected for the ceremony of agreement. A table banked with flowers stood in the center of the platform, on it were the white sheets of paper—the contract. Jim sat at the table, and grouped around him were the headmen of the villages. One by one they stepped forward to sign, except a very old man who held back, fearful now at the last moment that he might be signing away his rights rather than gaining them. But finally, urged on by the others, he took the pen and laboriously put a cross on the line Jim pointed out.

Then the musicians of the village took up their drums, beating out the ancient rhythms of their people, and behind the priest the procession formed. It had been the villagers' request that the water be blessed. Concha and her old nurse walked behind the priest, carrying lighted candles. Then came Jim, beside him Francisco and the headmen of the other villages in the white, loose, Mexican trousers and bright-colored shirts. Sometimes single file, sometimes walking together, the rest of the men and women straggled along behind. The children brought up the rear. The brilliant Mexican sun made pale the yellow flame of the candles but brightened the colors of the men's shirts. The women in heavy, black, woolen skirts, their dark *rebozos* close drawn over their heads like cowls, seemed to take into themselves the sunlight.

And now that the priest was here, there were christenings and marriages. Another day had to be taken for these. All this delay, thought Jim, with the rainy season so near!

Even when the work was begun he found that regular hours were difficult to maintain. Life was not measured in the village by the tickings of clocks. The cadences of nature made the cadences of their lives. The coming and going of the moon, the coming and going of daylight, the coming and going of the rain—these were the ample rhythms to which they naturally responded. Appointment was too sharp a concept for them. It was associated in their minds only with servitude. Nobody would hurry; nobody would lengthen the hours of the working day. Often Jim would come upon one of the men sitting under a tree, lost, so it seemed to him, in animal contentment. In most of them he knew it could be attributed to laziness, brought about probably by an unbroken diet of corn and chile, but not in every case. He had seen that same look in Concha's face sometimes when she looked out over the land.

But whatever it was, he must find some way to combat it. For Jim there was a very thin edge between success and failure. He had come to depend on a man named Fidel. He was a good worker. He could never be called lazy. Fidel's hut was the finest in the village; his fields were the cleanest and best cultivated. Jim had seen him day after day, when his quota of labor on the irrigating system was done, working the soil in his own corn patch. No, Fidel was not lazy.

"Fidel," he said, "put in an extra two hours beyond your quota and I'll pay you with a good foreign hoe." Fidel, he knew, for a long time had coveted a hoe to use in place of his long knife that served him to loosen the soil.

But Fidel made the usual reply: "No, I am going to my house now." When Jim told Concha, she said, "Perhaps Fidel wanted to watch the sunset."

"The sunset!"

The next day he questioned Fidel more closely.

"Yes," the Indian told him, "I sit before my door every evening to see the sun go down."

Jim had a flash of understanding why so often in the years he had lived in this country some Mexican had said to him, "You North Americans are a materialistic people." That a man should find it necessary to sit and look at the sunset when fields cried out for water was a conception Jim would never be able to share!

Would he ever understand these villagers? Would he ever understand Mexico? Here was a man who cared more for a sunset than for possessions. In the States it would follow that he would be gentle. Fidel was gentle to all appearances, and yet he held the record for killings. Only a few weeks ago without remorse he would have cut Jim's throat if he had had opportunity. Well, at least that danger was past, and Tito could be brought to the hacienda. Concha had gone up to Mexico City to get him.

Fidel's wife, Alejandra, was helping in the kitchen now. As Jim went by the door this afternoon he saw her lifting Teresita, her daughter, so she could look into the oven.

"Isn't she too little to work?" he asked. "She seems just a baby."

"If I train her now, you'll have her for a time before she begins bearing children. I am very old, Señor. I will train this little one to take my place."

"But, Alejandra, she should not bear children for many years yet," Jim protested.

Alejandra nodded her head knowingly. "It isn't long before the young men take them whether you want or not."

Fidel loved his little girl. By all rights he should have loved his son— a fine, strong boy—better, but it was tiny Teresita who followed him about and of whom he boasted. This was another inconsistency in Fidel, but one Jim understood more easily. Teresita has the quality that builds a shell of security around those whose lives touch hers, he reflected, watching her and thinking with gratitude of Concha. It's not to race or class this gift is especially given.

He had not realized how completely Concha formed his world until she went away to get Tito.

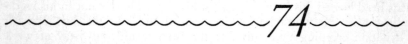

In Tito's small, autocratic mind, coming to the hacienda was a personal outrage. Menacing wings of insecurity beat around him. The tall, dark rooms threatened him. The crowlike children perched on the wall frightened him. Where were the children he liked to play with? Why wasn't his Aunt Louisa here to give him everything he wanted? And then he discovered Teresita. With her small brown hand thrust into his, his proud male superiority returned to him. The plan to make her cook had to be given up. Tito demanded her presence from the moment he woke until siesta time and again until he went to bed.

Every afternoon while Tito was asleep Teresita took her treasures, a few pieces of cloth, and poured water into a small depression in a cluster of rocks outside the kitchen door. Then she did her washing, hanging the blue and pink scraps to dry on the bushes. Always she was busy about something, looking like a diminutive woman in her long, full skirt and loose blouse, replicas of her mother's clothing.

One windy day Concha saw Teresita outside Tito's room waiting for him to wake. She was looking up at the sky under half-closed, swollen lids. Her face was blotched. Measles, thought Concha, and she sent Alejandra and Teresita home for fear Tito would get the measles too. "Keep her warm and in the dark," she admonished Alejandra. The woman gave polite assents. But how could she keep the child warm when it was not night? With the other children Teresita slept under the corner of her mother's spread-out, voluminous skirt, but in the daytime Alejandra's warmth and the covering of her skirt were gone. Better call on the witch doctor for a charm against the evil of sickness.

A few days later Jim came on the child outside her father's hut, cuddled up, trying to warm herself with the feverish heat of her own small body. Jim talked to Fidel this time, and he called Alejandra to listen. "You must keep her warm and in the dark."

Again the polite acceptance, but later to Fidel Alejandra said, "That is the training of the rich; poor people have to be trained to hard ways. So my mother taught me, so I must teach my children."

Daily Tito demanded his Teresita. "Soon . . . tomorrow perhaps," Concha kept telling him. "Alejandra says she is almost well."

And then on a wet, windy morning, at the beginning of the rainy season, Jim met Fidel as he came through the gate toward the house, his head bowed, his hat held against his chest. He was not in his working clothes. He wore clean white trousers and a bright shirt. Jim felt irritation creeping upon him. If the men would only stay at work instead of going off to fiestas in other villages. Fidel was a master musician, one of the *harpa grande* men. He was often desired. Such nibblings at the hours of labor, Jim knew, were depleting to the danger point their thin margin of financial security.

"What is it now, Fidel?" he asked.

"Señor, I was coming to ask you to lend me the money for a coffin. My little kitten . . . now she is dead."

Later Jim went to carry flowers to Fidel's dark and cramped dwelling. The hut was scrubbed clean. The table was covered with a cheap, knitted counterpane bought in installments from a Syrian peddler. Jim had seen him come every week for the loan money. On the table in a circle of flowers lay the waxen Teresita, looking like a doll, her small, once busy hands folded in passive death. She wore a white dress and veil. Fidel, Alejandra said, had not returned yet. Maybe he had difficulty in finding what he sought. There was always so much demand for children's coffins.

"Why do you feel sorrow?" asked one of the villagers standing outside as Jim came out. "She goes to God. She is much better off."

"Perhaps she is," Jim answered.

"Undoubtedly so," the man replied. "What did she have to live for? Just poverty, many children, probably a cruel husband." He smiled, showing his beautiful white teeth when he mentioned the husband.

"How do you know she might not become the mother of a great leader like Zapata who would carry on the Revolution?" Jim asked.

"That is very remote, very remote." The man walked away.

Jim was silent, caught, himself, in the blighting indifference which was so common among Mexico's poor. Why struggle for improvement? All effort seemed so easily dissolved among these people trapped in a kind of premature old age, exhaustion of the body from the eternal eating of corn, corn, corn, washed down with *pulque* with its dual offering of needed vitamins and narcotic oblivion that dulled the brain. Mexico could be described with three letters C— corn, cacti, and churches.

He reached the hacienda's inner gate, went into the patio. The tall jacaranda trees shaded it from the sun, shining fiercely now after the rain. The columns of the hacienda veranda were casting long shadows on the house wall. A villager dressed in clean, white pants and a fresh shirt stepped out from the shade of a tree, his great hat held against his chest.

"There is a delegation here to see you. Now that we have the irrigation system almost done, we would like to build a schoolhouse and petition the government for a teacher. On fiesta days and Sundays we could bring down the stones from the mountains for the walls. The timbers we thought would be the señor's share of the undertaking."

How strange! A new desire for improvement springing up out of seeming indifference. It was hard to have a request for a second project come before the first was completed. Jim felt every energy should be concentrated on the irrigation system. But he must not discourage them.

The conference was over; the long evening had begun. In these evenings unmarked by any outside event, Jim found his own urgent need for haste giving way to the slow pace of ancient ways, like footfalls out of the past establishing their own cadence in him.

His thoughts went back to the school. How adroitly the village delegation had put its proposition, assuming he would wish to share the expense of the school as he had of the irrigation system, although he would not share in its benefits! Yes, they are wily, he said to himself, as all people trained in servitude are. Their very survival has depended on trickery. He suddenly gave a low laugh, tinged with irony.

"Of what are you skeptical?" asked Concha. "You laughed as my people laugh."

"At myself," Jim answered. He hesitated to explain. Concha might not be amused, for his amusement was related to Tito and to the child's place in the community. Jim had assumed that the school was not for his son. But why shouldn't he attend the school and sit on the benches with the others? Concha would probably insist on the traditional Spanish aloofness from the Indians when it came to Tito's upbringing. And yet she had let Tito play with Teresita. Why shouldn't she let him go to the school? It would be good for him to run up against boys of his own age.

"How shall we break it to Tito that Teresita is dead, Jim?"

Jim started. Absorbed in his own affairs, he had forgotten about the dead child. "I'll explain it to him if you wish, but it's hard to explain death to children."

"Not to a Catholic child. He will think of it only as a separation. But I don't know how to keep him happy here alone."

"Why should he be alone, Concha? There is Fidel's son. Why shouldn't he play with him? And the villagers want to start a school. If we see there is a good teacher, he could go to the school until he is old enough to be sent away." Jim waited anxiously for Concha's reply.

"I don't want him playing with the village children. They might teach him bad things."

"Good ones, too, perhaps," Jim countered.

Concha remained silent.

"Suppose we let him go to the school and come directly home."

"Jim, don't you understand? The *hacendado's* family must be kept separate if it is to maintain its prestige."

"But ours isn't a hacienda family really. It is neither necessary nor advisable with this new conception of co-operation to keep ourselves so separate. . . . Is it?" he urged quietly when she did not answer.

"Jim, I have gone all the way so far with you in this co-operation you talk of, but when it comes to my child—it is hard, Jim." Concha felt some inconsistency in her attitude, remembering how, when they undertook this work, she had realized she must submerge her own proud Spanish heritage. But that was for herself, not for Tito.

"Suppose we let Tito work it out for himself," Jim answered. "But I must tell him about Teresita."

"I am Tito, and I am here." The words came from the recessed window just behind them. "What do you want to tell me about my Teresita? It is time she comes back to me."

"You should be in bed, Tito, not listening at the window," Jim said, lifting the child in his arms.

"Why should she go away?" the boy demanded. "I did not say she could." If death was a going away, the small imperious Tito would have nothing to do with it. But when he finally understood he could not call her back, he experienced his first sense of defeat, and wept.

"You could have Teresita's brother to play with," Jim suggested.

"He is an Indian boy. I don't play with Indian boys."

"But Teresita was an Indian girl," Jim expostulated, "and you loved her."

"Teresita is my playmate."

"Couldn't her brother be your playmate?"

Tito shook his head obstinately. "He is Indian."

"Suppose you were an Indian," Jim ventured. "Would you feel any different, Tito?"

"But I am Spaniard."

"And American," corrected his father.

"My Uncle Ramón told me Spaniard." Tito stood before his father, his feet firmly planted, his head held high, his eyes defiant, challenging his father to deny it.

Jim had a moment's sense of a tragic future for his son. Was Tito to suffer as Nacho had suffered because of his divided heritage? Jim had never considered such a possibility. He had thought of Tito heretofore as endowed with special opportunity, with the background of the best three peoples could give him. Somehow he must bring to him knowledge of the three strains of blood that flowed in his veins, teach him to be proud of them all, teach him to find harmony in his triple birthright. "Tito," he said, ignoring the boy's challenge, "you are six now, almost a man. How would you like to help me here at the hacienda?"

"I must be Spaniard," Tito answered, still maintaining his aloofness.

Jim realized now with a sense of loss that he had been too occupied during the years his son was growing out of his babyhood to spend much time with him. But he would rectify that now. "All right. You may be a Spaniard. And ride on my saddle tomorrow."

The next morning when Jim rode out to see how the work was going on the irrigation ditches, Tito sat in front of him, his short, plump legs scarcely reaching beyond the curve of the saddle. He was aloof in his manner to all around him, the only Spaniard among them.

But when Jim got down from his horse and joined the men in the opening of the sluices, Tito followed close at his heels.

"The little *patrón*." Fidel smiled, showing all his white teeth. "Place your hands here and help us to open the gates."

Tito stood among the men, his face red with exertion.

On the ride home, sitting on the saddle in front of his father, he forgot Jim was not Spanish. "I and thou," he said, using the singular "you" of the Spanish language translated literally into English.

"I and thou and the men," Jim answered.

"I and thou and Fidel." Tito turned, a mischievous smile lighting up his face. Jim rubbed the child's small nose upward.

"To be like thine," said Tito.

His father laughed outright. His nose did tilt upward. He was going to find his son a good companion.

Jim was certain now that his choice had been good to come to the hacienda. He could here forget the competitive business world. He smiled a little bitterly as he remembered his futile efforts at diplomacy. He was satisfied to live this simple life. There was this new companionship with his son, and as the weeks and the months had gone by a deeper and deeper relationship between himself and Concha had developed, without either of them striving for it. The time before Tito's coming had thrown them apart rather than drawn them together. But in waiting for their second child there was a deepening intimacy between them, a shared joy in their joint creation. "She," as they called the unborn child, seemed to both only cradled against the day when she would take her place among them at the hacienda.

"She is very gentle," Concha would say. "Tito pushed and struggled. Sometimes I felt nothing would make him wait his time. That frightened me. But this feminine one moves so gently."

It was at night when Concha lay in Jim's arms that she said things like this. And once Jim whispered, "Might I feel her?" And Concha had taken his hand and laid it over the place where the child rested. But he could feel no movement. He was about to withdraw his hand; this must be an experience out of the range of a man's perception.

"Wait," Concha whispered, putting her hand over his.
And then under their two hands Jim felt a stirring.

~~~~~~~~~~~~~~~~~~~~~~~~~~~~~~~*75*~~~~~

THE school, it was decided, was to stand at the end of the village
nearest to the hacienda directly across the road from the church.
Compared with the great Spanish edifice with its two bell towers and
thick masonry walls, exquisite carved entrance supports and massive
carved doors, it would look inconsequential. It was to be a low, one-
story building of stone with a slightly sloping, shingled roof—a plain
wooden door in the middle of the long front wall, a window at each
end. Jim wanted windows in the unbroken wall at the back. The
village claimed that winds laden with rain came from that direction.
In the rainy season windows on that side would make the room cold
and drafty.

The priest who had come to bless the waters of the irrigation system
advised against the school. These government schools were the work
of the Devil. They put a thing called science ahead of God. He
reminded the villagers of the teacher Soledad, whom they had expelled
long ago. "If you go on with this ungodly work, you will lose your
souls," he told them.

But the men wanted the school. Other villages had them. A government that donated them land could not be evil. The priest must
be misinformed of its ungodliness. In their trouble they came to the
patrón, as they insisted on calling Jim, asking if he thought the school
evil. "The priest says, *patrón,* that the school is a dangerous influence.
We want you to tell us why it is evil."

Jim was silent for a little. He saw that in spite of all his effort to
establish the equality of co-operation the relationship between the villagers and himself was becoming more and more one of children to
father. Too long subservient, they fell back into submission as cloth
once folded tends to fall back into its original creases. He was a good
patrón, but a *patrón* just the same, one on whom they were beginning
to lean.

"You must decide for yourselves. You know what is good and what is evil," he told them.

The priest came to see Concha, asking her to speak against the school, but she knew that this particular man was a bad father to his people, and she refused. He had been one of the priests Mamá Grande had supported. As he had been indolent and self-indulgent in the old days, she had no reason to believe he had changed. Furthermore, she had come to feel that the school would be of benefit to the Indian children, although in the beginning she had leaned to her family's idea that education would spoil the Indian. Only she insisted the teacher must not be like the godless woman that had installed herself in the village just after the Revolution.

Again the priest talked to the village fathers. For a long time, sitting back on their thighs, they gave no sign of agreement or disagreement with what he said. Then at last Francisco, the headman, spoke. "This government seems not to wish to harm us. If it wants us to have a school, I see no evil in it." And after one among them had been brave, each in turn spoke for the school.

During the rainy season, whenever the sun came out they gathered materials. When the children went into the hills, they brought back small stones. The men carried in the heavy ones, and on Sunday after they had been to the church, kneeling before the saints and the Christ, they built the walls of the school. For the ceiling Jim offered them beams from an old outbuilding he was tearing down. The floor boards —for there was to be a floor—were brought on the backs of burros from the Sunday market in the distant capital of the state, one or two at a time when they could get together enough money to buy them. Wood was scarce and therefore expensive. Pleased with themselves, often a little drunk, the men came home running at the side of their burros. The boards were so long that they hit the ground with a rhythmic *tat-tat* as the burros trotted forward.

Sometimes for weeks the work lagged, then again it moved forward, then stopped altogether when the rainy season was over and the cutting of cane began. It was the first yield since Jim's coming, and on it so much depended. If he could make his initial payment to Nacho for the land, he would be satisfied. And yet even at that important moment there was need in the village for time for a fiesta. The ears of corn in the *milpas* were shaping. A day must be taken to present the young ears to the Virgin. The women in a long procession came to the church with baskets of the newly conceived ears. Afterward there was feasting.

In the midst of harvesting the cane it was necessary for Jim to go to Mexico City with Concha. The time of her confinement was very near. Could he trust his laborers? He *must* trust them. He called Fidel in. "Fidel, I must go to the capital with the señora."

"I understand, *patrón*. The señora wishes now to be with her own people. There will be no slackening of effort here." With his hat held firmly over his breast, Fidel bowed and went out.

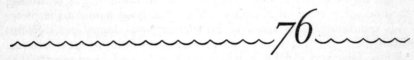

76

FROM the very moment of his return to Mexico City the clock dictated Jim's activities. There was a stated time when he could visit Concha at the hospital, a time when his friends were free, a time to get up. He wished himself back in the country with life set to the ample rhythms of a people marking their days by the sun, their nights by the moon, to which he was now accustomed. Here in the city there seemed to be no opportunity for what Fidel called fellowship of sorrow, fellowship of joy. Was Mexico losing its special flavor?

But after a few days Jim realized that his lack of pleasure in the city was due to its changed attitude toward him. It was because he was a gringo. He was dumbfounded, then alarmed, as he realized how great the hatred toward his country had become. It screamed at him from newspapers and *corridos,* bitter editorials, little remarks with a sting in them about the iron hand within the Good Neighbor's soft glove. As he went back and forth from the hospital to the hotel where he was staying, people looked at him with distrust. In this city where he had experienced so many kindnesses, so many courtesies, he now found himself treated with rudeness. Once he spoke English to a passer-by, asking his way. Why he had not spoken in Spanish he did not know. The man half snarled, "Why do you speak English? This is Mexico." At the time he thought nothing of it except that he was thankful Tito was not a witness to the little scene. That Louisa had snatched the boy away as soon as they had arrived he was now thankful. "Until Concha is strong again," she had said. "Until I go back to the hacienda," he had answered. But might not his sense of separation from this people lie closer home? In fact, lie in Louisa's act of taking Tito into her home? Perhaps it was in reality the separation from Tito that troubled him. Immediately Louisa had the child in her care she had arranged for his first Communion. On the day of that Communion as Jim, sitting in church, had seen Tito with a strange new expression of submission on his face go forward to the altar rail, he had felt as if his son were entering a world that would separate him from the world he lived in. Yes, undoubtedly that was why he was disturbed and what he felt of distrust in this city was nothing more than he had always felt.

But in the days that followed, Jim came to know it was something beyond the personal that troubled him. The good name of the States was crumbling. This scorn of his country was something different from the anger that had arisen at the time of the struggle over oil rights. That was a fight in which each side aired its grievances. As much as he had deplored it, it had the wholesome elements of a fight, but this was fanatical, unreasoned hate. He felt a growing alarm.

He noticed that there were many more Germans than previously in the throngs on the streets. In the shops he saw Germans and aristocratic Spaniards mingling in great camaraderie. Passing he often heard, like a refrain, "Latin America belongs to the great Spanish world." Was the Old World trying to drive a wedge between Latin America and the States? Or was there hatred toward his country simply because an embargo had been placed on Mexican silver since the confiscation of the oil wells? Or because the oil companies in the States had refused to buy Mexican oil? He wanted to ask some of his American friends, but he held back, not wishing to introduce the question. So many of them were bitterly against Mexico for her act of confiscation.

One evening as he came into the hospital he found Ignacio sitting with Concha. It was the first time he had seen Ignacio since his return to the capital. He was startled by the change in him. There were hairlike lines leading out from his eyes. His face was thin. He looked as if he had been driving himself to the point of exhaustion. The warmth of Ignacio's embrace made Jim realize with gratitude that the friendship persisted which had developed between them when they had worked together those last days before the expropriation. Then there was one Mexican, at least, who had not been affected by the emotion of hatred sweeping over the city.

As they left Concha's room, Jim burst out: "Nacho, what is happening to *my* country here in the capital? We have made grave mistakes, as you know, but there has always been respect between us. This picture of the States I get reflected from the minds of the people is foul."

Ignacio's face was drawn with emotion. "With Franco in power in Spain we are at the crossroads. It is a question now whether we are to belong to the New World or the Old. What you feel is the pull to the Old. Strong forces are urging us in its direction and for the first time in our history we are important to the States. As goes Mexico, goes South America."

Jim could not tell whether there was anguish or triumph in Ignacio's voice. "And *we* are important to *you,* if you believe in democracy," Jim countered.

"Yes," said Ignacio, "you are important to us, although by religion, language, and culture we belong to Europe, Franco or no Franco."

"Do you? Are you sure?" asked Jim. Once Ignacio had seemed entirely Spanish to him. But now, knowing the villagers, he saw likenesses to the Indian in Ignacio as well as in Concha. "You yourself, Nacho, your mother, everyone clear to the heads of the government is bound by your Aztec blood to the American continent. As I am," he added after a pause, "through Tito. Concha once said you came up out of the pores of the earth."

"But to get down to some of the causes of distrust. Did you know that oil sales to the States have been completely blocked?" Ignacio spoke as if he had not heard Jim's last words.

"So I understand," Jim answered.

"And I believe that the man who is the brains of that blockade is von Brenen who is negotiating for those stocks to go to Germany!"

"It can't be!" Jim exclaimed. "He hasn't enough power in the States."

"There are many ways of approach. The people he manipulates may not know they are being manipulated."

"But what can we do?" demanded Jim.

"If you could help, would you? Could we call on you?" asked Ignacio.

At midnight Jim was called back to the hospital. A few hours later Concha gave birth to their second child. If there was question whether Tito looked like Louisa or his father, there was no question about this boy. When the nurse held him up for Jim to see, he immediately recognized that his tiny features were a small replica of Mamá's.

This beautiful, brown boy had her well-modeled head, high cheek-bones, splendid forehead.

"He deceived us, didn't he?" Concha's voice held a note of amusement. "It's because he is so gentle. He doesn't assert himself as Tito did."

Jim thought suddenly of his last words to Ignacio: "I am bound by blood to Mexico through Tito." More so through this second son, he realized.

"What shall we call him, my husband?"

Jim, from some impulse born out of the last hour, answered, "After your brother."

Concha smiled. She was too weak to feel any surprise. All the intricate relationships of her family were swallowed up in her weakness. "Yes . . . Ignacio—and for everyday we'll call him Palito, Little Stick. He is as straight as a little stick. Most babies are all cuddled up into themselves."

Jim went out into the crisp morning air. The sky was so clear it seemed almost transparent, no roof at all over his head. Dark men and women were just arriving from the floating gardens to the south of the city, bearing huge baskets of vegetables and flowers. The church bells clanged. Two minutes and again the silence. He felt suddenly the mystery of the birth of a nation taking place here in this city of two million inhabitants, a new race compounded of Indian and Spaniard, both proud, both touched with poetry. Tito and Palito, Concha's and his sons a part of it, but a part of him too.

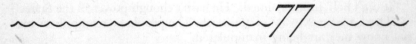

After Ignacio left Jim he dropped in at his sister Louisa's *sala*. There was always an aristocratic gathering there. Smart women, professors from the established universities, artists of the old school, men of leisure, representatives of the aristocratic inner circle. Whatever his aspirations for Mexico, Ignacio was born to this elegant life and felt at home in it. In the glow of his second cocktail he settled back into its superiority and sense of separateness. But tonight there seemed to be a great number of alien faces around him. Someone, speaking

Spanish with a German accent, was saying to a group standing a little to one side, "If we could break the Americas in two at the Rio Grande, then——" Ignacio strained his attention to catch the rest of the sentence, but the speaker had lowered his voice.

Ramón's younger brother Augusto came toward Ignacio. It was the first time Ignacio had seen him since the boy's return from his studies in Europe. After a few minutes' conversation Ignacio, delighted with his intelligence, said to him, "I am interested in what you think of present conditions in Spain. Of course, I know your family always supported the monarchy, but at present the currents of thought are so crossed. How do you feel about Franco's coming into power?"

"I am interested only in restoring the Church to the position it held before the Revolution here."

"You wish all the Revolution has done destroyed?" Ignacio asked.

"I come as an emissary for the spiritual reconquest of Latin America," Augusto answered. "One race, one language, one culture, and especially the Catholic faith, the one religion throughout, and division at the Rio Grande. Democracy is a sin against the Church. My mission is never out of my mind. The way will be opened for my work, so they told me before I left Spain."

"Who told you the way would be opened?" asked Ignacio.

"The Falangistas of Spain. We want nothing of Pan-Americanism." Augusto lifted his head proudly.

"You call this a spiritual conquest!" Ignacio exclaimed. "I should call it a militant crusade."

Augusto's expression changed, his ardor sinking back beneath a protective attitude of well-bred indifference. He began talking of superficial changes in Spain.

Leaving Louisa's house, Ignacio decided to see Pablo. More and more of late had he and Pablo collaborated in their efforts to defeat a reactionary Spain dominated by Germany getting a hold on a free Mexico. "I have learned a little more of Spain's plan," he told Pablo. "Augusto is back from Spain. He talked of work to do here for the Church. I think he does not know that he and others like him are being manipulated by Germany through Spain. But Ramón knows. The Falangistas of Spain and the Sinarquistas of Mexico will be welded together through young and ardent youths like Augusto, who think they support the Church when in reality they are supporting Fascism."

"I can add to the picture," said Pablo. "When the hatred of the

States is stirred to white heat, then the time will be ripe for Franco and his Mexican satellites to take over here. But even if Franco's plan for South America and Mexico is defeated, much of the work of the Revolution will be undone. The Sinarquistas now number fifty thousand. The Indian villages through them are being urged to give up their schools. This movement needs ignorant people."

Pablo did not wish to acknowledge how valuable Ignacio's information was. His knowledge came from a survey of the city's *pulquerías* and workingmen's cafés, where he listened to the gossip brought in from hundreds of villages. He had no access except through Ignacio to the talk of aristocratic Spaniards of the city. He had not known until now how closely the Sinarquistas were connected with aristocratic Spain.

"If necessary to keep what we have won, we will go back to the Revolution." It was Pablo's wife speaking. "Then we had enthusiasm, and the power was with the people. This movement to bring back the temporal position of the Church is really meant to bring back power to the great landowners. Maybe we'll have to fight again."

"We don't want to go through another revolution," Ignacio protested.

"Not for all of us, not for Mexicans, is it so bad," she answered. "We are not afraid of death. Didn't I watch it take place outside the windows of my father's house? I was just seven, and there was a soldier who used to come to our house, and he was very gay." She looked up stubbornly from under her downcast eyelids. "There's something in us that does not mind dying."

Her words brought to Ignacio the vivid remembrance of Soledad saying, "We should be afire the way we were when we were fighting." A kind of thrill of recognition came to Ignacio of a common quality in people like Soledad, Pablo's wife, and even the gentle Guadalupe. And in people like Berta and her father. He had a sudden longing to be one of them. The substance of sacrifice was in them. Then he remembered the men in the government, those who had surrendered to the temptation to become the new rich. If only these separate contradictory entities, including himself, could be fused enough to hold the line! "If the States would just reach out their hand to us now instead of raising it against us!" he said aloud.

Pablo got up, making a gesture of impatience, and walked off across the room. "The Americans are not sincere." As he turned, Ignacio saw his face was flushed with anger. "With one hand they offer us democ-

racy and a place in the new world; with the other they boycott oil and
refuse to buy our silver. A good neighbor with a blackjack hidden in
the folds of a scholar's tunic. If things go on as they are, those of us who
have fought for the people will be out. That is why I have taken care
to put something aside."

So, thought Ignacio, he too has made money, and this is his justification. He laughed.

Pablo's wife smiled and shrugged. That was the laugh of skepticism
she knew and understood.

Pablo seemed not to notice the interruption. "If the independent oil
companies would buy from us . . . but they won't! They've been
made to believe in a Mexico which is bad—that we never pay for anything, that we are a lot of cutthroats. They've been fed the idea that
Mexico likes nothing but a brawl, that we are chaotic and disordered.
If their people stood with our people, we could do something."

"If a man—" Ignacio looked up, his attention caught, an idea taking
shape in his mind—"could be sent to the States simply as a representative of Mexicans—a man neither rich nor poor—maybe he could stir
the United States to voice its protest against what is happening."

Pablo turned and faced Ignacio. "We need a more practical demonstration of friendship than that. If some independent oil company
would break the boycott—then we could believe and perhaps not scoff
at the idea of the Good Neighbor."

As Ignacio went out he saw great lines gathering before the corn
shops. Corn was scarce and had doubled in price. In the murmurs of
discontent he heard the words *"Norteamericanos. The norteamericanos* did this to us."

He came at last to the gates of his own home. They stood open now
all night that the many occupants of the house might go in and out.
Instinctively he longed for the security of his childhood in this
house, his family closely guarded, shut away into their sheltered
privacy. He paused just for a moment before the door of the flat where
Berta used to live. He wished she were here. Why had she thought it
necessary to go away? Well, he would forget himself in study. Reaching the door of his grandfather's library, he heard a low murmur of
voices. Then he was not to have its quiet and security tonight.

When he entered, he saw that his grandmother and some friends
were playing cards. The faded black of their old-fashioned dresses
seemed to enhance their faded eyes. As he kissed their hands in greeting, he saw on many the gleam of jewels. A very aged woman came

into the room, and with one motion all the others rose. He went forward to bow over her hand and raise it to his lips. No one spoke her name, but a faint memory from his childhood gave him the clue. She was the widow of Mexico's last dictator, the great Díaz. Her black dress of rich stuff was made in the style of that period, as were the dresses of those who paid her homage. This was the passing of the old order. Or was it only being revitalized for a new struggle? This woman was supposed to be in exile in Europe. Pablo's wife had said these once rich landowners were hoping again, through Falangist Spain, to reinstate themselves and regain their once enormous wealth. How much was his family involved in it? Augusto? Ramón? Yes. But Louisa? And Mamá Grande?

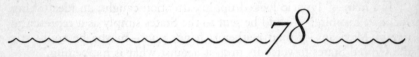

Jim was very happy as he and Tito went together to inspect the fields the day after their return to the hacienda. Already, the night before, Fidel had given Jim his account of the amount of cane they had cut to the *hectárea*. It was sufficiently good to guarantee that at the end of the season Jim would be able to meet his payments on the bank's loan and pay something to Ignacio.

"And now," Fidel said, when they came back from the fields, "the village asks of the *patrón* a holiday to finish the school."

By the time Concha and the baby came the building was completed —the wooden benches and the teacher's desk—a rough hand-made table—in place. But month after month the school stood empty, awaiting a teacher.

The village had asked the government for a man who could teach them new methods of agriculture as well as reading and writing. They had heard there were such men. When six months had gone by and no teacher had arrived, Jim wrote Ignacio, asking him if he had any influence with the Department of Education would he not exert it.

Ignacio took the matter up with Pablo.

"I've just the person, a man—that's what your brother-in-law wants, is it not so? He's trained as a surveyor, knows the country and something of agriculture."

"Yes. But what gives you such particular satisfaction in your choice?" It seemed to Ignacio that his half brother looked at him with malicious delight.

"Simply my desire to select the suitable person for an undertaking . . . and," he added, "an opportunity really for you to pay a debt you owe—shall I say to the village? Even your North American brother-in-law may find he has an opportunity to set right certain acts of his through this man."

Ignacio was puzzled by Pablo's cryptic remarks and his general attitude of elation. Would Pablo never really be friends with him? Sometimes he seemed to have real affection for him, and then, as today, in its place was a dislike that seemed as venomous as a snake bite. What kind of unique pleasure did he get out of such a relationship? Ignacio especially wanted his half brother to be friendly this morning, for he needed Pablo's co-operation.

"Pablo," he said, "the time has come when whatever may have divided us should be forgotten, and we should work only for Mexico."

"Yes?" answered Pablo. "And you have a desire to work?"

Ignacio ignored the reference to his leisure. "I have the opportunity through my connections to know certain things that are of value to the government. All who call themselves Spaniards in Mexico, all who have any connections with Spain, are to be forced into the Falange party. They must give money for its support. But worst of all, they have been instructed to hoard food supplies, force prices up. Then the cry is to go out when corn is really scarce that the States are to blame. You know the Spaniards of this city are the shopkeepers. If this group succeeds in its purposes, they will destroy everything liberal in Mexico."

"The President has deported the three leaders of the movement You are telling me nothing we don't know," Pablo answered.

"But I am certain," Ignacio insisted, "that the movement has only gone underground. Together, Pablo, we could help to weaken its force."

But all Pablo would say was, "If you have any information, bring it to me." Out of the dark broodings of his illegitimacy, jealousy of Ignacio stalked through his mind this morning, keeping him from co-operation.

~~~~~~~~~~~~~~~~~~~~~~~~~~*79*~~~~~

THE usual flower-decked arches had been erected. Concha and Jim had been asked to sit on the platform among the dignitaries who were taking part in the ceremonies connected with the opening of the school. As they ascended the platform Concha saw to her delight that Ignacio was one of the government's representatives. He came forward, and they embraced.

"I had not thought to be here today, but a friend of mine asked me to take his place," he said in explanation, and added in an aside to Jim, "Pablo was to have come, but at the last minute found he was too busy." Looking at Concha, Ignacio suddenly wanted to be with her for a while, and suggested he stay with them a few days.

Later, as she was taking him the rounds of the hacienda, she exclaimed, "See what Jim has done?"

"And you," he added.

"Yes. Together we have done it," she answered. "And now you must come and see your namesake!" She led him to the room which she had made into a nursery. But no one was there. Following Tito's voice, they came upon him in the patio beyond, his bright hair flying as he pushed forward a baby carriage. "Charge!" he shouted, and obeying his command he rushed wildly toward an imaginary army. Over went the carriage.

With the directness of an arrow Concha reached them. "He is not hurt," Tito cried as she lifted the baby from under the carriage, felt him over, and held him close. Tito leaned against her insisting, "He is not hurt. He's a stallion of a man." Concha looked down at him, shaking her head but smiling.

The three made a picture with the sun throwing the pattern of the trees down on Concha's pale-green dress. Palito's dark head was nestled under her chin, and Tito's red-gold hair tousled by his play was caught in a shaft of sunlight. Concha is really happy, thought Ignacio. There is some deep understanding between her and Jim. He remembered her now as she had run down the stairs to tell him she was going to marry Jim. She was happy then, but this was something

different, deeper, more satisfying. With Berta he could have a relationship as satisfying. If he could only make her believe in him!

Later when he sat alone with Jim he said, "And what we feared
would happen is happening. I suppose, sheltered here, you have forgotten what Mexico City was like when you were there eight months
ago. You haven't been up since, have you?"

"My work is here. Concha and I together are building something
worth while, are we not? But I have not forgotten."

"What you are taking such pains to build may be shattered any
moment," said Nacho.

"What do you mean?"

"What did you think would happen when your country boycotted
our oil? It has given the Falangistas just the excuse they wanted. Now
the movement has gone underground, but the Falangistas are operat-
ing through a secret organization here called the Sinarquistas to destroy
the union of the continent, stir up trouble in the villages, bring back
the old regime."

"I can do nothing about it," Jim answered, as he had that evening
in Mexico City when Ignacio had asked him whether he would help
if he were needed.

"But would you, if you knew you really could help?" persisted Ignacio.

"If such a moment comes, that will be time enough to decide." Jim
was unwilling to commit himself blindly to any quixotic plan that
Nacho might be sponsoring. "Let us go over to see if the teacher has
arrived," he added, changing the subject.

In the room at the back of the schoolhouse, where the teacher was
to live, they heard someone moving about. Jim knocked on the door.
A man, thin almost to the point of emaciation, opened it. "Will you
come in?" he asked in a gentle voice.

Neither Jim nor Ignacio found words to answer. Neither moved.
The small man before them was to both a man raised from the dead,
a man both of them in the innermost recesses of their hearts felt they
had harmed.

"Guadalupe!" gasped Jim at last. He held out his hand. "I am glad
to welcome you," he said frankly. "We need a man like you here in the
village—as we did in the oil business," he added, making full retribu-
tion for the past, or as full as he could. A man like Guadalupe in the
village! It was more than he deserved.

Still Ignacio did not speak, simply stood watching Jim and Guadalupe. "And your wife—" asked Jim, "is she with you?"

"I think she must be dead," Guadalupe answered, "or she would have left some word for me with the friend who managed to get me free—or perhaps you did not know that I was one of the labor men sent to the penal colony."

"I suspected it," said Jim. "Few come back."

Guadalupe turned to Ignacio. "It was Pablo who succeeded in getting me free and took me into his house until I was strong again. He tried to find Soledad but could not. And yet I cannot believe she is dead. She was so strong, so alive. Yet I have come to accept her loss." He spoke with quiet resignation. "But the school . . ." Quietly he led the conversation into a less personal channel.

With a low, bitter laugh Ignacio turned and left them. So this was why Pablo had acted as he had. He must think Soledad was still with him. What a trick for Pablo to play on him! Raising Guadalupe up from the dead to confront him. He knew no more than Guadalupe what had become of Soledad. But he could hear her voice saying now, "I will build the Revolution into your heart. You won't ever be able to escape it." Or her, he thought bitterly.

In another hour he was on his way back to Mexico City. He would not accept such an insult from Pablo.

"What did you expect to accomplish anyway?" Ignacio demanded, confronting his half brother. "What kind of a mischief-maker are you—having Guadalupe released from prison, nursing him, getting him into my very family, and then sending me down to meet him? What did you think I'd do? It's none of your business what happened between Soledad and me. I'd shoot you if you weren't my brother."

"And I'd shoot you if you weren't mine." Pablo got to his feet and moved out from behind his desk. "What did you do such a dirty trick for—take a decent woman like Soledad, treat her as if she were in the world just to serve you? She meant something to all of us. She stood up to things when the rest of us didn't. And you—a son of your father all right! It's time somebody teaches you you're not entitled——" Pablo swung out with his fists.

Ignacio struck back with a blow that made Pablo reel. Then Pablo came on again, charging like an angry bull. Ignacio, trained in the technique of bullfighting, neatly evaded him, and then let out a blow which landed on Pablo's jaw.

Blindly, furiously, the two fought, neither winning, neither sur-
rendering. At length someone separated them, pushed them into chairs.
Panting, exhausted, they sat facing each other.

"I guess we had it coming," said Pablo.

"Yes, I suppose so. I'd better be going now." Ignacio rose to leave.

"Sit down," said Pablo. "You said something the other day about
a man to send to the States. Was it your brother-in-law?"

"Yes," Ignacio mumbled. His lips were swollen and bruised.

"Do you think he'd go? My idea would be for him to approach the
independent oil companies and see if he could get them to break the
blockade."

"If I could go to him with a clear proposition I rather think he would
consent."

Together they planned ways and means. All their distrust of each
other seemed to have been resolved in their physical struggle.

80

As soon as Nacho was sufficiently recovered from his bruises, he went
down again to the hacienda to see Jim. "I am going to put it frankly
to you this time. We are in need of an envoy to your country, and we
believe you are the man. We want somebody who understands the
oil situation, and we want somebody who also has sympathy with
Mexico."

"Before we go farther in our talk," Jim interrupted, "I must know
who you mean when you say 'we.' I can make no promise of any sort
or undertake any mission for a mysterious 'we.'"

They were pacing the paths of the patio. A large banana leaf hanging
out over the path obstructed Jim's view of Ignacio for a moment.
Impatiently he thrust it aside, for he did not want to miss a single
expression in his brother-in-law's face, but already Ignacio had turned
away.

"If I tell you, will you promise to keep the matter secret whether
you undertake the work or not?"

It was Jim's turn to hesitate, but he consented finally. "Because I trust you, Nacho." Not until he had said this did he realize how strong the bond between Nacho and him had become, nor how much he had come to respect him.

"But this is no place to talk." Ignacio walked quickly toward the winding steps leading to the roof. "I ask that you do not jeopardize us by a single loud tone," he cautioned, once they stood together looking out over the village and the cane fields.

Jim considered the precaution excessive, but he nodded his assent and Ignacio, after first going over to see that no one listened on the stairway, began: "The secret organization I told you about when I was here last is at work in all the Indian villages. They call themselves the Sinarquistas—a Greek word. It's a military organization. You cannot tell where they have planted their spies."

"Not in this village," said Jim. "It is too contented now with its lot." From somewhere below men were singing the ballads of love and war.

> "I am a rebel, and I fight against the government,
> Because in the end it has not fulfilled anything,
> With my Winchester, my horse, and three cartridges,
> And I display the Virgin on my banner."

Even Ignacio would have been surprised to know that Ramón's brother Augusto the evening before had met with the men of the village. "To men like you," Augusto had said, "do I give this sacred trust. You must court sacrifice. You must be willing to kill, if necessary, to save your faith. This school you started against the counsel of your priest. It must be done away with. It is against God. For Mexico there is only one Church. All others must be driven out. Spain is your mother country. The country to the north of you is an evil one without God. Work against it and serve God."

Nacho on the roof was saying, "I do not need to sketch for you, Jim, the intricate pattern of oil superimposed on the political pattern of the world—or should I say, woven into it?"

"I know your views," Jim broke in. "And I know what has been happening since Mexico took over the oil fields. You've not been able to sell your oil in the States or in England, and you've not been able to get machinery or tankers. I understand as well as you do that Mexico thinks the oil men of England and of the States have not given up hope of breaking the President by bringing upon the country an economic crisis and thus getting back their wells. But what can I do about it? What was I able to do before?" Jim laughed derisively. "And for whom are you speaking anyway, Nacho?"

"I am speaking for the President."

"The President!"

The two men stood facing each other. "At least for a small inner group of men close to the President. You met one of them—Pablo, my half brother." Ignacio, after again taking the precaution to see that the stairs were clear, went on: "It is a desperate last-minute effort to see if we can't break the boycott somewhere. It is so important, Jim. Barter contracts will be signed with Germany if it isn't broken. If a man like you were sent to the oil independents now, and he could get them to break the boycott——"

"I am not strong enough; the independents are not strong enough," Jim answered. "You do not know as I do what you are fighting. Besides, I have Concha and the children to think of."

"That is why I urge you to go. A good Mexico for them to live in." There was pleading in Ignacio's voice.

"Suppose these Sinarquistas do teach hatred of my country, suppose they do try to destroy the fruits of the Revolution, bring back a ruling class and a downtrodden peasantry, as you insist they intend to do, Nacho—surely the peasants who fought for the Revolution could not be inflamed with fanatical hate against the very things their own Revolution has brought them."

"And yet one after another has given his oath, taken up the salute— arm crossed over the breast, hand extended over the opposite shoulder —Jim, surely you have seen them give it as they pass on the road, as they enter their churches."

"Well, what of it?" Jim countered. "May it not be purely a religious movement?"

"I tell you," said Nacho, "the dangerous lower fringe of society is catching fire, fanned to life by the fear that God, the saints, and their beloved brown Virgin are threatened. Ramón's brother Augusto and others trained as he has been in Spain to live a life as rigorous as that of the monks who first came to Mexico are seeing to it that it is more than a religious movement. They sleep on the ground in Indian huts, eat the Indians' coarse, monotonous food, attend the Indian churches. They give oil so that the altar light may be kept burning. Then, when they have won the people, they teach the doctrines of hate and violence. Men like Augusto are dupes of Ramón and others of his stripe. For your own sake, Jim, for Concha's sake, undertake this mission to your country. Get them to give us a sign of friendliness that will convince the common people of your country's good faith."

Jim shook his head. "No," he said. "I cannot do it."

81
~~~~~~~~~~~~~~~~~~~~~~~~~~~~~

THE six months following Ignacio's visit passed swiftly for Jim. He worked, he believed, with greater delight than he ever had before. The justification for his answer to Ignacio lay in bringing the hacienda to the highest point of efficiency he could, raising the standard of living for the Indians, increasing the amount and the quality of sugar cane taken from his own fields and those of the villagers. He decided to make an investment in machinery and put the sugar mill in condition. It would give employment to more men and be another co-operative venture to interest them all and hold them against exploitation by the Sinarquistas. He was beginning to hear more and more of them. Bits of gossip, *corridos* picked up at the market. Guadalupe spoke to him of it. "Pressure is being brought to bear on the village to join," he told Jim. Jim had found in Guadalupe another link with the Indian men. They had liked the teacher from the start and listened to his counsel much more readily than to Jim's.

Concha made no objection to Tito's attending the school with Guadalupe as teacher. All that Soledad had told her of him she found true. His gentle, quiet ways, his kindness to every child and animal made him in Concha's eyes a good companion for Tito.

As the child had once claimed Teresita, he now claimed Guadalupe for his friend. He followed him daily into the school, and set up a small desk for himself beside Guadalupe's. Sometimes he forgot to separate himself from the other children in his interest in what was going on.

Guadalupe was a good teacher. He took the things of the village and the fields into the schoolroom. His years of surveying and Soledad's love of flowers had contributed to his knowledge of the country. His young pupils listened to him eagerly.

But it was harder to teach the men and women of the village new ideas. He and Jim often discussed how to go about breaking the mold of tradition. One day Guadalupe remembered Rivera saying, "You will not need to teach Mexico to read if you cover the walls of the schools and public buildings with pictures." Guadalupe wrote a friend who had once assisted Rivera, asking for a few sketches for the walls of the school. But he received no answer.

It was corn-planting time now, and the benches in front of Guadalupe held only an occasional occupant, a few too young to work in the fields, and sometimes Tito. Guadalupe had time to dream of the future.

"Someday," he said to Jim, "we'll build white houses such as you have in your country and plant trees, and our village streets will be beautiful. But just now," he added innocently, "if you would let us tear down the hacienda wall in front of the side patio which you do not use, we could make a splendid square for the village. The church would fill one side, the school the other. The gallery of your house which faces that patio could be the third side. There we might hold a little market of our own someday, bring people here instead of their going off to other towns. That tall tree in the center of the patio would make nice shade for the children to play under."

"Let the village express some desire for it, Guadalupe," Jim answered. "Let us leave the initiative for village improvements to them."

His dreams seemed too ephemeral ever to be translated into reality, Guadalupe was thinking one morning as he sat before the empty desks. Neither Señor Jim nor his artist friend could be won to his plans. He heard the tread of a man's shoes outside on the steps. The men of the village wore huaraches or came barefoot. Jim Buchanan's step was lighter than this.

"Where is my welcome?" cried a voice at the door. "I come and find an empty school, and my friend sitting idly at his desk with his back to the door. I was told there was a school that needed beautiful walls. Here I find not even plaster. Must I mix my own?"

"There are walls ready for you," cried Guadalupe, embracing his friend. "I shall go over to the hacienda immediately and ask for walls in an unused patio to be put at our disposal. Later you can do me some sketches for this room on canvas that we can fasten by wooden pins to chinks between the stones."

Jim felt he could not well refuse Guadalupe this time. The wall shutting off the wing of the hacienda house bordering the unused patio was taken down, and on the wall beyond the colonnades of the deep veranda the painting began. Not only the children but the men and women of the village stole time to watch the glowing colors grow under the hand of the artist. They saw the history of their people appearing on the wall, things long held in their hearts but not spoken. At the other end of the space they saw a new world—corn twice the size of theirs and bearing many ears. "Just a picture," Fidel and Francisco said, smiling and showing their white teeth.

But Guadalupe, standing near, answered: "I can get seed for you to grow ears like that."

There were splendid plows, their silver blades laying back the soil in heavy black swaths. Then news spread through the village that the painter was making a machine that ground the corn. The women hurried to look at the golden grains so easily turned into meal. "Just a picture," Alejandra said, echoing her husband's words about the corn. But Cleofas, once maid in the Navarro house, spoke with superior knowledge: "I have seen corn grinders in the city."

"We might get one for the village sometime," suggested Guadalupe.

"A machine grinding my corn!" cried Fidel. "I can tell Alejandra's *tortillas* from anyone else's. Her grinding is better than any other." Alejandra had thought the machine wonderful until Fidel spoke.

In the evenings the men gathered in the schoolhouse, and after a time Jim formed the habit of strolling over, for the talk was good. There was no master nor laborer here, and they drew closer together.

Sometimes after the villagers had gone the artist talked of the world to which he and Guadalupe had once belonged. "We spent ourselves in disillusionment in the days of the Millionaire Socialists. Now when we are needed, we are poisoned with our own inertia." With a wave of the hand he dismissed the subject.

That evening Jim, who had almost succeeded in burying himself in the life of the hacienda, felt uneasiness stirring within him. Was he, too, caught by inertia? "Damn Nacho!" he swore under his breath as he walked across the square to his own gate. "Why do I keep thinking of him and what he wanted me to do? I have enough to do here. If we can educate the villagers, they will be the safeguard of the country. President Cárdenas has always claimed that enlightened farmers are one of Mexico's most urgent needs."

He walked along the veranda to the window of the children's room. "Concha," he called softly, "I'm restless. Come and sit with me on the roof."

Together they went up the winding stairs. To be with Concha was to catch in part the sense of fulfillment which enveloped her these days. Fullness of life had settled over her like a garment of plenty. Here on the roof only the sounds of village life and the sounds of nature accented the silence—the occasional soft footfalls of men returning to their huts, the *rub-rub* of wet corn under the rolling pin of a late worker, a light wind in the trees, the chirp of insects. Concha put her hand in Jim's. There was the abundant earth and her abundant self—a rich fertility. The night, the splendid productive earth, Jim, herself were one throbbing, harmonious entity. Before they had come to the hacienda to live, they had been too aware of each other for perfect welding together.

Lights suddenly appeared in the dark hills, merging into a long serpentine line snaking over the hills, and faintly on the wind came the watchword of the Sinarquistas: *"Fe y Patria! Viva Cristo Rey!* Faith and Country! Long live Christ the King!" The sound was high-pitched, the cry of fanatics on the march. Jim sucked in his breath.

Concha shivered. "What is it, Jim?"

Then Jim told her all he knew of the organization and what it was trying to do, everything that Ignacio had told him except the plan to send him to the States as an envoy.

"Don't blame the poor people, Jim," begged Concha. She was conscious of a deep hurt that men like Augusto and Ramón, professing the Catholic faith, should teach hate and intolerance to the Indians just emerging from ignorance. It hurt her too that Jim—not a believer—should know of the part Catholics like Ramón were taking in this movement.

Guadalupe standing on the steps of his school, Jim on his roof, alike were wondering if they had wrought well enough. Could they hold the village against a doctrine that would, if it took root here, repudiate them? It had already claimed the villages of the mountains —stirred as only primitive men fearful for the survival of their faith can be stirred.

Guadalupe heard stealthy footsteps, then a pause, an interval as if to make certain no one was in pursuit. Moving quietly, he followed the sound. Evil was abroad tonight. He knew how Pedro lurked in the hills, a man obsessed of one idea—the harm done the village by the Navarro family. In him now was the fiery faith of the Revolution and the fiery faith of Sinarquismo. That the latter destroyed the former he tragically did not see. Perhaps he meant to kill tonight. There were others in the village Guadalupe did not trust. Yes, the footsteps moved toward the hacienda gate. Carefully now Guadalupe followed the

crouched figure he could just discern skulking along in the shadow
of the church wall. He must reach him, grasp the man's arm before
he could fire at the two silhouetted against the sky on the roof of the
hacienda.

The figure crossed a patch of moonlight, hurrying toward the
shadow beyond. It was a woman! Something familiar in the movements—Guadalupe's heart leaped within him. A familiar straightening
of the shoulders. No one could so straighten the shoulders to meet
disaster except—— He had seen her do it so a hundred times when
they faced want or unemployment, or when she thought the Revolution was in danger.

"Soledad!" Guadalupe sprang forward. The woman swung around
and then dropped to the ground at his feet. Guadalupe bent over her
crumpled form. Her right arm hung limp when he tried to lift her.
Her dress was torn and wet. Her feet were bare and bruised. I should
get help, he thought numbly. I should knock at the hacienda gate and
get help to carry her in.

But he could not relinquish her to anyone . . . no . . . not now. Not
anyone but him must touch her now. He leaned over her. "Soledad,
it's Guadalupe," he whispered.

He did not know how many times he had said it before she opened
her eyes, looked at him. "Guadalupe?" she gasped. "Guadalupe is
dead."

"There, there!" He soothed her as he would a child. "God led you
here to me. I have searched for you everywhere. And now God has
brought you when I ceased to demand it of him."

Soledad raised her left hand, running her fingers over his face as a
blind man might have done who wished to fix in his mind's eye what
he could not see. Across his forehead to the edge of his heavy black
hair her fingers moved, touched lightly his eyebrows, and finally the
serene line of his mouth. Then she settled quietly back in his arms. "A
miracle," she whispered and closed her eyes.

He carried her to his room in the school, his thoughts in chaos. How
had she been hurt? Where had she come from? With fingers that
shook he undressed her, laid her in his bed. She roused once, frightened by some sound. "I must get away!" she cried. Then she sank
back. "They drove me out. I had been in the village for years. I had
cared for them when they were sick. I helped to get the land for them.
But someone told them that once I had trampled on the Cross. You
know once, long ago, they used it against me."

"You are safe now," Guadalupe soothed her. Her eyes closed again.

In the light of a shaded lamp he studied her face. With her eyes closed, the Soledad he knew seemed almost completely obliterated. This woman was far older than his Soledad. He forgot that he was older too. Her skin was yellow with the dread malaria. Her face showed the marks of never-ending flagellation of the spirit. Why should she bear that look? In the days they were together no matter what tale of the Revolution she told, she never entered that dark chamber of the soul where guilt dwells. Even her relationship to the father of her child was to her simple and natural. Evidently she had expended her life in his absence to teach the ignorant. What guilt could she feel? Suddenly he realized it was from this very village where she now lay that she had originally been driven, this village that would not listen to her when she told them it was not she but the overseer who had drawn the Cross on the dirt floor of the school. She was not safe here!

He started, as he heard a sudden knocking on the hacienda gate. He went quickly and opened the door of the school, standing tense, listening.

"They are after me!" cried Soledad. She sat up, a look of panic and torment in her eyes.

Quickly he moved to her side. "There, there!" he murmured. "You have nothing to fear." Gently he pressed her back against the pillows. Soledad was immediately asleep. He sat by her side through the night, joyous and fearful.

AT THE knock on the gate Jim and Concha hurried down from the roof. Who could be coming at this hour?

"Why, it's Nacho's car!" exclaimed Concha, as the runabout came to a stop at the foot of the gallery steps. She ran forward, crying, "Nacho, is anything wrong at home?"

Ignacio slammed the door of his car, came quickly up the steps, embraced Concha, then Jim. "No, nothing is wrong at home, Concha. I've come to see Jim. It's important."

Once they were within the *sala,* with the doors shut, Ignacio stated his business, his sentences shorn of all the usual Latin politeness. Turning to his brother-in-law, he said, "I have come to you for the last time, Jim. The mission to your people cannot wait longer."

Concha clasped her hands, looking at Jim, waiting for him to speak. His silence seemed unbearable. What was it that he had not talked over with her? A sense of disaster took hold of her. When they had planned to come to the hacienda, she had seen so plainly that Jim was to be the conserver of the family. In the world outside let Nacho be a ferment. But now she realized that the ferment was greater than Nacho, greater than any of them. It was pushing against the family walls.

Nacho was speaking. "We need you desperately. We believe if you go to the oil independents you could make them see the necessity of breaking this boycott. So far there have been no contracts made with Spain or Germany, but von Brenen is here again and pressing hard for one to cover a period of ten years. So far the government has sold only by the shipload, but it needs money, and the price offered is very generous."

"I don't know the independents," said Jim. He was sitting with his hands clasped and hanging between his knees, his eyes intent on the pattern of the rug.

"You understand the oil business, and you know our predicament," answered Ignacio. "The boycott is increasing the hatred between the two countries. What is happening in the hills tonight is only the beginning. Unless we who stand between the fringes of society—those too rich and those too poor—do something, we shall be hopelessly tied to the Old World. We need understanding with the States, and you, Jim, you could start that, break the dam of hatred that is building up."

"It would be dangerous." It was Concha who had spoken.

"Why do you say that?" asked both men, almost in unison. Jim's voice was gentle, but Nacho's was impatient and a little angry.

"Do you think that man von Brenen would give up easily?" Concha looked straight at her brother.

"He will know nothing about it until Jim is safely across the border —and know nothing then unless the independents act."

"You think so."

"Nacho, if I do it," Jim interrupted, "it means giving up here at a crucial moment. The support of my family depends on my success in this undertaking. And, also, if we leave the village now, what will happen?"

"If you go, Jim," Concha spoke quietly, "I shall stay and look after things here."

"I cannot leave you and the children here. It's not safe. The village is not proof against the fanatical hatred spreading so fast. You never know what men will do at such a time."

"It does not matter in a crisis like this whether one village more goes over to the Sinarquistas," Nacho answered. "Give up the hacienda for a while. Concha can come to us in the city."

"I am not afraid. No one in this village will hurt me. It is Jim who will be in danger." Again it was Concha who was answering Ignacio.

"It is unnecessary for you to keep harping on Jim's danger. It's a simple mission." As in his childhood, Ignacio grew irritated with his sister for thwarting his plans.

"You don't know what you ask," cried Jim. "Suppose I get the independents to break this boycott, I shall have done it at the expense of the company for which I once worked. I shall be able to do it in part because I have certain knowledge I gained while working for them. Some of these men are my friends. I didn't agree with them before, as you know, and I don't agree with what they are doing now. They are men of property who believe that in the name of property they have a right to do what they are doing. These are hard men, but they have their code. And I shall be breaking it. It will seem traitorous to them."

"I think you exaggerate. However, does what you say change the situation?"

"You mean——"

"I mean civilization is at stake, and you hesitate."

"Perhaps it is you who exaggerate. Civilization is a big word." And then after a pause Jim added, "If I go, how soon do you think I should start?"

"As soon as you possibly can." Ignacio rose to leave. "I must be back early tomorrow morning. I do not wish to be missed just now. I am sorry you will make no commitments. If you decide to undertake the mission, come up to Mexico City immediately."

That night, after Ignacio left, neither Concha nor Jim mentioned Nacho or his mission, but both knew that they had come to a crisis in their lives. Concha could not bring herself to say, "Go, Jim." Why

should he risk his life, all their happiness, all they had wrought together to carry out a plan that neither he nor Nacho was sure would
bring any results?

The night dragged on into day. Jim sat in his office trying to think
through his dilemma, for dilemma more and more it seemed to him
as the hours passed. Every instinct in him at first had rebelled against
the undertaking. Innate caution, innate dislike of radical methods,
innate distaste of any act that might be interpreted as disloyalty combined to make him view the undertaking with aversion.

And yet as the day wore on, Jim's mind slowly veered as if a mag-
netic needle swung it to the opposite point of the compass. Were any of
the reasons for holding back as great as the reason for undertaking the
mission? What did he place first? Was he to act for what he believed,
or act as seemed expedient? He was carried back to the days when
his ambition was to serve his country as an envoy. It would be in keeping with that ambition to go to the States now. He began to see ways
of approach, arguments he could use. Then he was suddenly brought
to a halt in his planning. Concha was against it. How could he ask her
to assume the burdens she would have to bear unless she were willing
for him to go? Hour after hour he trod the treadmill of conflicting
demands.

Toward the end of the day Concha rode her horse to the field where
the men were working so that they would not miss Jim's presence.
It would be fatal at a time like this with the village again critical of
them to appear to have lost concern in their mutual undertaking.

By the suspicion which those close to the primitive have, the villagers interpreted the *patrón's* sudden lack of interest. And Guadalupe they had not seen all day. The two were no doubt hiding from
Sinarquistas, as well they might, for they were godless men. The
Indians lounged at their work. "Why should we labor for men who
are bad?" some among them kept urging. "Let us join the Sinarquistas.
The hacienda has always been our enemy."

When Concha drew in her horse by the side of the men in the fields,
she knew immediately that their attitude was changed from friendliness
to guarded watching. Their blank faces told her of their passive
opposition. As she rode back, it came to her that as she was a Catholic
she could handle the situation among them better with Jim away. His
leaving would aid, not hinder, peace just now.

Then it was not for the good of the hacienda and to hold the village against the Sinarquistas that she was keeping Jim from this mission—and keeping him she was. By that subtle understanding come to them through years of adaptation of one to the other she knew that all Jim's life had been a preparation for this moment. Born in her country, deeply committed to it through her and through his children, and yet never relinquishing his loyalty to his own country, he would be the perfect emissary for a mission that, were it successful, might bring accord between the two nations. And yet she could not let him go.

She knew too if he did not go, something would die within him. His sense of purpose and usefulness would be injured. Yet she could not let him go. It was dangerous business. Jim, Jim, she cried to herself, I can't do it! I can't!

All at once she hated the United States because of what they had done to hurt her Mexico, because they had made it necessary for Jim to go off on this venture. It was futile for Jim and Nacho to assume this was not hazardous business. If as much was at stake as Nacho said, then it was important to those men from Europe to see that the journey was not made. She had met some of them at Louisa's. They were arrogant, proud, and ruthless.

As she reached the village on her return from her ride, she saw Guadalupe coming toward her, and she reined in her horse. "Did you want to speak to me?" she asked.

"Yes, I need to see Señor Buchanan. I have been twice to knock on the office door, but he does not answer."

"Perhaps I can take him your message."

"Señora Buchanan, it is a hard thing that I have to say, and I should rather say it to Señor Jim, but I have no time to waste. I must leave the school and immediately. I must go tonight."

"The danger is that great?" Concha asked quietly, but her heart was pounding with joy. Whatever she said now, Jim would not go and leave her alone. Without Guadalupe, Jim would consider her unprotected.

"It is not for myself," Guadalupe hurried to explain. "It is that last night a schoolteacher was driven out of a village beyond us in the mountains. She fled here for help. She is my wife! She is Soledad!"

"But Soledad is brave," said Concha, wondering why she was arguing with Guadalupe to stay when on his going hung her right to keep Jim. And then to her own surprise she heard herself saying, "Guadalupe, this can be arranged, but not now. Hide Soledad, if necessary, for a day, and if my husband sends for you say nothing about this. He himself must be absent for a little, and he needs to go feeling that you are here to help me. He leaves this evening. After that we can make arrangements."

Guadalupe hesitated. "I must explain to Señor Buchanan." Looking up, he saw he was speaking to space.

Concha spurred her horse across the little plaza where church and school faced each other, cantered across the park, dismounted at the foot of the gallery steps, and hurried in to Jim before she could change her mind. She found him listlessly toying with a paperweight on his desk. Standing behind him so he could not see the effort it was costing her to speak, she said, "I won't hold you back, Jim, from anything you feel you should do."

Jim swung round, facing her. "Concha, the United States is not set against Mexico as you think. My people are not greedy. They would not hurt Mexico if they understood. It is only that certain men who have power use it badly just as sometimes they do here. If we can stand together in this emergency——" But even as he talked he was getting ready to leave, moving about the room, throwing a few things into a pile to be packed.

"I should start tonight. Do you really think you can manage, Concha? I won't be gone more than two months at the outside. Fidel and Guadalupe and you together can manage. I'll talk to them before I go." But even as he spoke, she could see his mind was taken up with other plans.

"If I am to take charge, perhaps it would be better for me to arrange matters with Fidel and Guadalupe," Concha urged. "You often leave for a day or two. Leave like that now. Later I can explain. Nacho cautioned secrecy. Such delay will give you time to get to the border."

For a moment he was with her, a part of her, a part of their undertaking. His eyebrows drew together. "No, I'd better talk to Guadalupe. I can trust him."

"Don't worry," she said. "I'll manage."

He went on to the closed door of the children's room. "I don't like to go like this. Would you mind, Concha, if I should wake Tito? There are things I should like to say to him."

"Couldn't I tell him? He is so little, so excitable," Concha began. Then seeing the look of disappointment that passed over Jim's face, she added, "But after all, he'd be terribly upset if you went without speaking to him. It might be worse for him in the end."

Together they entered the room, Concha shielding the lamp's blaze with her hand. Jim sat down on the edge of Tito's bed, laid his hand on the child's shoulder. "Tito." He said it three times before Tito's eyes opened. When they closed again, Jim lifted his child into his arms, saying with sudden urgency, "Tito, I must speak to you. It is about our work."

"I am here." Tito's eyes opened wide this time. A scowl set between his brows as he looked into his father's eyes and then up at the shadow of his mother extended across the wall and ceiling.

"I have only a few minutes to spare, Tito. I am being called away on important business. I want to put Mother and Palito in your care until I return."

"And the care of the hacienda, if you are going away." There was a proud lift of Tito's head.

"Can I trust you, Tito?" Jim put his hand under the child's chin. "Will you be friends with Fidel?"

A look of stubborn resistance came into Tito's eyes. "I am the *patrón*." His voice rose.

"Jim, he is too little for such a decision." Concha had not meant to speak. The words seemed to have said themselves.

"Yes, I am too little," echoed Tito, nestling his spirit into the soft subterfuge his mother offered him.

"Then I must choose Guadalupe to take care of things while I am away."

Tito laid his hand caressingly against his father's cheek. "A wee *patrón* no bigger than a tiny fairy."

Concha stood at the hacienda gate to watch Jim's car cross the dimly lighted plaza, watch it disappear down the street of the village until it was swallowed up in the distance. Finally she turned, barring the gate behind her. Through the thick foliage of the patio an old moon sent dim, uncertain patches of light, making her stumble—or was it that she did not see clearly? At the very fullness of their lives Jim had let himself be drawn away from her. How could he let it happen after these months when they had been so closely bound together that it seemed nothing could ever separate them?

Scattered about in their bedroom lay the things he had discarded. Slowly she picked them up. There were not many, and when she had finished putting them in the drawers, there was nothing in the room to remind her of Jim. How swiftly he had disappeared from the life that had been going on in this house for centuries.

That night Concha dreamed that she and Louisa were young girls again and that they were staying here at the hacienda with Mamá Grande and Mamá. Bright red blossoms of the bougainvillea hung in festoons from the great pillars of the veranda. Somewhere a white honeysuckle sent out its perfume. She awoke. She could still smell it. There must be a spray somewhere in the room. How young that girl of her dream was! Suddenly apprehension swept in upon her. She had neglected to caution Jim against Ramón. Ramón was working with the Germans she was certain. Then her thoughts veered to Louisa. Was Louisa their dupe, or did she share in the intrigue? Oh, Louisa, Concha cried in her heart, don't let anything happen to Jim!

Duties pressed in upon her. There were Guadalupe and Soledad to see immediately. That business could not wait.

Very early, even before the village was stirring, while Tito and Palito were sleeping, she slipped through the gate and over to the school and knocked on Guadalupe's door. It was opened so quickly that she knew he had been waiting for her. Soledad was sitting on the bed, and Guadalupe went and sat beside her, after placing the one chair in the room for Concha.

At first Concha did not recognize Soledad. She was dressed in the garb of the villages, full skirt and loose blouse, and her hair was braided as the village women wore theirs. Everything that identified her with the city had disappeared. She was older and quieter. Her disguise was complete. Then Concha noticed her bandaged arm. "You have been hurt. Guadalupe did not tell me."

"It is nothing," said Soledad. For the moment she hated Concha. She had forgotten that bond of friendship which once existed between them, remembered only what she had suffered at the hands of this family. And now she was afraid Concha would try to keep Guadalupe—Guadalupe who belonged to her and who by a miracle had been given back to her.

Concha rushed on. "You are safe here. We'll take every care of you." The old liking for Soledad had come back to her, and she added, "I am alone. It would mean much to me to have you here."

The thin layer of ice covering Soledad's natural warmth dissolved. She leaned forward eagerly. "It would be lovely!" she exclaimed.

"You forget," said Guadalupe quietly, "we cannot stay here. Soledad was driven out of the village just above us in the mountains."

"But that has nothing to do with our village," cried Concha.

"But if the people here learn this——"

"We can make them understand. I am a Catholic as they are. They will listen to me." Concha was determined now to keep Soledad.

"Señora Buchanan, we cannot yet say whether the old trust will hold here in the village against this new distrust. I am a Protestant. Their cry, you know, is for one religion, the Catholic. Such as I are to be driven out," Guadalupe reminded her.

"I know," said Concha. "I am a Catholic, but I am not of this new movement. Neither need they be."

Then Guadalupe saw that they must tell her the truth. But before he could speak, Soledad had jumped to her feet crying, "I was driven out of the village because they were told that once I was driven out of *this* village for a heinous crime."

Concha drew back. She remembered her grandfather, how he had looked when he told her of the terrible blasphemous act of the teacher.

Soledad's old bitter laugh broke from her. "Once in a little hut here I tried to teach the children. At night the overseer made a Cross on the floor under the table I used as a desk. I did not know it was there."

"So you did not step upon it?"

"I did, but not knowingly."

"I see," said Concha, "and now——"

"And now," Soledad interrupted her, "there is no other way but for us to leave."

"The village is stirring. I must go. Tonight will be safer than now. Please, Guadalupe, go about your work for today." Concha's shoulders drooped with discouragement as she moved toward the door.

"There is a way," said Soledad. "My husband is needed here, while your husband is off on business of the Revolution. Lupe—" she swung around now, addressing him—"stay, my husband, and finish your work. In the city I will find something to do for the Revolution."

"If I can be spared long enough to take Soledad to friends in Mexico City, I will come back," Guadalupe said, turning to Concha.

Suddenly Concha sensed this was a solution of more than her own needs; a note of relief in Guadalupe's voice, the recovered life in Soledad's, meant more than willingness to help her. What tragic happening of their separation was holding them apart now?

"Go about your duties today, Guadalupe, as if nothing had happened. I thank you both for such loyalty." Quietly Concha left them.

Once the door was closed Soledad began to deplore the necessary parting. "So soon after our meeting . . . but you are needed here, Lupe."

"Yes, yes, it would not do to leave now," Guadalupe answered her. "It was brave of you to suggest it, my wife."

So, mercifully, did Soledad and Guadalupe each hide from the other a secret. Soledad, when the first fright and the first wonder of their reunion had passed, knew that she did not want to give herself completely to Guadalupe. Ignacio, the exquisite, stood between.

To Guadalupe those first hours of ministering to Soledad had been hours of transcendent happiness. But as morning came and Soledad's vitality and vigor returned to her, anguish had settled over his spirit. The years of his imprisonment with their exhausting hours of labor had taken their toll. He wanted to care for Soledad—that was all. And he wanted his work. That what each had to give to the other would be acceptable they did not yet know.

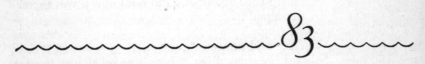

When Jim reached the city, in order not to arouse any suspicion he carried out his usual program. Leaving his bag at the Majestic Hotel, where he always stayed when in town, he went immediately to see Mamá Grande and bring her news of the hacienda. "Yes, everything is quiet in the country. I have come up to the city on a little business."

Mamá Grande, now that she had no part in the affairs of the hacienda, assumed indifference, but in reality she was eager for every detail. After a little, forgetting the part of bored listener she had put on, she prodded him with questions. She knew too much about the hacienda to be satisfied with generalities. "So you are not getting out of the land what we got with the old methods? Pampering the Indians, you'll learn someday to your sorrow doesn't pay. You and Concha are fools, to be carried away by the crazy ideas of this government. Nacho too is a fool. Louisa's the only sensible grandchild I have." She was in a better humor now, and he felt he could ask where he would find Nacho.

"You have not learned yet that Nacho holds to one tradition of his family, if to no other? No? You might go and wake him."

Nacho stirred lazily at Jim's entrance. Then, as he realized it was

Jim standing looking down at him, he sat up, and his inertia left him. The muscles of his face tightened. "You are ready?"

His hand moved toward the bell. "I'll ring for coffee. No, I had better not," he said; "there should be no semblance of a conference between us here. I am not certain of all the members of this household. Meet me just after the siesta hour at Pablo's. And will you tell Mamá Grande as you go out that I'm not ready yet to get up?"

Jim had not liked Pablo on the occasions he had seen him before. He seemed too full of suspicions and prejudices; but today, as he and Ignacio conferred with Pablo, he had a different impression of the man. He had grown in stature, or else his real quality had not shown before. But there *is* a difference, Jim told himself. He no longer feels inferior to Nacho. There is comradeship between them and understanding.

"I know that in the States labor is often suspect as it is here," Pablo began. "That is why we have felt you would represent us better than one of our own men. How to reach the independent companies, we leave to you. You know the oil business, and you know our dilemma. I believe Nacho is going part way with you. That is very good. In an emergency it would be better to have one of us along. We think those working against us know nothing of our plans, but we wish to take no chances." He spoke with considerable dignity and with a degree of friendliness that warmed Jim. And then, after every detail of the trip was settled, he again, as in the past, seemed restrained and uncertain of himself.

Late in the afternoon Jim drove up to his old home on the heights to call on Louisa. No act of politeness must be neglected today. The house, as usual, was full of people.

"Have you seen Nacho lately?" asked Ramón, scrutinizing Jim closely.

"I looked in on him this morning, but he was still sleeping. He rarely comes to see us. Like you," he added lightly.

"How is Concha?" questioned Louisa. "You should have brought her with you. You know she would be much better off in the capital. You shouldn't have left her alone, Jim, even for a night. Did you say you were going back tomorrow?" Jim had no recollection that he had.

It was just as he was leaving that he encountered the German whom twice before he had met in his sister-in-law's house. "I speak the

English now," the man said, "and the Spanish. We need no longer the interpreter. No? You have visited your own country since we last met, is it not so? No? I see. The time is not good. Too many of the accident on that fine new road to Laredo. *No es verdad?*" He laughed. "You see I mix my two new languages. But yes, you are wise. Mexico is the good country. Here we all stay together like brothers. No?" He passed on.

Jim went away deeply troubled. Concha was right, then, in her misgivings. This trip *was* risky. He was certain the reason for his presence in Mexico City was known, and he was being warned that if he carried out his plans, efforts would be made to stop him. His adversary was keen-witted and clever. He would need all his own cleverness to outwit him. A strange, odd excitement took hold of him as he admitted to himself there might be danger even to his life.

After leaving Louisa's, he went to Mamá's small shop. The excitement left him now. Her presence sobered him. He began to wish she knew more of what was going on behind the scenes, and just what part he was to play in it. Perhaps she did. Was Mamá ever entirely ignorant of anything affecting her children?

As on the day she had proposed he take over the hacienda, Mamá was sitting in the high-backed Spanish chair. He seated himself on a corner of a table near by, pushing away a clutter of china and glass. As he talked, he kept picking up pieces from the table, bits from colonial Spain and Maximilian's France. There was a tall porcelain vase from the Orient—come in probably on one of the ancient Manila galleons. The clutter around him seemed somehow to emphasize Mamá's repose, her strength. If anything happened to him on this trip, he wanted her to understand something of his plans both for Concha and his sons. Briefly he told her of his financial position, the safeguards he had taken for his family's future.

"I promised, as you know," he began, "to bring my children up in the Catholic faith."

"Yes," she said. "It was the only way you could marry Concha."

"But there was this understanding between Concha and me—my sons should go to my university, know my way of life as well as their mother's."

"And Concha consented?"

"Yes."

"You must remember," she said, "it was I who made possible the union between you and Concha. When I lived in France I had to make the same decision. We could not agree . . . and parted."

Perhaps through Concha Mamá had righted something in her own life. It would explain why she had gone against Mamá Grande's wishes, insisting on Concha's marriage to him. Jim wished Mamá would tell him something more of that part of her life. Instead, after a short silence she asked, "Why do you tell me this now?"

"Something may happen——"

She rose, signifying the conversation was over.

"Would you go to dinner with me?" he asked.

"If you will give me time to dress?"

He sat for an hour in the library of the old house, waiting for her. It was quiet here, and his taut nerves relaxed a little. He had turned out all the lights but one. The shadows were deep, hiding the pilgrim over the mantel. A small yellow flame burned at the far end of the room at the feet of the Virgin. Danger seemed unreal here in the still room.

"May we go to the restaurant Ramón is always talking about?" Mamá asked as they went out.

"Why, certainly." Jim was a little surprised at her request. The café's ultra-sophistication and smartness, he thought, would not be pleasing to her, nor would she wish her family to go there. Wealth and fashion of both Mexico and the United States gathered in it; with them the refugees from Europe more interested in preserving their money than their countries. Intrigue both personal and political made the café its meeting place.

Few people were dining when they arrived, but by the time they had finished dinner the place was full. Jim looked at his watch, fearful that he had overstayed and Nacho would be waiting.

"We had better stay another hour," Mamá said quietly.

How much did she know?

Dancing had begun. Jim studied the strange murals that gave background to the scene—soft, pale colors of twisted, broken trees that, when he looked at them more closely, became headless women, their breasts the enlarged joints of broken trees. He had a peculiar feeling of frustration as he stared up at them. These pale, distorted figures were the work of that artist who, in the days when the spirit of the Revolution was strong and there was a renaissance of art, had painted in throbbing blues and flesh tones the colossal figure of fertile woman.

Was it his own frustration or a frustrated people the artist sought now to portray?

"How extraordinary to find you two here!" It was Louisa's voice, and looking up he saw that she, Ramón, and their German friend, von Brenen, were standing by the table.

"Mamá! You are very handsome in that outfit." Louisa looked with approval at her mother's close-fitting black dress, relieved by pearl necklace and earrings.

"And you, Louisa, are very beautiful. But the scene does not suit you." Her mother's voice was low and stern.

"I think it does," said Ramón. His eyes appraised his young wife with her clear olive skin, her heavy mass of gold hair caught with a diamond bar at the nape of her neck, her tall figure, small hips, well-rounded breasts faintly outlined under the shimmering gold of her dress.

As they turned to go Jim caught a glimpse of Ramón's eyes leveled on him under half-lowered lids. They held a venomous hatred. I suppose, thought Jim, he has always hated me. How odd that I should not have realized it until now.

When he took Mamá home, she insisted that he come in, but when they were once within the patio she did not cross to the stairs. "I do not believe you have been in our chapel since your wedding," she said. "I have a desire to see it with you tonight." They stood silent for a few moments within the door. Only the light before the altar illumined the darkness. "There is a little door which Father Cristóbal used formerly," she said. "I'm going to let you out there." So she did know their plans! The knowledge brought a sense of strength and comfort to him.

But despite it, once he was outside he felt nervous. Was he being followed? Nonsense, he told himself. No one knows that door out of the Navarro mansion but the family. It is to be assumed I am spending the night with my relatives. That is why Mamá wanted to go to the restaurant, so Ramón's crowd would see us. However, better not take a public conveyance. He would walk to the hotel by a roundabout route, get his bag, and join Nacho at the agreed meeting place.

Along narrow old streets paved in cobblestones, bearing Indian names, he went, finally coming to the wide paved street named after the great Indian Juárez, leader of that part of Mexico's Revolution which paralleled in time the Civil War of the United States. He came to Madero Avenue—Madero, a leader in the late epoch of the Revolution. At last he stood on the steps of the hotel at the corner of the Zócalo. Across the great square bulked the cathedral, solidly planted upon the ruins of the Aztec temple destroyed by the Spanish invaders.

It was quiet here in the dead of the night, and with that quivering of his heartstrings which the sense of danger in his mission had brought him, Jim looked out on the old square, so often in its long history saturated with blood as step by step through the centuries the country had moved toward liberty. Surely his mission would be successful. His country, which had also fought for freedom, surely would now be on the side of freedom, imperiled as it was over the world.

The twin towers of the cathedral were dark masses against the sky, towering over the Zócalo. A man went by, muffled in a ragged serape. The night air was filled with the scents of spring. The hour had come to meet Nacho.

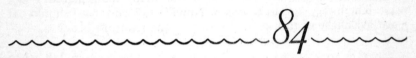

84

JUST before dawn Jim's car slid out along the great new highway that led to Laredo, over the flat land that came before they reached the piled-up mountains. It had not taken Nacho long to give him the last details he wanted him to know. Nacho had ended, "In the States, so the labor men tell me, all of Mexico's labor movement lies under the stigma of Communism. It is for that reason we asked you to go in an unofficial capacity. An American and a non-labor man would not meet with the prejudice otherwise easily aroused."

"I can't go as a representative of the Communists!" Jim exclaimed.

"You are not," Nacho answered calmly. "You complain about the picture of your own nation drawn here in Mexico. A master hand you say drew it. The same master hand has drawn for the States the picture of us as Communists. Think, Jim. I do not fit into such a picture, do I?" A delighted chuckle escaped him. "It's a tremendous thing you are going to do for our two countries," he added quietly.

Jim knew at last that there was complete understanding between him and Ignacio. Differences of nationality and outlook seemed finally to have been resolved in this night's journey and their joint undertaking.

They were in the mountains now, following one and then another curve in a series of switchbacks, circling down, then up again. Day had come. The sun's slanting rays lay on the flanks of the mountains, but the wind blew cold.

"I shall leave you at the next town and take the train back. I am convinced no one is following us any longer," said Ignacio.

"Has there been?"

"As we left the city I thought so. We shook them off when we stopped to eat."

Two Mexicans, the desperado type, with heavy black mustaches and thick black hair growing low on their foreheads, squatted on a high promontory. Below, the road made a succession of hairpin turns.

"Ought to be coming by this time," said Juan, peering through field glasses. "Sticks in place?"

"*Sí, sí.* I light now, Juan?"

"No, José, we get the wrong car maybe. Only the gringo's car we want. There they are! In that gap! Now!"

An avalanche of rock poured down on the road just below the two men.

Jim had heard the sound of an explosion not far away. "Somebody's up early," he remarked. "That was a small charge of dynamite going off, wasn't it? Working on the road probably."

He slowed the car as they rounded the next curve. "Nothing—I guess the way's clear." The car began to pick up speed on the clear stretch ahead. Then the road swung out where a rocky promontory forced it to hang over the valley far below, then cut back and out again. Skillfully Jim maneuvered the last abrupt turn. Halfway around he saw rock and rubble falling in an avalanche, blocking the way. "Jump, Nacho!" he cried, jamming on his brakes.

Juan and José clambered down the mountain. "Get the flags up, José!" shouted Juan. "Accident on the road."

Juan ran toward the slide. Yes, there the car was, jammed into the rocks, one door swinging drunkenly on a broken hinge. He peered in. Yes, there was the gringo, bent across the steering wheel. The windshield in a thousand splinters stuck up garishly from his blood-matted blond hair.

"Dead, all right." Juan grinned. "Now we get our money." He

jumped. There was someone groaning. He swung round. The thin, long body of a Spaniard lay sprawled at the very edge of the precipice. He was to kill only the gringo. He knelt beside the unconscious figure. Should he push the man over?

He heard men running behind him. "Saw your flag. Can we help?"

Ramón nervously paced his room, waiting for word. Now at last would he be revenged on Jim. He had hidden his hatred in his heart and hidden it well. But now his revenge and his loyalty to Franco's Spain, to the Sinarquistas and to the *hacendados* of Mexico flowed into one pattern. This outside, presumptuous man who thought of his country as the colossus astride all America, the bounder who had stolen Concha from him, would no longer take what he wanted.

He heard the telephone ring. He would show no impatience. Then he heard Louisa's light step running along the hall. She threw open the door. Her face was white, and she was wringing her hands. "Nacho, Jim!" she gasped.

"Nacho! What do you mean?" he cried, and he took her roughly by the shoulder. "You told me the servant brought word that Jim left your mother's house alone last evening."

Louisa backed away from him, her eyes large and frightened. "What has that to do with the accident?"

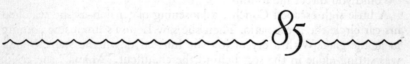

AT THE hacienda Concha waited for news. No word had come to her of Jim's arrival in the States. He had said it might be delayed. But if she did not hear today, something must be wrong. She went to the roof of the hacienda. Far away a dot was in motion on the road. It was an automobile. She knew by the speed it traveled forward. Long ago she had learned the characteristics of each moving thing seen from this roof. Quickly it took shape. Yes, it had turned off at the beginning of the old hacienda land, there where the road divided. A hand seemed to be squeezing her heart. Word about Jim, but not *from* Jim. Jim would have written. His letter would have come in the regular mail.

Slowly the car drove the length of the village street, stopped at the gate of the hacienda, passed in. With her feet almost refusing her bidding she went down the twisting stairs. The car was standing before the steps. By it stood a short man about her own age. He turned slowly from scrutiny of the patio to look at the great columns of the veranda, the wide beautiful entrance, as if to fix them forever in his mind. His interest seemed in the house. Then he had not come on personal business.

As she approached he turned, regarding her. There was something familiar about the man, that way of taking off his hat, and something about the black eyes.

Pablo surveyed his half sister with the same close scrutiny he had given to the house. The old bitter hatred rose in his heart. He forgot his love for Nacho, his admiration of Jim, brought to the surface by Jim's death and Nacho's injury. He was here to tell this proud woman who stood so silent on the step above him that there had been an accident and that she too was now bound by suffering into the cause of the common people.

Concha did not speak, could not.

Suddenly Pablo knew compassion. If only he had come as a beloved brother, then he could take his sister in his arms as Ignacio would have done and helped her to bear it, but convention held him from claiming that right. He remembered Guadalupe. Guadalupe with his gentleness could make it easier for her.

"I have come on an errand to the teacher of this village," he said. "Would you direct me to him?"

A little sigh escaped Concha, a loosening of tension as she watched his car circle the great patio. Then she saw Louisa's limousine coming in at the gate. With a cry of joy she hurried down the steps. Mamá was sitting alone in the seat behind the chauffeur. "Mamá," she cried, flinging open the car door. "How lovely to have you while——" Then she saw her mother's face and the words froze on her lips. Quietly Mamá walked up the steps, her daughter's hand clasped in hers, turned looking across the park. "It is here happiness came to you, Concepción."

Jim was dead. Mamá didn't need to tell her. Past and present were blended: the day she had released Jim for this mission she had known. But how could he be? Jim was so alive, his gray-blue eyes looking into hers, his strong, fine hands holding hers. The sound of his quick, un-Mexican step as he crossed the patio. What was Mamá saying? He was dead. The colonnades of the gallery seemed to be reaching up into unlimited space carrying the children's voices, near a moment ago, far away. She brushed her hand across her eyes, gave a long, low moan.

It was late now. Night had fallen. Mamá had told her that Jim had been instantly killed. His last thought had been to save Nacho. They had buried Jim in the near-by town at sundown in order to comply with the law that burial must take place within twenty-four hours after death. They could not reach her in time, as word of the accident had not come to them until late afternoon. This Mamá believed was divine Providence saving her daughter from knowing how broken had been Jim's body. Mamá had gone up from Mexico City for the burial and to bring Nacho back. There were long weeks of suffering ahead of him, for his back had been injured.

Night after night Concha dreamed an ever-recurring dream. She was standing by a door about to turn the knob. It came off in her hand. Filled with terrible anguish she tried to call out to Jim, but her voice was only a whisper. Then she would wake sobbing to find herself standing in the middle of the room trying to open a door that was not there and find Jim who was not there.

It was Friday of Holy Week. The church had changed in many ways since it had been entirely in the keeping of the village. There was a certain indefinable Indian atmosphere, erasing a little its Spanish origins. The high vaulted ceiling had been painted in Indian designs. No longer were there gorgeous expensive flowers on the altar brought by the Navarros. Instead small village offerings were placed there. Over the church was the pungent odor of herbs and green tree branches. Red paper pots filled with sprouting barley—sign of life—stood before the saints.

The figure of the Mater Dolorosa, miraculously come to their church from the hacienda chapel, had undergone little change. She was still Spanish in bearing and in feature, her skin very white. As the villagers had long accredited her with special healing powers, the heavy, black silk robes had never been changed except for the intricate border at the hem of small silver *milagros*—arms, legs, more intimate parts— offerings of those who had been healed of bodily injury. Only on this day of the Virgin's great suffering did they add to her costume a small lace handkerchief placed in her hand. In her great sorrow undoubtedly she would need it. Her black eyes seemed to look inward to sorrow. The lines around her nose, the quiet mouth, all indicated grief.

Last night the villagers had arranged for her to watch today's Crucifixion. The hill of Golgotha had been erected, Christ nailed to the Cross. The Mater Dolorosa stood a little out from her niche, half facing her anguished Son. Now it was night again. The Cross was empty, and the Mater Dolorosa mourned alone.

Concha walked slowly along the village plaza and entered the church, dark except for the candles that burned feebly in the vast empty space. She shivered, then moved quickly to the Mater Dolorosa, falling on her knees before that other sorrowing woman. She wept.

A hand was laid on her shoulder. "Concepción." It was Mamá speaking. "You have not told me, but I know your secret. You are again carrying Jim's child. You have work to do."

"Jim did not know. If only I had told him, he would not have gone."

Softly Mamá began her prayer. "Holy Mother of God, our Lady of Sorrows, intercede for this small suffering child of mine that she be given strength to suffer."

86

IT WAS all Concha could do through the summer to hold the villagers from joining the Sinarquistas. They were beginning to talk against Guadalupe, to call him an infidel, to make the sign of the Cross to protect themselves against him.

"I am of your faith. I would send Guadalupe away if he were not a good and righteous man," Concha told them over and over.

For a time this would satisfy them, but then again she would have to repeat it. Sometimes she was terrified, sometimes simply bewildered. What would she do without Guadalupe, and yet what would she do with him? Violence seemed to be like a monster ready to spring out of the darkness of minds long downtrodden. Thirty million Indians in South America. Suppose they should be united against Jim's country, Concha would think, forgetting her own difficulties in the larger issue. Sinarquismo was no longer a secret doctrine. Openly now it stood against Protestantism, against democracy.

One day Guadalupe said to her, "It was Señor Buchanan's idea to put the sugar mill into condition this year and run it as a co-operative undertaking. If they begin new work, they will forget the violence existing all around them. We could clear away the ruined parts of the mill and set the place in order, and then later, if I could be spared to go to the city, perhaps we could interest the government in helping us with the machinery."

It took hours of conference with Francisco before the idea was made acceptable to the village. Then, in the midst of their planning, Francisco died. He was a very old man, and his voice carried great weight with the village. Patiently Guadalupe went to work to win Fidel to be his mouthpiece among the men. Fidel had been inclined to join the Sinarquistas. It was a doctrine that appealed to him. He liked fighting. Guadalupe's gospel of peace gave promise of no dramatic night meetings—no march over the hills making a flaming cross, a living cross made by men carrying torches.

In the end it was Tito who swung Fidel over to Guadalupe's side. Fidel loved the little *patrón* who strode so proudly over to the mill with him, explaining earnestly that this work was to be a surprise for his father on his return. Tito allowed no one to tell him his father was dead. Fidel would not bring unhappiness to the little *patrón,* and let him believe his father would return. So the work on the mill was started, and after a while Fidel forgot he wanted to be violent.

In the child's game of bossing, the men good-humoredly played their part. The *patroncito* they affectionately called him. He came to sit among them when they talked, and though he did not realize it their ways of thought crept into his. Often afterward, by some remark of Tito's, Concha or Guadalupe entered more fully into the village life.

"My father will come back when he is ready," he insisted. Each night he waited at the gate of the hacienda for him. Tito was no more willing to accept the death of his father than he had been to accept the death of his playmate Teresita. Like his great-grandfather Julián Navarro, death offended his proud little soul.

One evening as he came back after his vigil at the gate and his father was not with him, he was very angry, and he slapped Palito. "Cease your babble!" he shouted. "Our mother is tired, and I am tired. We need our father, and I am the only one to watch for him when he comes." Then he turned and went out of the room.

Later, when she searched for him to put him to bed, Concha could not find him. Going to the gate she saw him making his way down the village street, a small bundle under his arm. He looked very lonely in the half dusk of evening. He was growing tall and thin, and his shoulders drooped a little. Suddenly Concha realized how much Tito needed something she could not give him until she surrendered her own sorrow. She would linger no longer at the hacienda. She would go up to the city, leave the care of the village to Guadalupe, prepare for the birth of her child. Mamá would help her with the children for a while. Louisa would make Tito forget. She could give herself to her grief.

"You must manage somehow," she told Guadalupe.

<center>~~~~~~ 87 ~~~~</center>

IGNACIO had been asleep. He woke with a feeling of physical well-being such as he had not had since the accident. But his spirit lagged. Having no desire to enter into the world around him, he did not open his eyes. He was sick with a mingled sense of defeat and guilt. Whether Jim's death had been an accident or had been engineered by the sinister forces of Europe, it seemed to him in any case that he was responsible. If only he had never had his crazy dream of breaking the boycott. It was he who had proposed the plan and the man.

Hearing his name, he opened his eyes. Concha was standing by his bed looking down at him—a Concha steeped in grief. In his blackest moments he had not imagined her so given over to sorrow. He had seen her in mourning before for their grandfather, for their father, but the garb she wore now seemed a part of her soul. The folds of her dress were girded loosely about her with a sash, heavy tassels weighting it down. There was no color in her lips or cheeks, her eyes were sunken, her nose pinched. Why did she have to come? What was there now left to say to each other? He closed his eyes.

There was a soft rustle as she seated herself in the chair beside his bed. "You will be well soon, Nacho." Her voice was drained of life, of interest.

"Do you regret it? Naturally you wish it were the other way around."

There was no answer. Ignacio's eyes flew open. He had spoken with the expectation that Concha would relieve him of his torment, and she had not.

Her gaze was on the floor, and she seemed busy with some torment of her own. "I should have come long ago." She spoke the words as if her only audience were herself.

"But you didn't." He finished her thought for her. "You didn't because you couldn't forgive me."

"It wasn't exactly a matter of forgiving you. You seemed futile to me. I just didn't wish to see you."

"If you had not meddled in my life, there would have been no chance that I would have meddled in yours," Ignacio answered.

"In just what way did I meddle?"

"I was meant to remain aloof from the sordid struggle this country is going through—I would have except for you. I never wanted to identify myself with it. It was you who urged me to participate. I did, and what happened? Jim is dead. The contracts have gone through. Our oil goes to Germany and Spain. Hatred against the States grows, and no one here has the brains to stop it, or the desire perhaps. So we become the wishbone between the New and Old World. Who gets the longest leg of the bone matters little to most Mexicans. Corn is all they are thinking about—and charcoal to cook it with. Except for you, I would have continued to live detached from such a spectacle."

"A detachment you have no right to. And you never really gave it up. Why didn't you undertake the mission you sent Jim on yourself?"

In low tones little above a whisper the accusations went on, each trying to find relief in condemnation of the other, each carrying on the arguments brooded over in the sleepless hours of many nights. Finally, all that either could say to pass sentence on the other and thus to clear himself had been said.

Concha was utterly weary. The child within her dragged at her back. She rose to go. But as she stood looking down at Ignacio, for the first time she noticed that his was the face of a man who had suffered spiritual as well as physical pain. Words he had just spoken came back to her, revealing more than he had meant them to reveal. He felt guilt for Jim's death, and it was destroying him. Nacho couldn't stand to be so humbled. A scene out of their youth leaped into her mind. Nacho, the would-be matador with red cape and sword, the look of triumph in his face. Nacho must be given back his sword, she thought cynically. She started to speak, meaning to restore Nacho's pride, then go away and keep her bitter grief to herself, stay beyond the reach of any further appeal to her sympathy. But she broke under the misery in his eyes. It was not a return of pride that would save Nacho. He must believe in something beyond himself.

"Oh, Nacho, forgive me! I have been cruel. It's just that I can't seem to live without Jim. I have no right to blame you for his death. I let him go. We both thought he could help save Mexico!"

Nacho reached up, took her hand, pulled her down on the bed beside him. "If I'd only been the one!"

Concha began crying now with an abandonment that frightened him. "You mustn't cry like that, Concha. Please, please."

"Let me," she managed to say. "It is the first time." But gradually her sobs ceased. "Nacho, please get well. Go on with what you and Jim started. That is why you were saved. A miracle!"

After Concha had gone, Ignacio lay listening to the noises of the city. For the first time since the accident, Jim's face did not haunt him, and he no longer heard Jim's voice crying, "Jump, Nacho!"

The door opened to admit Pablo. He stood for some time without speaking, looking down at Ignacio. "They tell me you are nearly well. It is time to talk of what you are going to do with yourself."

Once the words would have been spoken with a note of raillery in his voice implying he was humoring his half brother, making him believe he was an earnest worker. But there was no such tone now; instead, deep affection. During Ignacio's long convalescence Pablo had come daily to sit for hours by his bed, silently helping him in his struggle. He had never been able to keep Nacho from expending precious strength in censure of himself. But today Pablo saw, on studying him, some tension of his soul had loosened. Now was the time to get him to consent to help in holding Mexico against reaction.

He sat down prepared for a long struggle. "I know what you are thinking. I'll tell you your thoughts," he began. "They run like this. The dream of democracy, a will-o'-the-wisp flitting over the New World, appears to have led our Mexico up to the very gate of freedom and then left her to struggle in a quagmire of half-realized reforms and outside disapproval. There is complaint on every side. People are saying the gulf between the rich and the poor is as great as ever. What good has it done to give the villages land? Mexico's harvests have fallen alarmingly. Corn has to be imported, for many villages have failed to cultivate their quota. The railroads and oil wells which we insisted be returned to us are badly managed. Negotiations have broken down with the foreign oil companies. Money to satisfy the old owners of confiscated properties is not forthcoming. There is danger that we shall stand discredited among the nations. Contracts to supply Italy and Germany with oil have been signed.

"Even the greatest dreamers are a little frightened," he went on. "They cling pitifully to the record of schools started, co-operative projects in the villages that have succeeded, the way Mexico City has improved. The gap between its elegance and its squalor still is great, but it is not so great as it was, they say. There is a more workaday look. There are rows of workmen's houses and small dwellings. In all the city few go barefoot. That is all the Revolution seems to have come to. Is it not so?"

When Ignacio did not answer, Pablo continued: "Tomorrow, you know, is the election of a new president. Cárdenas has promised it shall be an election by the people, not the military."

"Yes?" said Ignacio. "How does he plan to accomplish it, when behind each would-be president the hand of Fascist Europe is felt? The most downtrodden men of the villages are going to be brought by thousands into the city, I understand. Illiterate, poverty-stricken, easily moved to fanaticism, they will be held in reserve by their bosses to bring terror to the city if it will help their side to win. Do you call that free election?"

"Wake up, Nacho. Face reality. We are not yet free. Sinarquistas are gaining power daily. It's been a long struggle, but we're still fighting. Are you going to quit when the struggle is fiercest?"

At the nurse's entrance, there was nothing for Pablo to do but leave. "Think it over," he said. "We can use you."

The day after the election he came again. "Well," he said, "a lot of men were killed here in the city and over the country yesterday. We're a bit shocked, but we're happy, too. Man, the people voted. What does it matter that men were killed. They were fighting for their rights as a free people." In his excitement Pablo walked up and down the room. "What's more, the Indians brought in from the villages made no terroristic demonstration. What Cárdenas has done among the people in the last six years is bearing fruit. We've elected our President, and he's for a Pan-America. No division at the Rio Grande."

Pablo swung round. "But in Madrid the Spanish World Axis has announced: 'One race, one language, one culture, one religion below the Rio Grande.' The Sinarquistas are its tool. And Hitler has overrun France. What's your answer, Nacho? Do you fight with us? If you don't, you're against us."

"What do you want me to do?"

"Get well first. Then accept a mission to the States for the government. Go as the others go, on a salary. Give up this free-lance business of yours, working only when it suits your convenience."

Ignacio hesitated. "I'll do it," he said at last.

Pablo walked out of the room before Ignacio could change his mind. The streets were full of people still celebrating the election. As always in Mexico, a medley of music drifted down from open windows. Someone was singing "Ave Maria," and someone was singing a version of the song of the Revolution:

> "In a democracy,
> Men are free and equal.

> "In our democracy,
> Now that the peacock has shed his tail,
> Every little animal has his say on Election Day."

Pablo turned the corner into his own street. He and Nacho were truly brothers.

It was late in the evening when Berta Mendoza came into the hospital and stopped at the head nurse's desk. "How is he tonight?"

"He seems better, much better. And he wants to see you. He asked no matter how late you came in to let you see him."

At the door of Ignacio's room Berta paused a moment. So many times she had come to help him through the black hours of the night, sometimes to find him sunk in discouragement, sometimes given over to cynicism. Would he ever completely affirm life? In this moment outside his door she waited a moment to regain her own deep, abiding faith. It had been a hard day. At her hospital in the poor part of the city emergency cases had been coming in—men and even women and children, injured in the election.

Softly she turned the knob.

"Come in, come in, Berta! Don't treat me like a sick person. I'm getting up tomorrow." Ignacio's voice had a new note in it, and Berta, tired to the point of exhaustion, felt her knees buckling under her. She was prepared to meet discouragement with optimism, cynicism with faith. But this buoyant voice—she was not prepared to meet happiness. There was a chair beside the door. She sank down on it.

"What is it?" she asked in a voice a little above a whisper.

"I'm going to the States, Berta, as soon as I am well. I've taken a position with the government."

"Nachito!" Berta felt as if wings carried her across the room. "And for how long will you be gone?"

"Berta, you are a fraud. You don't want me to go after all." His black Spanish eyes were full of laughter.

"When do you come back?"

"When I come, I shall marry you."

88

THESE were difficult days for Guadalupe, alone and under suspicion from the village as the enemy of their God. On All Souls' Day he brought his offering of flowers to the churchyard, but in the afternoon he withdrew into his room, leaving the village to its special celebration for the dead. Laying the marigold petals the villagers thought to make a last decorous call on the gringo Señor Jim who had worked side by side with them and now was dead. They did not share their sacred Indian rites with outsiders, and had Concha been at the hacienda they might not have carried out their plan. But Señora Concepción with Tito and Palito had gone for a while to the great city. There was to be another child.

Petals were laid across the new plaza to the hacienda gate. There they set up a straw booth that resembled their own huts. In it they placed a table and bowls of foods, black candles, and bright marigold blossoms. At evening, as the bell tolled, they crossed the square from the church to the door of this improvised house, their great hats held against their chests.

"We have harvested a good crop. You will be pleased to know that, Little Dead One." Thus they addressed Jim. "Fidel is going to the capital of the state to speak for us in the Assembly of Cane Growers. We wish you to know the school is a good school." In this manner they informed him that they had not joined the Sinarquistas and had not driven Guadalupe out. "All is well, Little Dead One." So for the last time they shared with the gringo the fellowship of the village.

It would have been good for Guadalupe had he known the meaning of the hut against the hacienda wall. Sitting in the quiet school-house, he planned how he would hold them all against Concha's return. He believed that Fidel, head of the village, might be interested in building himself a better house, something on the order of the school building. An undertaking of that sort would engross the whole village.

In the weeks that followed the house was started, but the men still appeared to have time for Sinarquismo. At night sometimes Guadalupe would see a cross of flame on the mountainside. Those nights there were absences from the village, and Guadalupe would kneel by his bed and pray, "Dear God, don't let them kill in Thy name! And take care of Soledad until I am free to do so! Amen."

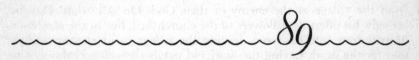

CONCHA's third child, though a girl, was not small-boned like Tito and Palito—she was built on a larger mold, more like Jim. Concha's labor was long and difficult. After the birth of the child, she lay motionless, exhausted, responding to nothing the doctor did. It seemed impossible to save her.

"I can rouse her to no effort," he said to Mamá. "There is no will here to live." He motioned to the nurse. "Bring the baby. Let us see if the child will rouse her."

"Wait for a little," Mamá begged. "Leave me alone with her."

When the nurse and the doctor had closed the door, Mamá leaned over Concha, smoothed her hair back from her forehead. Very gently she spoke her name. "Concepción, I have pleaded with you before to be concerned with life, not death."

There was no response from Concha. Her lips moved. Mamá leaned close. "Death is here . . . standing . . . waiting."

"Where is your faith?" Mamá challenged her. "Where is your responsibility? Would you leave Jim's children for Louisa and Ramón to bring up?"

Concha's eyes opened. "Won't you——"

"No, Concha. I will not assume your responsibilities. But Louisa will. She will take the three in order to have Tito. Ramón wishes it."

Ramón! Father to Jim's child! A faint spark of returning life shone in Concha's dull eyes. As once before, she struggled to live, to fight off death. But her spirit drifted—no anchor to hold it to earth. Jim—her strength—too weak alone. Somewhere far off she heard Tito crying, "I want my mother." Commotion at the door. Then Tito near her demanding, "It is not so, is it? Tío Ramón says you are going away like my father. He lies. Please say it is not so."

"No, it is not so."

Concha was sitting up for the first time today. She looked very beautiful, Louisa thought, as she entered the room. She wore the negligee Jim had given her for her trousseau. Imagine keeping it all this time!

The nurse was just lifting the baby from Concha's arms. There was a light in her eyes that erased the ravages of her sickness. "I have named her after her father," she said. "Jim told me in the South of his country they often name girls after their fathers. James—it sounds strange, does it not? Jeem." She tried it tentatively. Her face lighted up. "When he was little, Jim told me they called him Jemie—" She lengthened out the "e"—"Jeemie. Yes, it shall be Jeemie."

"You are stronger today, but you must remember that it will be a long time before you are well," Louisa began, "and I have come with Ramón's desire and my own to lighten your burdens. A family, he says, is as one person. When one suffers, all suffer. When one has plenty, all should share in that plenty. We want to help with the care of the children. We thought if we educated Tito—— Let us have him, and we will educate him as a gentleman should be. He's too strong-willed for you to manage alone. Ramón will be a father to him."

Concha shook her head.

Louisa rose, walking around the room with that restless energy so characteristic of her. Finally she came back, picked off a flower from a bunch on the table by Concha's side, tore it to pieces. With one of her sudden darting movements, she dropped on her knees at Concha's feet, burying her face, crying out in a muffled voice, "Concha, it isn't fair! You have two sons, and I have none. Give him to me, Concha."

Concha put out her hand, smoothed Louisa's hair with its glint of gold. She was filled with pity for her sister. It always had seemed worse for Louisa than anyone else to be deprived.

Then Concha stiffened, remembering what it was Louisa wanted.

"I can't do it. Not this time, Louisa, can I give you what you want."

But when Louisa was gone and the nurse helped her into bed, Concha was frightened. Somehow Louisa always had her way.

The very next day Louisa came with a new proposal. "When you go back to the hacienda—you *are* going back to the hacienda, aren't you?—let Tito stay with us until his school closes."

I must hurry and get well and take my children home, thought Concha. Aloud she said, "I think it is better for Tito to go back with me. Guadalupe can teach him until he is older."

Ramón had come into the room unnoticed. Now he spoke. "You remind me of your father, Concha. You will remember he did not accept my offer. It was a pity. I could have helped him."

Concha stared wide-eyed at Ramón. Did he mean he had brought about her father's ruin? Was he threatening her, if she did not give up Tito? What could he do? There was the village. And he belonged to the Sinarquistas. He might turn the village against her . . . bring harm to the children. Her hand went to her throat.

"Perhaps it would be wise to listen to me about Tito, Concha." Ramón's tone was soft, even solicitous.

Louisa, standing by the window, moody over her sister's refusal to give up Tito, heard the silken voice she knew so well, used so often to make her do his ugly bidding. All the years of her marriage seemed to marshal themselves into this moment—the suffering, the humiliation he had meted out to her. Now, now at last, her opportunity to strike back had come. As much as she longed to have Tito for a son, she wanted more to revenge herself on Ramón. Because she had not been able to give him a son, in a thousand ways he had inflicted humiliation on her for what she could not help. He had set his heart now on having Tito to bring up as his own son. She would see he did not have him and that he lost any respect Concha might have had for him.

She turned sharply, walked over to him and stroked the sleeve of his coat. "So Ramón would atone to Concha for Jim's death," she said in a voice as silken as his.

Ramón turned pale, threw off her hand, but his words were still smooth. "Louisa has always felt we should have warned Jim when he told us about his trip to the States," he explained.

"You mean I should have warned Jim against you. . . . But there is no need, my husband, to tire Concha with my regrets. Tell her now that you did not mean to take Tito from her. Or——" Again her hand stroked his sleeve.

"Be still!" commanded Ramón. "You don't know what you are talking about, Louisa. It is better, as you say, that Concha should keep Tito. You are too overwrought a woman to take care of a child."

"Just as you say," said Louisa, and with her light tinkling laugh she turned and went out of the room.

Ramón for a moment did not move, but stood looking at Concha. He could see she loathed him. He could not bear it. He must have Tito.

"Concha, it's all a mistake. I——"

"Please go," cried Concha.

When the door closed behind him, Concha sat motionless. Only her brain seemed active. Ramón had had something to do with Jim's death. Somehow Louisa knew it. What might he still do to hurt her, to hurt the children? She could not free herself of that final picture of Ramón, overfat, flabby-jowled, as venomous-looking as a snake. Somehow he'd find a way.

The door opened, and Mamá came in with Tito and Palito. Looking into Mamá's calm eyes, Concha grew calm herself.

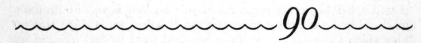

It was Christmas Eve when Concha arrived at the hacienda. To the last child the villagers welcomed them. The house was alight for their coming, and the church for the coming of Christ. As dusk fell men and women and children entered the church, candles in their hands, joy showing in their dark faces.

Around the village Fidel, as Joseph, walked with dignity at the side of Mary, seated on his old burro, seeking a place where the child might be born. At every hut someone within sang refusal. At last Joseph, shoulders bent under his discouragement, and Mary with her face anxiously peering out from her *rebozo,* came to the church. "There is room within," sang the kneeling people.

Over at the school Concha and Guadalupe prepared the traditional swinging jar of toys, hidden this year under the skirts of a beautiful

Spanish doll. From the church the villagers trooped to the school. There was laughter and fun when the blindfolded children tried to break the jar. It was Tito who finally succeeded. Concha, seeing how happy he was, gave a sigh of relief. That afternoon he had said to her, "My uncle Augusto told me once we should not have this school." Here in the village with his friend Guadalupe he would forget such teaching. Now that he had come home, she would see that he remembered how his father had said to him that last night, "Thou and I and Fidel."

On New Year's Day Concha and her three children were gathered on the gallery overlooking the fountain. Palito was playing quietly at Concha's side. Jeemie lay asleep in her lap. Tito, expressing his independence, put on his bathing suit and went alone into the pool.

A car rolled up the drive. It was Ignacio. "I've come to tell you my great news, Concha," he called as he got out. "Next week I leave for the States." Ignacio paused after this dramatic announcement.

"For long?" asked Concha.

"It may be a year, maybe two. It's important work for the government. I have been chosen by the Minister of Foreign Affairs. I'm going as a part of a mission to bring about understanding with the States. This Ezequiel Padilla is a man I admire. His ideal is continental solidarity. I shall work hard . . . and," he added, "for the first time earn my own living. It's a stimulating idea."

Concha, looking at her brother, saw that his long years of indecision and doubt had come to an end. "Is it safe?" There was a slight tremor in her voice.

"Yes," he replied, and then after a moment he went on: "My friend Pablo would have sent Jim openly and with the government's endorsement. He would have been guarded then. But I . . . to identify myself with the government . . . or have Jim——" He turned away, unable to complete the confession he had determined to make to Concha.

Concha reached out and took his hand.

Tito had been a little angry that his uncle whom he admired had not noticed him or his prowess in the water. He came to him now. "I heard what you said to Mamá. You are going to the States."

"Yes."

"It's my father's country. Father told me I must go there, so will you take me with you?"

Concha swept his small wet body close against her. "Not now, my little one."

"But I promised."

"And I promise I will take you when you are old enough."

~~~~~~~~~~~~~~~~~~~~ *91* ~~~~~

THERE was an air of expectation about the hacienda this morning. After two years, Ignacio was back from the States and was coming to see them. The gardener had framed the doorways with tuberoses and white honeysuckle. Tito had gone down the road to meet the car. Palito had taken the baby to stand at the gate with him. Palito was old for his four years, with the gravity and sense of responsibility which many Mexican children have, and he was very gentle. He could always be trusted with Jeemie, who in her desire to see everything was as likely to follow one of the bright butterflies which flitted over the patio as to wait for the car from town. Concha came often from the hacienda office to catch the first distant throb of a motor engine and as often went back to her work.

There seemed an endless number of things to do this morning. A man from the hills had come to receive his village's share of the last sale of sugar cane; a delegation from another village had arrived a little later, proposing they too enter the co-operative which managed the sugar mill. An Indian had injured his leg cutting cane; he came asking for medicine. Concha had a cupboard now in the office filled with simple remedies.

At last everything was done. She picked up the mail which had just been brought in. On the first page of the newspaper was a picture of two men shaking hands—a North American and a Mexican. Underneath it said, *"Mexico makes her first large payment for the expropriated oil. There is accord between us."* The goal for which Jim had worked. If only he were coming home with Nacho today!

The years since his death had been fruitful years. The co-operative effort had prospered. Most of Jim's plans she had been able to carry out. But they had been hard, lonely years.

There was the sound of the car! Then a halt to take in Tito and a second one at the gate to pick up the other children. Concha's heart grew tight with longing. The car swept up the drive. Tito, now a tall, slender boy of ten, tumbled out. "Mamá, Mamá," he cried. "He is here. Our *tío!*" Palito followed close behind, grasping Ignacio's hand; and Jeemie, not to be outdone, hugged him about the knees. Ignacio, leaning across the children, embraced Concha. "Mamá, Mamá." Tito stood on tiptoe touching her cheek lightly with his hand. "Look, he is a *Norte Americano* like Father!"

"Not a Mexican any longer then?" Her eyes looked deep into Nacho's.

"Very much one. More than I have ever been before. I'll tell you all about it, but first let me give the children what I brought them." There were watches for Tito and Palito, their names engraved on the back, and a set of toy ducks for Jeemie to float in her bath.

"And for my namesake there is on his watch my name too," said Ignacio, as the small boy held his gift up for his mother to see.

"I am Nachito, not Palito any more, Mamá." His black eyes were very bright.

"May we go and show Guadalupe?" cried Tito.

"Concha, let us sit down and talk," said Ignacio when the children had gone. "At last the things Jim and I sought to accomplish are coming to pass. I stood in the room and saw our own ambassador and America's Secretary of State sign an agreement, a Mexican-American agreement. We'll let them call themselves Americans, shan't we, if they think of us as Americans too, which we are?" he put in as an aside, smiling. Then he went on. "The agreement guarantees us sovereignty and control of our natural resources. And in our own senate yesterday I heard Minister Padilla say it marks a change in the international policy of the United States, not only toward us but toward all the Americas.

"Concha—" Ignacio leaned forward—"I have something more to tell you. Only Mamá knows it. I am to be married soon."

"To Berta?"

"Yes."

Ignacio's heart smote him. How alone Concha seemed! And so very young, not quite thirty. Tragically beautiful in her sheer black mourning dress. "Let us make one big family again. You know it's the Mexican way," Ignacio pleaded. "Surely you are not always going to stay here alone."

"And the hacienda?"

"Let it go. The city is where this nation is being shaped. It is there that exciting things are happening. We've a new and liberal Spanish colony, refugees from Franco's Spain—the best brains of Spain. They and our own liberals will shape us to greatness."

Concha shook her head. "It is in the village that our final strength or weakness lies. Palito definitely belongs here on the land. Tito maybe belongs to the city or to the United States. He will have to decide when he comes of age. But first I want to understand my husband's country. I want to go and see it, take Tito with me . . . see if it is a good place for him to be while he goes to school, for I must fulfill my promise to Jim. Then I'll come back to the hacienda to live."

"You mean you want to go to the States!"

"Yes, if you, now that you are to be married to Berta, will take the two little ones while I am away. That, too, is Mexican," she added, smiling. "And, Nacho, while I am gone for a few months, will you live here at the hacienda?"

Ignacio hesitated.

"Marry now, Nacho, and bring Berta here. Begin your life together close to the land."

"Mamá said that." Nacho frowned. "I had other plans."

"They can wait. Please, Nacho. Not one more village must join the Sinarquistas. All you say about unity between us and the States may be true, but after you are at home a little while you will learn how deep the hatred has grown in these two years. The Falange is making the Sinarquistas believe that war against the States would be a holy war. You must hold things here until I return. We cannot ask Guadalupe to stay longer. He and Soledad have been parted long enough. They wish to go to the new land the government has opened up and start their life together again."

"Yes. For you I will do it, Concha." And then he added, "I speak now the truth. When I was away I knew this land we have owned so long was my mother."

92

THE day for Concha and Tito to go north had come. Ignacio and Berta were to drive them as far as San Antonio. Nacho had opposed the automobile trip at first, divining that Concha wanted to go by car in order to see where Jim had been killed and to stop in the town where he had been buried. He would have spared her the ordeal. But when she insisted, he had said, "Then I will go with you as far as the border." Since the day they had talked at the hacienda, both Mexico and the States had entered the war against Germany. The Old World had not triumphed. Division had not come at the Rio Grande.

Berta suggested they take Palito and Jeemie with them. She believed that it would be easier for Concha if she had all her children with her when they came to the place in the road where Jim had been killed.

Quietly they all left the car where the road circled the last craggy mountain, and all knelt for a moment in prayer for Jim. Even Jeemie folded her little hands and was quiet. But when they reached the town, Concha asked that she might go alone to her husband's grave. It was a bitter, lonely experience.

It was the last day of the journey together. The land slipped away mile by mile under the wheels of the car—desert flatland of Mexico merging into the desert land of Jim's country. They came to the border town on the Mexican side, crossed the bridge into the States, passed through its frontier city out into the wide reaches beyond. They were nearing San Antonio.

Everyone had grown very quiet. Ignacio took out his watch. "There won't be time to go to the hotel. I'll have to take you directly to your train, Concha."

The warm soft pressure of Jeemie asleep in her lap was all Concha could think of. How had she ever thought she could give her baby up even for a day? And Palito—his eyes told her the parting would be terrible for him.

Gently Berta lifted the sleeping child from Concha's lap. "I'll write you every day how they are getting along," she whispered.

To Concha it seemed almost immediately they were at the station. Then they were on the steps of the train. They were in their compartment. Outside Ignacio was holding the baby up for her to see. She was laughing and throwing kisses. Berta had Palito's hand in hers. He was calling to her but she could not hear what he said, separated as she was from him by the windowpane. The train began to move, leaving the little group behind.

The next morning when Concha raised the blind in her compartment, she looked out into a strange and frightening world. Tito pulled at her sleeve. "I think my father would want us to go back to Mexico," he urged. All that day the scene grew stranger. The flat, spread-out plains of the Middle West, the scattered houses, the towns, the bustle. The heavy gray sky, seeming to hang like a pall over the brown earth, depressed her, used as she was to sunshine. Why had she insisted that she and Tito come to the States? She had a legitimate reason for turning back, one Jim would have recognized—the children she had left behind.

Night came. They were waiting in the station at St. Louis for a train to take them farther north to Jim's old home in Virginia. It was hours late. Tito was asleep, his head in her lap. The huge waiting room filled and emptied. Everywhere around her she heard the sharp, clipped English, the kind the man at the lunch counter had used when she had tried to get sandwiches for Tito. People had been three deep around the counter. The man next to her shouted, "Ham-on-rye."

"Next!" the man behind the counter shouted, looking at her.

"If you please, we would like——" she began.

"Make up your mind, lady. Next."

Three times she had tried. Each time her speech was too slow with its polite beginning. "We'll have to wait, Tito; maybe when we get on the train."

With the going of her own flowing, graceful language went Concha's last bit of assurance. She felt herself alone, shut out from the people around her, shut away from Jim. This was Jim's country that she had come to, hoping to find him again. But she had lost him completely now, shut out from his world.

She heard someone crying. With pity she looked at a young girl standing a few feet away. Her arms were about a young man's neck, and he was crying too. The man was in uniform. Finally he took her hands, placed them at her sides, and walked away to a train.

The room filled and emptied, filled and emptied. The scene repeated itself, changed in detail but not in its element of suffering. A man and a woman, a man and a woman, over and over in anguished embrace. Then a woman walking away alone. Separation like hers when Jim left her, never to come back. I understand this, she thought. What Fidel called the fellowship of suffering. Is that how I will come to understand Jim's country?

She woke Tito. "Come," she said, "we must get something to eat. It is very late, too late to be served anything on the train." She took her place in the crowd at the lunch counter. "Next!" the man called out, looking at her.

"Ham-on-rye," she shouted.